Drawn Together

Robyn Russell

Black Lace books contain sexual fantasies.
In real life, always practise safe sex.

This edition published in 2003 by
Black Lace
Thames Wharf Studios
Rainville Road
London W6 9HA

Originally published 1998

Printed and bound by Mackays of Chatham PLC

ISBN 0 352 33269 7

Contents

For Ginger & Sugar

Prologue

The Adventures of Katrina Cortez

From behind the grimy windows of her nondescript Chevy pickup truck, Katrina Cortez studied the two men. The dark-haired undercover detective was dressed in her usual combination of Texas Goth and retro-punk. She recognised the shorter blond-haired figure of Pete Regan, a local businessman. Many photographs of him had been included in her briefings by the narcotics squad detectives in the Dallas Police HQ.

In the dimming dusky light, Katrina observed her quarry greeting a taller brown-haired man who had been waiting in his own vehicle, a pearl-grey Lexus, at the arrivals area outside Terminal B at Dallas-Fort Worth International Airport. As they sped away, Katrina put her truck in gear and spoke into her two-way radio. 'Cortez here. Regan's just leaving with some new guy who showed up to meet him. I'm on his tail. Anything more I need to know? Over.'

The disembodied voice of Damon, her contact inside the airport, who had watched Regan disembark from his Mexico City flight, squawked in reply, 'No. As far as we could see, he was travelling alone. He didn't make contact with anyone here. He went straight to the exit. He's all yours, Cortez. Be careful!'

Signing off, Katrina brushed aside her shiny blue-black hair and pursed her lips. The seasoned private eye removed the handset from her ear and placed it on the seat beside her, focusing quickly on the task in hand. She concentrated on following the Lexus as it moved smartly through the automated toll booth at the airport exit and headed for downtown. With care, she drifted inconspicuously into place four cars behind, mixing with the early evening traffic on the John Carpenter Freeway. This accomplished, she reviewed her assignment.

At first glance, it had appeared quite straightforward. The Drug Interdiction Task Force commander had put it bluntly to her. 'Follow Regan, and get to know him, casual-like. Inveigle yourself into his confidence. Seduce the guy if necessary; he thinks of himself as a great one for the ladies,' the policeman had said with a grimace. 'You never know what he might let slip, in an . . . intimate situation. That's why we brought you in again, Cortez. He can smell a cop a mile off, the tricky bastard.'

Katrina recalled the commander's scowl as he had continued, 'I don't normally like PIs working with cops. But you come highly recommended from my boss, so I'm making the best of it. Don't screw up. We need enough information to nail him good. You don't act like a cop. You certainly don't look like one. If you're careful, he'll never catch on.'

Katrina smiled. Steering expertly through the maze of traffic, she considered her outfit. No, she certainly didn't look like a cop. For starters, she wore considerably fewer clothes than a regular undercover detective, and the accrued heat of the Dallas summer, even towards nightfall, provided her with the excuse to go scantily clad. Today's ensemble included a cropped black silk T-shirt that draped her otherwise unfettered firm round breasts and stopped short of her slender waist, revealing an expanse of pure white skin. This item was twinned with a short black denim mini-skirt that matched her exhibitionist tendencies by showing off almost every inch of her trim muscular thighs. Her calves fitted snugly inside a pair of black leather high-top Frye boots.

No cop could get away with this revealing garb, even under cover; nor did many female police officers wear their hair dyed a striking blue-black hue, or cut to the chin in sleek and sexy asymmetry.

Keenly aware of her vibrant sexiness, especially to men, Katrina shifted back comfortably and opened her legs as she drove, stroking the inside of her thighs; their paleness was accentuated by her black outfit. With pleasure she felt the compact firmness of her muscles beneath her skin, a product of long daytime hours in the gym, kick-boxing under the tutelage of Lang Van, her enigmatic Vietnamese trainer. Beneath her short skirt she wore only the smallest of string bikini panties, barely covering a vibrant bush of pubic hair, dyed blue-black to match her sleek tresses, and manicured to an exact geometric triangle. Katrina's fingers toyed beneath her skirt and brushed the soft silk that covered her mound.

With a start, her foot stabbed the gas pedal as the Lexus ahead of her darted through the remnants of the notorious Dallas rush hour stampede and on to the maze of ramps that joined the Carpenter and Stemmons Freeways. She was instantly on full alert, but Regan and his companion seemed interested only in outracing other commuters and, once through the tangled interchange, they settled down at a brisk seventy-five m.p.h. in the outside lane.

Katrina followed six cars back, still heading downtown, but after only a few miles the lead driver peeled off on to Harry Hines Boulevard and then on to Oak Lawn Drive, moving more slowly in the posh residential suburbs north of the city centre. Katrina hung further back, watching from a safe distance. The pearl grey vehicle she was trailing turned on to Turtle Creek Parkway, one of the most exclusive addresses in Dallas's in-town neighbourhoods.

The two men swung into the curved driveway of an elegant federal-style mini-mansion and slid to a stop. Katrina parked two blocks down the street, under a canopy of overhanging oak trees. To the casual eye the Chevy she drove looked like any one of the countless similar work vehicles to be found in all Dallas neighbourhoods; the souped-up V8 5.6 litre engine under the hood was a well-kept secret. She switched off her lights, but kept the motor running, the air-conditioning cooling her on this typically Texas midsummer evening; it remained 95 degrees Fahrenheit, 95 per cent humidity, even at nearly eight p.m.

She didn't have to wait long; within minutes, Regan and his host returned to their car and headed across town, beneath the infamously clogged Central Expressway, and now paralleled by the new rapid transit rail line. Katrina was surprised when the shiny Lexus headed towards the intersection of Lower Greenville and Ross Avenue, an area well known for its seedy bars and clubs. Not generally a part of Big D frequented by the Turtle Creek smart set, she thought, although she knew it well. Her pulse quickened. This might be interesting.

Katrina wasn't disappointed. Regan and his companion parked the Lexus in a bleak lot between two structures that lacked any architectural pretensions whatsoever. To Katrina they were depressingly familiar, ubiquitous dingy buildings found in similar districts in every city across America. Unloved and unlovely, they looked more like bunkers than buildings, but she knew from experience the kind of things that usually went on inside. With a mixture of excitement and disdain, the sleek and sexy detective pulled into a neighbouring lot across the street, and watched the two men walk towards the less ugly of the two structures.

While she waited for them to go inside, Katrina applied dark red lipstick and slipped her small hi-tech two-way radio into her purse. She hopped out on to the baking tarmac, then locked the truck with her remote electronic key and deftly dodged the traffic to follow on foot. She felt completely at home now; she shunned the harsh sun of the Dallas summers, preferring the lush darkness of the night as the medium for her work. And she felt a familiar tingle of anticipation as she headed for the seamy side of pleasure, where the middle-class got their kicks, slumming it with their less fortunate brothers and sisters.

The club whose portals she approached at a discreet distance behind Regan and his companion declared itself as 'Boobs'n'Boots! Dallas's Best Titty Bar!' This large garish neon lettering on the front of the otherwise windowless façade flickered in a virulent chartreuse green. Other lighted signs above the flat roof, straggling amid a mess of vents and ducts and chillers, depicted gigantic pink neon breasts with flashing magenta nipples. These throbbing images competed for attention with the words 'Topless! And More!' pulsating in large script in a random rhythm that had more to do with faulty electrical connections than sensual suggestion.

Whereas Regan and his friend paid the club's cover charge at the door and slipped straight inside, Katrina had to endure the leering stare and suggestive comments of the heavy-set doorman. He feasted his eyes on her body, drooling at the whiteness of her skin in sharp contrast to her black clothes, but more upon the shape of her breasts, visibly outlined beneath her T-shirt; finally he let his eyes travel slowly down her body to enjoy the sight of her firmly muscled calves and thighs, so invitingly exposed from the tops of her Frye boots almost to her crotch.

'Working tonight, darling?' The apeman winked and laughed at his home-grown humour, his eyes suddenly widening as he discovered the intertwined snake tattoo high on Katrina's inner thigh as she stood, legs slightly apart and arms akimbo, waiting for him to finish his visual plundering of her body.

'What's it to you, King Kong?' Katrina answered offhandedly as she posed for his salacious study. She certainly *was* working, but not at the game this cretin thought.

His misunderstanding was further made evident by his next utterance. 'Now listen, Pale Face, any hookers I don't know have to pay double the cover. Sort of like a deposit,' he chortled, pleased at his droll wit. 'Of course,' he added ponderously, 'the deposit's always returnable . . . if you know what I mean.' He leered greedily, his teeth bared in what Katrina supposed was his version of a sexy grin.

It was easier just to go with the flow, Katrina decided. Besides, if she could fool this guy into thinking she was a hooker, others would probably think so, too. It fitted well with the expectations of the clientele in a place like this.

'Maybe later,' she replied carelessly, tossing her shiny blue-black hair in the ogre's face as her almost black eyes flashed against her light ivory skin. 'It depends who's here tonight and how horny I am.' She paid the twenty dollars cover and the twenty dollars 'deposit' and stalked into the darkened interior, feeling the doorman's eyes boring through her sexy outfit to undress her in the hallway. Not that she required much undressing, she thought gleefully. She could divest herself of all but her boots in seconds flat. And she loved sex with her boots on.

Inside the club, Katrina stood for a moment at the top of a short flight of black iron stairs that led to an unexpected semi-basement level, and assessed the crowd swirling at her feet. It took her a few minutes to locate her prey; both men were sitting together at a table close to a small raised stage that formed the focal point of the main room. A smaller bar area was visible through a further set of swinging doors. As she cased the club, she noticed only a smattering of other solitary women, apart from the topless waitresses who ambled to and fro with patrons' orders.

Those other women, fully dressed like herself, or at least not topless, certainly looked like hookers; ostensibly here for sex, they managed to look very un-sexy, with expressions of lethargy and boredom written all over their faces. Maybe a couple lines of cocaine was what it took to start them up, Katrina thought dourly. By contrast, some of the waitresses were very sexy and pretty indeed. Her eyes fell upon a particularly fetching waitress advancing towards her with an empty tray. The young woman's cupcake breasts bobbed pertly as she stood at the foot of the stairs, looked up and asked, 'Want anything to drink, Pale Face?'

'What's with this "Pale Face" routine?' Katrina snapped back, with barely concealed irritation. But she quickly disciplined her lips into a smile as she came down a step and gazed unblinkingly at the brown-haired girl's nakedness.

'Because you're so damn pale, sweetheart,' the waitress replied insolently. She added with the hint of a sneer, 'Don't you ever see the sun? You must do *your* work at night.' As if to emphasise her point, she flexed her torso and arched her back, showing off her tanned skin, bronzed all over, with no tan lines from a bikini to pattern her torso. Her little upturned breasts were firm and her belly taut above the briefest of skirts.

'Very lovely indeed,' commented Katrina, enjoying the sight of the young woman's pretty semi-naked body.

The waitress looked up appraisingly at the white flesh of Katrina's exposed shanks and continued dismissively,

'I suppose it turns on some guys. There's no accounting for taste. Me, I prefer the sun on my tits; it feels so-o-o-o good.' She closed her eyes and smiled, as if in remembrance of a torrid solar embrace. She twirled around in a graceful pirouette, balancing the tray, her nipples taut with the memory of the sun. Coming to rest, the girl opened her eyes and stared directly back at Katrina, as if snapping out of a sexual trance. 'What'll it be, lady?' she asked.

Katrina found the girl's sexual antics quite appealing, yet something disturbed her. The girl's hyped-up sexuality seemed partially faked, or perhaps artificially amplified by chemistry. There was little doubt in her mind that drugs would be freely available here; it was probably no coincidence that Regan had made this his second stop since getting off the plane only a couple of hours ago. But she kept these thoughts to herself as she descended the remaining few steps and stood beside the waitress. 'Just bring me a Perrier,' she ordered.

Katrina looked around at the leering faces in the room and, before the waitress could turn to leave, she added, 'Make that two. And point me to a dark table.' She slapped a ten-dollar bill on the drinks tray.

'Follow me, sweetheart,' said the waitress, who sashayed across the room, nonchalantly swaying her hips. Most of the men at the tables turned their heads in avid appreciation as the woman slipped by.

Katrina kept a few paces behind, shadowing the waitress to a table that was too far from the stage to get a really good view, and therefore unoccupied.

'Expecting someone, dearie?' the topless waitress asked.

Katrina slid into a seat from which she had a good view of Regan and his friend. They had their backs to her. Without answering, Katrina turned off the table light and leant her chair back against the wall. 'What's your name?' she enquired.

'I'm called Cupcake,' giggled the waitress.

Katrina let her eyes drop slowly and deliberately to the petite woman's small upturned breasts with their pink areolae. 'I can see why,' she observed. Then she spoke confidentially. 'I'm expecting someone later, Cupcake, but in the meantime I'm not interested in picking anyone up. I want to be left alone. Understand?'

'OK,' Cupcake drawled, with a shrug that communicated complete indifference, and sidled off towards the bar, returning some minutes later with the drinks.

Katrina added a five-dollar tip to keep in the waitress's good graces, and watched the impudent serving wench saunter back through the crowd. The detective stretched her long legs and placed one Perrier across from her as if a companion had just stepped away from the little round table; this usually discouraged casual pick-ups. In any event, it was still early, and most of the club's evening clients were still in their nearby motel rooms, rustling up the courage to pursue a night of casual illicit sex.

Suddenly, the heavy beat of loud rock-and-roll assaulted the ear-drums of the assembled audience, and the stage lit up with red and pink lights. A brilliant spotlight enlivened the herringbone pattern of wooden blocks that comprised the stage floor.

Settling back, well out of the glow, Katrina observed a woman with a fine sweep of thick auburn hair and great dancer's legs mount the stage. The audience's chatter stilled as the performer, dressed in a tightly fitted blue fringed leather cowgirl outfit, executed a series of carefully orchestrated and frankly sexual gyrations. Katrina was disappointed to see that the dancer wore no authentic cowgirl boots to complete the outfit, opting instead for black-and-white snakeskin high heels.

The dancer's antics built slowly to a striptease, and the curvy red-haired woman tempted her audience with a variety of cunningly suggestive actions, including the provocative use of toy water pistols and a lariat. Slowly stripping down to only a blue leather G-string and a cowgirl vest studded with turquoise, the woman prompted ribald cheers from the audience. As she shrugged back her shoulders, the bejewelled vest opened to reveal a pair of large breasts with pert nipples.

While her naked breasts played peek-a-boo beneath the vest, the dancer hopped off the stage and moved around each of the nearby tables in turn, treating their occupants to a tantalising display. She lingered at the table where Pete Regan and his friend sat, and after paying especial attention to the taller man, displaying her breasts in his face, she blew him a kiss, and moved on to arouse other eager customers.

Returning to the stage, the woman divested herself of her last two items of clothing, and tossed them casually on to the two men's table. She gyrated fully nude in front of a howling lusty audience, mostly of men. This must be the 'And More!' referred to in the pulsating flashing neon outside the building, thought Katrina dryly. Her detective's eye for detail didn't fail to note that the woman's auburn hair was matched by her tight thatch of pubic curls.

When the sexy dance routine quickly reached its end, the woman vanished off-stage. She was briskly replaced under the spotlight by a buxom brunette, who extracted a shiny chrome dildo from her skimpy costume, to the evident satisfaction of the front row of overweight businessmen.

Detecting movement at the table where the two men sat, Katrina shifted her eyes. Pete Regan stood to follow his tall dark friend, who scooped up the remnants of the dancer's costume, and strode through the set of swinging saloon doors that separated the dance floor from the adjacent bar-room.

A few moments later, Katrina followed them and established her next vantage point, a seat at the far end of the bar from where she could observe the pair in a long framed mirror. She ordered another Perrier from the female bartender, whose opulent breasts, like Cupcake's, were displayed in all their natural glory.

After only five minutes or so, the auburn-haired dancer reappeared, dressed in ordinary, though scanty, clothes: a halter top, shorts, and ridiculously high-heeled pumps. She made straight for the men's table, where she greeted the dark-haired man with a long kiss and shook the hand of Pete Regan before sitting down between them in their booth.

With little delay, the boyfriend's hand strayed to the woman's thigh, his fingers tracing ever smaller circles towards the hem of her artfully frayed shorts, and coming to rest near her crotch. The woman said something in a low voice, and all three laughed.

Katrina glanced surreptitiously over the top of her Perrier at the mirrored reflection of the action in the dimly lit booth beyond. Her eyes danced with delight as she observed the woman's hand move between the tall man's thighs, stroking up and down what could only be a substantial erect cock hidden beneath the table. As the darker man eased back slightly in his seat and spread his legs wider, he exchanged glances with his girlfriend, and nodded to Regan. The woman responded with a lusty grin and, within moments, her other hand was similarly employed. In the dim half-light she deftly opened Pete Regan's zipper, and, being careful to keep a tent of material over the pole of his penis, expertly masturbated his shaft in an almost imperceptible rhythm. The merest ghost of a smile passed across the woman's face as she studied her two companions from under lidded eyes.

Katrina licked her lips. Both men were good-looking lusty types, and the woman's own physical attractions had been clearly displayed only moments earlier. The voyeuristic act of watching this display of sexual lust excited the detective; she enjoyed a distinctive throbbing in her own loins, accompanied by warm juiciness as she tried to concentrate on her next move. If any of the other patrons or waitresses noticed the covert sexual activities in the booth, they weren't paying much attention.

Both men were splayed out in their seats, happily fixated by the attentions of their companion. Within a few minutes, Katrina put together a plan. Adjusting her silk T-shirt so that her nipples were clearly visible through the fabric, she hitched up her own short skirt, unobtrusively checked the hi-tech walkie-talkie and her trusty Lady Smith .38 nestling comfortingly together in her purse, and sauntered towards the trio, getting close before they noticed her in their self-absorption.

When she stopped beside their table, the threesome turned to stare. Pete Regan jerked upright in his seat and batted the woman's hand from his fly. But his two companions just paused momentarily in their actions, and then resumed, the woman's agile fingers flagrantly stroking the dark-haired man's phallus under the table, defying Katrina to intervene.

In spite of his evident arousal, Regan's friend looked Katrina squarely in the eye and spoke with cavalier coolness. 'Something I can do for you, lady?' His dark brown-lashed gaze didn't flicker.

Katrina held his eyes and smiled. By way of reply she slid into the booth and blatantly uncovered Pete Regan's penis, now somewhat flaccid and, locking her arm through Regan's, she trapped him in his seat as he started in alarm. In her hand, she felt his thick rod jump in response to her expert ministrations. 'No, not a thing,' she murmured seductively, stroking Regan back to full tumescence. 'It's rather what I can do for your friend here.'

Chapter One
Katrina Revealed

'Katrina Cortez is a wild woman!'

As she stepped out of the lift, graphic artist Tanya Trevino was startled by the exclamation coming from the young man who stood at her drawing table across the wide expanse of the sunlit studio. From where she hovered in the mirrored foyer of Studio V, Tanya recognised the speaker, even though all but the top of his head was obscured from view. She knew that the shiny chestnut head of hair, just visible above the screens that carved out her private workspace, belonged to Stephen Sinclair, Studio V's newest young artist.

She passed through the foyer, with its many framed awards substantiating the firm's claim to be one of Dallas's top-flight commercial art and graphic design studios, and nodded a friendly greeting to the firm's pretty receptionist. On the wall behind the ever-smiling Carmen Sierra, who sat demurely behind her desk reading a Spanish language magazine, the office in/out board revealed that almost everybody else in the firm had just gone to lunch, and weren't expected back for an hour or more.

Tossing her sleek shoulder-length brown hair, Tanya

instinctively checked her reflection before entering the studio, noting with approval her trim figure and pretty face. With her velvety fringed dark brown eyes, friends often said she bore a striking resemblance to the late actress, Natalie Wood. She still ached from last night's punishing kick-boxing workout at Gold's Gym. With a wry smile she straightened her short summer cotton dress over the tops of her tanned thighs.

Quietly, she entered the lofty studio space and approached her workstation, taking a roundabout route past several vacant drawing boards. Studio V occupied the top floor of a large converted brick warehouse in Deep Ellum, the avant-garde arts district of Dallas, Texas. Tanya's drawing table was positioned at one of the tall windows that overlooked Elm Street, the phonetic corruption of which gave the district its name. While most of her colleagues liked to work in the open studio space, Tanya preferred some privacy, and had positioned colourful head-height screens around her board. Within her little enclave, north light flooded across her drawing board, now littered with the latest proofs for the next episode of *The Adventures of Katrina Cortez, Girl Detective!*

Tanya moved softly, her low-slung pumps soundless on the hardwood floor. She sneaked a glimpse of the younger man whose words had caught her ear, admiring his tall handsome good looks. Such an appraisal had become a habit of hers since Stephen Sinclair had joined Studio V a couple of weeks ago. She liked his pleasant blue eyes and long, soft-looking reddish-brown hair, and thought he, too, probably worked out; his confident bearing and manner bore witness to a trim and lean physique beneath the crisply pressed ensemble of button-down Oxford shirts and linen slacks that he always wore to the studio. But their schedules had kept them apart; Tanya surmised she probably hadn't shared more than a few polite greetings with him since his arrival. For a young guy just out of art school, he sure was cute and sexy.

Rapt in close study of her drawings, Stephen had spoken aloud to no one in particular, and was unaware of Tanya's return from her early lunch. Tanya moved closer, and saw his figure in profile. She stifled a gasp, for the physical attribute most noticeable to her gaze was her young colleague's erection. The outline of his penis was clearly visible through his lightweight summer slacks. As she watched, holding her breath, he rubbed his hand along the length of his shaft as he studied the drawings in front of him. Tanya's pulse quickened at the sight, and she felt a pleasing ripple of response deep within her. She fought down a sudden desire to feel that firm erection between her own fingers.

To her annoyance, Tanya noticed from the corner of her eye another occupant of the front room in the studio. Beth-Ann Bodine, a buxom blonde and a fellow graphic artist, was at work in the far corner of the well-lit space. Though Beth-Ann was absorbed and didn't seem to have heard Stephen's exclamation, Tanya's heart sank; she really didn't like her co-worker. Office rumour had it that the big blonde and Stephen were already lovers, and Tanya tried to ignore her resentment that Beth-Ann had moved in so quickly to claim the new man. But, Tanya told herself firmly, I already have a boyfriend.

Tanya had to admit the other woman did good work when she got around to it. But that wasn't often. One of Beth-Ann's tasks was to do the inking of Tanya's pencil master sketches for the *Katrina Cortez* series before they were scanned into the computer for colouring and lettering, but the blonde assistant seemed to spend as much time polishing her nails as she did her drawings. Tanya didn't see why Hiram Pease, owner and creative director of Studio V, put up with the woman.

As she carefully edged towards Stephen Sinclair, Tanya glanced again in Beth-Ann's direction, and was startled to see her colleague staring fixedly at her. Tanya smiled uncertainly, but received no acknowledgement. Snooty bitch, Tanya thought uncharitably.

Ignoring Beth-Ann's distant hostile glare, Tanya stepped quietly between the screens to stand at the young man's side. She spoke softly. 'Hello, Stephen. It's nice to see you.'

Suddenly aware of the artist's presence, Stephen Sinclair jumped in surprise and swung round. 'Oh . . . hi, T-Tanya,' he stuttered, glancing this way and that as if looking for an escape route. He placed one hand on his chest as if to still his beating heart, and colour rose in his cheeks. The other hand reached for his groin and then hastily drew back. He leant forward slightly over the drawing board to disguise the evident bulge in his trousers. 'You . . . you gave me a start! I didn't hear you come in,' he said with a weak smile.

The flustered young man made to rearrange Tanya's drawings. 'I didn't mean to pry,' he continued in a rush of words. 'I hope you don't mind. They just looked so . . . interesting, lying there on your drawing board.' He turned further away from her, affecting nonchalance as he tried to conceal his arousal from the beautiful young woman.

Tanya smiled, trying to reassure him, and studiously avoided any gaze in the direction of his crotch. She said quietly, 'It's fine, Stephen. I don't mind. In fact, I would appreciate your opinion about something.' She wanted to touch him, to run her fingers through his lovely hair, to feel his cock snuggled in her palm, but she controlled her urges. Tanya didn't need a new complication; she lived with her new boyfriend Eric Janovich, with whom she made love every day – or at least every day he wasn't away somewhere on business. And anyway, Stephen Sinclair was only a sweet young kid. She was nearly thirty. She had no place dating someone almost seven years her junior.

Yet just being near this youth, and enjoying the uncharacteristic shyness beneath his polite and confident everyday manner, made Tanya shiver with delight. She felt the vague attraction for Stephen that had slowly permeated her consciousness during the last two weeks stir into something more directly physical. She inhaled his distinctive lime cologne, and gently took her drawings from his hands. His fingers grazed her arm.

She liked the tightly wound and sexy feeling he gave her. Having him stand there made her want to show off, flirt, act clever and sexy. She took a firm grip on herself, and tried to revert to a more colleague-like demeanour.

'Here, Stephen, sit down for a minute,' she invited and offered her companion the draughting chair. From the introductions that Hiram Pease had made when Stephen joined the studio, Tanya knew that this boy, who was unexpectedly setting her body tingling, was a talented artist himself. Their boss had displayed examples of Stephen's commercial artwork, and Tanya had been duly impressed. She tried to put some of this into words, elaborating, 'I really liked your use of colour in the portfolio that Mr Pease showed us.'

Stephen's smile broadened with obvious pleasure, making Tanya glow inside. Nudging up close to his side, her traitorous body once more overrode the warning signals from her brain. 'I'm trying to capture a tense and sexy atmosphere, where Katrina is in control, but only just,' she continued. 'I'm searching for something that's glamorous, yet sexually explicit enough to make the reader's pulse race a bit, and I also want to communicate something of a gritty quality all at the same time . . . sort of "elegant *noir*" with an edge to it.'

'Sort of *Omaha the Cat Dancer* meets Dashiell Hammett and *Phoebe Zeit-Geist*?' Stephen suggested. His smile was unguarded and disingenuous.

Tanya was impressed. 'Not many people know about Reed Waller and Kate Worley's work,' she said. 'But I've always admired it, especially the stuff they did in the late eighties. *Omaha* has a great blend of sex, mystery and action. I've been influenced a lot by *Phoebe Zeit-Geist*, too. But tell me,' she asked, with a quizzical look at Stephen, 'how do you know about *Omaha*? Her exploits are pretty explicit.'

'Oh, I've . . . just come across them. I've seen them around; one of my old girlfriends had a few . . .' His voice tailed off.

Before Tanya could question him further, either on his taste in erotic images or old girlfriends, Stephen himself changed the subject. 'Isn't this a bit unusual for our normal workload?' he asked. 'I mean, all I've seen since I joined the firm have been corporate reports, advertising brochures, magazine inserts and that kind of stuff.'

'Yes,' Tanya agreed. 'I began this assignment a few months ago when one of our other employees left. It's something Mr Pease has been doing for several years for an old college friend. This guy, Joshua McNally, is a publisher of specialist comic books. He and Pease were fraternity brothers at Southern Methodist University, back in the seventies.'

'SMU?' queried Stephen. He seemed unimpressed.

Tanya smiled at her colleague. 'If I were to take a wild guess that you don't come from Texas, Stephen, would I be right?'

Stephen grinned and nodded. 'It's easy to tell, isn't it? Actually, my family's from Atlanta. I have a sister who runs an art gallery there. My family gave me a hard time for taking this job in Dallas!'

Tanya smiled. She found this handsome young man easy to talk to. 'Well, Stephen, you'll find out that anybody who claims to be anybody usually boasts about going to SMU. It's a passport to business success in Dallas.' She didn't add that she'd gained her own Master of Fine Arts degree from that very same august institution.

'So that's why the firm does these comic-book illustrations, as a favour to an old fraternity buddy?' asked Stephen.

'I think it used to be like that, but now it's becoming a bigger deal. Frankly, the strip used to have weak storylines and the drawings were grim. I've tried to spice it up a bit, add some sex, and develop Katrina Cortez into someone more complex as a character. Originally, I only drew the panels to match someone else's text, but recently I submitted a whole parallel storyboard to Pease, along with the one I was supposed to do. Pease thought mine was much better and he showed it to McNally, who liked it a lot, and since then I've had more freedom to work with the script as well as the drawings.'

Tanya paused, and felt a flutter of pleasure as she added, 'The drawings you've been looking at are my first set entirely on my own. I'm also writing the plot for the next *Katrina Cortez* story. If this goes well, I hope to do a lot more. It's really cool to draw and write, but the character does sort of take you over. I think Katrina is starting to dominate my life!' She laughed nervously in her excitement.

Tanya picked up a couple of drawings and laid them in front of Stephen for his review. 'Look at these two,' she murmured, leaning over him and deliberately allowing her fingers to brush his arm. She felt his muscles tense at her proximity and then slowly relax. Once more, the fleeting touch of skin sent astonishing vibrations through her.

Stephen gazed at the drawings spread before his eyes, then looked up at Tanya, smiled shyly and observed, 'These are really sexy drawings. I like them.'

Tanya glowed in response. 'I'm glad. I have a lot of fun drawing them.' The illustration was an explicit sex scene from the current *Katrina Cortez* story, in which the character of Pete Regan was rampantly making love to the daring and decadent investigator. The pale-skinned black-haired woman, naked except for her treasured black boots, rode roughly astride the man, whose engorged penis was buried in her vagina.

Stephen looked at the next frame, in which two other characters, a tall man and a well-endowed woman, were engaged in complementary sexual gymnastics on the same giant king-sized bed.

In a subsequent picture, the naked quartet improvised a carnal concerto. Through the bedroom window was a view of the night-time Dallas skyline, seen across the flashing lights of an elevated freeway. Above the characters' heads the word bubbles still stood empty, but it wouldn't take much imagination to fill them with appropriately sexy dialogue.

Stephen smiled up again at his attractive colleague. Tanya's heart skipped a beat as her eyes held those of the chestnut-haired young man next to her. His eyelashes were long and thick, like his hair. She was mightily tempted to scratch her fingers along his spine, exploring the contours of his sculpted shoulder muscles beneath his crisp blue shirt. She controlled her wayward hand just in time, and folded her arms to keep them out of trouble.

'Your line work is so vivid. What kind of pencil leads do you use to keep it that sharp?'

The question sounded banal but Tanya noticed the slight quaver in his voice. She seized on the commonplace query and gave it her full attention. 'Actually, I'm a bit of a fanatic about my pencils,' she replied enthusiastically, as eager as Stephen seemed to be to disguise the sexual tension building between them. She firmly reminded herself that she already had a boyfriend, and she enjoyed all the great sex anybody could wish for. Why was she flirting with this handsome kid? She clutched for something intelligent and non-sexual to say. 'I use only Derwent Graphix. There's a Pearl Paint store here in town that imports them from England. The density of the graphite gives much crisper blacks when they're scanned into the computer.' Her words sounded strained and stilted; this whole conversation was getting a little farcical, she thought.

However, Stephen Sinclair nodded in earnest agreement. He swung round on the stool and looked her in the eye. 'You're really into it, aren't you?'

Tanya hesitated, and then took the plunge. 'Do you mean "really into" drawing or "really into" sex?' she asked him boldly.

Stephen paused, as if carefully weighing the import of the question. Tanya held her breath as she waited expectantly for his answer. But the moment, pregnant with possibilities, was shattered by the sudden sound of Beth-Ann Bodine's loud Texas twang from across the studio. 'Steve, honey? It's lunchtime, and you said we'd go to that new Thai restaurant over on Commerce Street.'

At Beth-Ann's brash intervention, Tanya stared between her screens and caught the woman's vivid glare before it was doused by a smile of saccharine sweetness. Tanya was surprised by the fleetingly ferocious look that belied Beth-Ann's seemingly innocuous words.

Alerted to Stephen and Tanya's incipient mutual attraction, the buxom blonde slid off her seat and posed provocatively at her own drawing table, making no secret of her bodily charms. Head high and tossed back, she boldly displayed her considerable cleavage, set off by a low-cut, sheer mesh leopard-print shirt that stretched too tightly over her amply curvaceous figure. She tapped one snakeskin T-strapped mule imperiously on the hardwood floor. Tanya expected her either to growl or slither towards her.

Tanya sensed Stephen stiffen at her side; he smiled slightly, but didn't meet her eyes. 'Excuse me, Tanya,' he murmured apologetically as he eased past her towards his lunch date, who radiated haughty impatience from the other side of the studio. 'I did promise to take Beth-Ann to lunch. I was so engrossed in your drawings that I completely forgot. Thank you for letting me see them. They are very good.'

Tanya murmured softly, 'I'm glad you like them. I do have a lot of fun with them.' She let the slightest of *doubles entendres* hang in the air between them.

Stephen moved diffidently through the small space, unavoidably brushing against Tanya's thigh, and Tanya felt a jolt as she recognised the briefest of touches by Stephen's penis, evidently still hard within his trousers. Their eyes met and Tanya knew Stephen had enjoyed the same reaction. She gave him a sly little smile, and sighed. She wanted to caress his cock but modesty stayed her hand.

'Excuse me,' Stephen repeated, and hurried away.

Beth-Ann intercepted him at the door, and firmly grasped him by the arm.

Feeling envy at the big blonde's flamboyant ability to emit sex appeal, Tanya followed the pair with her eyes and, as the lift doors closed, the big-haired blonde flashed Tanya a look of gloating triumph at the recapture of her quarry.

Chapter Two
Conversations with Carmen

Tanya stared at the closed lift doors for several moments. She wanted to run after Stephen and Beth-Ann and ask what the hell was going on, but she restrained herself.

Tanya looked around the studio, her thoughts in a whirl. Her thigh still bore the memory of his penis brushing against her. What had she been thinking of, coming on to young Stephen like that? Her survey revealed, to her relief, that she was alone. Predictably, Hiram Pease was nowhere in evidence. The director's erratic hours and insubstantial workload were the source of much sarcastic comment among the staff of Studio V.

Tanya, Stephen and Beth-Ann shared the studio with another four artists, who divided their time between the tall loft space and the firm's computer lab, where they turned concept drawings into sophisticated production graphics.

With the exception of Beth-Ann, Tanya found her fellow employees to be a convivial bunch. The two men, Leon Clarke and Chuck Greenberg, were in their early thirties; both had been with the firm for several years. The other two Studio V artist-designers, Gloria Sanchez and Hillary Hightower, were attractive, quiet women in their mid-thirties. Firm friends, they shared a house in the ethnically diverse Oak Cliff neighbourhood south of downtown. Both seemed inoculated against Hiram Pease's post-modern brand of male chauvinism.

And then there was Stephen Sinclair.

The suite of spaces that Hiram Pease reserved as his luxurious lair was empty now. In typical Dallas fashion, the man's office was opulently over-done, and reflected his swaggering style. The burly Pease was also a sharp businessman, with a flair for hiring good graphic designers and a canniness for real estate. Together, these talents had made both him and Studio V very successful.

The building that housed Studio V had begun life as a humble cotton warehouse, built next to a rail siding that had curved off the main line to serve the old industrial district. Some years ago, Pease had invested shrewdly in several such buildings; under his guidance, the high-ceilinged spaces with their authentic brick walls and hardwood floors had been cleaned and subdivided, partitioned, rewired and replumbed. He had then advertised his projects to the trend-hungry Dallas hipsters, and waited for them to come.

To the man's smug but justified satisfaction, his investment had paid off handsomely; within a year, all his spaces had been leased at near premium rates. His tenants were mostly small businesses like himself, establishing their reputations in the fields of architecture, design, visual arts and communications, all willing to pay high prices for being where the action was. The success of the venture was assured when the prestigious Palinzetti furniture company had leased street-level space for their new Dallas offices and showroom.

From his office, Pease conducted business electronically with the world outside his windows. Inside, he could gain quick access to his studio and computer lab. For someone his size, the man could move very quietly;

he would materialise silently, peering at drawings or computer screens, checking what his workers were doing.

Tanya had been startled several times by Pease's touch on her arm, not hearing his approach. She was alternately attracted and repelled by his magnetic personality. But the boss paid well and kept Studio V employees satisfied, despite his irritating mannerisms.

Apart from Pease and his artists, the remaining office staff numbered two young secretaries and Carmen Sierra, the friendly receptionist-cum-bookkeeper. Tanya assumed the attractive woman, in her mid-thirties, to be Mexican, but she didn't know for sure. She made a mental note to pay more attention to details like that; her absorption in the *Katrina Cortez* stories had begun to detach her from the daily life of the studio.

Sitting at her drawing board, Tanya's mind was filled with frustrating thoughts about Beth-Ann Bodine's rapacious designs upon young Stephen Sinclair. With a sigh, she turned to Edward Bear, a small brown teddy bear who was her constant companion at work. He sat placidly on the windowsill and watched the daily life of Deep Ellum go by.

'Well, Edward, it looks as if that young hussy already has her fangs into our sexy young Stephen,' she said in a low voice. 'What the hell does he see in her?'

Edward gazed back intently, but remained mute.

Tanya supplied the bear's answer for him. 'I know, it's obvious, isn't it? She probably fucks the living daylights out of him, and he loves it.' If Edward was shocked by Tanya's language, he gave no sign.

'But why should that bother me, Edward?' Tanya continued. 'I have a steady relationship and I get great sex. Just what is getting into me? Why am I acting like a horny teenager around the handsome Mr Stephen?'

Like a furry Buddha, Edward remained impassive,

and Tanya placed him back in his customary position, supervising the world around her.

Tanya knew she was highly sexual. She had often wanted sex more than her boyfriends, and was sometimes abashed by her erotic desires, but at least in her current relationship that didn't seem to be a problem.

On her windowsill next to Edward Bear was a framed photograph of Eric Janovich, but this afternoon Tanya studiously avoided looking at it. Only three months earlier, Tanya had put most of her belongings in storage, terminated her apartment lease, and moved in with Eric. A high-flying executive with Travis Bank and Trust, Eric owned a luxurious condominium in an apartment building on Swiss Avenue, and Tanya now enjoyed the trappings of yuppie luxury that defined Eric's lifestyle.

In spite of the sudden bounty of wealth and beautiful objects; in spite of gifts like the sexy Italian lounging pyjamas with their gorgeous silky plissé finish that Eric had bought her last week; and even in spite of the delights of Eric's bedroom, with its full-length gilt bevelled mirrors and other attractive ensnarements, the apartment didn't feel like home to her. Tanya was unaccustomed to many of Eric's personal and precise routines and habits, and she sometimes found herself doing the wrong thing, or putting things in the wrong place, according to Eric's rigid system of order.

Tanya told herself it was only a matter of time before they resolved things, and that Eric was very generous in letting her share his space. And his appetite for sex matched her own. This only made her feel guilty all over again for flirting with Stephen Sinclair; but despite her discomfort, Stephen's distinctive lime fragrance wafted deliciously in her memory.

Lost in meditation, Tanya stared across the rooftops of Deep Ellum, which spread for several blocks beneath her studio window. In her mind's eye, her tall multi-paned window became part of Katrina's loft apartment in the refurbished Adam Hat Factory nearby, and she picked up one of her favourite pencils from her clutch of drawing instruments.

Tanya quickly sketched the skyline and the nearby freeway as seen from Katrina's fictitious bedroom. But instead of make-believe drug smugglers lying naked on the bed, she drew the face and figure of Stephen Sinclair, eagerly submitting to the sexy investigator's brisk removal of his clothes; together they flung the garments joyfully to the corners of the room in their abandon.

In her sketches, the character who was Katrina, or Tanya, was already naked, her firm full breasts standing proud in anticipation of the man's touch. Tanya felt her own nipples tingle in sympathy beneath her light summer frock.

The woman knelt commandingly over Stephen, and leant back to provide him with an erotic panoply, shamelessly stroking her love-bud. In Tanya's rendering, the sexy female enjoyed Stephen's fierce groan of desire as his rigid penis pulsed against her curves.

Putting down her pencil, Tanya closed her eyes. She was excited by Stephen's interest in her drawings, and she wondered whether his obvious arousal at lunchtime was caused by Katrina Cortez or by herself. She imagined lying in bed, naked, grasping Stephen's tall staff of flesh, bending her body across his naked torso to use the plump purple tip of his penis to massage her clitoris. In her all-enveloping fantasy, Stephen's dick slid deep inside her, penetrating to the very opening of her womb, and he screamed and shuddered with release.

The force of the fantasy orgasm was all the imaginary Tanya needed to propel her to climax, and she peaked with equal gusto, shaking with emotion and physical sensation as she spent herself atop her new-found lover. She held her fingers firmly on her still vibrant clitoris, feeling the spasms of desire echo in a glorious symphony of sensation.

With a guilty start, the flesh-and-blood Tanya jerked upright in her chair in her studio enclave. She had been leaning back, legs spread, and with an embarrassed shock realised that the sensations in her clitoris were not part of her vivid daydream. Her hand was inside her panties, where she felt her wetness on her fingers. She hastily peered around her screens but, to her great relief, the studio was still empty. Everybody but Carmen was still at lunch, and the receptionist's desk was tucked out of sight to one side of the foyer. Tanya hoped she hadn't given audible vent to her powerful fantasy and, seeing that she was alone and unobserved, in the partial privacy of her screened enclosure, she subsided thankfully over her drawing board. With a long sigh, she let her head relax on her arms, her body still quivering from the sensual aftershocks of her desire.

She was alerted moments later by a soft movement at her shoulder. Looking up, she saw Carmen Sierra peering around the screen. The attractive Hispanic woman's normal smile was replaced by a worried look.

'*Como está usted*, Tanya? Are you OK? I was walking back from the ladies' room, and I heard you sigh; and when I looked, I saw you slumped over your drawings.'

The receptionist's lilting accent conveyed her concern, and Tanya smiled reassurance. 'Thank you, Carmen. I'm fine. Really. I was just . . . exasperated.' Tanya grasped for an innocent explanation of her condition and, to her relief, the slight, dark-haired woman nodded sagely, as if in sympathy.

'*Si. Comprendo.*' Carmen tossed her thick, almost black, wavy shoulder-length hair from her face with a dismissive gesture. 'That *hechichera*, that witch, Beth-Ann. She has her claws into *Señor* Steve. She is no good for him, that one. She will milk him dry! She wants him all to herself.' The receptionist treated Tanya to a conspiratorial wink and then grinned wickedly. 'All that Beth-Ann thinks about is sex.'

Tanya blushed, and Carmen giggled. '*Si*. You and me, too, *chicita*, we think about sex a lot. Am I not right?'

Tanya grinned and nodded. 'Yes,' she admitted. 'A lot, and right now about Steve Sinclair.'

'*Si*, he is *hermoso*, handsome. I agree.' Carmen raised her eyebrows and asked frankly, 'But what of your banker friend, *Señor* . . . Eric?'

Suddenly serious, Tanya said, 'Oh, Eric. Right,' and looked down at her drawing board.

Carmen's eyes dropped to Tanya's sexy sketches of *Katrina Cortez*. 'Oi, oi oi, *chicita*! Did you do these?'

Tanya nodded, both proud and embarrassed.

'*Madre de Dios*! They are so exciting.' Carmen paused and glanced at Tanya, seeking permission. 'May I look?'

'Sure, pull up a stool.'

The two women studied the drawings for several minutes, Tanya pointing out details and filling in some of the plot lines for Carmen's benefit. The older woman's surprise and delight was evident in her muffled exclamations and giggles.

'How long have you been doing this?' she asked.

'Oh, just a few months. I took the strip over when the previous artist left. I was just telling Stephen that it really wasn't very good before. I knew I could do better. I had better ideas for stories and I can certainly draw better!'

Carmen nodded appreciatively. '*Si*. You make these drawings real sexy.' She giggled once more. 'They turn me on, and I'm sure they excite men, too.'

Tanya nodded. 'I remember the day I walked into Hiram Pease's office and suggested that he ask the publisher to give me a chance to write and draw the strip the way I wanted. I was so nervous, but when I put my sketches in front of him, I could see he was impressed. In fact, he made sure I saw his erection. He even joked about it.'

Carmen rolled her eyes.

Tanya grinned, and continued, 'Yes, Pease is anything but subtle! But he did say they were dynamite, and he called Joshua McNally at Quantum Comics right then and there. We Fed-Exed some samples over to their office in Fort Worth that afternoon and, two days later, we had a deal. And we heard the other day that the magazine's circulation increased dramatically. This new *Katrina Cortez* is a big hit.'

'*Caramba, chicita!* So now you are famous, yes? Does your *Señor* Eric like them, too?' Carmen's smile faded as she saw the sparkle of delight dim in Tanya's eyes.

'Yeah, mostly he does,' Tanya said with a shrug. In truth, Eric had never shown as much interest in her work as she would like, although he often boasted of his well-developed taste in art.

'Ah, he thinks of you more with his *polla*, his big dick. *Si*?' Carmen gestured to the enlarged penis of one of Tanya's drawings.

Smiling wryly, Tanya nodded. 'That's right, but it is a beautiful one.'

Carmen giggled, but fell silent when she saw another look of irritation cross Tanya's face. 'What's the matter?' the small olive-skinned woman asked. 'Have I said something wrong?'

'No, it's not you, Carmen; I'm pleased you like the drawings. It's that bastard Pease! He let the publisher believe that he was the author of the new characters and storylines. I'm so frustrated! *My* sexy plots and *my* drawings are reviving this strip from the doldrums, and I receive absolutely no credit.'

Carmen looked suitably shocked, even angry. Tanya continued, 'According to what he told the guys in the Fort Worth office, I'm just some cute little chick who does sexy drawings and screws the boss. He more or less mentioned to them over the phone that he got the ideas for the various sex scenes by trying them out in his office with me.'

Carmen's eyebrows curved in the slightest of questions.

'No,' said Tanya, with a shake of her head. 'I've never had sex with Hiram Pease, and I'm not about to start now. Maybe I should file a complaint for sexual harassment. But I don't want to leave the firm; I like the work so much. There are not many jobs around where you can put your sexual fantasies on paper in detail *and* get paid for it!' Despite her anger, Tanya managed a wry smile.

'Ha!' said Carmen, looking Tanya straight in the eye. '*Chicita mia,* I believe that you and *Señor* Pease haven't had sex. But even if you did, you wouldn't be the first. I could tell you some things . . .'

Tanya's ears pricked up at the thought of further revelations about her boss's sexual exploits, but Carmen's narrative was cut short by the return from lunch of their co-workers, including Pease himself, who could be heard regaling the party with some risqué joke. The receptionist cursed in Spanish under her breath and looked up at Tanya. 'You and me, *chicita,* we need to get together one evening after work. We need to talk. I must get back to my desk before *el patrón* complains!'

Carmen quickly walked away, leaving Tanya to ponder her mixed emotions. The brunette designer opened the screens around her board and smiled at her colleagues as they sat down to resume their afternoon's work. She gazed down at Katrina Cortez spread-eagled on her drawing pad, and remembered the touch of Stephen Sinclair's penis brushing against her own thigh. With a quick gesture, she swept the drawings into a drawer and dedicated herself to other tasks that needed attention.

Chapter Three
Making her Bed

When Tanya arrived home that evening to what she still thought of as 'Eric's apartment', she was disappointed to find the well-equipped spaces empty. She switched off the alarm system and checked the messages. There was one from Eric himself to say that he was delayed at a meeting in Plano and would be home late, after eight.

To compensate for her boyfriend's absence, Tanya took a bottle of Caymus Vineyards' *Conundrum* from the refrigerator, opened it with a satisfying pop and poured herself a tall cool glass of pale golden liquid. She shuffled a collection of k.d. lang CDs into Eric's new stereo system, housed in its reproduction Louis Quatorze cabinet, and put her feet up to listen to the singer's poignant lyrics.

As she looked at Eric's extensive collection of paintings and small sculptures, Tanya reckoned the investment in the alarm system was a wise one. The art was cleverly integrated into the designer-decorated spaces. Compared to Tanya's previous one-bedroom efficiency in a featureless apartment gulag near Central Expressway, this condominium was a palace.

One of four condos, cleverly converted from a mansion built in the 1920s, about one mile from Deep Ellum, it sported a separate entrance, two thousand square feet of tall-ceilinged space, and maid service twice a week.

Early-evening sun streamed through the west-facing windows of the second-floor spaces. Under grand oak trees, cars and limousines cruised the plush boulevard below. Outdoors, the temperature was still over ninety degrees, but the noiseless air conditioning maintained a constant internal temperature of seventy-two degrees Fahrenheit. Tanya closed the blinds to cut down the glare of the hot low sun.

She picked up the business section of the *Dallas Democrat* and, to her delight, a page one item mentioned Eric Janovich, and a deal that his bank was putting together. Her boyfriend was a rising corporate star in the Texas banking world; as a Senior Vice-President for Real Estate Services, he was charged with the acquisition and development of land for the expansion of new bank offices across the south-eastern United States.

Tanya looked at the clock; Eric should be home in an hour. She placed the portfolio she had brought home upon a low table in the living room. It contained the same sketches she had shown Stephen, and Tanya would choose her moment to show them to Eric, after supper.

She fantasised about his response: he would peruse her work thoughtfully, and signify his loving approval with a deep lingering kiss. Then she would lead him into the bedroom and undress him slowly, rubbing her hands all over his body, tracing her fingernails through his thick dark hair in the way that made him purr with sensual enjoyment. With deliberate, teasing slowness, she would take his wonderful penis between her fingers.

Tanya smiled at these anticipations; she desired Eric's body as much as his approval. As befitted a young executive on the make in the cut-throat business of banking, Eric was fit, lean and just over six feet tall. His ebony eyes matched his hair, which was trimmed neatly, but deliberately just a shade longer than corporate etiquette specified. She loved nuzzling into the forest of curls that covered his torso and extended down to the wiry mat of pubic hair that framed his long and handsome staff.

Like everything else Eric undertook, his lovemaking technique was bold and dashing, and Tanya shivered at the memories of what he did to her body. Moistening with desire, Tanya shrugged out of her few clothes and, with a long slow swallow of wine, sauntered into the shower. The drawings could wait. The first order of business would be to take Eric to bed, to satisfy her lust. She wanted to banish the memories of her disturbing attraction to Stephen Sinclair, burying those unfaithful thoughts beneath Eric's appreciation of her art and her body.

At a few minutes after eight, Tanya heard Eric's key in the door, and moments later he swept into the bedroom, to find his lover spread before him on the bed. A short silk dressing gown, tied loosely to reveal her breasts and neat triangle of pubic curls, was all she wore. Tanya smiled seductively up at her lover. Eric stood there for a moment, his features coarsened by the day's growth of heavy beard on his square jaw. His banker's eyes glittered in appreciation of the sight before him and, uttering a low growl, he cast aside his briefcase, kicked off his shoes and threw his dark linen jacket across a nearby chair. With one lithe bound, he covered Tanya's body on the bed with his own, and slid his tongue deep into her mouth, one arm encircling her shoulders while his other hand urgently cupped her breast.

Tanya scrabbled for the buttons on Eric's shirt and bared his chest. She breathed his scent and bit a mouthful of hair between her teeth. With her free hand, she dived between his legs to grasp his penis, which was already long and hard. She pumped him with urgent strokes, feeling the ridged veins on his shaft even through his clothing.

Briefly, he took his hands from her body and divested himself of his trousers, underwear and socks. 'Oh, my sweet pretty baby,' he crowed softly. 'This is what you've been waiting for, isn't it, my little harlot? Come on, baby, suck my dick.'

Tanya obediently took him inside her mouth and felt her vagina clench with desire as she sucked him expertly. Sometimes she liked it when he took charge of their sexual games, pretending that she was a pampered trollop whose only task was her master's bidding. She held Eric's balls in one hand, and he moaned with delight and swivelled around to bury his nose in Tanya's muff of dark-brown curls, already matted with her sex-juices.

'Ah,' breathed Eric fiercely, 'my little harlot smells so good tonight. She looks so pretty and she tastes so good, too.' His agile tongue lapped Tanya's labia, probing her moist pink folds; his chin rubbed her clitoris as he rocked back and forth.

Eric paused only to insert two fingers deeply into Tanya's vagina, and to find her throbbing clit again with his thumb. He started a hard rocking rhythm that brought Tanya to a peak of excitement. She groaned aloud, her cries muffled by Eric's cock filling her mouth. Matching his tempo with strong strokes on his shaft, she felt herself building to a crescendo under her lover's strong and insistent fingers, but he made other demands that took priority.

'Make me come, Tanya. Make me come now!' Eric shouted, wild with ecstasy. 'I'm going to come all over your sweet little harlot's face!'

True to his word, Eric came with long pulsing streams of white semen, which filled her mouth and spilt down her cheeks. She pleaded, 'Now me, Eric! Make *me* come.'

She led her lover's fingers back to her tender labia and eased them inside. She felt once more the insistent pressure on the hard carmine nub of her clitoris and, within moments, she was over the edge into the sweetest bliss. Her body exploded with release, a cataract of sensation sweeping from the inner recesses of her womb to the extremities of her limbs. With a gasping, shuddering sigh, Tanya relaxed as Eric rolled to lie at her side, breathing heavily. Tanya nuzzled against her lover, kissing him passionately, transferring some residual semen from her mouth to his. Eric groaned with delight, his eyes tightly shut.

'Welcome home, darling,' said Tanya. 'Did you have a good day at the office?'

Still aglow from their vigorous lovemaking, Tanya and Eric weren't in the mood to fix supper; instead, they enjoyed a delicious meal delivered from the Rangoon House on Greenville Avenue. They lounged around a low table in the living room in their matching silk dressing gowns that Eric had bought in celebration of Tanya moving in with him. Eric opened a bottle of Gewürztraminer, its sweetness a mellow complement to the hot and spicy Asian food. They shared chicken satay with peanut sauce, pud Thai noodles with tofu, and a delicious green coconut curry.

Eric was excited by a successful land deal for a new financial office park he had put together during his lengthy meeting in Plano, a fast-growing community on the northern edge of the Dallas Metroplex. 'You should have seen those suckers, sweetheart,' he said proudly. 'They agreed to sell the land for thirty dollars a square foot. I'd have been willing to pay up to fifty, and I could even make the numbers work at fifty-five or sixty.'

Tanya searched for an appropriate question that wouldn't appear too dumb. 'Is this project for a new branch bank?' she enquired.

Eric paused, his wineglass at his lips. He looked first annoyed, and then rolled his eyes; when he spoke his tone was patronising. 'No, Tanya, it's *not* for a *branch* bank. I get my assistants to do those simple deals, buying up out-parcels in shopping centres. This is much bigger. It's for our "back-office" operations: credit cards, mortgages, what we call consumer banking services. We're building 500,000 square feet of space up there. That's why it's so important. I do wish you'd pay more attention to what I tell you.'

Tanya bit back an injured retort. Eric told her only fragments of his business dealings, yet expected her to know everything. Instead, she said meekly, 'Yes, Eric. Sorry.' She put on her best smile. 'I've got some things to show you from work today. Would you like to see them?'

Eric looked at his Rolex. 'Sure, sweetheart, if it won't take too long.'

'Oh, no. Just a few drawings.' Suddenly nervous, Tanya brought her portfolio to the table and spread out the sexy storyboard for the newest *Katrina Cortez* adventure.

Eric picked up the drawings and carelessly shuffled through them. 'Hmm, very sexy,' he commented but, to Tanya's dismay, he tossed them back casually on to the table. One fell off and tumbled to the floor, damaging the corner of the thick paper.

'Oh, Eric, be careful,' gasped Tanya, scrambling to retrieve her artwork. 'Look, you've crumpled the edge.' She held out the damaged drawing for his inspection, an accusing expression sharpening her features.

'Don't be so precious, Tanya baby. It's only a sketch. Look, it's not as if it's real art, is it? You don't need to get so worked up about this commercial stuff. What's it for? Just some dumb comic book. Lighten up, for God's sake!'

Tanya was stunned, then angry, and then hurt. 'Not

real art? Not real art, you say?' Her voice rose as the shock of Eric's abrupt dismissal washed over her. 'What do you know about "real art"?' She stood up and faced Eric belligerently, stung by his cavalier attitude.

Now it was Eric's turn to be offended. 'Just look around,' he said gesturing to the walls hung with his many acquisitions. 'I know a lot about real art. How do you think I chose all this?' He strolled to a large oil painting that depicted a variety of jungle animals, rendered in a vigorous expressionistic style with vibrant brush strokes. 'This is by Mack Beaty, one of Dallas's best painters. This is real art. It's not commercial stuff, hacked out for advertisements or comic books. Beaty's got real vision and a unique style. You could learn something from him, Tanya.'

Tanya bristled with anger. 'I know a damn sight more about Mack Beaty than you do, Eric!' she flared. 'And I *did* learn something from him; I studied under him at SMU for two semesters. *He* liked my work. Which is more than you do, evidently.'

Eric stood his ground defiantly, but made some effort at conciliation. 'Now look, Tanya,' he said. 'Don't get so worked up. I didn't mean that I didn't like it. I was just saying that there's a difference between commercial art and the real thing.'

'Oh, yes?' retorted Tanya, not pacified in the least. 'Is that what you think I am, a commercial hack? You're as bad as Hiram Pease. He just thinks I'm some cute bimbo who does sexy drawings.' She paused. As suddenly as it had flared up, Tanya's anger faded, only to be replaced by an emotion more painful. She felt her pride and belief in her work shrivel in the face of Eric's thoughtless onslaught; she wondered how she could have ever been proud of the drawings.

'You sure know how to crush somebody, don't you, Eric?' Tanya said sadly. 'I'm not one of your precious business deals. I'm your girlfriend, and I don't deserve this.'

Distraught and depressed, Tanya rushed from the room, slammed the bedroom door behind her and flung herself face down on the bed. On the same silken sheets where, less than two hours before, she and Eric had enjoyed such exuberant sex, she buried her head in her arms and sobbed. She couldn't help comparing Eric's cruelty to Stephen's genuine excitement over the same drawings.

When Eric came to bed some time later, she pointedly ignored him and lay rigidly at the far extremity of the bed. Neither spoke; Eric turned out the light with a theatrical sigh, and lay down with no attempt to heal their breach.

Sleepless, Tanya tossed and turned until finally, as Eric slept, she rose from the bed, turned on the light in the kitchen and took her sketchbook from her tote bag. She sat at the dining table with a glass of milk; idly at first, but with increasing concentration, she began drawing the female detective, caught in a difficult and stormy relationship with her cartoon lover. Suddenly, Tanya perceived that she was drawing Eric into the *Katrina Cortez* story as a manipulative man who always liked to be in control. Like Tanya herself, the character Katrina, infatuated with the great sex she enjoyed with her lover, overlooked his major personality flaws.

She drew page after page, her quick and confident line effortlessly capturing the mood-swings between the two protagonists. Katrina, normally self-directed and competent, struggled to retain her own identity amid her emotional entanglements. When Tanya glanced up at the kitchen clock, she was startled to see it showed 3.30 a.m. She yawned and stretched, feeling deeply tired and emotionally drained as the stress of the evening caught up with her. But at least, she thought defiantly, she had rebuilt her faith in her artistic abilities. She knew the drawings were good, and not even Eric could take that away from her.

At home alone in his apartment, Stephen Sinclair was also sleepless, and he rose from bed to make himself a post-midnight snack. He was thinking about Tanya Trevino, whom he found both bright and beautiful. Her intelligence included a sense of humour; her beauty contained a sexy fitness. And she had a sexy attitude.

He ate a small salad with goat's cheese, sun-dried tomatoes, radicchio and mesclun, topped with a tangy pear vinaigrette. He had mixed feelings about being alone. Beth-Ann Bodine would gladly have joined him in his bed, he knew. But despite the undoubted attractions of the woman's body and her ravenous appetite for sex, he found it awkward being with the buxom blonde for more than an hour or two. By the time they had satiated themselves with each other's bodies, there didn't seem to be much else to say or do.

Stephen acknowledged that, at twenty-three, his sexual experiences were limited, and Beth-Ann was by far the most expert and inventively salacious lover he had ever met. In fact her sexual aggressiveness had bowled him over; he had never been pursued so relentlessly before. It was very flattering and, as he sat naked at his small dining table, he found his cock hardening at the memories of the woman's expert hands and tongue ministering to his pleasure. Stephen absently stroked himself, solid and firm between his thighs.

But rather than recalling the enveloping sensation of Beth-Ann, his thoughts turned to the imagined touch of Tanya Trevino's fingers along his shaft. He wanted very much to get to know Tanya, and to take her to bed, to be Pete Regan to her Katrina Cortez. He sensed the depth of personality and intelligence behind Tanya's sexy beauty, which intrigued him more than Beth-Ann's superficial seductiveness, exhilarating and exhausting as that was. But what about Tanya's boyfriend, Eric? Stephen had heard that the bank executive was rich, handsome and successful. The dream of pursuing Tanya and breaking up that relationship didn't seem wise, or even possible. He was more attracted to Tanya, but as luck had decreed, it was Beth-Ann who had seduced him and who kept pursuing him so relentlessly.

With a sigh, he carried his few dishes to the sink, and left them to soak. He lay on top of his futon with the sheets flung aside in the night's sultry heat. Taking his still-plump penis in his hand, he stroked himself hard again with the speed of youth, and pumped his shaft excitedly. He filled his mind with a vision of Tanya Trevino, naked and straddling his torso. When he came, he imagined Tanya taking him, hot and pulsing, deep inside her body. He fell asleep with a smile of wistful longing on his face.

Chapter Four
Chocolate Lust

Early next morning, Eric slipped out of bed while Tanya was sleeping. He gave her the merest peck on the cheek before letting himself out the front door. Struggling to wake up, Tanya vaguely remembered her boyfriend had an out-of-town business meeting, and she arose also. But he was gone, without giving them a chance to make up.

She walked to the bathroom and looked gloomily at her reflection in the cabinet mirror. Dark rings under her eyes betrayed her lack of sleep. She staggered under the pulsating spray of the shower, which did something to revive her.

After drying off, she went into the kitchen, brewed a pot of strong, dark coffee, and opened the morning paper. It was another bright sunny day, with a cloudless Texas blue sky, and even at 7.45 a.m. the temperature was hovering near eighty degrees. Tanya let the large bath towel fall from her shoulders and sat naked with her coffee and corn flakes.

As usual, she studied the morning comic strips, but today's crop of drawings and story segments neither pleased nor riled her. She caught sight of her portfolio, and flipped through the sheets of sketches that Eric had dismissed so casually the previous night. Still depressed from arguing with her boyfriend, Tanya searched for solace in the memory of Stephen Sinclair's enthusiastic response to the same drawings. Last night's initial feelings of resentment against Eric gradually crystallised into something hard and lucid.

Thus preoccupied, Tanya faced the demands of the day. Her little Pontiac was still in the garage, having a recent dent removed. That meant she would have to walk in the uncomfortable heat. She made a face; she was bound to get sweaty, and that meant taking a change of clothes. With a sigh, she walked back to the luxurious bedroom with its *en suite* bathroom and dressed simply, in a sports bra and a white silk T-shirt, completing her preliminary ensemble with a pair of black hip-hugging bicycle shorts, white ankle socks and running shoes. She stuffed a pair of skimpy panties, a lace bra and white banded leather sandals into her exercise bag, and laid over them a carefully folded light cotton dress in a summery pastel print.

Thus equipped, Tanya tucked her small handbag into the outside pocket, zipped up the bag, set the code for the security alarm and double-locked the front door to Eric's apartment before taking the stairs to the street. Gasping a little at the heat already radiating from the asphalt surfaces, she hitched the bag high on her shoulder and set off at a brisk pace for Studio V.

As she jogged towards the studio, Tanya wondered how she could get some time alone with Stephen. She wanted to ask him more about his responses to her drawings, more about his background, his new life in Dallas, and even perhaps what he saw in Beth-Ann. But her vague plans failed to reach fruition. As soon as she arrived, she saw the studio was in something of a frenzy. Hiram Pease was everywhere, haranguing his small staff to meet an urgent deadline on an advertising layout for an important client. Pease paused only to cast a lascivious eye over Tanya's moisture-soaked figure as she headed for the rest-room to change.

'Be quick, Ms Trevino,' he shouted from across the room. 'There's no time to powder that pretty little body of yours. Get changed and get back in here!'

Tanya, blushing with embarrassment, glared back at Beth-Ann, who was watching with undisguised amusement. For once, Tanya was pleased she couldn't see Stephen Sinclair anywhere.

In the ladies' room, she speedily stripped and washed, rubbing body oil delicately scented with pear fragrance into her skin. She changed into her clean underwear and summer frock, and lingered to brush her silky hair back to its natural beauty.

When she returned to the studio, Tanya found herself drafted to help one team that included Leon Clarke, Chuck Greenberg and Beth-Ann, while Stephen was working across the studio with the two other women artists, Gloria Sanchez and Hillary Hightower. Tanya's consolation was that Beth-Ann was at her elbow. She couldn't get to Stephen, either.

Later that morning, Pease toured the office again, discussing the particulars of the work with each group. As he perused the final double-page layouts from Tanya's team, he nodded approvingly. 'This looks good,' he said, smiling at the circle of four anxious faces. 'I think you're on top of it. Well done!' He paused, as if considering an important decision. 'As you're in such good shape, I think I can afford to take one of you away for a little while to work on something new that's just come in.' His eyes roved across the group and came to rest on Beth-Ann. 'Ah, Miss Bodine, you'll do nicely. Would you step into my office for a few minutes?'

If Beth-Ann was surprised, she didn't show it. 'Now, Mr Pease?' was all she asked.

Pease nodded. 'Yes, now would do just fine, my dear.

I'm sure Tanya can finish your piece as well as her own.' Pease's eyebrows lifted with the vestige of a question, but not one that invited disagreement.

Tanya nodded glumly, trying to fix a smile on her face, but not quite succeeding. 'Certainly, Mr Pease. It won't take long.'

'Good. Good,' mumbled Pease, and loped off to his office. 'Miss Bodine,' he said, 'come along. We've got work to do.' He called over his shoulder to Carmen, sitting at her desk in the foyer: 'Carmen, sweetie, hold my calls.'

Beth-Ann's face was expressionless as she picked up her big leather shoulder bag; she adjusted the spaghetti straps of her yellow square-neck tank-top and followed the boss into his office, shutting the door behind her. Tanya, watching her colleague's retreating back with idle curiosity, caught a questioning glance from Stephen to the buxom blonde, which was met with the merest shrug of her shoulders. As the heavy oak door closed, Tanya fancied she heard the tiniest click of the lock sliding into place. But her attention was distracted by her colleague Leon, who was asking her something; she dragged her mind to the urgent work before her.

Once inside his office, and according to a well-planned routine between the two of them, Pease removed his clothes while Beth-Ann filed her nails, watching him. Her eyes did not miss the sight of a crisp new fifty-dollar bill on his desk.

Within a few minutes, Pease eased into the reclining chair as the big blonde woman put aside her nail-file and knelt between his legs. He was sitting naked, propped up in the luxuriously padded leather chair; the lighting in his office was subdued, and his clothing neatly folded on the stool beside him.

'Beth-Ann . . .' murmured Pease.

But Beth-Ann was already engaged in the process of

giving her employer a masterful blow-job, his second of the week. The young woman knelt before him, sucking and licking and stroking his partially tumescent penis. Watching with delight, Pease stayed her hand after a few moments and ruffled her golden hair. 'Take off your top, honey, and I'll give you a bonus,' he whispered.

Ceasing her hand and tongue motions on the man's growing cock, Beth-Ann sat back for a moment on her heels, her hands on her hips. 'Double or nothing, Hiram,' she said, her voice teasing and seductive.

Hiram Pease smiled at his employee. He knew the rules of this game.

Teasingly, Beth-Ann ran her thumb over the outline of her nipple through the layers of her thin clothing. She leant forward again to cradle Pease's penis, now proudly erect, and commented, 'My tits always make you hard.'

Pease nodded and gestured to her to raise her tank-top. She did so, revealing a strapless white lace bra. 'That too, honey,' he exclaimed eagerly, as he grasped his member in one hand.

But Beth-Ann lowered the yellow shirt over her large lace-covered breasts and demurred. 'Show me the money first, Hiram,' she requested, fluttering long mascara-dark lashes over pale blue eyes.

Gesturing impatiently with his free hand, Pease pointed to his folded trousers. The woman withdrew his wallet from the pocket and handed it to him. He dropped his pulsing cock with reluctance, drew out another crisp fifty-dollar bill and gave it to the blonde. She placed it on top of the first and quickly sat back to commence pulling the cotton top over her head.

He snapped his fingers. 'Come on, come on, honey!'

'OK, Horny Hiram,' said Beth-Ann, tossing aside the yellow top. She unceremoniously removed her bra and flung it on the floor, too.

As her big tits bounced before Hiram Pease's eyes, he leant forward and caught them in his hands. Sighing, the woman wiggled closer, across his knees, and let him pull her up into his lap. She knew what he wanted and snuggled close. 'If you want to fuck me, Hiram, it's more money.'

'OK, OK,' he said, pulling at the woman's clothing, trying to dislodge her panties from her heated pussy, wanting to slide her on to his distended cock.

'When do I get the money, Hiram?' breathed Beth-Ann as Pease reached inside her panties. She clamped his hand with hers before his fingers could slide inside her moist vagina.

'After, afterwards,' he mumbled, panting with desire.

'How much, Hiram?'

'More, more.'

'Double or nothing,'

'OK. OK,' he agreed.

The agreement settled, Beth-Ann released his hand, and allowed Pease to undress her, stripping off her short skirt. He slid her panties down to her ankles and held them as she stepped out.

Wearing only her high-heeled sandals, Beth-Ann straddled his thighs and arched her back as he caressed her rounded buttocks. The naked girl masturbated him under the halogen light of his desk lamp. Pease's member was very thick, but it was shorter than Stephen Sinclair's lovely cock. She dismissed the comparison to concentrate on her lucrative sideline.

The blonde took the condom he handed her, rolled it skilfully on to his penis, then eased herself on to his erection. She reached behind to fondle his balls, making her boss groan with pleasure. She dutifully rode the older man, feeling her excitement begin to mount, when suddenly Pease exclaimed, 'I'm going to come!' Immediately, his body spasmed; he spent all his energy before she was really started. Blind to his employee's desires, Pease sat up and playfully pushed Beth-Ann off his lap as his penis quickly folded in its latex sheath.

'I bet that was good, sweetheart,' he said, blithely ignoring Beth-Ann's pouting look of frustration. 'It's not every woman who gets laid by her boss *and* gets paid for it.'

'But Hiram, I haven't come, yet.' Beth-Ann was pulsing with the desire for more sex.

'Use that little vibrator I gave you,' Pease suggested off-handedly, as he reached for one of the fluffy towels he kept in a desk drawer. 'It's right here. You know how I love to see you bring yourself off. If you're lucky I might just get hard for you again.' He leered at her, dangling his flaccid penis provocatively in one hand while holding up the small white vibrator with its gold trim around the shaft.

'Oh Hiram,' groaned Beth-Ann, but she took the Turbo Rocket mini-vibe. With relish, she twisted it to the high-speed mode and sat on her boss's desk, spreading her legs. She inserted the twitching cylinder inside her pussy and masturbated blatantly in front of her employer.

Sweat broke out on Hiram Pease's brow. He watched, transfixed, his right hand feverishly stroking his flagging member back to a state of visible arousal. Before he could achieve more than a semi-firm erection, Beth-Ann came with a shuddering gasp. She lay panting theatrically on Pease's expansive cherry-wood desk, with one arm flung wide and one knee raised. With a strangled moan, Pease removed the vibrator and lapped at Beth-Ann's labia. He frantically pumped his unresponsive penis until a drop of semen spread over his fingers.

'Oh, Hiram,' said Beth-Ann sardonically, 'you're such a man.'

Satiated and deaf to his employee's mocking irony, Pease fumbled for his wallet and casually tossed two more fifty-dollar bills in the direction of the first two that now lay scattered on the floor. He stood up and began to get dressed.

'Come on honey, get back to your drawing-board,' he

said and reached in another drawer. In addition to the money, Pease handed Beth-Ann a small gold box of chocolates. 'This is a little extra for the, er, entertainment.'

Still squirming and peevish, in spite of the mouth-watering chocolates, Beth-Ann dressed; eschewing her bra, she pulled the Spandex tank-top over her ample breasts. She whined, 'Hiram, you know my blouse you ripped last week?'

'Mm?' he mumbled unconcernedly as he towelled himself and reached for his clothes.

The big blonde didn't bother with her panties either, stuffing them in her bag with the bra and the box of chocolates. 'Well,' she continued as she adjusted her skirt, barely concealing her lush loins, 'you said you'd buy me a new one.'

With a shrug, Pease laughed at her pouting expression and slipped on his shirt. There was not a wrinkle anywhere. Carefully, he stepped into his crisp blue and white striped boxer shorts. He pulled up his trousers and adjusted his belt before snapping on the lights and extracting his wallet again; handing the girl yet another fifty, he said, 'Maybe that'll keep you satisfied for a while.'

Her sullenness suddenly vanishing, Beth-Ann blinked at the crisp bills piled up in the brightness of the room. Cheerful again, she licked her lips and inserted the wad of money in a small purse, where it joined the hundred she had received from Pease for Monday's ministrations.

'Hiram, you're a sweetie,' she said and blew Pease a kiss, before unlocking his office door and prancing out.

Through the opening, Pease watched Beth-Ann walk across the studio to Stephen Sinclair's table and whisper something in his ear. As she bent over, her short skirt rode up to expose her naked arse to Pease's view. He smiled at her brazen behaviour. The blonde then sashayed out of the office to the ladies' room down the hall, young Sinclair's eyes following her all the way.

Pease fastened his tie as he watched the tableau. He was pretty sure the girl was also fucking Sinclair. Not that he minded; his regular sex sessions with Beth-Ann were nothing more than casual satisfactions of his sensual cravings. But, he thought, that sex-crazy blonde didn't waste any time. And he'd have thought Stephen might have been more attracted to Tanya Trevino. She was more his type.

For all his vulgarity, Pease considered himself a shrewd judge of his employees, and recognised that Tanya was someone with hidden depths to her character. A sudden mental picture of the slim brunette with creamy skin arose in his mind. It was time to talk to Tanya about the new developments with *Katrina Cortez*. If he played his cards right, he just might be able to plumb some of those hidden depths. The big blonde girl forgotten, he picked up the phone and smacked his lips with anticipation of new prey. He punched the number of Tanya Trevino's workstation.

The phone rang at Tanya's elbow when Beth-Ann re-entered the studio. Airily, the blonde greeted Stephen with a small wave. 'Hi, Steve,' she said insouciantly, ignoring Tanya as she waltzed past with a wiggle of her hips.

Beth-Ann hid her smile when she saw him blush, knowing that he was gazing fixedly at her as she returned to her desk in the corner next to him.

Tanya picked up her phone. 'Yes? Tanya Trevino.'

Beth-Ann listened absently to Tanya's end of the conversation, settling on to her seat, minus her underwear. She removed the chocolates from her large leather purse and set the gold box on her drawing table, taking off the golden lid. Extracting a succulent dark chocolate, she looked seductively at Stephen Sinclair. She felt a strong desire for more sex.

Tanya was speaking again. 'OK, Mr Pease. Yes, I'll be ready to leave for lunch in five minutes. Should I bring the drawings?' A pause. 'Fine. Goodbye, Mr Pease.' Tanya put down the phone.

Beth-Ann's ears pricked up; she slowly licked the chocolate from her fingers. Having just had sex with the boss, she was a little surprised and more than a little miffed that he was already on the phone to another girl – and skinny little Tanya, at that. The little bitch did have a good pair of tits, thought Beth-Ann begrudgingly. She wondered if Tanya drew her own tits in the *Katrina Cortez* illustrations. Beth-Ann had slyly started to alter the character's breasts when she took over the inking stage of Tanya's concept drawings. She especially liked rounding them out to match her own, and making the nipples larger and more pronounced, just like they were when Stephen Sinclair sucked them.

Still moist from today's hurried sex session with Pease and the Turbo-Rocket, Beth-Ann relished her horniness as she watched Stephen at his board. She wanted him. Hiram sometimes gave her a good time, but he was a selfish man, more concerned with his own release than anything else; often, she didn't even get off with him. Now, she lusted after little Steve.

Jealousy magnified her sexual neediness as she observed Stephen walk over to Tanya's desk to ask her opinion about a drawing. He glanced appraisingly at some of the *Katrina Cortez* sketches littering the brunette's board. Beth-Ann's finely tuned antennae picked up Tanya's attraction to Stephen Sinclair from across the room.

Beth-Ann felt tremors building in her clitoris as she fidgeted on her stool, skirt hiked up, hungrily watching the attractive young man as he consorted with that skinny little filly. But there was something *she* had over precious little Miss Tanya. She could fuck Pease one minute, and then Stephen Sinclair the next. God, her pussy would feel so good with first one and then the other man inside her . . .

She wanted Stephen. And she wanted him now; she would take him away from right under that silly Tanya's nose. It would be so easy, she smiled to herself. She dreamt about him; at home, when she masturbated in the shower, just thinking about sex with Stephen made her come. Beth-Ann reached between her silky thighs as she listened to Tanya's low murmur.

Beth-Ann was pleased when Stephen moved back to his own board, next to her in the corner bay that held their two desks. She swivelled on her chair and faced him. None of their colleagues could see when she parted her legs wide, giving Stephen a naked display of her curly bush. Staring fixedly at the young man, Beth-Ann made a kissing motion and massaged her labia, dipping her fingers in her vagina and then plucking a chocolate from the gold package in front of her. She held the sweet in her sex-drenched fingers. 'Want a taste, darling?' she asked.

Stephen was non-plussed, just as she'd planned. One minute he was looking at Tanya's enticingly erotic drawings, and the next he had a sight of the real thing, a semi-naked girl displaying herself right before his eyes. She could see his dick hardening in his trousers as he became increasingly turned on by her blatant sexual antics. He rose to stand beside her table.

'Thank you,' he said, reaching with his lips for the chocolate in her outstretched hand and tasting the spice of her sex juice. His penis strained in his linen trousers; it was obvious that he was enjoying the succulent double delicacy.

'Enjoying the chocolates, are we, Stephen?' said a quiet voice behind them. 'I think you'll find they have a very special flavour.'

Stephen and Beth-Ann both jumped in alarm as Hiram Pease stepped into their space, his quiet approach unnoticed in their mutual lust. Stephen once more shuffled awkwardly to disguise his arousal, but Pease shifted his attention to Beth-Ann, who froze like a deer in the headlights of a car.

'I'm glad to see you're hard at work, Ms Bodine,' he observed with a chuckle. He examined her flushed cheeks then studied some ink sketches on her board. 'Very good,' he drawled. 'A nice sensitive touch. You're no computer-aided cookie, are you my dear?' His manner was flirtatious and familiar.

Beth-Ann recovered quickly and responded in kind. 'No, sir, Mr Pease,' she confessed with a sly smile. 'I'm strictly hands-on.'

Pease laughed, then turned away to face Tanya, who was still working doggedly at her drawing board. He padded across to stand at her elbow. 'Are we ready, Ms Trevino?' he asked, his tone now formal and strictly business-like.

Tanya looked up from her drawings. 'Yes, Mr Pease, quite ready,' she replied, setting aside her pencils and picking up her purse.

To Beth-Ann's annoyance Pease smiled at his employee's promptness. 'I thought we'd go to that new Mexican restaurant on Knox Street,' he said. 'We have some important business to discuss, my dear. Come, my car is outside. Fernando will drive us.'

Chapter Five
Sex for Credit

The latest trendy little Mexican restaurant on Knox Street represented the 'down-market chic' that was booming in the Dallas area. Instead of a plush and sophisticated interior, *Across the Border* cantina sported bare walls with artfully crumbling stucco, rudimentary chairs, tables and fittings, all topped off with surly waiters. Tanya thought it looked rather like the Alamo after Generalissimo Antonio Lopez Santa Anna had finished with it; it was, she mused, the logical extension of the recent fashion for 'distressed' surfaces on furniture and walls and, before that, of torn jeans and frayed seams.

Pease commandeered a booth at the rear of the dining room. 'Tanya, my dear,' he gushed, 'don't you just love this latest deliciously avant-garde look? I know the interior designer who did this. He's from LA. He's the hottest thing around Dallas.'

In light of Tanya's thoughts a moment before, Pease dropped several notches in her estimation. 'Yes, Mr Pease, very nice,' she replied, with barely a hint of irony.

Pease looked hurt. 'Oh, tut, tut, my dear Tanya, we're out of the office, now. Please call me Hiram.'

Tanya cringed, but felt it wise to humour her boss. 'Thanks ... er, Hiram.' She struggled for more conversation. 'But didn't we come here to talk about work ... my work on *Katrina Cortez*?'

Pease frowned, and fiddled with the salt and pepper shakers on the white tablecloth. 'Yes, that's true, Tanya. But first let's treat ourselves to a good lunch. I think you'll enjoy what I have to say, but I'm hungry. I've had a *hard* morning. Let's eat,' he proclaimed.

Pease ordered Mole Ranchero and a giant Margarita on the rocks. Tanya contented herself with Chicken Fajita Salad and a Perrier. Throughout the meal, which Tanya had to admit was very tasty, Pease kept up a banter of office gossip spiced with none-too-subtle innuendoes concerning his virility and sexual prowess. He was, however, silent about his affair with Beth-Ann Bodine.

Their plates were cleared and they ordered coffee. Pease slid across the seat of the booth, moving closer to Tanya. 'Now, my dear, let's get down to our real business,' he said smoothly. He traced the contours of her biceps with his fingers and, despite herself, Tanya felt a *frisson* of anticipation echo down her arm. 'I wanted you to be the first to know,' he continued. 'I've been working really hard on this deal, and it's just come through.' He paused to move his fingers to Tanya's triceps. She followed his movements with her eyes as if hypnotised. She made no move to stop him.

Pease spoke again. 'Joshua McNally and I have optioned the revived *Katrina Cortez* strip to an independent film company that's interested in developing it for an erotic film noir. What do you think of that?'

Tanya was stunned. This was more than she'd hoped; imagined royalties and copyrights danced before her eyes. 'That's wonderful, Mr Pea ... Hiram,' she said. She could feel her cheeks redden with excitement. 'Who is it? Someone from Hollywood? Does this mean I'll be working directly with the film company?'

Pease held up his hand. 'Whoa, my dear,' he replied. 'It's not quite as simple as that. The deal is with Studio V, and that means with me. *Moi.* Myself. After all the hard work I did to sell this idea, the film producers need me as a cornerstone of the arrangement. I'll pass on their requirements to you, and you can churn out lots of your cute sexy little drawings. Then I'll work with the film people on the final production details. That's how it's done in the big leagues. Don't worry, Tanya,' he added, at her expression of doubt. 'It will be very good experience for you, my dear.'

He moved to stroke her shoulder, but now Tanya shrugged him off with an abrupt gesture. A sudden spurt of animosity overcame her natural reticence when dealing with her boss. 'Are you taking all the credit yourself?' she enquired fiercely. 'You know very well it's all my work, the drawing and the storylines. I should be involved in this right up front. It's my work, dammit, not yours!'

Pease appeared unperturbed by Tanya's outburst. In fact he looked as if he'd been expecting it. 'Tanya,' he said soothingly, 'don't get so upset. It will all work out. What's good for Studio V will be good for you. This could lead to higher and greater things for both of us.'

'Not for me, it won't,' stormed Tanya. 'Not if your name is all over the credits. So far I've received no recognition for my efforts, none whatsoever. I insist that you and the film company acknowledge my authorship.'

Pease, anticipating such a demand, refused. 'As the principal of the firm, my dear, all artistic copyrights belong to me.'

Tanya paused in her tirade, a look of uncertainty on her face.

'Now, Tanya, Studio V owns all the rights,' he said, 'but I'm sure we could arrange something between ourselves. Most women say I'm an attractive man . . .' Oblivious to her look of alarm, he preened slightly before continuing. 'And you are certainly a beautiful young woman – a very sexy young woman, if you'll permit me to say so. We could be partners, you and I. I'll agree to acknowledge you as the author, if you'll agree to get to know me better. How's that? That way, you'll get the best of both worlds.'

For the second time in as many minutes, Tanya felt as if the breath had been knocked from her body. She felt a surge of anger, at herself as much as at Pease. She should have seen this coming. Before she could muster a reply, Pease's cellular phone interrupted their *tête-à-tête*. With a muffled curse, Pease fumbled in his jacket pocket and flipped open his slimline handset. Turning away from Tanya, he spoke *sotto voce* into the little machine.

Shocked by the blatant sexism of Pease's tactics of 'sex for credit', Tanya moved away in the booth to get some literal and metaphorical breathing room; Pease's pre-occupation with his conversation on the cell phone allowed her a speedy review of her position. In quick succession, she considered giving in to her employer's demands (after all, he wasn't too bad looking for a guy in his mid-forties), filing suit for sexual harassment, and resigning on the spot. But Tanya knew just how caught up she was in the world of Katrina Cortez. More and more it was her world. And Pease, the crafty bastard, showed that he understood this very well. Tanya was afraid that if she didn't agree to his demands, she'd lose her job, and all the hard work she'd put into her new career would be for naught.

Tanya was perspiring. But Pease needed her. Without her, she thought feverishly, the deal couldn't go through. Without her, there would be no stories, no *Katrina Cortez*. She had to get McNally and the movie people to understand that.

In her quandary, Tanya imagined what her alter ego Katrina Cortez would do to turn the situation to her advantage. *She* would have no qualms about having sex with a man like Pease; she'd find some way to turn the tables, just like her adventures with Pete Regan and the drug smugglers.

The more she thought about it, the more she considered that sex with Pease might indeed be the best way to advance her own professional future as an artist. But, just as she was about to commit her body in the cause of art, she drew back. What would Eric do if he found out? It would be very unlike Pease to keep quiet about his latest sexual conquest. With a start, Tanya realised she wasn't too concerned about Eric's feelings: what was more important to her was Stephen Sinclair's opinion. What would he think if he found out she was sleeping with the boss?

Hiram Pease finished his conversation and turned to face her. 'Sorry about that little interruption, my dear,' he said smoothly, picking up where he had left off. 'Now where were we?' A lascivious smile greased his face.

Tanya knew in that instant she could never have sex with Pease, even to save her job; but, intuitively, she felt she could fool him, string him along – at least for a while, until she and Katrina Cortez came up with a better idea. Taking a deep breath, she replied in a voice that sounded unfamiliar to her own ears.

'You'd just asked me to fuck you, Hiram, in return for giving me authorship credits on the movie deal.' She struggled to catch the right note of irony and tease. 'Tell me, did you have in mind just one fuck, or perhaps a series? One per chapter? Or one per scene? How much is a blow-job worth these days? I confess I don't know what the going rate is "in the big leagues". But don't tell me, Hiram, that a man of your prowess hasn't worked all this out?'

Tanya relished the look of utter bewilderment on her boss's face. Of all the possible reactions to his proposition, it was clear he hadn't expected this one. He'd expected shock and denial, or some such coy display of womanhood.

Hiram Pease opened and closed his mouth to no effect before regaining control of his vocal chords. 'Well, Tanya, I . . . thought we'd just work it out, so to speak, as we go along . . . as we get to know each other better, you might say.'

'Hiram,' said Tanya, silkily, 'you can't manage this strip without me. You can't possibly pass yourself off as the creator of Katrina for more than a few minutes.' Her pulse thudded like a drumbeat in her ears. 'But if you play fair by me, we might just get to "know each other better", as you so quaintly put it.' She reached out to stroke Pease's arm for effect, and noted with alarm that her hand was shaking; she couldn't keep up this act for much longer.

If Pease noticed Tanya's nervousness, he gave no sign. 'Well, sweetheart, I think we have ourselves a little deal,' he cooed, snuggling up closer to her side. He reached for Tanya's hand and brushed it gently with his lips, before placing it deliberately over the growing bulge in his pants.

Tanya tensed, but forced herself not to pull away. She allowed herself to squeeze Pease's dick in response to his light nibbles on her neck; feeling the ridge around his glans, she schooled herself to stroke it gently. This had worked for Katrina.

'I see we understand each other perfectly, my dear,' Pease murmured appreciatively into her ear. 'This is going to be a most stimulating partnership.'

Tanya didn't want to give Pease the impression that all was decided, bar the sex. She removed her hand from his lap, sat up straight in the booth, and shook free Pease's hand, which was fingertipping its way towards her breast. 'Hiram,' Tanya said with more confidence than she felt, 'that's enough for now. I want to see some evidence of good faith, on your part.'

'You won't have to wait long, Tanya,' he said, with a knowing wink. 'I was just coming to that part. I would like you to join a special little business meeting over dinner tonight. We're gathering preliminary ideas for the screenplay. And as artistic partner,' he added, with a leer, 'I'm sure you could add a lot to the discussion.'

Tanya forced herself to be business-like. 'Who's "we", Hiram? Who is going to be there? And where is this dinner going to take place?' Irritably, she remembered her car was still in the shop. 'I'll need a ride.'

Pease couldn't keep the condescension out of his voice. 'You already know Joshua McNally, the publisher,' he replied. 'The other people at the meeting will be Sheila Sorensen, the film producer, and her assistant. Sorensen heads up Ganymede Productions. They're based in LA, but have a branch office near the studios at Las Colinas. That's where we're having supper, at the Venetian Piazza on the Manderlay Canal.'

Tanya knew the restaurant by reputation. It was located on the bizarre little waterway that bisected the peculiar office and housing complex at Las Colinas, an instant 'edge city' created during the nineteen eighties. In many ways this urban recreation of Venice was indistinguishable in its glitzy PoMo superficiality from the stage settings of the nearby film studios. Katrina Cortez had driven nearby, tailing Peter Regan and his companion from the airport.

'Be there at eight,' commanded Pease. 'Why do you need a ride?'

'My car's in the shop.' Tanya didn't elaborate.

'Can't your fancy boyfriend drop you off?'

Tanya bit her lip. 'No, he . . . has a meeting out of town. He won't be back in time.' She realised that she had no idea what Eric's plans were for the evening. They usually checked their diaries over breakfast, but not this morning. Tanya's heart slumped at the memory of their argument.

She knew that none of this was lost on Pease, who watched her under lidded eyes, like a hawk. No doubt he'd guessed that all was not well on the romantic front. His eyes glittered in seeming anticipation, but his tone was annoyed.

'I need Fernando to drive Joshua and me. I'll get young Sinclair to pick you up. I'm sure he won't mind doing me this one small favour.' Pease continued to watch her and Tanya shut down the conflicting emotions that flickered across her face. Even so, she had a nasty feeling that her eyes had sparkled at Sinclair's name and that Hiram had filed that away for further reference.

'I'll call young Stephen right now, and fix it up.' He teased Tanya with a malicious grin. 'He's such a handsome young boy; I think our friend Sheila will find him very amusing. He's just her type. Do you want to talk to him?'

Although her pulse raced with alarm at the thought of Stephen being seduced by this other woman, Tanya held her emotions and her unreliable poker face in check. 'No,' she said offhandedly. 'Why should I?'

Pease flipped open his cellular phone and speed-dialled the studio. 'Carmen?' he said brusquely. 'Put me through to Sinclair.' There was a pause while Stephen came on the line. Tanya could hear him faintly over the handset, but not clearly enough to make out any words.

'Oh, Stephen,' purred Pease in his most unctuous tone, 'I wanted to give you the opportunity to meet some important new clients this evening. I hope you don't have any plans.' He nodded into the phone at Stephen's reply. 'Good, good. I knew I could rely on you, my boy. We're eating at the Venetian Piazza in Las Colinas; you know it? These are important clients on a film deal I'm busy negotiating.' He unconsciously groomed his hair under Tanya's watchful stare. 'Be there at eight. Oh, and one more thing. I need you to bring along the star of the evening. She needs a lift.'

The phone squawked a question.

'Who is it?' repeated Pease, with a nasty little grin on his face. 'Why, it's our very own little Tanya.' Tanya winced at the proprietorial tone in her employer's voice. 'Your colleague, Miss Trevino,' Pease added, to make sure Stephen got the message. He reached over and stroked Tanya's firm, bronzed thigh. 'She's very much in demand, now. You'll need to pick her up by seven-thirty.'

Pease turned to Tanya. 'What's your address?' He repeated Tanya's directions into the phone. 'Got that, Stephen? Yes, that's all. You won't keep the lady waiting, will you?' He snapped the handset shut with a practised flick of the wrist. 'There, my dear,' he said with a sly grin. 'Things are coming together nicely.' He looked at his watch, sighing with an exaggerated slump of his shoulders. 'Time to get back on the treadmill. Places to be, people to meet. Got to bring in enough money to pay your salary, my dear.' He stood and helped Tanya slide out of the booth, holding her arm a little longer than was necessary, and letting his fingers as if by accident slide down her back and brush her buttocks. Tanya grimaced but said nothing.

'Come, I'm sure Fernando will be waiting with the car. I'll drop you back at the office. Oh, and by the way,' he added, as if an afterthought, 'why not wear something special this evening? You know these film people.' Pease shrugged as if to disclaim any responsibility for their tastes. 'They respond so well to sexy young women.'

The drive back to Studio V was brief, and Fernando pulled to a stop outside the building's main entrance, opening Tanya's car door for her to climb out. She realised that he was admiring her long legs and firm breasts as she gathered herself from the sumptuous seats of the limousine. He caught Tanya's eye; her flicker of response was quickly quelled, but she was sure that he'd noticed.

Pease spoke through the open door. 'I'm looking forward to this evening, Tanya,' he said. 'To our combined efforts, and to . . . working out all the details of our little arrangement. Don't be late.' Fernando closed the door and, a moment later, the car pulled silently away into the traffic of Elm Street, leaving Tanya standing on the pavement, her emotions upside down.

Tanya walked slowly to the front door, excited by the opportunities opening before her. The entrance was deserted, and she absently pressed the button to summon the lift. But as she ascended, her elation turned into anxiety. How far could she go to mislead Pease into thinking she really wanted to have sex with him? Was there any way to do this and still retain some shred of integrity? It was all right for Katrina Cortez; Tanya could draw her an escape route from any difficult situation in the next chapter. If only life was like a comic book!

Wrapped up in her own thoughts, Tanya didn't notice Carmen's smile of welcome, Beth-Ann's look of poisonous spite, or even Stephen Sinclair's look of troubled yet eager enquiry as she walked back to her drawing board.

Perching nervously on her tall stool, Tanya tried to concentrate on the drawings in front of her. With a start, she saw amid her scattered sketches a clever little cartoon depicting a young man holding a car door for someone who looked a lot like Katrina Cortez, dressed in a revealing black evening gown. As the young man helped her into the back seat of the limousine, the dialogue bubble above him read, 'Seven-thirty on the dot, Ms Trevino!'

Chapter Six
Learning Lessons

Alerted by muffled giggles across the studio, Tanya saw to her annoyance that Beth-Ann and Stephen were engaged in a furtive conversation over the blonde's drawing board. The other artists were watching, too, Leon and Chuck with amused smiles, while Gloria and Hillary exchanged disapproving looks. Stephen flushed when he saw himself the centre of silent attention and, with attempted nonchalance, he ambled back to his drawing board. But Beth-Ann ruined the effect by flashing the young man a conspiratorial wink and blowing him a leering kiss.

Watching Beth-Ann and Stephen play cat and mouse gave Tanya a sudden wicked insight into their activities over the lunch hour. While she herself had been manoeuvring around the issue of future sex with Hiram Pease, the pair of co-workers had probably been having sex right here in the deserted studio. Tanya couldn't stop her active imagination filling in some crucial details, and she pictured the taut line of Stephen's buttocks contrasted against the woman's fleshy curves.

Further deliciously carnal thoughts simmered in her libido, igniting a stirring tingle between her legs. Tanya struggled with a rising unrequited desire to make love with Stephen Sinclair herself. But her eyes fell upon the framed photo of Eric, still propped up next to Edward Bear; her boyfriend's black-eyed stare bored into her, and the little stirrings of guilt returned. Tanya wrenched her gaze away from Eric's picture and turned his photograph face down on the board, shutting him out of her mind.

But the public game of billing and cooing between Beth-Ann and Stephen wasn't so easily ignored. Frustrated with her growing obsession, Tanya slammed down her drawing instruments and stomped to the ladies' room. Carmen Sierra was there, washing her hands. She looked up at the artist's heavy-footed entry.

'My goodness, Tanya, what's wrong?' Her voice was tinged with alarm. 'You look ready to hit someone.'

'Oh,' shrugged Tanya, 'it's nothing. Just an ink blot on a drawing.'

'I don't believe you, *cara mia*. Only a man could make you look that way. Is it Eric?'

Tanya shook her head. 'No,' she said. 'It is not Eric. It's Stephen Sinclair.' She turned to face Carmen and blurted, 'I want Stephen Sinclair! I want to touch him, kiss him, lick him, make love to him . . .'

Carmen's eyebrows rose theatrically. 'This is a recipe for serious trouble, Tanya. You know that?'

Tanya agreed. 'Yes, Carmen, it is trouble – and it is serious. I keep thinking about having sex with Stephen. I'm jealous as hell of Beth-Ann, and now all of a sudden Eric isn't enough for me.'

'Oh dear,' said Carmen. 'You sound hot and horny.' She frowned. 'Perhaps you don't have to decide between them, Tanya. Many men have more than one lover at a time; why not we women, too? Is Eric faithful to you?'

Tanya's eyes opened wide in surprise. 'I've never thought about it. I assume so.' She laughed self-consciously. 'I was about to say, "he'd better be!", but here I am wanting to have an affair with a guy at the office. What a cliché.'

Absently, Tanya rinsed her hands in the basin. The hum of the hot-air dryer drowned out Carmen's next words. 'Pardon?'

'I said, I don't know your *Señor* Eric, but I have got to know Stephen a little, and he's wasted on Beth-Ann.' Carmen's tone was haughty in her dismissal of the blonde Texan's attributes. 'Stephen needs a girlfriend who's more than just a sex-crazed *bambina*. All Beth-Ann thinks about is her next orgasm.'

Tanya laughed out loud at Carmen's merciless description of their colleague.

'You know, Tanya,' Carmen said, her head cocked to one side in appraisal, 'you could take Stephen away from Beth-Ann and open up a whole new world for the young boy. The experience would probably do him good. But the real problem is not Miss Kissy-Face out there, but your friend Eric. Does he deserve you? Are you happy in his fancy apartment?'

Carmen smiled at the look of surprise on Tanya's face. 'You were the talk of all the office when you moved in with him, you know. There were stories of what a palace his home was, how he had gilt mirrors on all the walls and ceilings so he could watch himself having sex anywhere, and TVs and stereos that came out of the walls at the touch of a button.'

Tanya laughed again. Talking with Carmen was fun; she was feeling a lot better already. 'It's not at all like that. Where on earth do all these rumours get started? It *is* pretty fancy, though. Lots of stuff, "and all in the best possible taste".' She parodied a Dallas socialite's airs and graces.

Now it was Carmen's turn to laugh, but she caught herself. 'I must go back,' she said. 'Pease will wonder where I am.'

'He's not in this afternoon; there's no hurry,' Tanya said.

'No, I must go. Tanya, don't take too much notice of me and my questions. I don't want to get you into trouble with your boyfriend.' She left.

Tanya stared at her reflection in the mirror. She imagined Stephen Sinclair standing behind her, his hardness pressed against her buttocks, his hands reaching round to cup her breasts. 'I think I'm already on my way there,' she said to herself.

Back in the studio, Tanya found it impossible to concentrate, and soon gave up the struggle. If she was going to get her act together for the evening, she wasn't going to do it at Studio V, constantly distracted by taunting eye messages from Beth-Ann and confused little smiles from Stephen. Tanya left the lovebirds to their little lovers' games for the time being. She couldn't face the hot and sweaty walk home in the glaring afternoon sun, so she called a cab and packed her bag, taking home sketchbook and pencils.

Moments later Carmen called from the front desk. 'Tanya! The taxi, it is here.'

'Be right there,' replied Tanya, but on her way out she detoured past Stephen's desk. 'Thank you for that beautiful little drawing, Stephen,' she said, conscious of Beth-Ann's eyes boring into her. She pointedly ignored her rival.

Stephen blushed and smiled, his eyes downcast. 'My pleasure,' he mumbled.

'I'll see you at seven-thirty, then,' Tanya continued, returning his smile. 'I'll look forward to it.' Only then did Tanya look in Beth-Ann's direction. 'Don't wear him out, Beth-Ann,' Tanya suggested ironically to the other woman. 'Young Stephen's got a busy evening ahead of him.'

She heard Leon's muffled snort of laughter, but Tanya

didn't look behind her as she walked briskly to the lift, pausing only to say a friendly goodbye to Carmen. 'I'm going out to dinner tonight with Pease and some movie producers. It's about the *Katrina Cortez* stories. Wish me luck!'

The receptionist clapped her hands excitedly. 'That's great news! Will you become famous overnight?' Carmen joked. 'Will you speak to us mere mortals in the morning?' She blew Tanya a pouting kiss. 'No, really, *chicita*, best of luck! I mean it.'

Tanya laughed as the lift doors closed and she was whisked to the waiting taxi in the street below. She hoped the joke wouldn't be on her.

During the brief ride to Eric's apartment, Tanya pondered the tangled web of lust that wove together the different personalities in Studio V's hothouse of sexual intrigue. Pease wanted to have sex with her and she wanted Stephen, who in turn was getting laid by Beth-Ann. To complete the circle, she thought with a grim little smile, Pease should be having it off with Beth-Ann.

That notion, which began in jest, hit her with a flash. Perhaps that was exactly what was happening. Tanya recalled Beth-Ann's lengthy private 'meeting' with Studio V's director in his office before lunch. She wondered if there really was a special project the big blonde was working on for the boss. If so, she doubted whether Stephen Sinclair was aware of his lover's probable duplicity.

Her train of thought was interrupted by the cab's arrival at Eric's Swiss Avenue apartment. She paid the driver and, once inside, moved quickly to deactivate the alarm. One day last week she had forgotten, and all hell had broken loose. Because the system connected directly to the neighbourhood police station, a squad car had come screeching to her door in only five minutes, siren howling and lights flashing. She had failed to pacify an irate police officer, who had lectured her about wasting valuable police time. Eric had walked into the middle of the fracas; he had apologised smoothly to the policeman, but then berated Tanya for her carelessness after the surly representative of law and order had driven away.

The memory disturbed Tanya. Why *am* I here? she wondered. What did I think I was doing when I moved in with Eric? She knew the answer very well: great sex. While they had still been dating, and the relationship hadn't reached the stage of firm commitment, she had found Eric to be a wonderful and attentive lover. After indifferent sex with several boyfriends, making love with Eric Janovich had been just glorious. Even now, in her grumpy state, Tanya felt a tingle as she anticipated his touch.

But soon after she had taken the plunge and moved in, instead of being a cherished lover, Tanya had felt more like a possession, a beautiful companion to decorate Eric's arm at social functions and to entertain him in bed at the end of the day. And yet when Eric smiled beguilingly, when his penis swelled at the mere sight of her body, when he pulsed inside her and kept her at a sensual peak for what seemed like hours, she was prepared to forgive him most things. Maybe, she thought, it's just a phase. Maybe he's under a lot of pressure at work. Maybe things will be better soon.

On that optimistic note, Tanya left her things in the living room, where she'd dropped them in her rush for the alarm switch, and walked lightly to the bedroom. She kicked off her sandals and lifted her dress over her head, unclipped her lace bra, and pulled down her silk panties. She left the clothes on the floor where they fell, and walked, naked, back to the kitchen; she poured herself a long cool glass of minty iced tea from the jug in the refrigerator.

Tanya stepped into the living room to pick up her sketchbook and pencils, her bare feet sinking into the dense carpet. She turned to Eric's stereo equipment, and flipped through the pile of CDs. Most were Eric's, Baroque concertos and cool jazz: fine in their own way, but unsuited to her current mood. Eric had pushed a few of Tanya's own discs to the back, mainly Texas blues, R & B and country rock; she considered Stevie Ray Vaughan and Bonnie Raitt before selecting her namesake, Tanya Tucker. At the touch of a button, the singer's strong voice filled the apartment, bemoaning unfaithful lovers and unrequited passion.

Am I going to be unfaithful to Eric? wondered Tanya. Would that make her just as bad as Beth-Ann, who might be having sex with Hiram Pease *and* Stephen Sinclair? With a cold-blooded resolve that surprised and alarmed her, Tanya knew without a doubt that she was going to lure Stephen to her bed, and to hell with the consequences. What was she thinking?

Sinking to her knees, she ran her hand across the smooth pile of the carpet, softly, as though petting a docile animal, recalling Stephen's arousal when he read her *Katrina Cortez* stories. Tanya squirmed with agitation as she imagined his cock unfurled from his tailored trousers, free of underwear, naked in the palm of her hand. Beth-Ann Bodine had held that same cock in the flesh, thought Tanya.

Lying naked on the soft carpet, Tanya experienced a fresh burst of untrammelled jealousy towards her blonde and busty co-worker, but enjoying at the same time the physically cooling waft of conditioned air from the floor vents. She grabbed a cushion for her head and made herself comfortable. She rationalised her anticipated betrayal of Eric as payback for his cavalier and dismissive attitude towards her art the night before; she nurtured a burgeoning resentment for his lack of appreciation of her professional accomplishments. It was all one way; she was supposed to play the Greek chorus to her lover's achievements, while never receiving any equivalent response from him.

Other thoughts troubled her. What would the two executives, McNally and Sorensen, be like this evening? How would she pull off her sexual manoeuvres with Pease at the forthcoming dinner? She rolled over on her stomach and opened her sketchbook, brushing aside her long brown hair as it fell over the pages. She needed to order her thoughts for the meeting; she needed desperately to impress McNally and Sorensen with her ideas for storylines and visual settings that would translate into a movie. But how far were they prepared to go with the sex scenes? What was their anticipated audience?

Many of Tanya's sketches depicted sexual acts, and the storylines of the *Katrina Cortez* comics were mainly vehicles for sex of one kind or another. But as she picked up her pencil, her personal thoughts and worries blended with the invention of new storylines with which to impress Joshua McNally and Sheila Sorensen.

Quickly sketching, Tanya imagined the actions of her man-eating character, Katrina Cortez, who would do anything to further her professional career and to satisfy her sexual desires. If Katrina wanted to take Stephen from Beth-Ann's boudoir to her bed and to keep Pease at arm's length, all the while making sure the film people appreciated her talent, what would *she* do?

The sexy undercover PI took off her red shoes as she watched the stranger in black withdraw an enormously erect penis from the darkness of his cape. She silently straddled a tall stool. The smooth pale skin of her firm inner thighs was marked with a single dark blue serpent tattoo. Dressed only in a suspender belt and red stockings, she watched the man masturbate as he moved closer to her. In return, she silently slid one finger between her pussy lips, visible within the triangular frame of her clipped pubic hair. As the man stepped into the pool of light before her, she saw he was naked beneath his cape, and the light brown of his pubic curls matched his lustrous chestnut hair as it flowed to his shoulders. In the background, the lush buxom blonde was tied securely to the bed. Stripped naked, she could only watch in seething frustration as Katrina slowly bent forward to take the head of the stranger's penis deep within her mouth.

After an hour of collecting ideas through drawing and writing, Tanya put down her pencil and sketchbook. Fed by her sketches, her thoughts veered straight towards Stephen Sinclair; her lusty fantasies ignited sensations in her loins that demanded quenching.

Tanya rose and moved purposefully into her boyfriend's adjacent home office. This was the space that most represented her lover's male charisma; normally just being here turned her on. The large sash window provided a view directly to the office towers of the central business district, just over two miles away. The branches of large oak trees created an elaborate frame.

Before this portal, Eric's desk was a deep rich oak, inlaid with red African padouk and black Peruvian walnut; the filing cabinets were matching oak and the chairs finished with beautifully aged leather. The walls, panelled in pale cherry, were patterned by the oblique rectangular shadows of the window mullions. But this afternoon Tanya had little time to admire the decor. She perched on the ergonomically perfect office chair and unlocked the central drawer of Eric's desk, feasting her eyes on the array of sex toys that he kept in the shallow velvet-lined storage space.

She noted with interest that Eric had purchased some new items recently; an illustrated catalogue from a San Francisco mail-order firm lay to one side. In addition to the pink, blue and red battery-operated jelly vibrators they used in their sex games together, Tanya noticed two new ones, astonishingly patterned in art deco tile motifs and wood grain. She passed these by with a shudder of aesthetic distaste. Eric would have to use those on himself!

The male aroma and aura of the office was working its magic. Tanya carefully adjusted the swivel chair, and picked out her favourite toy, the purple jelly G-spot vibe. She coated it with the new lubricant, Liquid Silk, that Eric had imported specially from a friend in England, and gave herself over to auto-erotic pleasures as she slid it deliciously deep inside.

Her fantasy characters filled Tanya's imagination. In her latest invention, Katrina Cortez was engaged in a complex ritual of sex games at the GirlZone, an Aladdin's Cave of erotic pleasures, to pry information from her quarry Regan, the drug smuggler, about his contacts and schedules.

But in Tanya's fevered creation, Regan's fantasy penis transformed into Stephen Sinclair's proud member, and she came with a crescendo, the young artist's name shuddering on her lips. Sensations of release, intertwined with continued desire, coursed through her limbs as Tanya slumped back in the chair, her legs splayed wide across the armrests. She stared in a trance through the window at the downtown towers of Big D. A large dark thundercloud was massing up behind the panoply of towers, its mass and ferocity enhanced by the slanting yellow flinty light. Charged with menace, it looked like a huge black caped nemesis looming over the city. Tanya shuddered again.

Chapter Seven
Katrina in Control

The black cape hung across the shoulders of the dark-haired woman like a spreading thundercloud. Beneath its folds, Katrina Cortez was naked, except for her cherished black knee-length boots. Their stiletto heels added several inches to the lean detective's height.

From her elevated position, Katrina smiled wickedly down at Pete Regan, who was naked and firmly lashed with indigo silk scarves to the four corners of a low futon and frame. Regan was not alone; two naked red-headed women knelt at his side, taking turns sucking and stroking Regan's energetically erect penis. Occasionally their hands detoured to his fulsome balls and the cleft of his buttocks. Over the previous hour, the sexy pair had brought the helpless man countless times to the brink of climax, only to cease cruelly at the critical instant, leaving Regan thrashing in frustration. To add to the exquisite torture, Katrina openly masturbated above him, standing with her thighs spread over his head, giving her tormented captive a tantalising view into the pearly folds of her pussy.

'Katrina, please! For Chrissakes! Let me come!' Her

hapless companion bucked his pelvis upward, searching for any friction that would trigger his ejaculation.

Katrina smiled cruelly and shook her head, unmoved by his pleas. 'Now Pete, play fair. You've had your way with me. Only an hour ago you had me tied down, teasing and tormenting me till I begged you to make me come. You refused, remember? And I was begging harder than you are now. These two ladies are every bit as expert with a woman's body as they are with a man's.'

Regan groaned at the very threshold between pain and pleasure as the two redheads traced their long fingernails over his flesh, assiduously avoiding any contact with his bucking penis and bouncing balls, denying him ultimate gratification.

'Just think how good it's going to feel when I do take that long thick cock of yours deep inside me, Pete,' purred Katrina, increasing the intensity of her own self-pleasure. 'But you know the rules of this game. I told you my deep, dark secret and earnt my reward at the hands of these two nymphs.' Hands and tongues, Katrina remembered deliciously. 'Now you have to tell me yours. To what evil deed will you confess, and gain release from my thrall?'

Katrina milked the melodrama for all it was worth. Indeed, she was determined to coax some important scraps of information from Regan's lips: names, places, dates. Something, anything that would enable the cops to penetrate the closed ranks of his organisation.

Regan remained stubbornly silent and, at Katrina's signal, the girls lay down on a matching futon, where Regan could watch them. 'Men like to watch girls getting it on, Pete,' she teased. 'Let's see how long you can stand it, seeing them come and not being able to touch your dick.'

The duo fell readily to their task, enjoying a well-practised routine of mutual cunnilingus and masturbation. Hands, fingers, tongues and shapely dildos probed every available orifice, till the two bodies were locked together in a frenzy of glistening lust. The women's moans and screams of pleasure rent the air of the closed room. Imprisoned on his bed of torment, Regan tried to avert his eyes, but Katrina could see that the full-blooded and sensual carnality of the spectacle overwhelmed him. He couldn't tear his eyes away from the beautiful women pleasuring themselves so deliciously. He groaned with such anguish, and went white with tension, that Katrina worried for a moment he might faint.

Katrina herself was sucked into the maelstrom of pleasure, rubbing and finger-fucking herself to a matching and shuddering climax. She taunted Regan. 'Oh, God, that was delicious! Oh, Pete I'm so wet!' Katrina slid two fingers inside her, in a ripple of renewed sensation.

As the waves of pleasure receded, Katrina spread wide the folds of her cape, highlighting her beautiful white body against its depthless indigo backdrop.

'One last chance, Pete Regan,' she intoned, towering over her captive. 'One terrible secret will release you; otherwise you will be condemned to stay here, spread-eagled with all that come in your cock and nowhere to shoot it.' She bent forward and pressed a finger gently on the tender place between Regan's balls and his anus. It usually drove him wild, and tonight was no exception.

'All right! All right! Enough!' Regan was yelling and squirming fit to burst. 'If I tell you something that's a secret, something that nobody else knows, you'll untie me so I can fuck one of you? Is that the deal?'

'Hell, yes, Pete. If it's a really good secret, you can fuck all three of us.'

Regan's wild eyes darted round the three beautiful libertines at his bedside. The two redheads stood with hands on hips, one to each side, flanking Katrina at the foot. Their firm round breasts and rosy nipples jutted towards the prisoner in silent titillation, reinforcing his sense of helplessness. Their fluffy forests of pubic curls were a matching deep auburn tint, in contrast to Katrina's closely cropped and geometrically exact triangle of dyed indigo. Katrina was a symphony in black and white, her naked body shining under the spotlights, her skin glistening.

Obviously salivating at the prospect of rampant sex at last with these three goddesses of lust, Regan could hold back no longer. 'This is a big secret. You must promise that it never goes outside this room.'

'Of course, Pete. That's always part of the rules,' Katrina lied. 'Trust us; our lips are sealed.'

Regan appeared satisfied. 'I'm not just a regular businessman like I told you, Katrina,' he began. 'I do a little import-export business on the side.'

Katrina snorted derisively. This was the understatement of the decade. 'Oh, sure, Mr Big-Shot. You expect us to believe that?' she taunted, pretending scepticism. 'You're just making it up. What do you "import-export"? Come on, give us some details.'

Regan was stung by Katrina's sarcasm, his macho pride punctured. 'Look,' he said, his penis bobbing with indignation, 'I'll have you know that you're about to get fucked by the guy who brings most of the cocaine and heroin into Dallas!'

Katrina tried to look surprised and impressed. The redheads' faces were expressionless masks.

Now Regan's boasts were coming thick and fast. 'And I'm going to expand. I'll be the biggest dealer in Texas in a few months. Next week I'm meeting a new partner from Mexico. He'll be at the airport on Wednesday, and I'll be there to meet him. With his contacts and couriers working with mine, I'll have access to every corner of the state.' He stared hard at Katrina to gauge her reaction, obviously wanting to see his high opinion of himself reflected in her face. She was ready for him; her expression was a mask of adoring delight and her eyes shone with glowing admiration.

'Ha! See, you didn't have any idea, did you babe?' gloated Regan. 'If you play your cards right, and stay by Pete Regan, you can get in on the big time.'

Katrina knelt by the bed and stroked the gangster's burly chest. 'Oh, Pete,' she crooned, 'that's so exciting. Let me go with you. I'll be there whenever you need me.' Her hands brushed down his body and grasped his penis, still rigid and urgent. Masturbating her lover slowly, she bent forward and took his glans in her mouth. 'Umm,' she murmured between mouthfuls, 'this is where you get your reward.'

The red-headed nymphs unleashed the silken cords that bound Regan's limbs, and he sat up, rubbing his wrists. He looked at the three women available for his pleasure. With a smile, he nodded to Katrina, 'If you're good to me, Katrina honey, sure, you can tag along.' He ruffled her hair and lifted her face from his penis. Then, none too gently, the drug smuggler pushed Katrina to the floor. 'Sorry, babe, that's all for you, tonight. I can fuck you any time. Now, I want to enjoy this delicious duo.'

Regan grabbed the nearest of the pair and pulled her on to his upraised penis; the redhead, right on cue, accepted him readily between her legs. Her face remained devoid of delight, but she was wet and ready. Regan twisted his head to call the second girl. 'You, come here!' he ordered, gesturing to his face. 'Let me taste you while I fuck your partner.' Obediently and without a word, the woman straddled Regan, obliging his tongue with access to her most private parts.

The girls faced each other, holding each other's shoulders to ride the bucking body of the drug dealer, now single-mindedly absorbed in his own and long-delayed sexual gratification. Only now, and for the first time during the whole evening's charade, did the two women's faces betray any emotion. Like fleeting sparks between two poles, flickers of amused contempt and disdain crackled across the short distance between them. But tonight they would be well paid for these efforts.

Beneath their lithe bodies, Regan at last released his pent-up frustration, bucking his hips like a wild bull; finally, he sank back with a low moan and lay there, exhausted.

The redheads exchanged glances and, with little ceremony, eased themselves in unison from Regan's recumbent form. To one side, where she had rolled on the floor when Regan had abruptly pushed her from his body, Katrina sat still and silent, cross-legged within the folds of her cape. Let the bastard have his fun while he can, she thought with grim satisfaction. Now we've got a new lead that will help us nail him.

Katrina stood and dismissed her helpers with a silent gesture. Without a sound they glided from the room, leaving the detective to study her recumbent prey. Regan's penis was flaccid now, curled on his thigh; his chest rose and fell in light slumber. Her deadly little Derringer was in her handbag by the door; it would be so easy to rid the world of this contemptible slime right now. But instead, Katrina knelt once more and stroked Regan awake. 'Time to get up, Pete,' she purred. 'You and me, we've got exciting times ahead of us.'

Chapter Eight
Beth-Ann's Parlour

The mood in Studio V was fractious. The office work ethic had crumbled in the vacuum created by the absence of first Hiram Pease, and then by Tanya's early departure. Beth-Ann's thoughts were unabashedly elsewhere.

'Stephen,' she whispered. The hands of the big studio wall clock crept around to 3.45 p.m. 'I'm horny again. Let's go back to my place and fuck.'

'I can't go yet.' Stephen was clearly embarrassed; Beth-Ann thought he was worried about the others finding out, or if Pease learnt he had left work early for sex. 'I've got to finish this layout,' he complained, and bent over his work, as if to shut out Beth-Ann's lewd suggestions.

'Oh, Stephen, don't be such a nerd!' Beth-Ann said disdainfully. 'Old Hiram will never know. He won't be back this afternoon.' She edged over to Stephen's board, pencil and paper in hand, and pretended to ask his opinion about some graphic design problems. She bent forward to give Stephen a private view of her breasts, swinging freely beneath her low-cut tank-top.

'Would you like to rub your dick between these,

Stephen?' she invited coyly. 'I'll let you come all over my face. I bet you'd like that.' She traced her fingers over her nipples, bringing them immediately to attention.

Unable to compete with this onslaught of carnal suggestion, Stephen surrendered to the inevitable erection already bulging in his pants. 'All right,' he hissed, peeking over his shoulder as if to check no one was watching. 'But you go first, and I'll follow in fifteen minutes. I'll meet you at your apartment. The others won't know what we're doing.'

Beth-Ann snorted with derision. 'I don't care if they do,' she said. 'It's none of their business who I fuck.'

In the afterglow of their lusty fervour, the couple rolled apart on Beth-Ann's king-sized bed. Stephen stretched his body and sighed; he was sexually replete. He reached down beside the bed to adjust a bouquet of artificial flowers he'd accidentally toppled during their love-making. Though Beth-Ann's bedroom was capacious, her whole apartment was stuffed with an assortment of such objects. From where he lay, Stephen contemplated pink- and green-glazed ceramics, floral chenille tapestry adorned with silk tassels, and clusters of chiffon roses set into plaster vases.

He looked at the woman lying beside him.

There was no doubt that Beth-Ann, splayed on the rumpled bedcovers, eyes staring up at the ceiling fan silently beating the air above their heads, was a physically alluring woman. Her breathing now was quiet, in contrast to the heaving gasps and cries of her climax just moments before. He had never known a woman who came with such gusto.

The fingers of her right hand were lightly folded into the opening between her labial lips, where her skin gleamed. A shaft of sun lay across her thighs and illuminated her thick wedge of darker blonde pubic curls. Stephen propped himself on an elbow and gazed down at her recumbent form. He traced his hand over the fleshy curves that hid her bone structure and created a voluptuous landscape of peaks and valleys. He had come, and on her face, as she had promised. She had swallowed it with apparent relish.

The blonde turned to look at the handsome lover who toyed so gracefully with her body; in that instant, Stephen grasped an inescapable fact. What he had originally taken for guilelessness in his lover's eyes actually reflected a sort of emptiness. The pupils, slightly dilated with lust, were opaque china blue, the colour of the big, vacant Texas sky. There was, he decided glumly, not a whole lot going on upstairs. Beth-Ann's talents were reflected in her luscious body, spread invitingly before him; her mind was unsullied by ideas.

She spoke, her voice a husky tone. 'I need something to eat and something to drink, honey,' she said. 'And it's no good looking in the fridge. There's nothing there.'

Stephen eased himself to a standing position. It would be nice to talk of intimate things after sex, to explore personal histories, and share details and anecdotes. But, for Beth-Ann, the whole purpose of making love was to fuck, and she did that superlatively well. Stephen wondered how long Beth-Ann would hold him in her spell of casual lust.

But now was not the time to evaluate that question. Like a baby bird in a nest, beak open, wanting to be fed, there was one hungry hussy at his side to be taken care of. Pushing the simile to one side, Stephen said gallantly, 'My treat. Where do you want to go?' He was suddenly eager to get out of the apartment. There was time for a drink before he went home and changed in time to pick up Tanya at seven-thirty.

Beth-Ann had her answer ready. 'I like the new Bar of Soap down McKinney.' She stood up, gave Stephen's penis a friendly squeeze, and sauntered into the bathroom. She didn't bother to close the door, and called him from the curtained tub. 'Stephen, can you wash my back?'

'Sure, be right there.'

As he stood behind her in the shower, Stephen massaged Beth-Ann's back and bottom with body scrub. The subtle scent of lavender permeated the steam-filled room as he gently scrubbed her back and worked his fingers into the cleft of her cheeks. Within seconds, he was hard again, pressing his shaft between her buttocks.

Beth-Ann bent forward, the shower spray bouncing off her back. 'Take me from behind, Stephen,' she encouraged. 'Put your dick right inside me. I want you again. I bet you can come a third time!'

She grasped the taps firmly in both hands and thrust backward towards Stephen; he felt his cock penetrate to the opening of her womb. He knew that she wanted every inch of him, to draw every ounce of pleasure from his long stalk. She came in moments, to the sound of the shower spray and to the rhythm of his balls bouncing against the tops of her thighs. He shuddered, his buttocks clenching with each thrust.

'There's a good boy,' said Beth-Ann. Turning to embrace her partner, she bent to kiss his still plump dick before standing to plant a long wet kiss on his mouth. 'What with lunchtime, that makes four times today.' Stephen felt an absurd pleasure in her praise, all reservations temporarily forgotten.

The sky above Deep Ellum was filled with dark thunderclouds. Stephen left his car on the street outside the apartment, and drove Beth-Ann in her car the six blocks to The Bar of Soap.

When they entered the spacious converted store front, Beth-Ann preened on the arm of her newest 'conquest' to an audience of friends and acquaintances. Stephen drank sparingly, mindful of his evening's responsibility as Tanya Trevino's chauffeur. He watched his companion polish off three White Russians in quick succession, followed by a platter of buffalo wings.

'Sex always makes me hungry,' Beth-Ann confided to her friends, an odd bunch of corporate preppies and post-punks, all of whom burst into approving giggles. 'And today,' she added, 'Stephen made sure I could eat a horse!' She nudged him hard in the ribs; he acknowledged the back-handed compliment with a wan smile.

Before he knew it, he was buying drinks for three or four other pals of his companion. He sat quietly beside Beth-Ann, sipping an espresso, the women eddying around him. Feeling smothered by the shrill females, Stephen was somewhat relieved to be called away from their fawning attention by the sound of his beeper. When he returned the call, he heard Pease reminding him to pick up Tanya and deliver her to the dinner meeting.

Beth-Ann was displeased. 'Why are you wasting your time on that stuck-up little bitch?' she enquired rudely.

Stephen was taken aback. 'It's work, Beth-Ann. I have no choice. Boss man's orders. You were there at lunch when the call came in.'

'Yes, and I told you not to take it.'

Stephen sighed. 'Pease knew I was in the office. Look, you're being silly. This could be a big night for Tanya; she could get a job with those movie people for the *Katrina Cortez* project. I think it's very exciting.'

'Well, I don't,' his lover spat. 'It's not fair her getting all the credit. I help produce those drawings, too. In fact, I improve them a lot.' Her voice rose in complaint, and she looked for support among her friends at their table, who formed a Greek chorus of assent and nodding heads.

Stephen shook his head, and continued to try logic; time was getting short. 'Be fair, Beth-Ann. You know Tanya invents the plot and storylines, as well as the concept drawings.' He checked his watch discreetly; if he left now, he would still have time to go home and change his clothes. He said as much to Beth-Ann.

Beth-Ann was angry at being left out, and at the growing recognition of her rival. 'Steve, darling,' she slandered silkily, 'how do you suppose precious little Tanya knows so much about the underside of the Dallas sex and drugs scene?' She smiled archly and continued, 'You don't know? Well, she tried to keep it secret, but she was once a call-girl herself. And a druggie. Do you know why she lives in that fancy apartment with her millionaire boyfriend? She was his cocaine connection. Then she moved in.'

Stephen frowned with disbelief. This couldn't be true!

But Beth-Ann wasn't through. 'And what's more, I know why she gets the best jobs in the studio.' Pausing for effect, she said more loudly, 'She sucks Pease's dick!'

Stephen looked at the girl with whom he'd recently shared similar intimacies. Her eyes had a depraved kind of fire in them. 'Beth-Ann! I can't believe such stories. You must be mistaken,' he said firmly.

'Are you calling me a liar, Stephen?' Beth-Ann proclaimed, with injured innocence. 'Well, go and do business with that skinny little bitch, and see where it'll get you. If you had any sense, you'd stick with me.' Beth-Ann stormed over to another table, where she had a more congenial audience for her malice.

Stephen followed, and touched her arm. With a maturity that belied his years, he gentled Beth-Ann like a frenzied mare. Stroking her hand, he turned it over, kissed her palm softly, and gave her back her car keys. He placed a ten-dollar bill on top and said with a small smile, 'Don't spend it all on White Russians. I have to go to work now.' He nodded to her intrigued companions, and walked quickly out of the door, leaving his lover among the eclectic entourage.

'What a sweet stud-honey!' he heard one of them say, and cringed. His car was only a few blocks away. He dodged some heavy raindrops jogging there; he still had time to stop at his flat and change into fresh clothing.

Chapter Nine
Holding Back

The thunderstorm brewing over downtown deluged the city just as Eric Janovich was driving home. Great curtains of water lashed the buildings as the blackened summer sky took on a yellowish tornadic tinge; raindrops as big as quarters hurled themselves at fleeing pedestrians in a manic aerial bombardment. Within minutes, the street gutters ran inches deep in swirling water. In the short dash from the kerb to his front door, Eric was soaked to the skin. Cursing under his breath, he unlaced his expensive wing-tips and shrugged off his wet outer clothing as he climbed the stairs to his front door.

Once inside, Eric hung his lightweight linen suit neatly on a hanger to dry before sending it to the cleaners, and quickly and quietly made tidy piles of his shirt, socks and underwear before putting each in its appropriate laundry basket. He placed his shoes precisely on their rack; he would have the maid pay especial attention to them tomorrow.

Eric padded naked and barefoot into the living room, where the recorded voice of Tanya Tucker sang plaintively sexy ballads to an absent audience, and saw to his displeasure several articles of Tanya's clothing strewn throughout the normally tidy spaces. When would that woman learn to be neat? This was too much, especially at the end of a difficult day like today.

Propelled by a flash of anger, Eric marched down the long angled hall towards the bedroom, but stopped in his tracks at the open door to his home office. His irritation was quickly replaced by lust at the sight of his girlfriend sitting in his chair, bent in deep concentration over her sketchbooks, an array of his sex toys scattered on the desk next to her. Her long brown hair was tucked behind her ear as she leant forward, focused on her task. Eric's eyes followed the contoured line of her shoulders, down her trim waist, to the firm cheeks of her buttocks. She was completely naked.

For a few seconds Eric stood and watched silently, playing the role of voyeur. Absorbed, Tanya obviously hadn't heard him enter, and what little noise he'd made had been effectively masked by the stereo system. The sight of the beautiful naked woman before him made Eric's penis stiffen immediately, and he gently stroked his shaft.

He coughed lightly, and Tanya swivelled round in the chair to face him. Her eyes grew wide with shock and delight as she drank in the sight of his fit lean body and rampant penis, already hard and poking straight at her. Suddenly wanting nothing more than sexual communion with her handsome lover, all animosities and hurts were forgotten in the magic of her lust. Just seeing Eric standing in the doorway, fondling his magnificent penis, made everything right.

Without a word, Tanya slipped off the chair and approached her lover, looking him straight in the eye. A small smile played at the corners of her mouth. She stood in front of him and kissed him, feeling the length of his penis push against her. She put a finger to his lips and shook her head to silence his greeting.

With no sound other than a low sensual purr, Tanya sank to her knees, and ran her fingertips downward, through Eric's dense black body hair until her lips made contact with the tip of his penis. With practised expertise, she took his shaft in her mouth, feeling his veins and ridges with her tongue.

When he was panting with desire, Tanya released Eric's cock from her mouth and pulled him down to the soft white carpet. She was moist and, needing no further preparation, arched to meet Eric's erect penis against her swollen labia. He pushed slowly and easily inside, filling her completely with his length and girth.

In sibilant silence they rutted together on the office floor, like anonymous lustful strangers, communicating only through their bodies, each passionately rediscovering the other's scents and contours. The only sounds were those of fleshly contact, lubricated by intimate liquids. The woman spread her legs wide and curled around her lover's body. It was she who came first, in bucking muffled sobs of desire. The man followed moments later, with a cry of pleasure racking his body.

They rolled apart and for some time lay together on the floor, unmoving, eyes closed, listening to the furious drumming of the rain on the roof and windows. The twilight thunderstorm deepened colours in the room to the purples and blues of dusk, and Tanya wanted just to lie there in Eric's arms, to forego her evening's task. That wasn't, however, a realistic option. Pease or no Pease, she had to go through with this dinner meeting, to impress the film people with her talent and personality on her own terms.

Her thoughts were interrupted by Eric nuzzling her cheek and licking her earlobe. 'Let's stay in tonight, darling. We'll call in some food, and spend the whole evening in bed. We can fuck some more.'

Tanya bit her lip, suddenly anxious. 'I'd love to, darling,' she said regretfully. 'But I have to go to a business dinner meeting, up in Las Colinas.'

'Who with? Why didn't I know about it? Can't you cancel it?' Eric asked querulously, stifling their emotional rapport with three brusque questions.

'No, I can't. It's with Hiram Pease, the boss; he wants me to meet some new people. I'm being picked up in –' she looked at the clock '– about an hour. But darling, listen. I've got big news! My *Katrina Cortez* strip is going to be made into a movie. That's what the meeting's about.' Tanya anxiously scanned Eric's face for signs of approval.

But Eric didn't seem too impressed. He turned away. 'That's all very exciting, Tanya, but it's a bit inconvenient, isn't it, just springing this on me? What if *I* had an important function this evening and I needed you to be there? I need to have things planned out well ahead of time.' He glanced at the series of unfinished sketches on his desk. 'Are these for the meeting?'

'I was just working out some ideas,' replied Tanya, trying to keep the irritation from her voice. 'The meeting's to discuss screenplay ideas. If I do well tonight, I might be taken on the team for the movie. And I only found out about the meeting today at lunch. Pease has been keeping it quiet.'

Eric became petulant, and made some sarcastic comments. He asked, 'Who's picking you up? When will you be back?' He rose to dress.

'Stephen Sinclair from the office; I'm not sure what time; fairly late, I expect.'

'Do I know this Sinclair?' Eric was frowning.

'I don't think so. He's new, a young artist. I think that's why Pease gave him the job of running me around.' She ventured a grin. 'Because he's the office junior, I mean. My car's in the garage, you know, and I thought tonight might be your basketball or racquetball night, I didn't remember which. I thought you'd be taking the Jag . . .' Tanya's voice trailed off. He didn't allow her to drive his precious Jaguar, anyway.

'Well, you'd better get dressed if you don't want to be late for these important people.' Eric said bad-temperedly, his voice laden with sarcasm; Tanya knew he found it hard to believe a meeting was important if it didn't include him.

She was stung, but she kept her mouth shut; now wasn't the time to have this row. She slipped into the bathroom to prepare a hot bath. In her debates about how to react to Pease's sexual blackmail, not once had Tanya thought of Eric as being part of a solution. She couldn't even bring herself to mention Pease's unsavoury proposition to him. Her pride required her to deal with this on her own, not to run to her boyfriend for help. And part of her mind nagged quietly that Eric would not be particularly sympathetic.

Tanya thought Eric would be even less amused if he knew of her sexual fantasies about the guy who was picking her up. She felt energised by their sex, though Eric had behaved rather childishly. Determined not to allow her boyfriend's selfish mood to spoil her plans for the evening, Tanya dismissed him from her mind, as Katrina Cortez would do. Floating some candles in the tub, she slipped into the fragrant bath.

She emerged aglow twenty minutes later, towelled herself dry and sprayed *Paris* over her skin. Eric was gone, in his silly pout. Tanya cursed him under her breath, and tried to dispel his selfishness from her mind. Slipping into her sensuous ivory silk dressing gown, she pondered what to wear. Something serious? Something arty? Sexy? High style? Pease had requested something 'sexy', but she was damned if she'd be his pawn at the meeting. Then it came to her. Why not take the part of Katrina Cortez herself? She could be sexy, but in her own way. This would get the point across that she was central to these proceedings.

Eagerly, she laid out her sexiest, vampish, most revealing evening outfits, and selected her one and only Versace original, an incredibly expensive short silk dress, patterned in silver and deep cinnamon. It featured a scoop neck and dozens of tiny baby buttons all down the front. The colours set off her warm brunette beauty: dark eyebrows and hair, lightly tanned skin, and deep brown eyes. It would be fun to have a sexy lover unfasten the buttons, slowly, one by one, finally opening the garment to reveal and fondle her breasts. Instead of Eric, Tanya pictured Stephen Sinclair doing this.

Tanya slipped the silken bodice of the dress over her body and pulled on tiny silk bikini panties. She loved not wearing a bra, and her opulent well-shaped breasts were clearly outlined by the sheer fabric. To complement the dress, she added a pair of ankle-wrap sandals in bronze, a faux-pearl choker, her favourite silk stockings and a suspender belt.

Finally dressed, Tanya elaborated her normally simple hairstyle by using lots of mousse, teasing it into a greater volume of wet-look curls and, as a final measure, threw over her shoulders a matching cinnamon silk jacket with sculpted shoulder pads. Its boxy silhouette added a dash of masculine bravado to her sexy feminine style.

It was almost seven-thirty when Tanya walked into the living room to watch for Stephen's car. At that moment he pulled up at the kerb. Stepping out, he looked up and saw Tanya outlined in the window. He waved and walked to her well-lit door, rang the bell of the entryphone, and heard the click of the lock release as Tanya buzzed him in.

Tanya greeted him at the upstairs front door. 'Welcome!' she called. 'Come in for a minute. I'm almost ready.'

* * *

Stephen, who hadn't seen Tanya out of her blue jeans or simple dresses, stared at her lustfully, his eyes following the pleasing curves of her bottom and legs as she led him into the apartment. He wondered where the banker boyfriend was lurking.

As if in answer to his thoughts, Tanya remarked, 'I'd introduce you to Eric, but he's –' she frowned and paused briefly '– gone.' She shrugged as if it were of no matter.

Stephen couldn't take his eyes off her; he knew he was staring but couldn't stop. She was wearing the most stunningly, unbelievably sexy outfit.

Tanya turned. 'Do I look all right?'

Snapping out of his trance, Stephen swallowed hard. 'Oh, God, y-yes,' he stammered, mesmerised by the sight of her outlined breasts and erect nipples through the thin fabric of her dress. 'It's . . . it's your hairstyle. It caught me unawares.' Her hair, usually so sleek, had been transformed into a cloud of tousled curls tumbling around her shoulders.

'Oh, a bit wild, isn't it?' she said with a smile, patting her untamed hair. 'I thought it would be an interesting change from how I wear it at the studio.'

But it was her whole outfit that struck Stephen. Unlike Beth-Ann, who dressed wantonly at the office, at home and on the street, Tanya rarely wore tight or revealing clothing to work. Stephen studied her lithe figure as she skipped gracefully around the spacious living room, switching on the alarm system and checking the air-conditioning. He marvelled at her prettiness.

He rose to follow her as she locked the front door and, side-by-side, they walked to his car through the final raindrops of the flash flood. He let her in and walked around to slide in beside her, his heart in his throat. Tanya's skirt grazed the tops of her thighs; he could see she wore silk stockings, attached to a black lace suspender belt. He swallowed hard. Was she wearing panties?

Utterly tongue-tied by her sexy appearance, he could only stare at her loveliness.

Tanya smiled at his bemusement. 'I'm vamping tonight,' she explained.

She spent much of their journey to Las Colinas surreptitiously studying her chauffeur. His driving technique was crisp and careful, his appearance handsome and elegantly casual. Yet he seemed nervous in her company, saying little and concentrating on the traffic. She wanted both to soothe and excite him, to ruffle his hair, to touch his leg where it lay tantalisingly near her left hand. She wanted to tell him what she couldn't tell Eric. As they neared their destination, her fingers fluttered, lightly caressing his thigh. Her hand was like a butterfly, gently darting, never landing for long.

'Stephen?' she said. 'I want to . . .' Her voice faltered. She wanted to trace her fingers all the way up to his crotch and feel his penis beneath his neatly pressed cotton trousers. She wanted to talk about her role with the *Katrina Cortez* comics, and how Pease was trying to blackmail her with his sex for credit proposition, but her heart was in her mouth. Unable to know what was going through her companion's mind, Tanya held back her impulses at the last minute.

Stephen took his eyes off the road momentarily to look sideways at his companion. She was smiling uncertainly at him. One glance into those lovely dark brown eyes told Stephen that the lovely creature next to him couldn't be the arch-villainess of Beth-Ann's loathing. How could Beth-Ann imagine he'd believe those wild accusations?

He quickly parked the car. His flesh ached for her hand to linger. He didn't trust himself to remain in the car with her a moment longer. She had a boyfriend. He had a sort of girlfriend. And it was time to go in. Pease would be arriving soon.

He got out of the car, stepped around and helped her out, enjoying the opportunity to touch her arm. They walked from the car park down a winding flight of steps that led to the canalside, where a festive atmosphere had been created by antique lamps, strings of coloured lights, and several tables occupied by diners along the water's edge.

Tanya took Stephen's hand as waiters bustled to and fro, and reflections danced in the ripples of black water. The canal made soft slapping sounds against its concrete banks, and from somewhere inside the restaurant came the sound of a Vivaldi violin concerto.

'Just like Venice,' said Stephen, with just the right amount of irony. 'Who needs to fly four thousand miles?'

Tanya grinned. 'I've heard the prices here more than make up for the air fare.' She pressed closer, leaning into his arm.

Stephen paused, absorbing her closeness, her fragrance. He could feel her breast against his side. Suddenly, he gently pulled Tanya close. 'Do you know what you do to me . . .?'

Tanya looked up at him and smiled. He was about to kiss her, but the chugging of a boat motor, loud in the warm moist evening air, disturbed their union. A vaporetto, specially imported from Italy, appeared around the curve of the canal.

'Ahoy, Tanya, my sweetie!' There was no mistaking that voice. Pease was disembarking before them. Tanya hastily released Stephen's hand and stepped smartly two paces to the right. Stephen had no chance to say, or do, any more.

Chapter Ten
Sex in Venice

'Hello, Hiram. Welcome to dry land,' Tanya called back, affecting a poise she didn't feel.

'Hello, Tanya, my dear.' Pease, wearing an expensive suit of Italian cut, clambered ashore. He kissed Tanya's hand with a bravura show of gallantry and then turned to Stephen. 'Hello, young Sinclair. Good timing. The others should be here any moment.'

Above their heads, a swoosh of sound announced the arrival of the monorail from one of the other commercial clusters around the lake that was the centrepiece of the development. The futuristic tram glided on its curving ribbon of track into a canal-side station housed, most improbably, in the topmost storeys of a fake medieval clock tower. 'That should be them now,' said Pease.

The remainder of their party, a trio of sleek, expensive-looking and well-dressed executives, emerged from the brilliant cube of a chromium-lined lift into the watery shadows of the quay. Pease made introductions all round. Sheila Sorensen, the film producer, was a beautiful older woman in her forties, wearing a sleek royal-purple chemise which zipped from neck to crotch. One tawny shoulder was bared in a striking diagonal cut of silk, and her tall stature was accentuated by black slingback sandals that added three inches to her height with their stacked heels. The woman's Californian complexion glowed. Her short curly brown hair was bouncy, and her grey eyes sparkled with humour, but Tanya recognised right away that this was someone used to being in control.

Two handsome men accompanied this woman, her assistant Michael Jardin, and Joshua McNally from Quantum Comics, the latter being the only one of the trio Tanya had met before. Both men deferred to Sheila Sorensen as they walked and in their speech. In this sophisticated company, Pease's brash bonhomie grated on Tanya's ears. She chafed for the opportunity to elude his stifling patronage and deal with these experienced professionals on her own terms. Tanya noted that Stephen had faded adroitly into the background.

The sextet entered the dining room, where the hostess led them to a secluded table on a dais above the main floor level. In this remote enclave, they could view the canal and its waterside festivity. Hiram's hand lingered on Tanya's shoulder before he pressed her into a chair to his right. Sheila Sorensen seated herself to his left at the table's head. Though Stephen was seated directly across from Tanya, she had difficulty catching his eye. He seemed abstracted about something.

'Call the *sommelier*,' Hiram insisted loudly. 'I want to order something special for this evening.' He leered at Tanya.

Despite being addressed in French, the Italian wine waiter appeared politely at their table, but his smile thinned when Pease dismissed the virtues of his fine Bardolinos and Valpolicellas from his home in the Veneto, and insisted on American reds. In revenge, the waiter led the unsuspecting Pease to the most expensive bottle, an excellent vintage, 1992 Duckhorn Vineyards Cabernet. Pease ordered two.

When the wine was tasted and approved, Tanya leant over to catch her boss's attention. 'Mr Pease,' she whispered in his ear, 'I'm expecting you to play fair and let everyone know the *Katrina Cortez* stories are mine, as we agreed.'

Pease bestowed on her one of his standard sly grins. 'And I hope you haven't forgotten *your* end of the bargain, Tanya, my dear. I'm looking forward to . . . shall we say . . . consummating our relationship?'

Tanya hedged. 'First things first. You don't lay a hand on me until you give me credit.'

The water-waiter scurried around the diners, splashing their tumblers full of naturally effervescent spring water. Pease's grin stayed in place, looking even greasier than before. 'Don't worry, Tanya; a deal's a deal,' he whispered out of the side of his mouth. 'But afterwards I get to lay a lot more than a hand on that luscious little body of yours!'

Tanya pretended not to hear.

The table settled into small talk about Dallas and Los Angeles, publishing and film making. As conversation flowed easily around them, Tanya and Stephen contributed little, and at times their companions seemed barely to register their presence. Sensing an imbalance in the dynamics, Joshua McNally took Tanya's request for some wine and turned the conversation to the young Studio V artist herself. He asked politely, 'Do you do much research for your drawings, my dear? I was thinking of some of the more famous "graphic novels".'

'Sure,' replied Tanya, reciting several examples, '*Modesty Blaise*, *Ms Tree*, and *Judge Dredd* . . .'

Stephen took the opportunity to chip in. 'How about *Sandman*, Tanya?'

'Oh yes, Stephen,' Tanya answered, with a sweet wink in the younger man's direction. 'Especially the *Season of Dreams* from the early nineteen nineties. In fact, I have a bound copy.'

'And *Phoebe Zeit-Geist*, from the late sixties, too,' added Stephen. 'I have several hardback versions of those stories.'

'Oh really?' interjected Joshua McNally. 'Isn't that a little before your time, young man? More a baby-boomer thing?' The well-dressed executive managed to give the remark a condescending ring as he examined the younger man's lack of a tie with his Oxford button-down shirt.

Stephen's simple attire was in marked contrast to McNally's impeccable tailoring. Tanya thought that McNally's ensemble of pearl-grey Italian silk suit, a shirt of a subtle paler shade, and a smoky-grey necktie with charcoal pinstripe, would probably eat up two of her Studio V monthly paychecks. Though he looked self-conscious amid all this sophistication, Stephen didn't back down. He smiled openly at the older man. 'I don't think my entire generation, all us infamous X-ers, necessarily conform to the stereotype of not caring about anything older than themselves,' he said quietly. 'I like history; in art and design it's very important. Is that not so in publishing?'

There was a flicker of amusement behind McNally's eyes at Stephen's riposte. He nodded, and turned with an easy smile to respond to Michael Jardin, who was asking him a question about the Dallas Cowboys.

Tanya flashed Stephen a little grin. '*Touché!*' she murmured. Then, louder, 'Hey, Stephen, have you seen the work of that new guy based in Seattle, Jason Lutes?'

'Yes,' Stephen enthused. 'I really like *Jar of Fools*.'

'I think Richard Sala's *Chuckling Whatsit* is superior.' Tanya was surprised to hear Michael Jardin chime in an opinion.

'Yeah, but it could be sexier,' grumbled McNally.

The chatter and gossip came to a temporary halt with the arrival of appetiser platters adorned with antipasto, fresh salads with goat's cheese and cherries, and warm garlic focaccia bread. All six diners fell to with exclamations of relish. The waiters unobtrusively placed fresh glasses and a couple of bottles of Pinot Grigio on the table to complement the food.

When the table was cleared after the first course, Sheila Sorensen and Joshua McNally turned to more substantial matters. Sorensen's first words made Tanya sit up and listen. 'Well, it's about time we got down to business. We called this meeting to discuss details about Hiram's *Katrina Cortez* project. I'm convinced of its movie potential, and I think we all agree that Tanya's sketches of Hiram's latest ideas work out very well.' She smiled graciously at Tanya, whose lips were stuck in a frozen grimace.

Now was the time for Pease to put the record straight. But her employer just sat quietly, a small smile on his face, nodding agreement.

'Yes,' he said. 'Tanya is a talented artist.'

Tanya waited for him to continue. But Pease just sat back in his chair, hands folded across his stomach, gazing at his companions from under heavily lidded eyes. He didn't look at Tanya. Stephen tried to catch Tanya's eye, but her attention was focused solely on the slimeball who was her employer. At last, he said, 'I think it's important that we retain Tanya as one of the artists on the film team. It will be good experience for her.'

Sheila Sorensen nodded. 'Yes, that makes sense. That leaves you, Hiram, free to come up with more of those wonderful ideas for plots and settings. Your Dallas connections will be very valuable to us . . .'

Tanya didn't hear the rest of the conversation; her mind was racing to confront Pease's verbal trickery. *One* of the artists? Pease was a sneak. While he appeared to give her credit, it was not the kind she wanted or deserved. Tanya had to do or say something, but with a major effort of will, she bided her time, trying to judge her best moment.

Her chance came when the main course was ferried to their table by a bevy of mustachioed waiters. Amid the cacophony and chatter and placement of plates, waiters' arms intervened between Tanya and Joshua.

The servers gracefully lifted plates and deposited platters of *scaloppine al marsala con funghi* and *petti di pollo alla fabrizio*, family-style, in the centre of the table. A large tureen of *verdure miste al forno* materialised at Tanya's elbow. Fragrances mingled deliciously.

Joshua McNally turned to Tanya.

'Hiram was telling me the other day about some of his latest ideas for the screenplay. Has he shared them with you yet, Tanya?' he asked. 'I'd be interested in your opinion of them.'

Tanya's pulse quickened. Pease's ideas? What ideas would those be? Before she could respond to Joshua, a covered dish of *patate alla friulana* completed the serving, along with more wine and breads. When the waiters were finished, Tanya returned sweetly to her questioner. 'Oh, Hiram has a lot of ideas he doesn't share with me,' she replied in a low voice. 'Which ones in particular was he discussing?'

'One episode was about Katrina as an undercover agent who seduced the male villain. It had some very good locales. Very *noir*, rather like *La Femme Nikita*, but with less violence and more sex.'

Tanya saw Stephen tense in annoyance on the other side of the table and make as if to say something. She reached out her foot and nudged him lightly on the shin. He stared at her in surprise, but closed his mouth.

Keeping her voice calm and friendly, Tanya said, 'Oh, yes, the scenes in which Katrina tails the two guys from the airport to Boobs'n'Boots? I want to do more with the waitress, Cupcake. She might have a role in some later sex action.' Tanya checked Joshua to see that he was listening acutely. 'I'm also considering whether the auburn-haired dancer is just a walk-on sex partner, or should develop into a more important character.' She smiled invitingly at the publisher.

McNally nodded. 'Interesting ideas. I'm glad Hiram shared them with you.'

Tanya cleared her throat. 'Yes, it is interesting,' she agreed emphatically. 'Those drawings are only a day or two old in my sketchbook. I didn't know he'd seen them.' The lousy creep, Tanya thought furiously. He's been rifling through my sketchbooks, behind my back!

McNally's brow furrowed in perplexity. 'Are you saying they're your ideas? Not Hiram's?'

'Yes, Mr McNally, that's exactly what I'm saying. *All* the recent *Katrina Cortez* ideas are mine.' Tanya looked the publisher straight in the eye, reinforcing her words with a hard level gaze.

Through the hubbub, Tanya studied McNally's thoughtful expression. She wondered whether he believed her. From the corner of her eye, she noticed Stephen step away from the table, and she took the opportunity to dig Pease sharply in the ribs. 'You bastard!' she hissed. 'You're not holding up your end of the deal. All you've done is reinforce your own position and keep me in the margins.'

'*Au contraire*, dear Tanya.' Pease smiled, managing to look hurt and smug at the same time. 'You heard me say that you should join the team, and everybody agreed. What more do you want?'

'Acknowledgement of my authorship of the character. That's what I want.'

'Well, you *did* say you'd sleep with me. I've got you on the team; now it's your turn for fair play. How about later tonight? We won't go into work tomorrow. We'll just screw all day. We'll go back to my place after the meal; how about it?'

Tanya was speechless. The Pease of her imagination was a beast, but the real man was even worse. She heard footsteps behind her and turned to see Stephen returning to his seat at the table. He looked pale. She tried anxiously to catch his eye, but he wouldn't look at her.

Tanya guessed that Stephen had overheard Hiram's suggestion – but surely he didn't think she was sleeping with Pease?

Surely he knew that what she wanted was to go back to his place after dinner and make love. Tanya looked his way, an anxious expression on her face. He pointedly ignored her and turned away, plunging into a conversation with Sheila Sorensen.

Tanya's stomach lurched with dread. He was avoiding looking at her, and his normal smiles had been replaced by an angry expression that vanished only when he was talking with Sheila Sorensen. She hoped Stephen's *tête-à-tête* with the alluring older woman would soon end.

Putting down her knife and fork, she drained her Pinot Grigio and swallowed a hefty sip of the Bardolino, and focused once more on McNally. He smiled at her.

'Joshua,' she began, 'I'd like to tell you about some of the latest plot ideas I've developed for *Katrina Cortez*.' She spoke in a firm voice, loud enough to carry over the buzz of conversation. Pease looked up, and Sheila Sorensen paused, her fork halfway to her lips.

Hiram Pease interrupted, 'Tanya, not now. We'll deal with that tomorrow. You and I can –'

Tanya didn't let Pease finish. 'No, Hiram. You've been very kind inviting me here tonight, but I think it's time to clear up a little misunderstanding. We wouldn't want Joshua and Sheila, and Michael –' she addressed the trio '– to think that you have to do all this work by yourself, would we?' Tanya smiled sweetly at her employer, although she would have enjoyed splashing the good red wine left in her glass all over his fine silk shirt.

'What do you mean, Tanya?' Sheila Sorensen's tone was sharp.

'I mean that Hiram has not been entirely frank about the *Katrina Cortez* concepts.'

'Tanya, I told you –'

'Hiram! Let the girl speak.' Sorensen turned her sharpness on Pease. He subsided, muttering into his wine, and glared at Tanya.

'Hiram has been very supportive of the *Katrina Cortez* stories,' said Tanya, offering an olive branch. No point in rubbing Pease's face in the dirt too obviously. 'And he's encouraged me to do more with them.' That was far enough. 'But the truth is, the drawings are mine . . . and the new storylines and characterisation are mine, too.' She had the rapt attention of her audience.

'Is that true, Hiram?' Sorensen's eyes bored her question in Pease's direction.

'No, of course not, Sheila. Like I told you, Tanya's a big help in production. But if I'd known she was going to start thinking it was all her own work, I'd never have brought her along.'

Tanya glanced at Stephen for support, but he was watching Pease, a scowl on his handsome face.

Sorensen's eyes turned back to Tanya. 'Well?'

Tanya stood up, adrenalin pumping. She could do this. She didn't need Stephen, or anybody else; she could control the events around the table herself. 'There's one way to demonstrate the creator of these stories and characters,' she said. 'Simply ask. I can give you all the details.' Standing erect, she tossed her hair, quiet and confident, dominating the ensemble despite her slight stature. 'Would you care to begin, Mr Pease?' She spoke with exaggerated politeness.

'I'm having nothing to do with this charade.' Pease made one last appeal. 'Joshua, let's sort this out in the morning. Young Tanya's had a bit too much wine. It's gone to her head.'

McNally turned to his partner. 'Perhaps that would be best. Sheila? Light of day, and all that?'

'Nonsense, Joshua. The young woman looks fine to

me. I want to hear what she has to say. Tanya, you've said the ideas are yours. Give us some examples.'

Tanya was ready. Sheila Sorensen seemed like a level-headed business person. Her straight talking was a relief after months of Pease's prevarications and innuendoes. She addressed the whole party. 'The latest piece I'm working on is located at a place I call the GirlZone, which is located in Oak Cliff, south of the city, in a transitional neighbourhood with an edge to it. Sometimes it's dangerous. Katrina's strategy is to use sex games to worm out information about the drug smuggler's organisation, and pass it on to the cops.'

Katrina Cortez came to life in the room as Tanya painted pictures with her words. 'The GirlZone, run by a bunch of neo-feminists, is a cross between a women's resource centre, an arts centre and a sex club. Katrina lures the character called Regan there for some very special entertainment.'

The group was silent, watching Tanya stride to and fro, her gestures carving space and outlining the action. Her body language changed from the lithe dominatrix Katrina, to the burly boastful Regan, to the submissive silent redheads.

At one point, she snatched a large white paper tablecloth from an unoccupied table and held it against the wall. One of the waiters moved to object, but Michael Jardin stayed him with a gesture. A twenty-dollar bill passed silently from Jardin's wallet to the waiter's back pocket. Tanya asked for a pen. Stephen uncapped a thick-tipped Pentel and passed it to her wordlessly.

'Hold the other side, please, Stephen,' requested Tanya. Without demur, he complied, and watched fascinated with the others as Tanya developed the characters with quick authoritative strokes of the pen. Particularly striking was the rendition of Katrina herself. The swirling form of her cape was captured in broad cross-hatching, and formed a deep contrast against the white nakedness of the woman's body. Tanya drew the detective standing above Regan, one booted stiletto heel resting on the bed-frame, just inches from his face. Within a network of fine lines that described hard muscled thighs and abdomen, the dense triangle of Katrina's pubic hair was the focal point of the composition.

Tanya's whole performance lasted no more than fifteen minutes but, at its conclusion, the energy suddenly drained from her body. She passed the pen back to Stephen, and folded the large paper drawing before tossing it on the table in front of Sheila Sorensen. 'There's plenty more where that came from,' she said simply, and returned to her seat. She barely kept her hand from shaking as she sipped her wine with what she hoped was the appearance of sang-froid.

McNally was the first to break the silence. 'Hiram, you old rogue! You've got yourself a talented little lady there. Why have you been keeping her all to yourself?'

Tanya opened her mouth to protest being referred to as Pease's little lady, but Sheila Sorensen beat her to it. 'Joshua, take that stupid grin off your face. You're not at one of your fraternity reunions now. The real question is why Hiram wasn't being straight with us. It's very clear that Tanya is the original creative impulse behind the work we like so much.' The woman turned to face Pease directly. 'Well, Hiram, what's your explanation?'

Pease met the challenge with aplomb. 'The reason is very clear, Sheila,' he said, framing his features into the appearance of a proud parent, whose child has just won a talent competition. 'I've nurtured Tanya's skills for the two years she's been with me, and I've taught her well. She is a tremendously talented young lady. If I've been overprotective of that talent, I had her best interests at heart. We all know,' he said, beaming at his colleagues, inviting them to agree, 'that the movie business can be tough. I thought at this stage in her career, it would be best for Tanya's creative energy to be directed through me and my firm. It's really for her own protection.' Pease finished his eulogy with a fatherly pat on Tanya's shoulder and an effusively large smile. But when his eyes met hers for a moment, they held no affection. She returned his dark and spiteful look, malice for malice.

McNally smiled. 'You see, Sheila,' he said turning to his partner, 'I was right about old Hiram. His company will do us proud.'

Sorensen didn't look totally convinced. But when she addressed Tanya and Pease together, sweeping them with her pale eyes, she said decisively, 'It seems we've concocted a temporary arrangement. Hiram will work with us to provide the graphic services we require, and Tanya will continue to play a very special role.' The others nodded. 'So, Hiram –' her gaze slid back to Pease and pinned him in his chair '– I expect you to provide Ms Trevino with everything she needs for her work, and I want her time devoted solely to this project. We can work out the financial details later, when we're sober.' She smiled fleetingly. 'That's the basic outline of my expectations.' She looked from face to face. 'Any questions?' There were none. 'Tanya, is that satisfactory to you?'

Tanya, sipping her wine, found her voice. 'Yes, Sheila. I appreciate your confidence in me. I look forward to working with you.' She kept her voice calm and professional, but deep inside she felt a warm glow of satisfaction. A sideways glance at Pease and Stephen, however, cooled her pleasure. The presence of these men was problematic. Even success came with its quota of difficulties. She drained her wineglass.

The party grew more relaxed and ribald as the wine flowed, and the business tensions took a back seat to more personal issues. After Sheila Sorensen's control of the situation had been confirmed, she developed a keen interest in Stephen's conversation.

Under glowering brows, Tanya watched them grow more animated, their voices dropping to whispers, full of smiles and laughter. The older woman was clearly setting her sights on Stephen, and she had covertly pulled down the zipper on her sleek dress to reveal a beguiling portion of her creamy cleavage. Stephen Sinclair made no secret of his interest and admiration. He acted as though Tanya were invisible.

Pease, on the other hand was quite mindful of his favourite brunette. He grabbed Tanya firmly by the arm. 'I need to talk to you, my dear,' he said softly into her ear. 'Come with me.' He steered Tanya to another room near the back of the restaurant.

Flushed with her success, and slightly drunk, Tanya was nonetheless on her guard. In the dim back room, she grew uncomfortable and refused Pease's offer of a seat, and stood restlessly, waiting for him to get to the point. She didn't have to wait long. Pease stroked her arm, stopping just short of touching her breast.

'Now Tanya, I've kept my part of the bargain. You're on the film team, and they know how good you are. But they're not ready to trust you on your own.' He smiled. 'I think that makes our little partnership agreement even more appropriate, don't you?' To her alarm, Pease unzipped his trousers and his penis sprang up from a thick nest of hair, above plump ripe balls. 'I think it's time for my payment,' he said greedily.

Focusing on the man in front of her, Tanya listened to a seductive little voice from the Katrina Cortez corner of her mind: he *was* sexually attractive in a physical sense, though a bit overweight, and she was tempted to run her fingers along the length of his plump penis. What harm would having sex with him do? She could get more control over the guy. Use him to her advantage. Besides, Stephen Sinclair was already getting it off with Beth-Ann; perhaps tonight he'd have Sheila Sorensen, too. She was a fool to pine after that boy.

Pease's eyes took on the sparkle of conquest as she stared at his dick. He guided Tanya's hand to touch its bulging purple crown; it pulsed beneath her palm as she stroked it gently. He moaned with pleasure, 'That's right, baby.'

But Tanya's tentative compliance was shattered when he crooned, 'Oooh. Do that some more. That's just like Beth-Ann, only better, much better!'

Tanya jerked her hand away as if scalded. Her wanton thoughts vanished in the face of Pease's gloating. He *had* been screwing Beth-Ann. Tanya stepped back and looked him up and down scornfully. 'You see me as just another bimbo, don't you Hiram Pease?' she hissed, cold and angry. 'If you think you can put me in the same category as Beth-Ann Bodine, you've made a big mistake. You just want sex – any way, any how, with anyone you want. But not me. Zip up your pants, old man.'

His face darkened. 'You need me in this deal!'

'And you need me if you want to keep this contract. Only McNally was rooting for you in there. No sex for you, Hiram. Not tonight, and not ever.'

'Wait, girlie,' he snarled, grabbing at her arm. 'Stop taunting me. I want you.'

She pulled away. 'You're in no position to demand sex. Back off.'

'If you won't fuck, then suck,' he demanded, blatantly waggling his plump penis at her.

'Hiram, go play with yourself. If we need each other for professional reasons, so be it. I don't like it but I can live with it. All other bets are off.' Tanya stalked out. 'I need some fresh air,' she exclaimed, and slipped out of a side door into the relief of the warm summer breeze blowing off the water. Her head swam, and she collapsed on a bench and closed her eyes.

Pease made no attempt to follow. He left hurriedly through the kitchen, avoiding his colleagues at the table.

He caught one of the waiters. 'Tell my party I've had an emergency. I'll call them in the morning.'

Tanya was absent from the table for so long that Stephen gave up on her. He knew she was with Pease somewhere in the back of the fancy establishment. Tanya must be having sex, he figured. Burning with lust, jealousy, or both, Stephen allowed himself to be claimed by Sheila Sorensen; the older woman exuded feminine power and sexual energy.

When Joshua walked away to join an impromptu conversation with some acquaintances at another table, Sheila laid her hands on Stephen's thigh. His erection, which had never really gone away since being teased to life by Tanya's presence in the car next to him, became large and hard in Sheila's hand.

'Let's go!' Sheila said, grinning at Stephen. 'What are we waiting for?' She played with his thick and eager penis. 'Is it Tanya?'

'Yes . . .' he croaked and blushed suddenly.

She took his arm. 'Don't worry about her. I think she's otherwise engaged.' She pulled Stephen to his feet and, hand-in-hand, they walked towards the door, pausing for Sheila to murmur some instructions to Jardin, her assistant, who in turn spoke briefly to the waiter.

'The dinner's on Mr Pease's account,' the waiter confirmed. 'It's taken care of.'

'Let's go then,' said Sheila, obviously impatient to be alone with the young stud. 'Come on!' She took Stephen's arm and propelled him towards the door. Outside, standing beside the canal, Sheila put her lips to his. Her voice was thick and seductive, warmed with alcohol, and very different from her firm, crisp manner of earlier in the evening. 'Shhh, Stephen, dear. Don't worry about what Tanya does.' She led him around the bend of the darkened canal.

* * *

Tanya walked slowly back indoors to rejoin the party, but found their table empty. She hurried outside. Michael Jardin was there, but she thought she could smell Stephen's lime cologne in the stillness. Around the canal bend, the click and echo of high heels receded in the background.

'Have you seen Stephen?' she demanded.

Michael Jardin had the grace to look embarrassed. 'I think he's busy, right now,' he said.

Tanya was furious and then deflated. How could he go off with that woman and just leave her here? She made to move after the retreating sounds of footsteps, but Jardin placed a gently restraining hand on her arm.

'Tanya, I think it best you leave them alone,' he said. 'Sheila would not like to be disturbed.'

'But he was my ride!' complained Tanya. And the man I was planning to sleep with this evening, she thought bitterly.

Jardin spoke briefly into his cellular phone. 'There's a cab on its way,' he said sympathetically. 'Don't worry about the fare. It's taken care of.'

Tanya nodded absently. 'Thank you; that's very kind.'

The taxi arrived and Jardin escorted Tanya up the stairs to the street level. She wrapped herself and her thoughts in the back seat and Jardin closed the door.

Her cab drove away into her successful, sad and lonely night.

In the water-rippled darkness that filled the canalside alley, Sheila Sorensen unzipped her dark violet dress and stepped out of it, leaning against the cool brick wall of a darkened building. Light from a single neon sign illuminated her body. She took Stephen's hand and placed it on the band of her panties. She looked at her young artist and said, 'Tanya's a very pretty woman. She can fuck whoever she wants to.' She kissed him hard and passionately. 'You can, too.'

She pressed the young man's hand inside her panties. 'I don't like underwear on summer nights,' purred Sheila.

Stephen pulled off her panties.

'Good boy,' she said. The tiny garment fell discarded to the stones to lie with her dress. She stood there, naked except for her high-heeled shoes. Pulling his body to hers, she deftly undid his belt and opened his trousers in one easy movement, to expose his cock to her waiting hands.

Stephen gently lifted Sheila's leg around his waist, and opened her sex to his waiting and rampant cock. With a groan of pure desire, he entered her moist channel, pinning her nakedness against the brickwork. He couldn't quite believe this was happening. Five times in one day was a record and, for all he knew, this was only the opener for a long night of sex. The pale neon now illuminated the movements of the young man's bare backside as he thrust inside his lover with sighs of pleasure. The couple's low moans drifted softly across the still, silent canal and echoed from the stone façades of the darkened buildings.

Chapter Eleven

Arrivederci, Eric

Tanya woke up to the insistent pressure of Eric's fingers between her legs, seeking her clitoris. Irritably, she closed her legs to his fingers, and rolled away, still wrapped in her bad mood from the stress and drama of the night before.

Moments later, the hand returned, gently massaging her shoulders and back, running all the way down to her buttocks. She opened one eye at the bedside clock: 6 a.m.

'Umm, Eric, it's too early,' she muttered. 'Go back to sleep.' She moved his hand away. She shuffled over to her side of the bed, but the silent hand followed her, stroking her arms until her flesh ran with goose bumps. It felt too good to stop, so she lay still, acknowledging the pleasant sensation.

A second hand joined the first, and together they traced the curves of Tanya's breasts for the longest time, squeezing each nipple gently between finger and thumb. Eventually one detoured down over Tanya's firm belly, playing hide-and-seek in her pubic curls and stopping just short of her precious folds.

Lowering her defences, she felt the remnants of her bad mood dissipate from simple lust. Tanya opened her legs, allowing the probing fingers to slide into the wetness of her vagina. A thumb circled her clitoris, bringing forth a moan from her lips. Tanya closed her eyes and lay back passively, thighs spread, inviting more liberties; she wanted this to last all morning.

But her mood of delicious sexy lassitude was shattered when Eric's penis nudged itself arrogantly against her face, seeking her tongue and open lips. 'Come on, Tanya. Wake up! Suck my dick; play with my balls,' Eric demanded. He was petulant, like a small child. His hand pushed deeper inside her, making her gasp, and his cock slid into her obligingly open mouth.

Tanya sucked with a reflex action and long habit, her lover's familiar taste soothing her irritation. Her tongue followed the ridge of his glans and tasted the pre-come. She raised her hips to encourage Eric's fingers, feeling her vagina clench with building desire. She was rewarded with increased pace and pressure, but she wanted more.

'Eric, get inside me. Please! I want your cock inside me.' Disgorging Eric's penis from her mouth, Tanya took his pulsing instrument in one hand, and pressed him to the lips of her vagina. She guided her rampant lover inside with a shudder; just feeling him enter brought forth a small spasm of joy.

Tanya wound her feet around Eric's shoulders and neck, providing him access to her most intimate recesses. The tip of her boyfriend's long penis reached far inside, and the muscles of her vagina contracted to weld themselves around his shaft. With a scream she filled herself to the hilt with his cock, her orgasm washing through her while Eric was still building towards his climax; her legs held him in a vice-like grip which rendered him powerless to finish until her hold relaxed. As she fell back against the pillows, Eric thrust with renewed frenzy, climaxing only seconds later. The sudden spasm triggered an aftershock in Tanya's womb and, moaning with delight, she marked Eric's muscular arms with her nails.

He knelt over her, a predatory smile on his chiselled features, and murmured, 'That's my baby. That's the Tanya I love, a sex hungry little whore.'

Tanya smiled slowly up at her lover, the languorous warmth of her satiated body spreading to every extremity. 'Is that what I am to you?' she asked jokingly. 'Your own personal nymphomaniac?'

Eric eased his still-firm penis from her vagina and rolled to one side. He propped his head on his arm. His indolent eyes feasted upon Tanya's open labia. He shrugged his shoulders. 'Oh, I wouldn't put it as bluntly as that, my dear,' he said. There was no humour in his voice.

A slow chill edged out the warmth inside her. 'Exactly how would you put it?' she asked, keeping her voice neutral. Her skin cooled; she reached for her svelte ankle-length *crêpe-de-chine* gown.

'My job is so stressful that I need your body for release, to relax. I need you here for me so I can fuck you whenever I want.'

Stunned, she rose and pulled her matching sheer silk chiffon jacket over her transparent gown. Finding her voice, she said, 'I think I'll fix the coffee.' She walked into the kitchen, filled the electric kettle, and plugged it in.

Eric, wrapped in his robe, padded to the front door, picked up the newspaper, and followed Tanya into their breakfast area. They sat at the table in simmering silence.

Eric glanced up from the newspaper. 'Be honest, Tanya. You know you love it, too. You can't get enough of my dick.' He reached across to tweak her nipple through the thin layers of fine fabric. His face lit up with a grin. 'And you know you won't find a more skilful lover in all of Texas,' he added.

Moving out of pinching range, Tanya found her voice.

'Is that all I am to you?' she asked. 'An ever-available piece of arse? Just when you want it?'

Eric put down the paper and grinned inanely, his eyes full of lust. He gestured around the well-appointed apartment. 'It's got its compensations.'

Her boyfriend's smugness reminded Tanya of his ungracious dismissal of her drawings. Flushed, she felt her anger building. 'Well, let me tell you, my Lone Star Casanova, I've got a career, too, and I'm on the verge of breaking into the big time,' she stated boldly. 'How about a bit of support for me, too?'

Eric proclaimed, 'Oh, yeah, those drawings are cute, but that commercial art stuff . . . let's face it, it's just fluff!' His eyes were back on the newspaper, studying an advertisement for men's clothing; he didn't see the fury that flashed across his girlfriend's face. 'The real power, now,' he continued, 'is in making a brilliant financial deal.' He was growing animated. He looked up, scanning the well-appointed and expensive dwelling. 'When you screw the last buck out of your competition and make them eat dirt: that's where the real big time is. Taking their money and living high. It's almost as good as fucking.'

Leaning forward proprietorially, he fingered the fine silk lingerie between forefinger and thumb. 'Anyway,' he murmured smoothly, 'I'm the one who brings the big bucks into this relationship. That should count for something.' He found her nipple again.

'You're ostentatious,' said Tanya, again in retreat from his probing fingers.

'And you're expensive,' he countered, finally looking into Tanya's angry brown eyes.

She stood up, cast off the silk robe and left it on her breakfast chair. 'You can have it,' she hissed, and stalked from the room. 'I'm late.'

Tanya showered and locked the bedroom door, hastily pulling on jeans and a lime-green T-shirt. Only when she was ready did she unlock the door. Eric was nowhere to be seen, but the sound of the shower came from the second bathroom. Tanya slipped quietly out the front door and down the stairs. Even though she had to walk six blocks to pick up her car from the bodyshop, she breathed a sigh of relief to be outside the apartment.

Half an hour later she drove to work in an angry daze, fuming over Eric's rampant ego and domineering attitude. There were serious problems in her relationship with Eric; their quarrels were becoming a troublesome pattern of events that she couldn't dismiss.

With a shock, it suddenly hit her that these domestic troubles had blanked her mind to an equally serious set of problems awaiting her at the studio. What would Pease be like, today? What would Stephen say? What would she say to Stephen? The confused currents of the previous evening had stirred the muddy waters of the office sexual politics still further. Tanya was so consumed with apprehension that she almost turned round and went back home, but she couldn't face another day in that luxury prison, where her primary role was to dance naked to Eric's tune.

Word of the dinner group's antics the previous evening had clearly preceded Tanya, and the atmosphere was strained upon her arrival at Studio V. Stephen pointedly ignored her and was reserved with Beth-Ann. In turn, the blonde, put out of sorts by Stephen's coolness, continually glanced over at Tanya with unconcealed hostility. Tanya returned her look with distaste and contempt; she toyed with the idea of telling her that, last night, her precious Stephen had been fucking a beautiful woman old enough to be his mother. But she was silent about that *imbroglio*, figuring the fall-out from that little sex-bomb might bring the design studio to a complete halt.

Pease, thankfully, did not appear that morning. Tanya couldn't have stood his nauseating presence. The other artists kept their heads down, and it was Carmen's day off.

Tanya worked introspectively at her desk for most of the day. She glowered at anybody who came near, thus discouraging conversation, and the other employees left her alone. As she glanced past the comforting shape of Edward Bear, at his post on the windowsill, her eyes fell upon the image of Katrina Cortez pinned at the top of her drawing board.

The familiar foxy face stared coolly off its page, seeming to speak to her, and Tanya heard the voice of Katrina Cortez reverberate in her mind. 'It was just another *noir* night!' she seemed to murmur, with wry understatement. Tanya drew those words in the vacant bubble above Katrina's head. They seemed a fitting tribute to her evening's experience.

During the day, the oppressive silence at her workstation was broken only once by the ringing of her telephone. It was Joshua McNally, with a message that revived Tanya's flagging spirits. The publisher made no reference to the previous evening's licentious goings-on, and instead told her, 'I'd like to confirm my and Sheila's delight at working with you, Tanya! You're the real creative talent; we need you to work with us.' He added, in an undertone, 'As directly as possible.'

'Of course,' Tanya responded, so ecstatic that she hardly registered Joshua McNally's next smooth request.

'Can you meet a 48-hour deadline for some new sketches, plus dialogue, by Saturday morning?' he asked. 'We want to get them to our partners in LA for first thing Monday.'

'Of course,' she said enthusiastically. 'Are you looking for any special content or theme?'

'Something typical with good dialogue and sex action between Katrina and Regan. Hell, I don't know! That's your department. You sold us last night. Now produce.' A convivial tone took the sting out of the publisher's words, but Tanya saw this experience as just the beginning of such demands.

'There's just one more little thing,' continued McNally. 'It's a bit awkward for me to deal with Hiram. He upset Sheila last night and could be out on his ear if he's not careful. I put in a good word for him, of course. We go back a long way, him and me. See if you can work something out with him, can you? Calm him down. It would be easier for us in many ways if Studio V could still handle some of the production graphics.'

'If he leaves me alone to do my job, I won't bother him,' promised Tanya. 'I don't want to pick a fight,' she added firmly, 'but I must receive proper credit for my work.'

McNally grunted assent, and terminated the conversation with arrangements for the drawings to be picked up by messenger on Saturday morning. Only after putting down the phone did Tanya pause to register the full portent of McNally's remarks. Forty-eight hours!

Despite the uncomfortable ambience at the studio, Tanya stayed at work for a long time after the others had left. It was her way of postponing whatever lay in store for her at home. She need not have worried; when she returned, the apartment was deserted. There was a brief note. *Flying to Houston on the shuttle. Not home till after midnight*. There was no name, no doodles of endearment, no sign of an improvement in relations. Tanya sighed, but in the face of all the new developments in her professional life, she decided to put personal things on hold: to wait and see.

Tanya knew Eric was resentful of the occasionally long hours she spent in pursuit of her own career, but in the past she had blocked these disturbing thoughts from her mind. With the next morning's coffee, however, Tanya was once again forced to contemplate the degree of Eric's selfishness when he walked into the kitchen and demanded, out of the blue, 'Tanya, I need you to come with me to an important business dinner this evening.'

Tanya's heart sank. 'Eric, I can't. I'm sorry, but I'm working to a deadline of midnight tonight.'

He looked furious, but Tanya mustered control of her own anger and explained, 'I'd like to go with you, but I must have work ready for a Saturday morning pickup. It's a big deal and I simply cannot put it off.'

'You refuse to go, then?'

'Eric, you are putting me in a difficult position,' she said. 'I simply *cannot* go with you tonight.'

'Has it occurred to you that my meeting might *also* be important? It's with the CEO; you know how he likes to invite promising young executives over from time to time, to sound them out, and evaluate them.'

'But what's that got to do with me?' Tanya asked. 'He isn't evaluating me.'

'Don't be so dumb, for Chrissakes!' Eric was agitated. 'The old boy's got this thing about pretty women. It will help my chances no end if he takes a shine to you. You need to wear something sexy, and low cut; let him see your tits and smile cutely. That should be easy enough for you.'

'Eric Janovich, you're a dinosaur. You're every bit as bad as Hiram Pease!' Tanya was mad now. 'That's all you see in me, isn't it? You see me as a bauble to impress people! Well, I'm sorry. I can't go, and that's that!'

Eric finally lost his patience. 'You're ungrateful and unreliable,' he barked. 'Finish your work by early evening. I'll pick you up at the studio and we'll go on to this dinner meeting. That's an order.'

Hot tears welled up behind her eyes, but she didn't let them fall. 'I'll try,' she said, fearing an out-and-out confrontation. But she wondered if she would bother.

'Don't just try; do it,' Eric demanded, his angry black

eyes burning. With more mutterings under his breath, he departed noisily for the bank.

Tanya worked at a furious pace all day, completely absorbed in her designs and storylines and not speaking to anybody, but by six o'clock there were still several hours of work in front of her. Stephen was also working late, helping Carmen Sierra with old job files for a report to the auditors that was due Monday morning.

Pease had obviously been in the office overnight, for there were notes in his handwriting on Stephen's and Carmen's desks. Tanya, consumed with curiosity, peeked at Stephen's before he arrived. She was disappointed; there was nothing juicy, simply instructions to leave the artwork he was doing to assist Carmen on the business files. Pease justified his instructions on the basis that it would help the 'new boy' understand the working of the firm better. But Tanya knew, and she suspected Stephen did also, that it was simply a dull job given to the most junior member of the staff because no one else wanted to do it.

Beth-Ann had left early. Tanya speculated she must have a date with Pease that Stephen didn't know about. She couldn't imagine why else the blonde witch would leave her lover behind, especially with Tanya still around in the office. She looked up as Stephen disappeared to the men's room. Quickly, she walked over to Carmen, whose smile was friendly as always.

'*Hola,* Tanya. *Como le va*? You seem very busy. We don't even have time to say hello.' Carmen wanted to ask a dozen questions, but she doubted this was the time for personal matters.

She was wrong. 'I am busy, Carmen. I've been such a grouch, muttering to myself all day over in the corner, but I'm on this deadline, and I might not make it. I have to have a bunch of stuff finished by tonight so I can leave it with the guard downstairs. Then a messenger will pick it up in the morning.'

Carmen nodded sympathetically.

'But I really need your help . . . with Stephen.'

Her friend's eyebrows rose enquiringly.

Tanya rushed ahead. 'I know Stephen thinks that I had sex with Pease last night; and I didn't. He tried, though. He even exposed himself to me! But I just walked away. I left him there, high and dry, so to speak.'

Carmen murmured approval. 'Well done, *chicita*.'

'But Stephen saw Pease take me into a back room, and I know he thinks the worst. Then he went off with Sheila Sorensen, and I'm sure they had sex.'

'Stephen and the film lady? *Oi, oi, oi!* He's been very quiet about that. I'm sure Beth-Ann doesn't know,' Carmen said, unable to squelch a small grin.

'And I'm not telling her,' said Tanya. 'But Stephen's been giving me the cold shoulder ever since. I'm going crazy, but I'm too embarrassed just to walk up and speak with him about it. Can you help me? Can you talk to him?'

At that moment, the women heard Stephen's footsteps approaching from the hall, and Tanya scooted back to her board. She gave Carmen a pleading look. With a small nod of her head, her friend smiled back encouragingly. Tanya busied herself with her drawings.

As soon as Stephen sat down, Carmen passed him a couple of files she had been working on. 'Check these, will you Stephen? I think we can discard them.' Her voice took on a tone of annoyance. 'I don't know why *Señor* Pease wants this. It is a waste of time.' She shrugged and shook her head. 'You know, I only think he made me stay behind to do this stupid work to get back at me.'

'Get back at you for what?' asked Stephen, more out of polite interest than any real desire to know.

'Because I wouldn't go out with him. He wanted to take me to a bar, "just to relax". Those were his words, "just to relax". I knew it wouldn't stop with a drink or two.' She tossed her hair contemptuously. 'He wanted sex.'

Stephen was dubious. 'Mightn't he have meant just what he said?'

'Ah, not *Señor* Pease, he likes sex. He boasts about it.' She dropped her voice to a conspiratorial whisper. 'Do you know, two nights ago, at dinner, he tried to get Tanya to have sex with him?'

Now Stephen was all attention. 'What do you mean? How do you know?'

'Tanya was so upset by it, she came to ask my help,' explained Carmen. 'Did you know Pease tried to stop Tanya getting credit for her work unless she agreed to sleep with him? He is *el cochino*, a pig!'

'What happened?' Stephen was whispering now, looking over at Tanya to see if she was paying attention. But she appeared to be engrossed in her work, head down over her drawings.

'Well, she pretended to agree, just to play him along. I heard that Tanya was a big hit last night with the movie people, *Señora* Sorensen especially. When they discovered how good she was, they wanted to work with her directly. So she could refuse that sex-mad *bastardo*.'

Stephen blushed at the mention of Sheila Sorensen. He wondered what Carmen and Tanya would think if they knew what had happened in Sheila's bed. He shook the thought from his mind, and concentrated instead on Tanya. It seemed as if he'd made a serious mistake.

Stephen replayed the evening's events in his memory. Tanya had certainly been in top form; she'd given a stunning performance of ideas for *Katrina Cortez*, almost becoming the character herself. But he'd overheard Pease discussing sex with Tanya as a prelude to the both of them going into a back room for what had seemed an age. He'd assumed they'd had a quickie, as part of their sordid little arrangement. But if Tanya had only pretended to agree . . . He turned back to Carmen. 'Where's Pease been for the last two days? We haven't seen him at all.'

'Hiding, if you ask me,' replied Carmen. 'I think he's too ashamed to show his face. But you can bet if Tanya had slept with him, we'd all have heard about his latest conquest, by now.'

Stephen nodded. He looked over at Tanya's board. She was busily working. 'I thought she'd been sleeping with Pease,' he said, looking back at Carmen.

'Is it any of your business who Tanya sleeps with?' Carmen asked with a curt nod in the direction of Beth-Ann's desk.

Stephen blushed and dropped his eyes. 'You're right. Not really.' He, too, looked at Beth-Ann's working area as a way of acknowledging his careless lust, and nodded sadly.

'Stephen, you must believe in our Tanya. She's been loyal to that boyfriend of hers. But it's you she hungers for.' She looked him in the eye. 'You don't think she let Pease lay her. Do you?'

Stephen returned her slow stare. A flush was high in his cheeks. 'I believe you, Carmen, I do, and I feel a fool for getting so confused about it. I really thought she was having sex with Pease as a way of getting what she wanted in the movie.' Stephen looked so contrite, so young and vulnerable, that Carmen didn't have the heart to tell him about Beth-Ann, who did sleep with the boss. Instead, she leant forward and gave him an affectionate kiss on the cheek. But she couldn't resist a getting-your-own-back jab.

'Talking of movie people,' she said in a sly undertone, 'how did your interview go on the casting couch with Sheila?'

Stephen was reduced to blushing incoherence. He

refused to look at either woman, for Tanya was looking up from her board, and Carmen looked ready to burst into laughter.

'Oi, Stephen, I have hit *el tragaluz*, the bullseye, no?' Carmen laughed at Stephen's discomfort. She pinched him playfully on the arm. 'All the time you were upset that Tanya might be in bed with *Señor* Pease, you were making love to the movie lady. Shame on you! I've heard she's old enough to be your mama!'

'Carmen, please ... don't tease me anymore,' he pleaded with a sheepish smile.

'Maybe another older woman is just what you need,' Carmen suggested with a giggle, but her merriment, Tanya's curiosity, and Stephen's growing embarrassment, were cut short by the arrival of Eric Janovich dressed in his best evening suit and carrying a small valise.

Without greeting the other two, Eric addressed his girlfriend abruptly. 'It's time to go. Look, I brought you a change of clothes,' he said, holding out the valise, 'because I knew you wouldn't be ready. Come along. If you change right away, we'll still be on time.'

'But Eric,' Tanya explained, 'I'm not finished. I said I wouldn't be.'

'But I told you to be ready! You knew I was expecting you to come with me.' Eric grew visibly angry and glowered at Tanya. 'Come on,' he growled, and took her arm.

Tanya, embarrassed by his tantrum in front of her colleagues, lost her patience. 'I cannot abandon my work just so I can decorate your arm at some boring banking dinner!' she said, standing her ground. 'Let go of me!'

Eric gripped Tanya's arm tighter and tried to drag her away with him. Stephen and Carmen stood and watched, uncertain what action to take. For her part, Tanya refused to budge and shook off Eric's arm.

'Look here, Tanya, you're coming with me. Now!'

Eric's voice and temper rose; he grabbed Tanya and pulled her off balance.

In retaliation, Tanya caught Eric a swift and stinging slap across his face. 'Don't touch me, Eric!'

Eric's face was livid, both from the mark of Tanya's hand and his own rage.

At that moment Stephen strode forward and grabbed Eric's wrist. 'Mr Janovich. That's enough. Tanya isn't going with you, she has work to finish. Please just leave the studio. That will be best for everybody.' His tone was a model of moderation, but there was no doubting his own rising temper.

Eric tore his arm free and pushed Stephen in the chest. 'Who the hell are you? This is none of your business. Tanya's coming with me. Get out of my way!'

Eric pushed Stephen to one side and grabbed at Tanya, who dodged and dropped into the kick-boxing stance she was learning at the gym. 'Eric, go away. I don't want to hurt you,' she said with the vain wish that she was further along in her lessons.

Eric laughed disdainfully and moved forward, but was seized at the elbow by the restraining arm of Stephen. The two men struggled together momentarily, until a short stabbing blow by Stephen's fist brought a bright sprouting of blood from Eric's nose. Within seconds, he was bleeding over his shirt and expensive suit.

'Jesus! I'm bleeding! You fucking maniac, I'm bleeding all over my suit. That cost $1000!' Eric's voice was a strangled shriek as he watched in horror as blood spattered over his wardrobe. 'You'll pay for this, kid. I'll sue you!'

'If you try that, Eric,' said Tanya coldly, 'I'll file a complaint with the cops. A charge of accosting your girlfriend should look good on your resumé. I'm sure your friend the CEO would be very impressed.'

Eric backed off, clutching a red-stained handkerchief to his face. 'This is it, Tanya, it's over between us!' He was yelling. 'Move out, bitch! Get your things out of my apartment by the time I'm back from dinner, or I'll throw your trash out on the street.' Eric turned on his heel, fumbled for his cellular phone and stormed out, one hand to his head, the other frantically punching buttons. The door slammed behind him.

Chapter Twelve

Bitter Fruits

'*Mia cara,* he doesn't really mean it, does he?' cried Carmen with concern, her mascara running, tears on her cheeks.

Tanya was stunned. She felt shocked. Mortified. She nodded dumbly, 'I think so; I think he really means it.'

Stephen said quietly, 'Tanya, I'd like to help.'

Tanya swivelled to face him. His blue eyes looked sad, yet oddly restful after Eric's nasty black ones. She felt like she was drowning in their limpid pools. With her relationship in ruins and nowhere to live, Tanya wanted to fall into Stephen's strong and comforting arms. He would console her with runaway kisses. He would . . . She pulled back, alarmed that she could think about going to another man so easily, mere seconds after her boyfriend walked out on her.

'I've got to finish this work,' she said. 'Even if he puts my bags on the street, I've got to finish these drawings tonight.'

Carmen suggested a solution. 'Look, *chicita,* if the drawings cannot wait, let me and Stephen collect your things. You can stay with me for a few days – a few weeks, if necessary. I have a big sofa. Give me your key, and we'll get your clothes and come back and pick you up.'

Tanya shook her head. 'Thank you, Carmen, but that would be too complicated. There's an alarm system, and my stuff is all over the place. No, I'll go and then come back and finish up. I've got this finished lettering to do.'

'I have a better idea,' said Stephen. 'You and Carmen collect your stuff; I'll stay here and work on your drawings. You've seen my lettering. It's pretty good, and I'll make it look like yours. Just show me your notes.'

Tanya was stirred by his willingness. 'Stephen,' she said, touching his arm. 'I haven't thanked you for standing up for me back there. You didn't have to do that.' She lifted his hand; the knuckles were beginning to show a slight bruise. He winced slightly. She asked, 'Did you injure your hand?'

Stephen shrugged it off. 'It doesn't hurt as much as Eric's nose, I'm sure.' He laughed to break the tension. 'In the movies you see guys fight all the time with their fists, and they don't wince. It didn't occur to me that it would hurt.'

'Well,' Tanya said softly, 'in the movies, they don't really connect.'

'Have you ever hit anyone before?' Carmen asked.

Stephen considered the question. 'No, I don't think so, except in playground scuffles as a kid in school. Anyway, that's enough about me.' He withdrew his hand, and Tanya realised she had been holding it for several minutes. 'I'll get on with your lettering. Why don't you get your stuff, before Eric gets back?' he suggested.

Tanya smiled her thanks at her young colleague. 'Would you mind? The rough sketches are on my board; the dialogue is worked out and pencilled in.' She paused. 'I'll be back in a couple of hours, and we could finish together. Then you could take me to Carmen's place.'

'Yes, you must stay at my apartment,' said Carmen. 'I insist.'

'Thank you, that would be a relief. You're a good friend.'

Stephen grinned. 'You go with Carmen, Tanya. I'll see you later.'

Tanya gave him a light kiss on the cheek, and let Carmen drag her away.

After two and a half hours of hectic packing, continually looking over their shoulders in case Eric returned, the two women drove back to Studio V with Tanya's belongings packed high in the trunk and the back seat. Tanya was grateful that her furniture and larger possessions were safely in a lock-up storage bin near her old apartment.

She and Carmen had found Eric's bloodied shirt soaking in cold water, and the suit and tie carefully bagged for the dry cleaners. Tanya thought it a shame the man took better care of his clothing than his girlfriend. Presumably he had changed into another immaculate suit and was now dining with his precious chairman. Tanya felt sure Eric would find a suitable explanation for his damaged face: probably walking into a door. Eric had never been very original.

Thinking of Eric in the past tense brought home to Tanya her first real sense of shock about her eviction. She hadn't grown to like Eric's apartment that much, but it had been her home, even if only for a short time. She began to cry softly to herself in the passenger seat as Carmen picked her way back to Deep Ellum through the maze of intersecting grids that confused the central areas of the city.

'Me, I wouldn't cry for that bastard,' scolded Carmen gently but firmly. 'It will be difficult for a while, but you are better off without that man! He is no good for you.'

'I'm so embarrassed that you and Stephen had to see that,' said Tanya, sniffling into her handkerchief. 'You must think me a wretched person, always in one mess or another.'

'Far from it, *cara*,' denied her friend. 'And I told young Stephen you didn't have sex with Pease. Look how he helped you. You don't know what Eric might have done, with that temper of his.'

At first, Tanya was silent. She was grateful to Stephen, and shocked by the instantaneous erotic feelings that she felt for him so soon after Eric had left. But for the last few hours, she had been fighting the urge to run to him. She wanted him.

As they pulled up at the studio, Carmen offered one other piece of advice. Putting her hand on Tanya's arm, the dainty Hispanic woman said softly, 'We have in my country a saying: "Even a good harvest can bring bitter fruit." There can be disappointment, even with good things. But it is still a good harvest in your life. Work is good, and I think if you take care with young Stephen, he might be a good man for you. And,' she added, almost as an afterthought, 'next week we find you a new apartment. That will be fun. We can see more of each other.'

Tanya smiled through the last of her tears. 'I'd like that,' she said.

Upstairs in the studio, they found Stephen finishing the lettering in the dialogue boxes. Tanya was impressed. 'That was fast!' she said. 'I was expecting to do another hour's work on it.'

Stephen proffered the drawings for her inspection. 'You'd better check them,' he said. 'I've been careful, but it's your work.'

When Tanya took the sheets of vellum and sat down at her drawing board, the first thing she saw was Eric's photo. She swore, throwing the frame forcefully in the direction of the large studio trash bin against a wall several feet from her desk. 'Get that jerk out of my sight!' The frame smashed against the brickwork and dropped into the bin. The glass cracked with the impact. 'Good riddance,' muttered Tanya. Stephen and Carmen exchanged glances but said nothing.

'Give me a few minutes with these, then we can go. OK?' Tanya didn't look at her companions. She was in rapt concentration over the *Katrina Cortez* drawings. By now, Katrina Cortez had the upper hand in the relationship, but her influence was well disguised. To Regan's mind, she was an attractive wind-up sex toy, to be enjoyed and indulged, but not taken seriously.

With a shock, Tanya saw that she had been unconsciously drawing aspects of herself and Eric Janovich into the characters. The fusion of fact and fiction sent a small shiver down her spine.

Stephen had done a first-class job with the final lettering and, with a great sense of relief, she packed the sheets carefully into a padded envelope, and added stiffening cardboard for protection. She sealed it securely, to give to the security guard downstairs on the way out. On the front of the envelope she printed in large bold letters: 'Special Delivery. Messenger Pickup. For Joshua McNally, Quantum Comics: From Katrina Cortez.'

Chapter Thirteen
Tequila Duet

Tanya, Carmen and Stephen stood together outside Studio V on Elm Street in the warm darkness of the Friday evening. No one spoke, each unsure of the next move.

Stephen broke the silence. 'I'll follow in my car,' he said, 'and help you carry all your things inside.'

'That's too much trouble; you don't need to do that,' said Carmen.

'Thanks, that would be great,' said Tanya.

All three laughed. 'Come on then,' Carmen decided. 'Let's go to my place.'

In a small convoy, Carmen led the way through downtown and the glitzy West End bars and nightclubs, past the Book Depository from which Lee Harvey Oswald had fired his fatal shot, and across the wide dry floodplain of the Trinity River, wending its narrow summer course beneath a plethora of freeway bridges and railroad viaducts. From there she headed south on Beckley Avenue and Zang Boulevard, towards the Oak Cliff neighbourhood. Tanya and Stephen followed in their respective vehicles. A right on to Jefferson and a left on to Montclair brought them to a stop outside a small brick fourplex, a two-storey building with two apartments on each floor, opening off a central hallway. Cheerful yellow light spilt from the windows upstairs, bathing the front lawn.

Carmen pulled into the driveway and, while the other two parked at the kerb, she ran ahead to open the front door to the hall and then an inner door to her flat. She returned to find Stephen and Tanya unloading boxes from her car on to the lawn. She picked one up. 'My place is on the ground floor. Tanya, we'll put your boxes in the living room and your clothes in the hall closet for the time being. Follow me.'

With three sets of hands, Tanya's rescued possessions were stowed against the wall in Carmen's front room within fifteen minutes. With relief, the trio relaxed in the three available armchairs in Carmen's living room.

'This calls for a drink,' announced Carmen, disappearing into the kitchen. The others heard the fridge door open. 'I've got Mexican beer, Negro Mondelo or Tecate, or tequila. I don't have Triple Sec for margaritas, so it'll have to be straight, I'm afraid.'

'I'll take a Tecate, please,' called Stephen.

'Do you have salt and limes for a Tequila Solo?' asked Tanya. 'That seems appropriate.'

Carmen brought in a tray with an open bottle of Tecate and a frosted glass, a half-full bottle of Cuervo Gold Tequila, a plate of quartered limes, a shaker of salt and two shot glasses. 'I'll join you, Tanya,' she said, with a smile. 'Welcome to my new housemate.'

Tanya poured a full measure of the light golden liquid into each small glass. She shook a little salt on to the back of her left hand between forefinger and thumb, and picked up a lime wedge with the same hand. Raising one glass in her right hand, she toasted Carmen and Stephen. '*Salud!*' Tanya looked them both in the eye. 'Thank you, both of you; it's been a difficult evening.' She looked around the modest but cheerful room. 'This is nice, Carmen. It's a surprise, ending up here tonight.' Tanya licked the salt from her skin, tossed back the fiery liquor in one swallow and bit hard into the lime, all in one fluid motion. The combination of fierce tastes sent a shudder through her body. 'God, that was good. Give me another.'

Carmen laughed. 'You drink like a *Latina*. Maybe there's hope for you yet.' She quickly followed suit. '*Salud*, Tanya! *Salud*, Stephen! Welcome *a mi casa*.'

Stephen acknowledged the greeting, and sat slowly sipping his beer, his eyes flicking from one attractive woman to the other. He surreptitiously compared Carmen's petite body and features, her dark, almost black hair, shoulder-length and curly, and her olive skin, with Tanya's tanned creamy complexion, long brown hair and slightly taller, trim muscular figure. They were both very attractive; and although they were older than himself by several years, he had developed a new appreciation for older women, after his night with Sheila Sorensen. Those memories, plus the open and natural sexiness of his companions, stirred him into semi-arousal. He cradled the beer bottle in his lap to camouflage the developing bulge in his pants, but couldn't stop luscious images of three-way sex with these lovely women from popping up in his mind.

He saw Tanya's eyelids flicker briefly. When he looked more closely, he could see tiredness and signs of strain around her eyes. Her eyes caught his gaze and smiled briefly before resting under closed lids. He wanted to say how beautiful she was, how sexy, and how pleased he was to be able to help. Tonight she looked like Natalie Wood from videos he'd seen of her early movies. Beth-Ann and Sheila receded in his mind, replaced with erotic imaginings of Tanya. But common sense told him this wouldn't be a good time to make those feelings known.

He finished his beer and stood up, careful to disguise

his partial erection from the women. 'It's late,' he said, putting the empty bottle on the table. 'I'd better get home. I'll call tomorrow, Tanya, to see if you need anything. Thanks for the beer, Carmen.'

'Thank you for helping, Stephen. And thank you for ... what you did with Eric.' Tanya clearly wasn't quite sure how to describe those awful moments. She stood up and walked Stephen to the door, taking his hand loosely in hers. 'Call me tomorrow. We'll talk more then.' She tilted her face up to receive his kiss, a warm soft touch of his lips against hers, with just enough pressure to set her tingling in anticipation.

'Good night, Tanya,' and he was gone, leaving behind the faintest trace of his familiar lime fragrance.

The women sat together in companionable silence. 'He's a nice boy,' Carmen said eventually.

Tanya smiled sleepily. 'Yes, he is.' She giggled quietly. 'Did you see his hard-on?'

Carmen nodded with a smile. 'I thought it best not to mention it. I didn't want to embarrass the poor guy.'

'He was probably sitting there imagining three-way sex: you know, the male fantasy where the man has his dick inside one girl and his tongue inside the second.'

Carmen smiled. 'Could be worse,' she said coyly.

Tanya's eyes opened wide. 'I've never done anything like that,' she said. 'Have you?'

But Carmen seemed to regret her innuendo, and stood to clear away the bottles and glasses. 'It's late, *chicita*. There will be plenty of time to talk more tomorrow. I'll get some sheets for the couch, and you can make up the bed.'

When Tanya awoke, the morning sun was already warm. She had slept fitfully in the unfamiliar surroundings, dreaming of Stephen, Eric, and Carmen, and also of Katrina Cortez. Her fictional heroine was becoming like a real person in her mind. In the other room, Tanya could hear the shower running, and Carmen's radio tuned softly to one of the local Hispanic radio stations.

For the first time she accepted her attraction to the 'sweet young thing', as she thought of Stephen Sinclair, without the complications of guilt. They had much more in common with each other than she and Eric. She slipped naked from the couch and tidied away her sheets. She was just pulling on a loose T-shirt when Carmen walked in from the bedroom.

'*Buenos dias, chicita*. Did you sleep OK?'

Tanya nodded, pulling the hem down to cover herself. Carmen seemed unfazed by the partial nudity.

'And dreamt of Stephen?'

Tanya nodded again. 'And of Eric, and you, and Katrina Cortez.'

'Ah, that woman, she is going to dominate your life. I can tell. Remember, she's only a cartoon.'

Carmen disappeared into the kitchen, where Tanya heard the low whir of a coffee-grinder and the sluice of water. 'I have to go to work this afternoon, Tanya,' called Carmen through the open doorway.

Tanya was surprised. 'You have to go into the studio on the weekend?'

'No, not the studio. I have to go to my other job. I'm a part-time hostess at the CowGirl Club; it helps pay the rent.'

'I had no idea. Where is it? What's it like?'

Carmen didn't answer straightaway, and busied herself pouring boiling water on to the coffee grounds in a big cafetière and pushing down the plunger. She poured two steaming mugs of strong black liquid and handed one to Tanya. The writing on the mug proclaimed 'Dallas! The Biggest and the Best' in slightly faded lettering. The bitter taste of Carmen's potent brew jolted Tanya to full wakefulness.

'How long have you had this other job?'

'Oh, just a few months. The place is really cool; it's not your typical strip club. It's run by a couple of women who moved here from Atlanta. They have all sorts of shows there, from fashion modelling to local bands. Sometimes they have dance and performance art, and sometimes it is just a straightforward striptease.'

'Do you dance? You've got a dancer's body.' Tanya admired her friend's physique.

'No, not really. I eat too many *enchiladas*. But, yes, once or twice I've helped when one of the girls was off, but I'd need more practice to keep a hundred horny men happy without my clothes on. Speaking of clothes,' Carmen said, changing the subject, 'you can hang yours up in here.' She indicated the hall closet. 'Make yourself at home. I'm leaving in a couple of hours, and I won't be back till very late. There's a spare key on the hook by the front door to use while you're here.'

Carmen occupied herself in the kitchen, leaving Tanya to settle in. Later, they shared a light brunch of scrambled eggs, bacon, toast and orange juice, and sat reading the newspaper. Neither woman seemed anxious to talk, or to pick up the threads from the previous night. When Carmen moved to tidy things away, Tanya forestalled her.

'I'll do the dishes,' she said. 'What time do you have to go to work?'

'Soon. I'll go and change now.' Carmen skipped to the bedroom.

Tanya washed the few mugs and plates. Carmen returned wearing a navy blue SMU sweatsuit and white Reeboks; she carried a small gym bag. 'I'm off to work,' she said. 'See you after midnight, if you're still awake. *Hasta luego*!'

On her own, Tanya slowly unpacked her suitcases, removing what she would need for a few days, and leaving the rest. Everything fitted in the hall closet, and she pushed her empty suitcases under Carmen's bed.

Tanya placed several CDs next to the stereo and some books on a side table. She took her make-up and toiletries into the bathroom, and drew herself a long hot bath. She'd discovered early in her relationship with Eric that he didn't like her to take baths; it took too long for his precise schedule. Now Tanya determined to pamper herself and, putting on some soft jazz by Keiko Matsui, she borrowed some potions from Carmen's collection and mixed up a scented pillow of suds. She lay back in the hot water with a contented sigh.

With her eyes closed Tanya pondered this new freedom thrust upon her. Her first priority was to find a place to live, but she wanted to think about Stephen, and how to make him hers. How could she overcome Beth-Ann's hold on him? A small voice in her brain told her to do what Katrina Cortez did. *You've got a better body than that chubby trollop; use it! Give him the best sex he's ever had!*

Tanya looked down at her nipples poking through the foam. Her breasts were full and firm, large for her slender frame. She stroked them, imagining Stephen's fingers rather than her own, until her nipples were hard.

After a good soak, she dried off, and padded naked around the small apartment. There was only the single bedroom, living room and a little dining-alcove plus the bathroom and kitchen. The dining area opened out on to a small deck and a well-treed back yard, fenced in from neighbours.

Picking up the tequila bottle and a glass from the kitchen, Tanya opened the sliding door and stepped on to the wooden patio. She enjoyed the warm late-afternoon sun on her naked body, and stretched out on a padded *chaise-longue*. She swallowed a shot of tequila down in one, and poured herself another. She drank that down with gusto also, and poured a third. This one she took more slowly.

The liquor tingled inside her, and the sun warmed her

skin. Unlike Katrina Cortez, who was a night person and whose porcelain flesh rarely sought the sun, Tanya's skin was lightly tanned. But her thoughts of sex matched those of her cartoon heroine. Katrina Cortez, decided Tanya, would have no hesitation in taking Stephen to her bed.

Imagining Stephen's large young manhood rising up before her, Tanya tingled at the thrill of masturbating in the open air. She closed her eyes, soaking up the sun, and curled the fingers of one hand, gently pressing against her clitoris. Lying naked in the waning rays of the sun, Tanya felt a slow orgasm build. She came long and hard, her pent-up tensions flowing out of her as she shuddered to her release. She lay panting; her clitoris was tingling and she kept a gentle pressure on her bud with her fingers, enjoying every last quivering note as it vibrated through her body.

Hungry for more, Tanya hurried indoors and returned with Carmen's cordless phone. She got Stephen's home number from Information, quaffed another shot of the Mexican spirit, sat down on the sofa, and dialled, holding her breath.

'Hello. Stephen Sinclair.' He answered on the second ring.

Tanya disguised her voice like she imagined Katrina's would be. 'Are you alone, Lover Boy?' she asked in the slow purr.

'Yes.' His voice squeaked ever so slightly. More deeply, he asked, 'Who's this?'

'Are you sure you're alone? No big blonde girlfriend with you?'

'No, I'm alone. Look, who is this?'

With simulated huskiness, Tanya announced, 'I want you, Stevie boy.' She reached between her legs. Her pussy was hot again.

He whispered, 'Who *is* this? Is this Sheila?'

'No, it's not Sheila, Stevie. She's much too old for you. Are you listening, Stevie?'

'Yes.'

'Do you know what I want you to do?'

'No.'

'I want you to ... lick my clit,' Tanya purred, the warmth of the several tequilas feeding the fires of her sexual lust. 'I'm playing with my clit right now. I'm wet for you, Stevie.' Fresh juices moistened the lips of Tanya's sex as she dallied with herself. It was like a long-delayed aftershock of her earlier orgasm. 'But first, Lover Boy, I want you to take out your penis, and play with it. I want to know you've got that lovely long thick cock in your hand.'

Stephen's hand went to his fly. The sexy voice engendered an immediate reaction. He unzipped his pants and released his fully hard penis into his right hand, just as his mystery caller demanded. There was something familiar about the voice, but he couldn't quite place it. He knew it wasn't Beth-Ann; nothing could disguise that nasal Texas twang.

Disguise! Suddenly Stephen caught on. It was Tanya! Was she drunk? She certainly sounded weird, but he liked what she was doing. This whole episode was like one of Katrina Cortez's antics. The voice on the telephone sounded like Tanya's enactments of Katrina's sultry speech at dinner the other night.

Playing along, he said, 'My cock's in my hand. What shall I do with it?' He didn't want Tanya to know that he'd penetrated her charade.

'Masturbate for me, Stevie. Tell me what your lovely firm staff looks like.'

'It's long and hard, I'm pumping ... I can feel the come rising up my shaft.' Stephen wanted to ask some questions himself. 'What are you doing? Are you rubbing yourself? Are you alone? Are you naked?'

'Yes, I'm all alone. I am . . . completely undressed; just for you.'

Stephen was pumping hard, his breath getting ragged. Thoughts of Tanya, naked and masturbating, filled his mind. 'I'm coming. God, I'm coming!'

'Me, too,' yelled Tanya as she concentrated on her labia.

Stephen's cock jumped in his hand, spurting semen over his fingers and on to the chair where he was sitting. He groaned.

'What's happened, Stevie? What have you done?' Tanya's own voice was now breathless with excitement.

'I've just come all over my hand,' Stephen whispered into the phone. 'And I know who you are, mystery girl. I know you . . . Katrina Cortez. I want you. I want to fuck you. I know where you are. I'm coming right over.'

Tanya gasped, and then smiled to herself. That was what she'd wanted all along. She put on her most Katrina-like purr. 'Little Tanya's out for the evening Stevie. I'll be waiting for you. I'll be ready for you. You can pump all your wonderful come deep inside me. Be quick!'

She clicked off the phone and lay back, her sensitive flesh still pulsing. Breathless, she sank into the cushions of the sofa. Wow, she thought, wouldn't that make a great little *Katrina Cortez* vignette? She reached for her sketchbook.

For her debut as Katrina Cortez, Tanya selected some sexy garments that she'd recently ordered from a catalogue. First, she slipped on a front-fastening black satin push-up bra that emphasised and swelled out her creamy breasts. To cover her mons, she chose the barest of thongs, black and embroidered with a red velvet rose positioned directly over her clitoris. The cheeks of her bottom were completely bare. Over this ensemble she draped a long silken red Chinese kimono, with a black dragon motif embellishing the back. As a final touch, she stepped into her one and only pair of black high-heeled ankle boots. Pouring herself another Tequila Solo, Tanya felt bold and very Katrina-like.

She put on a CD of Anúna's mystical *a cappella* vocals and lit some of Carmen's aromatic candles. The atmosphere became charged with eastern spices and an air of sensuality.

Outside her window, the evening sky had darkened. In her provocative costume, she walked out into the shared hallway and switched on the lights. She unlatched the outer front door and left it ajar. Tanya heard a car pull up outside and the car door slam. Footsteps hurried up the path and there was a faint squeak as the outer door was pushed open. A faint click marked its closing behind her visitor.

Through the peephole, she could see Stephen walking down the hall towards her. She flung open the door, stopping the young man in his tracks, where the halo of the lobby lighting illuminated him for Tanya's study. His blue eyes, enhanced by dark eyebrows and lashes, seemed brighter in his handsome face. His chestnut hair flopped back from his broad forehead.

Tanya felt a warm, liquid sensation radiating between her thighs. She cast off her robe. Her breasts were thrust forward; the minuscule thong did little to hide her body. 'Come in,' she invited.

Stephen simply stared. His bright blue eyes darkened with desire.

Tanya licked her lips and touched herself between the legs, her fingers sliding behind the velvet rose to stroke her own bud. Stephen's eyes followed her hand's every movement. 'Unclip me,' she commanded.

'T-Tanya,' he managed to stammer, staring at her lovely, radiant semi-nakedness. His hands fumbled with the satin bra, then peeled it away, revealing her full breasts.

'Now my panties.'

Stephen knelt, easing the tiny thong down over Tanya's thighs to her ankles. She stepped out gracefully. His eyes were level with her sex.

'Stephen,' she sighed deeply, and closed her eyes, tracing the outline of his face with her fingers. She ran her index finger down his chin and on to her own flesh. She found her clitoris, circling it for a moment before softly pushing her finger inside her vagina. She was so wet, it slid in easily.

Tanya heard Stephen's sharp intake of breath, and felt his face nuzzle amongst her tight brown curls. She eased her finger from her pussy and placed it against his lips. 'Lick me clean,' she commanded. His lips took first one knuckle and then the whole finger into his mouth. 'Let's go inside,' she said.

Chapter Fourteen
Change of Heart

The warm glow from the hallway flowed through the fanlight above the front door, illuminating the small living room and the fold-out sofa where two naked bodies lay entwined. Stephen Sinclair was pinned beneath Tanya Trevino, who knelt astride him, her mouth locked to his, her hands enmeshed in his hair.

Her legs spread wide, Tanya reached to hold the young man's rigid penis in her hand and pressed its tip against the petals of her sex. She sat up slowly and eased her body back so that Stephen's penis was buried deep within the wide open folds of her vagina.

'You feel so good in there.' Tanya smiled down at her lover. Stephen's impressive rod never seemed to falter; he stayed hard for her.

Stephen reached up to claim her breasts, palming their smooth creamy contours, pinching the nipples gently between his fingers. He tilted his pelvis upward, pushing his thick staff into Tanya as far as it would go. 'Ride me, Tanya. Make me come again.'

Tanya complied by pressing her groin into his, mashing her clitoris against her lover's pubic bone. She eased her buttocks up and down in a rocking motion, never once releasing the pressure against her swollen love-bud. She cried out with pleasure as Stephen matched his rhythm to hers; their bodies moved in a syncopated symmetry of carnal desire.

Tanya reached behind to find Stephen's balls. Encouraged by his cries of ecstasy, she ran her fingers back and forth along his cleft. Having learnt from Eric the effects of teasing his anus as he was approaching climax, she tried the same trick on Stephen, with amazing results.

The young man cried out in surprise and delight. His body jerked and spasmed, bucking Tanya in the air.

She grabbed his shoulders to keep her balance above him. She clenched her internal muscles, enjoying the sensual warmth inside. Her own tremors built fast and, with renewed vigour, Tanya ground her clitoris against Stephen's body, rubbing back and forth in a rapid motion. She climaxed with a scream of pure pleasure; sensations of delight coursed through her. The walls of her vagina vibrated with the force of her orgasm, racking her body as she exhausted her passion.

Stephen slowly faded inside her, and he slipped out. Tanya lay back, lingering over the aftershocks of their lust, wondering if she could capture that sumptuous sensation in the *Katrina Cortez* cartoon.

Stephen drifted into sleep, splayed across the sheets in all the wantonness of the truly satiated lover. Tanya cuddled next to him and was soon asleep herself. She woke only once during the night, disturbed by a small noise in the room. She opened one eye to see the figure of Carmen tiptoeing past the couch into her bedroom.

Monday was a Texas state holiday and Tanya and Stephen stayed in bed, on Carmen's couch, for most of the morning. The dark and overcast sky was redolent with humidity, foreshadowing the heat to come. Of Carmen there was no sign: Tanya assumed her friend was sleeping late after her long hours at the CowGirl Club, or had slipped out before they awoke.

No breeze stirred the air, no movement brushed the bright green leaves on the willow oaks and the blossoms of the crepe myrtles outside the window. As her lover's tongue and expert fingers spread her sex-lips wide, she heard the stuttering patter of the first heavy raindrops on the foliage. Above the quiet hum of the fan that paddled the heavy air across their bodies, she listened with delicious languor as the muted soulful strains of Richard Stoltzman's flute wove a haunting melody deep into her soul.

Tanya enjoyed their lovemaking for its very spontaneity and she gloried in the satisfaction of sex for sex's sake. But she became alert to a subtle change of mood during their conversation later in the morning.

While nibbling a very late breakfast in bed, trying to keep the toast crumbs from dropping into the sheets and forming a prickly layer between their bodies, they discussed Tanya's need to find a new apartment.

'We could look for something this afternoon,' Stephen suggested, his eyes sparkling with anticipation. 'And tomorrow I could take a day off work, and chase down some possibilities in the paper.'

Tanya was touched by her lover's concern, but found his eagerness to help her in this chore a bit puzzling. 'That's very nice of you, Stephen. I do need to move quickly so as not to burden Carmen's hospitality, but I'll have to visit places and look them over myself.'

'Of course, Tanya. If I saw something that seemed right, you could come along afterwards and check it out.'

'But how would you know what was right for me? I won't know till I see it.'

'But if I like it, I think there's a good chance that you'd like it, too.' Stephen displayed the eagerness to please of an overgrown puppy.

'Stephen, you don't need to go to all that trouble to find me a place to live. I certainly appreciated your help moving my stuff in here. But that was an emergency. I have a few days to sort things out.'

Looking down at the rumpled bedclothes, Stephen blushed. 'Tanya, I . . . thought we might . . . move in together. You and me,' he said plainly. 'After all, you need somewhere to live, and the crummy little house I rent over at McCommas and Greenville isn't very special. It's only three houses down from the main drag; it's very noisy. I don't like it much. This would be a good chance for us to join forces, so to speak. Then we could be together all the time.'

Tanya had a sinking feeling in her stomach. She took a moment to order her thoughts before suggesting, 'We can see each other a lot without living together. I've just tried that with Eric, and it was a disaster. I want to be on my own again.'

'But you're not on your own, Tanya,' Stephen cajoled. 'We're together, you and me. We're lovers. I love you. I want to be with you always.'

Despite the heat of the day, Tanya shivered with apprehension. She looked up at Stephen, and found him gazing devotedly into her eyes. She closed her eyelids tightly.

'I like you, Stephen,' she said, slowly and carefully. 'I like you a lot. And I really like having sex with you, but that's not the same as being in love with you. I'm not ready for that.' She opened her eyes and looked straight into her lover's face. 'I told myself I was in love with Eric, but I misread my feelings in a big way. I won't put myself in that position again.'

'But Tanya, this is different. This is me, Stephen, not Eric. I love you! Tanya, tell me you love me.'

'Stephen, don't push! I told you. I'm not ready. It's too early. It's too fast. I feel like I love you, but I don't trust my feelings. Let's stay friends and it'll be cool.' Tanya sat up straight and pulled a sheet around her waist. Her pulse was racing, but she tried to remain calm. It was difficult.

'But Tanya, I love you. Don't push me away. Take me into your heart. I know everything will work out.' The young man's tone was pleading.

'Stephen, don't spoil it all by rushing me. I want to be your lover, but I don't want to live with you. Do you understand?' Her tone sharpened.

With aggravated sarcasm, he suggested, 'You want to have me around as your toy-boy, is that it? A cute little guy to fuck when you're horny?'

Tanya shook her head in annoyance. Why did men always have to mess up everything, just when things were beginning to work out? 'Stephen, everything is fine as friends and lovers, making love and having laughs.'

'But I want to be with you all the time. I can't live without you.'

'Stephen, last week you lived quite well without me. If my memory serves me right, you made love to Beth-Ann, probably several times, and to Sheila Sorensen at least once. Did you tell them you loved them and couldn't live without them?'

'No, of course I didn't. That was different.' Stephen looked abashed.

Tanya smiled to reduce the tension building between them. 'Look, ever since the beginning of last week, I've wanted you. You're cute and sexy. You're also nice and gentle and kind. I like that. I like it a lot. I've just left a bad relationship, and now I can take you to bed without feeling that I've betrayed a trust. We've had a great time this weekend, but that's not enough time for us to know whether we want to commit our lives to each other.'

'It is for me.' Stephen was adamant.

'Be realistic. You're young. You're impatient. Slow down. Let's stay the way we are, friends and lovers. No commitment, yet; just fun and company.'

When Tanya felt that she was finally making things clear to her young lover, Stephen's next question caught her completely off guard.

'Will you promise not to see other men?'

'What?'

'I want your promise that you won't see other men.'

'It's too soon for me to give a promise like that. That's not fair.'

'If you loved me enough, you wouldn't need to see other men.'

Tanya felt her patience slipping away. 'I can give you friendship and sex, but, no, that's not enough for you. You want more. You want love. You want to tie me down.'

Stephen jumped up and walked about the room, gesturing helplessly. 'Tanya, what's wrong with love? It's not a dirty word. I want to be with you, all day and every day.'

Suddenly, that very possibility, which had seemed such a pleasant thought only yesterday, was threatening to Tanya. 'What about my independence?' she demanded. 'What about my desires? Everything is suddenly subservient to your needs.' Jeez, she thought, I've been here before. This may just as well be me and Eric; we had great sex and then argued about everything else.

She got up from the bed, and stalked naked into the bathroom. 'I'm going to take my shower,' she announced.

Ten minutes later, Tanya emerged from the bathroom, a towel around her hair and a larger one draped loosely over her shoulders. She sat down on the edge of the unmade bed. Her breasts swung free as the towel slipped off her shoulders, and she picked up her old T-shirt, pulling it over her wet hair with a brisk movement. 'Why don't we make up the bed, so we can have the place more or less tidy for when Carmen comes back?' Tanya suggested. As they made up the sofa bed, she continued, 'I think commitment has to build slowly between people. It can't just be traded in words. It can't be rushed.'

Stephen didn't look happy. 'I'm confused; you give me all sorts of hints and flirts, then you seduce me.' He made it sound like an accusation. 'Then, as soon as I want to get serious, you start pushing me away.'

Tanya tried to explain one more time. 'Stephen, I like you. That's pretty obvious, considering the way we've spent the last twenty-four hours joining our bodies in almost every way possible. But I'm on the threshold of some new situations that are a big deal for me. Katrina Cortez is starting to dominate my life, in terms of my creative work, and also, in a funny way, my personal life as well. When I write and draw the comic strip, I find that I can work things out, about myself as a person. I'm growing up, becoming liberated from my old assumptions and values. I'm changing; it's exciting, and I don't want to miss this opportunity.'

Stephen scowled. 'I don't want you to change. I love you just as you are. I don't want you to change into some cartoon character.'

Tanya scooted over on the bed and put her hand on Stephen's shoulder. 'I'm not saying that I want to become Katrina Cortez: just that exploring the character opens up new possibilities for me. When you ask me for commitment, for guarantees that I won't see other men, that goes against all these new opportunities. If I'm going to make a success of this movie venture, I've got to develop the character and explore.' Tanya's eyes shone with anticipation. 'I'm afraid that your conditions will hold me back, just when things are moving ahead.' She looked at Stephen, but he turned away and shrugged off her hand. He made a point of looking at his watch on the side table.

'I'd better be going,' he said in a neutral voice that saddened Tanya. 'It sounds like you've got places to be and people to see. You don't need me around.' He picked up his clothes and pulled them on, briskly and carelessly, studiously avoiding looking at Tanya as he dressed.

Tanya became agitated. 'Stephen, can't we still be friends? Can't we still go to bed together when we feel like it? I don't want to break up. Don't walk out like this.'

With exaggerated patience, Stephen said, 'No, Tanya, you can't have it both ways. I want to be the man in your life. The only man in your life. I don't want to sleep with you one day, and wonder if you're with someone else the next. I'm not going to be on call just for those times you want me.'

He walked to the door. 'See you around. If you change your mind, you know where to find me.' Without looking back, he turned the latch and stepped out into the hallway, shutting the door behind him.

Tanya stared at the closed door. Part of her wanted to cry, part wanted to run after him and do whatever he wished, but the strongest voice was one she recognised. 'Let him go. He's just like all the rest; he wants to control you. Sure, he's nicer than most, but it's always the same with men. We've got new worlds to explore, you and me.' It was the voice of Katrina Cortez.

Tanya straightened up, and swept her hair back from her face. Quickly, she tidied the room, pulled on some panties and a pair of jeans. She grabbed her sketchbook and a clutch of pencils, then opened the door and headed for her car. There was no sign of Stephen. 'You're right, Katrina,' she said to herself. 'This is going to be interesting. Who knows where we'll end up?'

Chapter Fifteen
Marking Territory

The atmosphere at Studio V was tense when the work week recommenced on Tuesday.

Stephen was pointedly polite but distant with Tanya, who in turn was stiff and formal with her erstwhile lover. Beth-Ann was alert to it all, trying to work out what had happened over the long weekend while she had been consoling Pease with her bodily charms and boosting her bank account. Carmen watched Tanya and Stephen anxiously, but held her own counsel.

Leon and Chuck, the other male artists in Studio V, watched the stilted play before them, and exchanged a few ribald remarks. The other two women, Gloria and Hillary, tried to float above it all.

Beth-Ann made the first move. She walked over to Stephen's board and snuggled up against him, rubbing her hips against his thigh.

'I thought we might get together tonight, Stephen,' she said softly, in a tone of voice that left no room for ambiguity about her intentions. If Tanya had taken her boyfriend to bed while she had been otherwise occupied screwing the boss all weekend, the best way to get Stephen back was to mark him again. She was under no misapprehensions about the power of her body, its scents and fleshly enticements. 'Let's talk about it at lunch,' the buxom blonde suggested. Giving Stephen a teasing bite on his ear, she sidled back to her board.

Tanya made a point of ignoring Beth-Ann's flirtation, and concentrated on her work. A fax from McNally arrived mid-morning. It read enthusiastically, 'Love the new material. The LA people tell Sheila they want more GirlZone stuff. Can you explore some new variations, with visuals and dialogue? Maybe some location stuff. As always, we want everything yesterday.'

Finding herself mooning a little over Stephen, Tanya threw herself into working hard, without much success, until one o'clock, when everyone else disappeared for lunch. Beth-Ann and Stephen predictably left together. Tanya politely refused Carmen's offer of a sandwich at the deli across the street, preferring to concoct some wild scenarios for Katrina Cortez at the GirlZone, but, after a few minutes, she took a stretching break, put down her pencil, and walked to the ladies' room.

Tanya rounded the corner into the hallway when she heard familiar voices from the open doorway to the storeroom where the studio kept its multitude of art and office supplies. The words were loud and clear, and Beth-Ann's nasal twang unmistakable.

'Oh, Stephen! You have the most beautiful dick in the whole of Texas. You taste so good. It's so long and hard. Umm, baby, give it to your honey-child . . .'

Tanya, mouth agape, was drawn magnetically to the doorway, knowing what she'd see before she got there, but lured to the spectacle nonetheless. Sure enough, there was Beth-Ann, topless, her breasts swinging free as she knelt between Stephen's thighs, her mouth around the young man's stiff penis.

Tanya knew that, from where he was standing, Stephen couldn't see her; his pants were down and his penis jacked, his eyes squeezed shut. He was turned away from Tanya, leaning rigidly against a stack of boxes. But Tanya could see very clearly what he and Beth-Ann were doing.

The blonde's eyes flashed when she saw Tanya standing in the doorway, but otherwise the semi-naked woman continued to suck Stephen's cock with insolent delight. Stephen, suspended in ecstasy, looked as if he were in another world.

In full sight of her open-mouthed audience of one, Beth-Ann gripped Stephen's shaft and pumped vigorously. Stephen's face was clenched with passion; semen coursed to the tip of his manhood and spurted suddenly and silently from his glans, some flying into Beth-Ann's open mouth, the rest stringing her face and hair, slowly running down her cheeks. At Tanya's involuntary gasp, his eyes flew open and he turned to see her ashen stare.

Holding her panicked stud stationary, Beth-Ann deliberately and sensuously sucked the remaining fluid from Stephen's throbbing stem, and slowly turned to face the shocked brunette. Semen decorated the blonde's face and body. With actions reminiscent of some tribal ritual, she smeared it over her bare breasts, rubbing it into her nipples. For what seemed like several seconds, no one spoke, the tableau frozen in time.

Moving jerkily, Stephen hiked up his trousers, looking embarrassed. Beth-Ann rose and walked to the doorway, stopping only inches from Tanya's face.

Tanya could smell Stephen's semen on the woman's flesh.

Holding her rival transfixed in her feral glare, the blonde smiled arrogantly, and spoke with barely controlled venom. 'This makes him mine, Tanya. Put that in your fucking cartoon! Now, get lost.' She moved slowly back to the hapless young man, and placed her hand on the bulge of his recently zipped trousers.

Tanya dragged her eyes from Stephen's groin up to

his livid face. His lips were working but no sound emerged, until he croaked, 'Tanya! I didn't mean –'

The rest of his sentence was cut off by the slam of the door as Tanya closed it behind her with a force that rocked the frame. She ran down the hall. She grabbed her sketchbook from her desk and stormed to the lift. As the doors opened, Carmen stepped out. 'I'm gone for the rest of the day,' shouted Tanya, before her friend could say anything. 'I'm on location. I may not be back. Ever.'

Chapter Sixteen
The CowGirl Club

'What the hell is wrong with me? Why do I mess up with men so often?' asked Tanya, glaring at Carmen as a prosecutor might intimidate a recalcitrant witness. 'Is it me? Or is it the men? First Eric and then Stephen; both wanted to control me.'

The two women were sitting in Carmen's living room, drinking Tequila Sunrises. In the few hours since witnessing the torrid spectacle in the Studio V storeroom, Tanya had ridden a roller-coaster ride of emotional swoops and plunges. Her frustrations and anger boiled over.

Carmen stayed calm in the face of her friend's outburst. 'It may seem like that,' she said, 'but I think both cases are different. Deep down, Eric didn't care enough about you. He desired you; he wanted to possess you. But young Stephen is different. Underneath his confusion, he likes you.'

'Then why the hell did he let Beth-Ann give him a blow job? In a place where I could see?'

'Have you ever met a man who could refuse a blow job?' asked Carmen with a smile.

Despite her ill humour, Tanya managed a weak grin

in return. 'You have a point. But . . .' Her frown returned. 'He didn't do anything to stop Beth-Ann from humiliating me. That bitch! I'll never forgive her.' Tanya's eyes flashed brightly in the glow of the table lamps. 'I loathe Beth-Ann. But I can't make up my mind about Stephen.' Tanya paused and spread her hands wide. 'He isn't the only one who's confused. Considering his actions, why can't I forget him?'

Carmen shrugged. 'Good question, *chicita*. Maybe you should just blow him off, so to speak.' She smiled at her own wit, but Tanya was not amused.

Each woman sipped her drink in silence until Tanya's impatience broke the stillness. 'I need to get away,' she said, 'and be on my own. I need to get my own place and work at my own pace. No Pease, no Stephen Sinclair, and certainly no Beth-Ann. I won't burden you with all my woes.' She looked at her friend with solemn eyes. 'I'm going to be self-sufficient, with no emotional entanglements to hurt me again. Sex is fine – the more, the better; but relationships are out.'

She put her glass down with a click on the coaster by her side. 'First thing tomorrow, I'll go apartment-hunting. You can tell Pease I'm working on location. He dare not give me any grief. He knows I'd go over his head to Sheila Sorensen.'

'Do you have much work?' asked Carmen.

'Yes.' Tanya rolled her eyes in pretended cynicism, determined to keep her excitement under wraps. Showing enthusiasm and being open about her feelings hadn't worked with Eric and Stephen. 'McNally & Co. want a bunch more stuff about the GirlZone club I invented for Katrina Cortez,' she said. 'I need to get out to some clubs and bars; develop character ideas and settings. I think Ganymede may want some more adventurous sexual variations.'

Carmen's eyes narrowed eagerly. 'I might have the perfect solution,' she said. 'It's right here under our noses, and would be a lot safer than drifting round a bunch of strange bars.'

Tanya read her friend's mind. 'You mean the CowGirl Club?'

'*Exactemente*. As I told you before, the club's new owners are two real cool women from Atlanta. You've got to meet them. Vivienne is a tall, sexy and beautiful redhead, and her partner is a small blonde, named Liz. She's cute.'

'You said they do performances?' Tanya hid her enthusiasm under a look of bored unconcern.

'Yes,' Carmen said, not put off by her companion's exaggerated ennui. 'Viv and Liz stage performance art, show films, and this weekend they're working on a film of their own.' Carmen smiled. 'They call themselves "sex-artists",' she continued, 'and they certainly do encourage creative sex. Bi, gay, lesbian, multiple partners . . . I've seen the whole lot. Everything is beautifully choreographed, like a ballet.'

Looking coyly over the rim of her tequila glass, Carmen added, 'You know, Tanya, watching some cute sassy girl sex at the CowGirl Club might help you forget about these *estupido* men!'

The possibility intrigued Tanya. Katrina Cortez would make the most of such an opportunity. The more she thought about the possibilities held by the CowGirl Club, the more this seemed a likely remedy for Tanya's woes. Her pulse quickened. She could watch and sketch, immersing herself in the sensual energy of the club and its performers. She might even participate, if she felt like it, forget Stephen, and start a whole new chapter in her life. The thought of sex without the hassle of men held a certain allure.

'When would be a good time to visit? Could I go with you?' Tanya tried to keep the curiosity out of her voice.

Carmen's eyes sparkled. 'Let's go on Sunday morning

when the club's closed for normal business. That's when they do the filming.'

'That sounds good. What time?'

Carmen considered. 'If you come by here at ten, we can be there in half an hour. It's located on Northwest Highway by Love Field. We'll get there before things start rolling and you can meet Vivienne and Liz.'

Tanya knew the area, but not well. Northwest Highway was the main cross-town route that linked Dallas's in-town commuter airport to the giant freeways. 'Is it close to the airport?' she asked.

'Yes. It's in an older brick warehouse along Bachman Lake, near the flight path. The lake is pretty, but the area's noisy. That's how Viv and Liz got the place cheap. They spent money soundproofing the film stage, but they've come out ahead on the deal. They do a real good club business, which subsidises their art work.'

Tanya thought it sounded pretty cool, but her growing mood of cynical detachment held her natural enthusiasm in check. She looked at her watch, and refused Carmen's offer of one more Tequila Sunrise.

'I'm going to get up early and find an apartment,' she said decisively, rising from her chair. But then she hesitated. 'I . . . hate to ask another favour, Carmen, but could you help me move my things out of storage when the time comes? I don't know who else to ask. Living all those months under Eric's thumb, and working so hard on *Katrina Cortez*, I've lost touch with my old friends. They just drifted away.' Tanya looked angrily at Carmen, as if it was all her fault.

Carmen's poise was unaffected. '*De nada*. Of course I'll help, *chicita*,' she said warmly and treated her friend to a big smile and a hug.

Tanya's body tensed beneath the touch before relaxing into Carmen's embrace.

Carmen stepped back, flexing her biceps in a weight-lifter's pose. Tanya admired the cut of her muscles. Her mind created a fleeting image of what Carmen would look like naked.

Her friend spoke again, breaking the spell. 'I may be small, but I have *los brazos fuertes*.' She tapped her arms to emphasise the point. 'You're not the only one who works out.'

Tanya tested Carmen's muscle with her fingers. Her flesh felt smooth and warm, but there was indeed a hard knotted core beneath the soft exterior. She let her hand dally on Carmen's skin, enjoying the little electric tingles in her fingertips.

Carmen moved close and brushed Tanya's cheek softly with her lips. 'I am your friend, Tanya. I am glad to help. It gives me pleasure.'

Tanya turned away to hide her emotion. 'I'll let you know how my apartment-hunting goes,' she said gruffly. 'But we have a date for ten o'clock Sunday.'

Tanya struck lucky; within a few hours she found a suitable new apartment. She liked to believe in omens, and thus interpreted her success as a sign that the gods were smiling on her.

She had chosen the University Park neighbourhood as a place to start, four square miles of pleasantly gridded streets around Southern Methodist University. She knew it from her days as a graduate student, and thought she might find a small flat in one of the many converted houses.

On a whim, she turned off Hillcrest, a major north-south artery, and drove down Rosedale, where some fellow student friends had lived several years ago. Two blocks along, a tweedy middle-aged man was hammering a sign into the front lawn. 'Apartment: 2-BR. For Rent', it proclaimed in handwritten capitals. Behind the man, a two-storey brick apartment building stood amidst well-maintained lawns and bushes. Tanya pulled to the kerb and jumped out.

'May I see the apartment, sir? Please,' she added as an afterthought.

The man squinted at her through bifocals. He was dressed in khakis, a button-down plaid shirt and, even in the summer heat, a woven bow tie. Tanya guessed he was a college professor. His first words confirmed it.

'You're not a student, are you, young lady? I hope not. I see enough students every day in class.'

Tanya duly denied the charge, but did lay claim to her alumnus status from SMU. 'I'm a designer,' she said, having learnt years before that calling oneself an artist scared promising landlords away. 'I work in Deep Ellum.' She decided to play on the man's sympathy. 'My boyfriend just threw me out,' she complained. 'I've got to find somewhere to live right away.'

It worked. 'Come up my dear,' said her potential landlord, leading the way. 'My name's Crockett, David Crockett.' He turned halfway up the front staircase. 'And before you ask, no, I'm not related to the hero of the Alamo.'

'I bet lots of people ask you that,' said Tanya.

David Crockett sighed resignedly and nodded. 'Yes. That's why I forestall the question.' He unlocked a door at the top of the stairs and ushered Tanya into a series of rooms, small, but high-ceilinged and well lit. A wide bay window overlooked the street and faced north, and two side windows let in the morning sun, highlighting the scuffed but polished hardwood flooring.

'The last tenant moved out in a rush and broke his lease,' grumbled Crockett. 'Now I insist on two months' rent up front.' He shrugged to disclaim all responsibility.

'How much?'

'Seven hundred and fifty dollars a month. All utilities extra.'

Tanya bustled through the other rooms. It would do. And the location suited her fine. 'Will you take a cheque?' she asked, reaching into her bag.

* * *

Over the next thirty-six hours, Tanya and Carmen retrieved Tanya's belongings from the storage locker where they had resided since the day she moved in with Eric. Together, they carried cartons and furniture into her new place.

On Friday night Tanya rejoiced in her new-found freedom. She slept soundly, alone, on a futon laid directly on the hardwood floor amid a mini-Manhattan of boxes. All day Saturday, and early on Sunday, she unpacked, cleaned and put away the mementos of her former lives. At nine a.m. she showered, changed into a white linen blouse and pulled a short skirt over a silken thong, strapped a pair of high-heeled mules to her feet, and grabbed her sketchbooks. By ten o'clock she was sitting in Carmen's car on Northwest Highway, heading for the CowGirl Club.

It was starting to get hot when they arrived at the shaded doorway in the centre of the club's understated exterior. A SouthWest Airlines 737 roared overhead; its fractured reflection shimmered over the surface of Bachman Lake before transforming itself into a solid shadow that swooped across the grass of the small park and the tarmac of adjacent parking lots.

The women stood on a small landing under a dome-shaped, elegantly fashioned awning with the initials, 'CGC' lettered in white on dark red canvas. Mercifully free of girlie silhouettes, Stetsons and lariats, the façade of the building was the simple unadorned brick of an old warehouse. Tanya noted that the masonry had recently been cleaned and repointed.

Carmen spoke into the small intercom by the door, and they were buzzed in. Entering the simple foyer through two sets of heavy double doors, Tanya was immediately surprised and delighted by the good taste and style of this reputedly decadent club. The polished industrial cement floor was handsome and the walls, enhanced by light sconces, were painted with warm

Mediterranean colours. A dozen large pots of Areca palms stood beneath a clever skylight. Off to the left stood a well-stocked bar with sumptuous seating, and straight ahead through some plush velvet curtains, Tanya glimpsed a large polished dance floor and stage area. It was very quiet after the noise of the street.

A tall red-haired woman greeted them. Tanya recognised her from Carmen's description before she spoke. The woman strode forward and shook Tanya's hand and embraced Carmen with a kiss.

'Hello, Tanya. Carmen's told me all about you. I'm Vivienne Dupree. I own half of what you see.' She turned with a proud smile to gesture at the surroundings, her red hair shining in the shafts of light admitted by the skylight. Her long slim legs were emphasised by a short skirt in vibrant green. 'Come through to the back. We can talk there.'

She escorted them to an adjacent chamber. 'The club spaces are up front, and we use these areas back here for our own film productions,' she explained. 'As you'll see, we're setting up a scene now. It's part of our new project: sex as performance art.' Their attractive hostess was clearly excited about the aesthetic and carnal possibilities of her work.

Ushering Carmen and Tanya deeper inside, she swept aside another heavy dark velvet curtain and led them on to the set, where assistants were in the process of preparing an interior shot comprising an elegant dining room. Several lighting and sound engineers were preoccupied with the installation and testing of equipment.

Wordlessly, Tanya pulled out her drawing-pad and did some quick studies of the activities. Vivienne watched, entranced by Tanya's pencil racing across the paper, transforming the set, with its special lighting, into an illustration for *Katrina Cortez, Girl Detective!* Later, at her board, Tanya would add other colours: strong saturated purples, deep greys, a light-reflecting indigo and red.

'You're good,' Vivienne said admiringly. 'Am I right in understanding that you'd like to make some sketches on site during our performances?'

'Yes, if that's OK,' said Tanya. When Vivienne nodded, she added, 'When does filming begin?'

'This afternoon. Oh, let me introduce you to Skip,' said Vivienne. 'He's one of the actors.'

A tall, dark and handsome man detached himself from a small knot of people and sauntered over. He had bedroom eyes. 'Hi, ladies,' he said pleasantly. 'Nice to meet you.'

'Skip,' said Vivienne, 'will you entertain Carmen and her guest Tanya while I go and find Liz?'

'My pleasure,' the actor replied. The three of them stood to one side of the space, observing the technical preparations before them.

'Do you have a good role?' asked Carmen.

'Yes, it's great fun,' he replied.

'What's the movie about?' Tanya asked.

'Oh, it's one of a series the girls are doing about the seven deadly sins. This one is *Lust and Gluttony*, my favourites.' Skip Braddock's face warmed with an easy grin.

'Is there a whipped cream scene?' Carmen asked mischievously.

Skip laughed and answered, with mock severity, 'Of course there's a whipped cream scene! It's a mandatory cliché.'

'Let me guess?' teased Tanya. She gave him a wicked wink. 'Does someone spray whipped cream on a naked girl and then get to lick it off?' She wondered if their joking host was gay or bisexual. He was probably very attractive to both sexes.

Skip winked back. 'Well, no, my dear,' he purred sensuously, 'actually *she* licks it from *my* naked body.'

Carmen tittered.

'Would you like to watch?' he asked.

'Sure,' Tanya responded.

'Me, too,' said Carmen.

An unbidden picture arose in Tanya's mind: herself and Carmen, both naked, licking thick whipped cream from Skip's very long and tumescent penis.

But before this fantasy could develop towards reality, Skip was called over by one of his colleagues. 'Excuse me, Ladies. Back to work, I'm afraid.' He waved. 'Enjoy the CowGirl Club, ladies. I'm off!'

'He is so debonair,' said Carmen.

'Fuckable, actually,' agreed Tanya.

Vivienne returned with a tray of coffee mugs and a large cafetière full to the brim of a deliciously flavoured brew. She ushered Carmen and Tanya into a dressing room where a petite blonde, wearing a red silk robe, sat before a wide mirror at a communal dressing table, studiously applying vampish stage make-up. Her pointed breasts were outlined by the silk, and her platinum crew-cut was freshly washed and groomed. A hair-piece with cascading curls of a darker blonde tint was placed on a wig stand beside her.

'Let me introduce you to my friend and partner, Liz,' said Vivienne, putting down the laden tray.

Turning away from her primping, the small blonde woman smiled at Vivienne and blew the redhead a kiss. Turning to Tanya, she extended a small, firm hand. 'Hi. I'm Liz Angelo.'

'Hello,' said Tanya, charmed by the woman's trim and diminutive figure, and by her decorum: for she was both sexy and poised before a stranger, even in a state of near-undress.

'Liz, this is Carmen's friend, Tanya. She's an artist with a graphics firm,' explained the tall redhead, 'and now she's working on a movie about a comic-book heroine.'

'Cool,' said Liz. 'Hi, Carmen.' She gestured towards the love-seat, 'Have a seat. Tanya, it's great to meet you.'

'We just had a look at the *Lust and Gluttony* set,' explained Vivienne. 'But that's for later. Let's have some coffee.' She handed each woman a mug.

Tanya sat beside Carmen on the love-seat and sipped the fresh, hot brew. She looked around the room, noting its leatherette stools appliquéd with rhinestones and a collection of pony-hide pillows. A heart-shaped hand mirror lay on the light-rimmed dressing table.

Liz followed Tanya's gaze. 'Aren't they deliciously tacky?' she asked, putting down her mug. 'They're things I've collected over the years and now I can't bear to part with them. She smiled at Tanya. 'So y'all work together at Studio V?' she asked.

'Yes,' affirmed Tanya. 'I'm working on a special project, based on a character called *Katrina Cortez, Girl Detective*. It's a *noir* thriller, very sexy.' Spontaneously, Tanya suggested, 'Perhaps you would like to pose for some sketches, maybe even for a portrait?'

Liz assented enthusiastically. 'Maybe you can do some of Vivi and me together,' she said, with a quick grin at her partner. Vivienne blew her a kiss in return.

Tanya penned *The CowGirl Club: Friday June 26* across the top of a page in her notebook. Sketching quickly and vigorously, she explained, 'I'm developing some ideas for my next storyboard that's set in an imaginary club. I'd like to know more about this club. A real club.'

'How can we help you?' queried Liz, sipping her coffee daintily.

'Do you strip all the way?'

Liz and Viv chortled merrily at the question. Liz replied amid the girlish laughter, 'All the way? Well, yes, of course, sometimes. For late shows in the club, the girls sometimes strip naked if there's a good audience. And then there's our film studio, where we're shooting

Lust and Gluttony. You could say that anything goes, there.' More easy laughter greeted Liz's explanation.

'Of course,' Liz continued, 'Vivi and I take it off only in the best of establishments. Nowadays, it's mostly my act, as Vivi is doing camera and set.' The petite woman paused. 'You can watch the film shoot from the Green Room. It has windows so you can see everything, but you won't be in the crew's way.'

Tanya replied eagerly, 'We'd love to. It sounds like great material for my project.'

'Yeah,' Liz said with a devilish smile. 'But I can show you now how easy it is to strip all the way.' In one supple gesture, she slid the red silk robe off her shoulders to reveal her small high breasts. She dabbed some rouge on her rosy nipples, which stood up like cherries. 'Do you want to draw me now?' she asked.

'Yes,' affirmed Tanya excitedly. 'Would you really like to pose?'

'Sure,' said Liz and, with that, the diminutive blonde stood up, leaving her robe as a puddle of red silk on her dressing room chair. Her porcelain skin glowed, smooth and pale but for dark pink rosebud nipples and a small fluff of blonde pubic hair that matched her platinum head.

'She's a former gymnast,' said Vivienne proudly, her eyes greedily feasting upon the sight of her partner's lithe and sexy body.

Tanya's pencil moved in quick confident lines, capturing the soft curves and harder planes of the woman's musculature, hinting at the hidden bone structure of Liz's body. She did three studies from different angles, and each time Liz teased her audience with poses of greater abandon and sensuality, fingering herself and parting the lips of her vulva to slide a finger inside.

Despite her professional concentration, Tanya felt a warm tingle between her thighs. For the moment, she suppressed her response. 'Be still,' she commanded, but

Liz dissolved into a fit of giggles. Her concentration broken, Tanya put down her pencil with regret.

Liz materialised at her elbow, her naked breasts brushing Tanya's shoulder. 'Let's see.' She studied the pages of drawings and whistled in appreciation. 'Tanya,' she said, 'these are great. I've never seen such beautiful sketches. Could I have a copy of that one?' She pointed to the last of the three, where her body was arched back, thighs splayed apart and her finger buried in her quim. The two other women gathered around appreciatively.

Tanya laughed to cover her embarrassment. She found it odd having people watch her draw, but she realised she'd have to get used to it on location. 'Sure,' she replied. 'Just lead me to the photocopier.'

Vivienne was obviously the business brain of the two partners. 'Tanya, could we purchase some of your drawings? I can see lots of ways we could use them in our advertising. You've captured Liz's eroticism better than most of the publicity photos we've taken.' The tall redhead ruffled her fingers through her partner's blonde crew-cut in a gesture of deep affection, and Tanya caught a look of adoration flash across Liz's eyes before the pair returned to business.

'Could you do a series based on our movie? Single actors, and then groups in couples and trios?' Vivienne's questions were always to the point.

Tanya was flattered and delighted to comply but she didn't show it. Her tone was all business; this was how Katrina Cortez would handle it. 'Sure,' she said, 'but I'll need you to sign a release saying that the copyright remains with me, and that I can use the sketches in my comic-strip drawings. I'll do you a series of ten studies for $1,000. Payment on the spot when I finish the drawings. You can set up the poses. If you want more, the same rates apply.'

Vivienne's eyebrows arched slightly. 'Can you start work today?'

Tanya shrugged. 'Sure. Can you pay me today?'

Vivienne laughed out loud. 'Carmen,' she said turning to her employee, 'your friend Tanya isn't only beautiful, she's one tough little lady.' She gave Tanya a hug to let her know this was a compliment. 'It's a pleasure doing business with you, Tanya. We've got a deal.' She thrust out her hand. Tanya shook it firmly.

Chapter Seventeen
Upstairs, Downstairs

'I'm ready for my bath,' Liz exclaimed, standing naked in the doorway. 'I'm going upstairs to the spa.'

Vivienne turned to Carmen and Tanya. 'Would you like to join us? Filming is always so stressful that we like to relax thoroughly before we start. It gets us in the mood.'

'Sure,' said Carmen and Tanya together. They followed Vivienne and the naked Liz up a spiral staircase at the rear of the building. Looking upward, Tanya studied Liz's body in foreshortened perspective, outlined against a bright skylight. The muscles in the small blonde's thighs and bottom rippled seductively as she climbed the steep stairs two at a time. Her hair caught the rays of the noonday sun as it filtered through the leaves of several palm trees on the top landing.

To Tanya's surprise, the quartet emerged into a roof-top conservatory and exercise room, full of light yet shaded by heavy Venetian blinds. The floor was lined in cool earthenware tiles; soft throw rugs of Persian origin lay scattered across the surface. Against one wall stood several Nautilus machines, with a small stack of floor exercise mats and a couple of benches. Opposite was a small bathroom, and in the far corner nestled a large sunken whirlpool tub, lined in soft pink marble and fringed with hanging plants. Liz danced across the floor and pushed a series of buttons. The water bubbled to life and, without waiting for the others, the petite blonde lowered herself gracefully into the warm bath.

'Last one in's a sissy,' she shouted playfully, and splashed in the water.

Tanya looked around for somewhere to change, but Vivienne, as if reading her thoughts, said, 'Just leave your clothes on one of the benches. We don't stand on ceremony around here. We have plenty of towels for afterwards.' Setting an example, the tall redhead quickly removed her clothes, to reveal a pair of large breasts and sleek hips. Tossing the garments across one of the benches, she walked towards the bath. Tanya instinctively checked out the colour of Vivienne's muff. True to expectations, it matched her deep auburn tresses, curling thickly over her mound.

While Tanya hesitated, Carmen undressed, too, tossing her clothing on the loose pile next to Vivienne's. Tanya admired her friend's body, which was much as she had imagined it, lithe and petite, with good muscle tone and small firm breasts, high on her chest. Rather like Cupcake's, a character from an earlier *Katrina Cortez* episode. Between Carmen's legs nestled a thick black bush of pubic curls.

'Your turn,' said Carmen, standing naked before her. Tanya kicked off her high-heeled mules and wriggled her blouse over her head. Without her bra, her rounded breasts swung freely. Carmen's eyes widened, and she licked her lips, but said nothing. She stood watching the impromptu strip.

Tanya slipped out of her short skirt and stepped out of her panties, remembering the last time she had been naked in company, in front of Stephen Sinclair. Images of his tumescent penis rose in her mind. Surprised at the force and vividness of the memory, she felt a tremor somewhere deep inside her.

Carmen misunderstood Tanya's frozen stance. 'Don't be shy, *chica*. We're all friends here. Come, take my hand.'

Tanya allowed herself to be led to the side of the hot tub. Liz and Vivienne stopped their cuddling and looked up approvingly.

'You and Carmen make a lovely pair,' said Vivienne with a smile. 'Come and join us.'

'Mind you,' interjected Liz with a giggle, 'we're going to be busy for a while.' She bent forward to kiss Vivienne's breasts, and took one nipple between her lips. Vivienne gave a small moan of pleasure.

Tanya turned back for her sketchbook, but Carmen touched her arm.

'Leave that for now, *querida*! You're always drawing. Just relax and enjoy yourself.' She slipped into the water and held out a hand for Tanya.

Tanya followed her friend and gasped as the warmth of the water touched her skin. She relaxed against the side of the tub, and spread her arms along the sides.

Wordlessly, Carmen moved close and snuggled up to Tanya, her olive skin fitting against Tanya's lighter curves. They nestled in each other's arms, and Tanya closed her eyes as the stress began to melt away. Gently, slowly, one of Carmen's hands found Tanya's breast, cupping it softly and rolling her nipple between two fingers. Tanya murmured assent and her friend delicately explored her body. Soon, the other hand stroked her thigh. With a sigh of acquiescence, Tanya moved her legs slightly apart and slipped deeper into the luxurious water.

The caress of Carmen's hands across her flesh sent ripples of pleasure through Tanya's body. Her nipples stood out and her clitoris tingled at the touch of Carmen's fingers between her legs. She reached in return for her friend's body, and found the soft small orbs of Carmen's breasts. The small Hispanic woman took one of Tanya's hands and placed it over her own vulva, pressing the heel of Tanya's hand against her clitoris in a silent request.

So this is what lesbian sex is like, Tanya thought appreciatively. Does the fact that I'm enjoying it mean I'm bisexual? The idea was rather exotic. Certainly *Katrina Cortez* could explore these areas of sensual pleasure with confidence from now on.

Tanya was content to cuddle intimately with Carmen, each woman's fingers resting gently along the sex lips of the other. Carmen seemed equally at ease. Tanya lazily opened one eye and was treated to a spectacle of active lesbian loving between their two companions on the other side of the large Jacuzzi. She nudged Carmen, and they watched in fascination as Liz sat on the edge of the tub, legs spread wide, with Vivienne's hair nestled amid the pale blonde of her lover's thatch.

The tiny blonde stood and eased Vivienne from the water, placing her gently on a soft towel. 'You're in dire need of some good sex, my darling,' she murmured. 'Here, let me help you.' She spread Vivienne's legs wide, revealing her pink lips. 'That's right, sweetheart. Would you like me to kiss you right here? Make you nice and wet inside with my tongue?'

Shivering softly despite the warm water, Tanya watched as Liz's pointed pink tongue licked Vivienne's pussy, her blonde crew-cut in stark contrast to her lover's dark red bush. The taller woman bucked her pelvis, demanding more, and Liz eased one finger deep inside her lover's quim.

'Turn over, baby,' she whispered, and reached for a small bottle of lotion as her partner moved and lay face down on the towel, her bottom slightly raised. With practised ease, Liz lubricated Vivienne's cleft with the scented oil and slid a finger inside her lover's vagina. A second digit caressed the lips of Vivienne's labia until it reached her puffy clitoris, and a third pressed the tight sphincter of her anus. With a moan of pleasure, Vivienne relaxed the muscle and allowed Liz's slick finger to penetrate the secret place.

Kneeling over her lover, the lithe blonde rocked her wrist back and forth, probing her lover's crevices, and creating a triple tension around Vivienne's sex. Her practised sensual technique brought Vivienne to climax in only a few moments, and screams of joy burst from her lips.

'Come, baby. Come, my sweetheart,' cooed Liz, as she slowed her movements but extended her partner's pleasure, allowing Vivienne to drift slowly down from her plateau of ecstasy. Vivienne's juices trickled down over her lover's fingers. Without her sketchbook to hand, Tanya tried to imprint the scene in her memory.

After a few moments, Vivienne rolled over and sat up, flushed. She threw Tanya and Carmen a foxy glance. 'That did me good. How about you?'

'Oh,' said Tanya with a straight face. 'It was very . . . interesting. Ouch! Let go!'

Carmen's elbow in her ribs and tickling hands reduced Tanya to a giggling heap. The little Hispanic woman turned to Vivienne with glee on her face. 'Don't you believe little Miss Proper, here. Her tongue was nearly hanging out. She was salivating over you two.'

Tanya blushed at her friend's teasing, and jumped out of the bathtub, pink and dripping. A thought struck her, and emboldened by the foursome's recent intimacies, the words flew from her lips. 'But what about you? Don't you get to come?' she blurted to Liz.

The small blonde, still naked, did a graceful cartwheel across the floor. 'Oh, I'm fine,' she said with a laugh. 'I've got mine still to come.'

Her lover made a pretend pout of jealousy from her

position on the floor. 'Oh yes,' she said. 'Liz gets her reward downstairs. You'll see.'

'Look at the time! I must get ready,' chirped Liz Angelo excitedly.

Tanya put down her pencil and closed her sketchbook. This afternoon's portrait of Liz was better than those she did this morning. Watching the titillating lesbian sex upstairs must have improved her graphic technique.

'What are you smiling about?' demanded Liz, slipping into her abbreviated costume: a fancy, hand-embroidered silver bolero over her breasts and a shiny G-string around her loins. The former gymnast completed her ensemble by stepping into incredibly high, shiny silver stiletto heels.

'Nothing,' Tanya said, keeping her thoughts private. She changed the subject. 'Are you going to wear that blonde wig today?' She gestured to a cascading tumble of dark blonde curls resting on a stand in the corner of the dressing room.

Liz nodded, and wrestled for a moment to fit the curls over her own short platinum hair. Then she gave up and protested, 'I need help with this!'

Vivienne stood in the doorway. 'I think Kevin's waiting for you next door,' she said, a wry smile on her lips.

'Oh?' replied Liz excitedly. She blushed slightly.

'I saw him,' replied Vivienne. 'He already has a hard-on.'

Tanya's head snapped up to see Vivienne wink broadly at her partner. Carmen, sitting across the room, smiled too.

Liz grinned happily and skipped to the door, opened it wide and called in a cheerful and breezy manner over her shoulder. 'Tanya, Carmen, you gals amuse yourselves while I visit my hair guy.' She added, 'When you hear the intercom announcement, that means the cameras will roll in ten minutes.' All three watched lithe Liz prance away, wig in hand, the cheeks of her bottom winking on either side of the silver thong of her G-string.

'This is her reward,' murmured Vivienne to the others. 'She's off for a torrid quickie with the Big Prick.'

'Who? What?' asked Tanya, curious.

Vivienne smiled as she explained to Tanya and Carmen. 'It'll only take a few seconds to get that wig on; she'll be able to have a quick fuck with Kevin, the hairdresser we use on film projects, before setting up with the guys on stage.'

Tanya almost gasped aloud at the revelation. Having assumed her new friends to be 'straight' lesbians, the graphic artist was startled to discover the bisexuality of at least one of the two beauties. She wondered what else they were into.

Licking her lips suggestively, Vivienne grinned at the women's surprised faces. 'Liz usually just sucks Kevin off while he masturbates her, but today she's really hot.' Vivienne smiled at the curiosity on the other two women's faces. 'Sometimes Liz and I have a very exciting threesome with Kevin the Big Prick, as Liz calls him,' she added casually. 'He's good in bed for two, maybe three fucks in a row.' She winked and asked them wickedly, 'Either of you gals interested? Maybe we could stretch it to four fucks of an evening.'

Tanya shot Carmen a salacious look, but Vivienne reverted to business. 'I've got to go and check some technical stuff on the set. I get nervous just before we start filming. Excuse me. I'll see you later.'

In his room, Kevin stood waiting, a slight grimace on his handsome face as he looked at his watch. But when Liz, in her state of temptingly partial undress, arrived at his door, a wide smile spread across his boyish features, and he moved his hand to caress his penis, immediately and noticeably thick through a pair of loose-fitting, soft cotton shorts. In expectation of sex, he wore no underwear. He stuck his thumbs in his waistband and grinned at the seductively attired woman entering his cheerful chamber.

She closed the door and leant against it while the tall young man assessed her costume.

'Lizzie, you're hot,' the hairdresser exclaimed. Taking the untamed cascade of hair from Liz, he placed it carefully on a wig stand on his high-tech dressing table.

Liz nodded and moved closer. Kevin's big cock was outlined and enlarged beneath the soft fabric of his shorts. She reached for it and squeezed it gently in her hand.

'Fix my hair later, Kev. I want your dick now,' she said. She was a good twelve inches shorter than the hairdresser; she grinned up at him, wiggling her lithe little body seductively. She tugged at the drawstring of his shorts with one hand, firmly masturbating Kevin's cock with her other. 'I want to fuck,' she purred.

She pulled Kevin's shorts down over his slim muscular hips, and eagerly grabbed his swollen cock. 'God, Kevin!' she breathed, pumping him, 'You're huge!'

He moaned and a bead of pre-come appeared at the end of his dick. Liz's tongue flicked out like a lizard's to lick up the first offering.

'Take me!' she cried. 'I'm already wet! Fuck me!'

Kevin's penis reared up and he grabbed the small woman around her waist, deftly pulling off her G-string. In spite of his lustfulness, he felt compelled to remind her, 'We don't have much time, sexy girl.' As if on cue, Vivienne's voice on the intercom announced: 'Ten minutes until dining shoot, take two.'

'We still have time for a quickie,' Liz said. Naked now, save the little vest and her high-heeled pumps, she wrapped her legs around his waist as he lowered them both into the salon's only upholstered chair. She parted her legs. 'Fuck me,' she squealed.

Kevin adjusted her on his lap and, clasping her breasts

beneath her unfastened waistcoat, eased the tip of his erect manhood between her wet pussy lips.

'Just hold on, Lizzie!' he panted, pressing his massive rod further inside her tight pussy.

Liz rode him hard, but screamed with lust, obviously wanting more. 'Harder, harder!' She squirmed with ecstasy as Kevin raised and lowered her body. His size and the power of his motion inside her brought her to orgasm within moments.

He was still hard inside her and, amid her fading ecstatic little cries, he murmured through his teeth, 'Hang on, Lizzie! It ain't over yet!' He groaned mightily; his orgasm spurred Liz to a second climax.

After quivering to stillness, she slid off his lap and settled naked in front of his mirror, to adjust her wig.

Kevin's breathing returned to normal; he, too, dried himself, quickly slipped on his shorts and a fresh T-shirt, and attentively adjusted the long blonde wig on to Liz's head.

She gathered her costume, and he murmured, 'Remember the flute, darling.'

'I'll never forget your flute, darling,' she said with a smile, and bounced out the door.

Chapter Eighteen
The Green Room

Only steps away from these carnal activities, the stage was coming to life. Film assistants, preparators and stylists busily prowled the set, adjusting, correcting, and refining. Eager to observe, Carmen and Tanya entered the club's adjacent Green Room.

Through the window of the viewing room, they watched the actors take their positions. Appropriately for a commentary on lust and gluttony, the setting for the film was a luxurious meal, and the current scene followed the main course, just prior to dessert. Tanya smiled to herself. Would Liz be dessert?

A circular table five feet in diameter was spread with a black lace tablecloth and set with four place-settings of fine crystal, china and silver. A large rotating silver platter was centred amid the cutlery. A stylist swept on to the stage and lit two dozen candles in wall sconces, adding a romantic ambience. Liz was nowhere in sight, but four male actors, all dressed in formal black tie and tails, entered the room.

'Wow! Four guys!' Tanya noted aloud. 'All good-looking. Oh, look, there's Skip Braddock, the fuckable one we met earlier.'

'*Si*,' Carmen echoed, excitedly. 'I also love the tall blond guy.' The tallest man's glacial colouring glimmered in the lights. 'Nordic Man,' Carmen sighed. 'Perhaps opposites attract!' Both women laughed.

The buzz around the set suddenly quietened. All eyes moved to the entrance from the dressing rooms. Several monitor screens flashed into life and were filled with the image of a beautiful blonde with cascading curls.

Vivienne was waiting. 'Your skin is so pink, Lizzie,' she teased, holding her lover at arm's length to assess her appearance. She muttered sexily, 'Looks like you've been fucked!' She slapped her playfully on the bottom, leaving a bright pink hand-print. 'Time to get out the dildo at home.'

Liz let out a yelp, and reached to kiss her lover. She was ready to roll. Drawing on silver gloves, she pranced on to the stage.

The crew was ready.

Unseen by the crew or the actors, a lone man stood amid the deep shadows in the hallway, greedily watching Liz's image fill the oscillating screen of one of the monitors at the rear of the space. 'God, what a sexy little bitch!' he breathed, and touched himself between his legs, feeling his penis rise. From his unobtrusive position, he glanced from the screen across the stage set, his eyes ranging to the windows of the Green Room. He stiffened and gripped his member tightly as he identified Tanya Trevino through the glass.

From her post inside the Green Room, Tanya barely recognised the petite blonde woman; the long, curly wig over her cap of platinum hair transformed the elegant performer into a big-haired doll. Besides the wig falling over her shoulders, Liz had added some jewellery to her provocative ensemble: hoop earrings, and a necklace dripping with faux rubies and pearls that glittered in the stage lights.

Matching the short silver embroidered waistcoat laced over her breasts, the tiny silver G-string and the silver stilettos, Liz wore silver elbow-length opera gloves, and carried a thin silver flute. Little silver bells encircled her ankles, and dozens of rings were fitted on her fingers.

'She looks distinctly fucked,' muttered Carmen, with more than a little envy.

The petite woman's rosy cheeks did suggest a quick tumble, thought Tanya, as did her full rosy lips. Liz leant on the edge of the table and looked over her shoulder, saluting the two women in the window of the Green Room. Liz held the small silver flute aloft for a moment, blew the women kisses and, clasping the thin rod in her teeth, like the proverbial rose, crawled on top of the table.

The crew adjusted the lights, illuminating the surface of the ornately appointed table without overpowering the candles. A still photographer approached the exotic tableau. The four actors took their places round the table.

Like a human still life or a delicious centrepiece, Liz perched demure yet provocative upon the large silver platter in the middle of the table, ultimately to be relished or ravished. She placed the silver flute across one knee and contemplated the men, as though measuring them.

From the Green Room, Tanya also appraised the men, who were clearly deliberately stylised. Among the diners, the blond Nordic prince with his ice-blue eyes, pale and handsome, sat beside Skip, whose coal-black hair and warm chocolate-brown eyes provided a visual contrast to his cool companion. On the other side of the table was another dark-haired man, huskier and darker than Skip, with a moustache, and with deep hooded eyes. Beside him was a striking redhead who had thickly lashed hazel eyes. All were handsome. They unfolded large square serviettes and spread them in their laps.

Two cameras rolled forward, one focused on the diners, the other on Liz. Vivienne, as director, stood next to one camera. A script girl was with her. They conferred in low voices. A series of deeply sensuous dramatic musical riffs on a solo flute drifted into the room. Liz shivered sensuously.

'Take positions!' barked Vivienne, very crisp and professional. Tanya compared the tall redhead's professional persona to that of the lustful woman writhing under her lover's tongue hours before. On the set, Vivienne gestured to amplify the music. 'Action!' she cried.

Several young male actors, dressed as slaves in leather jock-straps, materialised to stand straight and stiff against the walls of the set, holding platters of food and jars of wine. Others, dressed in Roman-style togas of transparent material, waited upon the long table, pouring flutes of bubbling champagne for the diners. Through the gauzy wisps of material, Tanya could see the outlines of the young men's genitals, hanging free and unclothed.

The candlelight flickered, the lenses bore down, and the cameras rolled in a single take, recording the actors as they enjoyed a feast for the senses, dining, chatting, and nibbling edible delicacies while Liz pantomimed under the lights.

She entertained them in an exclusive 'dinner theatre'. On cue, she raised the silver instrument to her lips and mimed a performance on the tiny flute, undulating languorously while the soundtrack music controlling her moves wafted across the set.

The activities on stage heated up when the tall Nordic-looking blond man at Liz's rear reached across his plate and grasped the edge of the silver platter she sat upon. Slowly, he rotated it until Liz faced him. Liz ceased to play the flute for a moment, balancing the small silver cylinder across one knee, and stayed the revolving plate with her foot. Making each small movement an erotic provocation, she stripped off one glove.

The room darkened and a single rose-toned spotlight focused on the Nordic man Liz faced; as it widened its scope to train upon Liz, its colour deepened to magenta, and the couple shared the spotlight. In a series of sultry gestures, Liz slowly removed the other glove, tossed them both away, and began to unlace the tiny waistcoat. Teasingly, she opened and closed the vest, allowing glimpses of her small but lovely breasts. Then in one graceful movement, she slipped the embroidered waistcoat over her shoulders, revealing her fully naked torso and a glittering zircon in her belly button.

'The Nordic blond man leant back in his chair,' wrote Tanya as she observed this erotically portrayed tableau, 'suavely folding his hands behind his head . . .' With a few deft lines, she sketched the glacial planes of his face.

Letting the waistcoat fall, Liz stroked and jiggled her small pointed breasts provocatively and, at a gesture from Vivienne, the camera pulled back to reveal all four male diners sitting up to wipe their mouths delicately on heavy white damask table napkins. The semi-naked slaves returned to the table, bringing liqueurs, bon-bons and fresh strawberries and cream.

Two beautiful youths serving Skip bent forward, allowing the actor to slip his hands beneath their togas and gently fondle their balls and penises. The other members of the quartet followed suit, and eight slaves stood like statues while their masters stroked them. The camera panned lovingly around the multiple masturbation before switching back to Liz. The slaves stepped away from the table.

The dark man was offering the seductive blonde a ripe red strawberry.

Liz rose to her hands and knees and arched her back, letting her breasts dangle in the diner's face. She pressed forward and the dark man fed her the fruit; a glowing circle of warm light tightened for a close-up of Liz's face taking the dark man's finger inside her mouth. Vivienne watched the action assiduously, conducting the timing of each actor and crew member.

Tanya scripted in flowing text across the half-finished drawing, 'Her small yet proud breasts, nipples like rosebuds . . .' To Tanya's right, Carmen was rapt and breathing hard.

Save the whir of the camera, all was silent on the set until a persistent drumbeat began. With their eyes on Liz, the quartet of men pressed back from the table, loosened their collars, and slouched comfortably in their chairs.

Vivienne murmured over a mike, 'Now, darling. I believe the gentlemen are ready.' One camera zoomed in.

Gracefully, Liz swivelled to support herself on her arms with her torso facing the ceiling. She thrust her pelvis into the air, contracting the muscles of her slim buttocks, where only the thin silver band of her G-string separated the twin globes of her beautifully sculpted cheeks. She toyed with the G-string, unsnapped it and tossed it away. Completely naked, she reclined.

Spreading her thighs, she rubbed the silver tube delicately against the lips of her sex. The sound man lowered the boom, and soft words issuing from Liz's carmined lips emanated into the Green Room as the actress moaned softly, 'Now . . . oh, now . . .'

The music swelled. Liz inserted just the tip, the mouthpiece, into her coiling body.

Tanya chuckled softly to Carmen. 'Liz is quite an actress!'

But Carmen was otherwise engaged. *'Madre de Dios,'* she moaned softly, wedging her hand between her legs in concert with Liz's musical masturbation. Thighs apart, the pretty Latina slid her fingers inside her panties to fondle her moistening labia. Tanya gasped and started a new sketch, ignoring the action outside for the moment.

Carmen, panting in her mounting excitement, stared doe-eyed at Tanya and lifted her skirt to her waist. She slipped aside the thin silk of her panties and eagerly fingered her clitoris.

Tanya smiled encouragingly at her friend's wantonness. 'Mm, that looks good, honey,' she cooed and, with a simple gesture of her pencil, encouraged Carmen to continue.

Carmen spread her legs wider and slipped her fingers deep inside her love channel. Her juices spilt over her knuckles.

On the set, following another cue from Vivienne, the four male actors rose from the table and slipped off their dinner jackets. Keeping their eyes glued on Liz, they placed their coats neatly on the backs of their chairs, and proceeded to strip off matching fitted satin waistcoats and wide cummerbunds.

To the continuing beat of the music, the men unfastened their belts in unison, and dropped their tailored trousers, revealing uniform white briefs. Each pouch was filled with the outline of a swelling penis. Still wearing their pleated shirts, the men paired off; they took turns pulling down each other's underwear and divesting themselves of shoes and socks. These potentially awkward movements were choreographed with skill, heightening the erotic tension within the tableau. Finally, the men slid their shirts from their bodies and stood statuesque, completely nude. Skip stepped into a pool of light, and blatantly fondled himself.

Tearing her eyes away from Carmen's sexy display, Tanya could have sworn the actor looked through the Green Room window at the moment his large erect cock was exposed to her view. Handsome and tanned, he seemed to look right into her eyes. She felt a direct response in her womb.

The foursome stood at the compass points of the table, a chorus of substantially erect penises in their hands; in time to the music, each man slowly began to masturbate. Four male slaves appeared and lovingly coated the tip of each member with a layer of whipped cream, spooned from a bowl.

Tanya, viewing them through the softly tinted glass, switched her attention back and forth between the masturbating men and the masturbating woman at her side. The sexual tension built inside her. 'Those are four of the prettiest dicks I've ever seen,' she said softly to her companion. Carmen nodded wordlessly, a rapt expression on her face as she stared at the orchestrated orgy unfolding before them. She rubbed herself rhythmically in time to the music.

Without missing a beat, the actors changed places around the table and continued their vigorous masturbation. The music intensified. The cameras whirred.

Liz, again the central element of the complex choreography, delicately caressed herself, and admired the tableau of handsome naked male flesh before her. She licked the shaft of the flute, and slid it deeper inside her plush channel. Lying on her back and raising her pelvis for the camera, she matched her rhythm to that of the auto-erotic male quartet. The men's penises were rigid, dessert topping still in place.

Against the very edge of the round table, the quartet of cream-tipped penises pointed straight towards Liz at the centre. Lying on her back, she stretched to her full length and rotated herself on the centrepiece. Facing Skip and the others in timed sequence, she paused at each man's staff, sucking and licking all traces of cream from the four purple tips in turn. Her cream-licking activities complete, Liz lay back, limbs spread wantonly across the table, her sex open to view, the silver flute again teasing the lips of her vagina.

Vivienne shouted, 'Now!' and all four men pumped

their towering erections in a vigorous and stylised ballet. As the music crescendoed, all four ejaculated with perfect timing, spurting shining arcs of come, spraying Liz's prone, sleek body, tracing lines of white across her belly, breasts and face. Under the lights, the male seed pooled on her skin, glimmering on her gleaming flesh.

The men slumped back in their seats, their responsibilities duly discharged. The cameras shot some final footage of Liz, who put aside her flute-cum-dildo, and made a production of smoothing the sticky milky fluid over her breasts and buttocks. The camerawomen happily captured several foxy images of the small, beautifully shaped woman's naked squirming body glistening sensuously as she writhed dramatically.

'Cut! And print.' Vivienne's commanding voice held a note of delight, and she jumped from her director's chair to assist in spritzing the come off Liz and patting her lover dry.

The surreality of watching four naked men climax in unison was amusing and titillating to the extreme. Tanya softly massaged her own erect clitoris, pressing her fingers against the damp silk of her panties, near to coming herself. Sweat beaded her forehead. Her clitoris tingled and she pulled her panties aside to feel her wetness.

She turned from the now-darkened stage set to the sexy woman beside her, and Carmen shamelessly elaborated her pose, rolling her shirt up to expose bare carmine-nippled breasts for Tanya's sketchpad. As Tanya drew and massaged her own clitoris, Carmen rolled her skirt high, too, and pulled aside her panties, revealing the lips of her vagina, which were as carmine as her nipples. Tanya grinned and followed her companion's rhythm. Soon the two women were deep in the throes of mutual lust.

Suddenly, the pair were startled by a muffled sound

as the door to the Green Room opened softly. To Tanya's utter horror, Pease was standing at the open door with a lascivious smirk across his face and his hand on his crotch.

'What the hell are you doing here?' Tanya yelped, taking her hand from her panties. 'Get out of here!'

But Pease ignored her. Stepping into the room and closing the door behind him, he smacked his lips with enjoyment at Carmen's semi-nudity. Gripping his erect penis through his linen trousers he strolled over to stand between the two women. 'You two little lezzies might like this better,' he crooned.

Carmen was still frozen in position, her skirt jammed up beneath her naked breasts, her T-shirt around her neck and one finger deep inside her vagina. In slow motion, she withdrew her finger from her dew; just as slowly she sat up and pressed her knees together. Her eyes were glazed in shock.

'Carmen the carmine!' jeered the man gleefully, and splayed his hands as if to touch her breasts and their bright pink nipples.

Pease's movement broke Carmen's spell and, still quivering from remnants of lust, now mixed with fear, she recoiled, hurriedly tugging at her T-shirt. Silently, her dark eyes burning, she smoothed the Spandex over her hardened nipples.

Pease relished the discomfort of his two employees. He taunted them. 'Well, well, ladies, looks like I've caught you . . . "in flagrante"!'

The women were silent.

Pease leant over Tanya's sketchbook to ogle her drawings of Carmen; his voice had an ominous undertone as he said, 'My oh my, what a pretty picture!' He continued to fondle himself flagrantly through his trousers.

Disgusted with his leering presence, Tanya was past caring what her boss said or thought. She stood up, and hastily stuffed her drawings into her bag. 'What do you want, Hiram?' she asked boldly.

'Well,' he answered, shifting his eyes to Tanya. 'I did want you. Past tense.' Standing near, he chucked Tanya under her chin, and murmured, 'But now I understand.' He laughed and looked meaningfully from one woman to the other.

Ducking his hand as it moved to caress her throat, Tanya parried. 'Understand what?'

'Now I understand why you won't have sex with me, Tanya . . . my pretty little lesbian,' he added, with a menacing chuckle.

Tanya gestured to Carmen to come with her, and summoning her dignity, she put her arm protectively around her fellow Studio V worker and pushed past their gloating employer.

'Fuck off, Pease,' she said with quiet fury, turning back at the doorway. 'I'm going where you can't touch me. If I hear you're making Carmen's life a misery at work, I'll make sure Sheila Sorensen yanks the film contract out from under you so fast you'll fall backwards on that fat arse of yours.' She pushed Carmen out of the Green Room and slammed the door. Pease's laughter echoed after them down the hallway.

On the set, Tanya found Vivienne and explained what had happened. The club owner was furious and stormed into the Green Room.

'Hiram Pease! How did a low-life like you get in here?' she demanded. 'You'd better leave immediately!'

'Don't you come all high and mighty with me, you stuck-up bitch!' yelled Pease. 'I just came over here to watch the movie. I've got lots of contacts in the art world here in Dallas; I heard about it through one of them. It's a free country.'

'Coming over here to watch the movie is one thing.

Sexual harassment is quite another. Now get out of here, before I call the cops.'

'You wouldn't dare,' jeered Pease, sniffing the air ostentatiously. 'All I can smell is marijuana and sex. The cops would have a field day if they came here now. They'd close you down. Anyway,' he added with another sneer, 'you don't want to believe everything these little lezzies tell you.' He gestured dismissively at Tanya and Carmen.

'That's it, you creep. I've had enough.' Vivienne's eyes blazed with anger. 'Skip, Malcolm, come over here.' Vivienne called two of the male actors. She gestured at Pease. 'Throw him out.'

Pease shrugged off the actors' restraining hands; he hesitated at the door, as if summoning a parting shot. Tanya intervened first.

'I meant what I said,' she hissed. 'I quit, right now, and I'm taking *Katrina Cortez* with me. She's mine. She always was, and always will be. You send me my back-pay or I'll sue you. If I or Carmen have any trouble whatsoever from you, remember, I'll get Sheila to cut your contract into little pieces.' Tanya drew herself up to her total height and glared at Pease full in the face. Pease dropped his eyes.

'Come on, Carmen,' said Tanya contemptuously. 'We need some fresh air.'

Sitting quietly in the car as Carmen drove away from the CowGirl Club, Tanya felt suddenly quite alone. The import of her actions slowly sank in. Over the last three days she had rejected her long-term boyfriend, Eric; on the rebound from that affair, she had started a new fling by seducing the young Stephen Sinclair, and that too, had failed. And she had just quit her job. A very good job. Even Carmen's friendship couldn't compensate for her recent losses. And her friend was very subdued, driving like an automaton.

Eventually Carmen spoke. 'You were very tough in there, Tanya,' she said quietly. 'I haven't seen you like that before.'

Tanya snorted. 'It must be the Katrina side of me coming out,' she said dismissively. 'She would make mincemeat of jerks like Pease.' Looking over, Tanya caught a look of concern from Carmen; her friend looked decidedly worried. 'Hey, lighten up! It was a joke. About Katrina, I mean.' Tanya tried to ease the conversation.

Carmen was silent for a few minutes, and then spoke again in a small voice. 'I appreciate your standing up for me. I'm more grateful than you can know. But I saw a new side of you; you were hard, almost vicious, towards Pease. You scared me a little.'

'Do you think I scared him?'

Carmen sighed. 'We will see, Tanya. We will see.'

Chapter Nineteen
Tanya's Transition

Later that Sunday afternoon, Tanya drove her own car fast across town, heading for her new apartment. She took stock of her options, now she had so precipitously quit her job. She telephoned Sheila Sorensen and Joshua McNally. She punched in their numbers on her cell phone and left identical messages in quick succession on their answering machines, giving them an edited version of recent developments, saying she'd call again first thing Monday morning.

In her apartment, she stripped and showered, studying herself critically in a full-length mirror. Her figure was different; it didn't look like her body anymore. Friends who said she looked like Natalie Wood would find that description too feminine, now. Carmen was right. There was a new hardness about her: the result, perhaps, of her martial arts training. She didn't know, but she rather liked it.

She twirled her hair between her fingers. The style wasn't right for her new physique. She extracted a pair of scissors from her unpacked boxes and stood before the mirror, deliberately hacking off her long tresses, leaving her hair with an asymmetrical butch-cut, full of hard unfinished edges. After a moment's thought, she took the scissors to her pubic hair, too, carefully trimming her curly thatch to a neatly clipped triangle of short fuzz. With shaving soap and razor, she tidied the edges of the newly defined shape with precision.

She stood back, studying the results. Better, but not right. There was one drawing of Katrina Cortez that Tanya especially liked and she taped this to the mirror. In the sketch, the half-naked figure of Katrina was pulling a sheet of thin body armour over her large firm breasts, which jutted from her chest. She also wore a black leather thong and boots that flared with metallic shin-guards. A nipple ring adorned her right breast.

Tanya regarded her own breasts. Her pectoral muscles were developing in a manner that made her tits project outwards and upwards, especially in profile. Though not as hard-tipped as Katrina's, they jutted out, shapely and impressive.

Next she analysed her hips, buttocks and thighs. The kick-boxing and weight-training were paying off. Katrina's hard thighs bulged more than Tanya's and the heroine's smooth waistline was as narrow and defined as a dancer's. Of course, a real human being couldn't compete with a cartoon character in terms of perfection. But Tanya's body was looking pretty good, and she drew in her breath, simulating the drawings she made of Katrina's midriff. Streamlining her physique was intensive work, but the punishing routines in the gym were showing.

There was one last important detail. She flung on jeans and a T-shirt and drove briskly to the local drug store, where she found what she wanted. Back in the bathroom, she mixed up the black hair colouring and applied it thoroughly to her cropped locks and, after a moment's hesitation, to her pubic triangle. After she was finished, she stood back to appraise her handiwork. A reasonable approximation of Katrina Cortez stared back at her.

Unlike Oscar Wilde's Dorian Gray, who remained unchanged while his portrait aged, Tanya saw herself transformed into her artistic depiction of fictional heroine. 'Yes!' she said triumphantly to her reflection. 'That's the new me.'

Very early the next morning, even before the office cleaners were up and about, Tanya dashed into Studio V to retrieve her supplies from her drawing board and desk. She left the screens; they were too big to fit into her car, but she snatched up Edward Bear eagerly.

'Come on Edward,' she said gruffly. 'This is no place for a bear like you.'

Tanya walked around the studio one last time. Most desks were clear of paper, but on Beth-Ann Bodine's desk two drawings for *Katrina Cortez* were in the process of development from Tanya's original sketches. Tanya snatched them up angrily.

'They're not yours, bitch,' she hissed to Beth-Ann's empty space. 'They belong to me.' Spitefully, black-haired Tanya dumped Beth-Ann's pens and ink into the trash, and carried the waste basket to the garbage chute in the hallway, where she consigned them to oblivion in the basement below. 'Go fuck Pease some more,' she snarled. 'He'll buy you another set. Maybe you can use them as dildos!'

With that parting shot, Tanya strode quickly to the lifts. The hazy reflection of a hard-faced woman in black stared back at her from the polished steel doors. Tanya felt a raw sensuality flowing through her. With the help of Katrina Cortez, she could make it on her own.

Two hours later, Tanya was on the phone to Sheila Sorensen. 'All hell's broken loose with Hiram Pease, Sheila,' she said bluntly. 'He's been sexually harassing me, so I quit. I want to negotiate a freelance arrangement with you and Joshua to continue my work with *Katrina*

Cortez.' She spoke with more confidence than she felt, describing Pease's lasciviously insulting behaviour. She left out some details of herself and Carmen. 'You can check with the women who own the CowGirl Club,' she urged. 'They will confirm everything.'

There was a lengthy silence at the other end. 'I'll do that,' Sheila said slowly. 'Come over to my office at four this afternoon, Tanya. We'll talk about it then. In the meantime, I'll phone Joshua.'

Tanya put down the phone and looked at her watch: seven hours till the meeting. Tanya absently ruffled through her wardrobe. It struck her that she had few clothes to match her new colouring and image. The tough, independent and sexy woman she modelled after the Katrina Cortez character wouldn't wear Tanya's collection of pretty flowered summer dresses and white blouses with brightly coloured skirts and sandals. Tanya stuffed these clothes into a plastic garbage bag, along with her faded denim shorts, pastel T-shirts, white ankle socks and tennis shoes. After stuffing the bulging plastic bag in the trash can, Tanya checked her credit cards and headed for NorthPark Mall.

At a store *en route*, she stopped and bought a dozen black cotton T-shirts, halter tops and skinny tank-tops with tiny spaghetti straps. With this haul on the back seat she pulled into the mall's parking lot.

Her first destination was Victoria's Secret, a sexy clothes store noted for its English ambience. Tanya had no idea whether there really was a Victoria's Secret store in London, but she didn't really care. She liked their selection of sexy underwear and street clothes in black. That was her criterion.

Her first purchase was a single-breasted black lab coat with peaked lapels, which fell to mid-thigh. To go under it, she bought two simple black sixteen-inch mini-skirts that exposed most of her trim thighs. She added a satin camisole, also black, and decorated with sensual red flowers. She smiled approvingly in the dressing room mirror. She managed to look dressed and half undressed at the same time. Adding a couple of simple black skirts with long slits up the side, two unadorned black camisoles and, on a whim, a short black dress trimmed with lace and graced by a plunging V-neckline, her outerwear tastes were temporarily satiated. She headed for the underwear department.

She picked out several front-closing black satin soft-cup bras and matching string bikini panties. A sexy silk bustier and silk G-string trimmed with lace went into her basket, along with several more satin thongs of minute proportions.

With her shopping basket filled, Tanya walked briskly to the register and signed the credit card slip without paying attention to the amount. If her new contract worked out, this was a legitimate business expense. And if it didn't work out . . . well . . . She did not pursue that line of thought.

One final stop at a shoe store added a pair of black strappy sandals with four-inch heels and slingback straps and buckles. Her arms full of bags, Tanya walked to her car, threw the bags in the back seat and drove down Central Expressway to a liquor store, where she bought a bottle of tequila, several bottles of Chardonnay, and some Californian Merlot.

With this pleasant ordeal behind her, Tanya treated herself to lunch at La Madeleine, a French bakery on Walnut Hill Lane, stocked with delicious pastries and fresh roasted coffees. With three hours remaining before her meeting, Tanya drove home, put the white wine in the refrigerator and laid out her new purchases on the bed.

Selecting her wardrobe for the real business of the day, Tanya considered the possibility of going out for dinner after her late-afternoon meeting with Sheila Sorensen. With that eventuality in mind, she chose her original purchases, the long open-cut jacket, the matching short skirt and flowered camisole with its seductive lace-up front. She needed no bra, and eschewed any jewellery that would mar the strong plunging line of the camisole and the swell of her breasts. As the final element of her wardrobe, she picked out the skimpiest of her thongs. These important details settled, she grabbed her exercise bag and dashed to the gym to do penance for the lunchtime pastry.

From Tanya's new apartment in University Park, Las Colinas was a straight shot west along NorthWest Highway, past Love Field and the CowGirl Club. Arriving within the surreal landscape of large steel and glass buildings plonked down in a former marshland, she turned south on O'Connor Boulevard, beneath the elevated monorail tracks that straddled the artificial lakes formed when the marshes were drained and the small streams dammed.

On her right, a tall trio of faceless modern buildings framed a vast barren plaza, happily relieved by some of the finest public art in Texas. Tanya had always liked The Mustangs, a small herd of larger-than-life wild Texas horses that galloped eternally though an ever-splashing fountain, spurting water from their bronze hoofs as they thundered across an artfully sculpted granite and marble *arroyo*.

But today she gave the giant sculpture and its appreciative audience of tourists and art patrons barely a glance. She found a rare parking spot at the kerb, locked the car, and hurried across the windy open plaza. Her confident bearing, her strikingly cropped black gashes of hair, and her sexy outfit competed with the art for the gawking tourists' attention. She stalked boldly towards the building's main entrance, head held high, sketchbooks protruding from her shoulder bag.

A portly uniformed doorman raised a tentative hand

to slow the stern-faced black-clad young woman bearing down on him. 'Miss . . .?'

Tanya paused, her clicking heels stilled on the cold marble. 'Ganymede Productions. Sorensen's office. Which floor?'

'Do you have an appointment?' The middle-aged doorman was sweating, not so much with the heat and his uniform, as from the waves of highly charged sexual energy radiating from the provocatively garbed woman in front of him.

'Yes,' said Tanya impatiently. 'Call up and check if you must. But don't be long. My meeting's at four.' She looked ostentatiously at her watch. It was the only accessory that didn't really match her ensemble, and she quickly shrugged it back under her cuff. Another visit to the mall loomed in her future.

The doorman wrenched his eyes away from Tanya's partially revealed bosom and gestured weakly to the lift. 'Nineteenth floor, miss. Turn left out of the lifts and it's on your left.' He took off his hat and wiped the back of his hand across his forehead.

Tanya flashed a small smile of thanks and felt the doorman's eyes follow her all the way across the spacious lobby, undressing her piece by piece in his middle-aged fantasy. 'In your dreams,' she muttered under her breath, thinking that Katrina Cortez would have had a better exit line.

It was four o'clock on the dot when Tanya presented herself to Sheila Sorensen's secretary. The fresh-faced assistant raised her eyebrows fractionally at Tanya's appearance, but rose and led her silently into the executive's office, on the front of the building overlooking the still-galloping mustangs and beyond to the lake and the Manderlay Canal.

Sheila Sorensen greeted Tanya warmly, but with a look of surprise on her face. 'My God! You've changed. I wouldn't have recognised you on the street.' She appraised the artist's sexy attire with an acute eye. 'Getting more into the Katrina Cortez character, are we?' she asked with a sly smile. Turning, she gestured to a sleek well-muscled man sitting to one side, lounging comfortably in a grey light-weight Italian suit. 'You remember Michael Jardin?' she asked.

Tanya nodded politely, and came right to the point. 'Will you consider taking me on as a freelance script-writer and design consultant for the movie?' she asked. 'I don't need Pease's studio. There are plenty of other firms in Dallas who could take my drawings and turn them into full renderings and computer images.' The words tumbled out in a rush, and Tanya fought to keep her breathing even.

Sheila's face bore no expression, and she sat silently for a few minutes. Tanya's heart lurched in trepidation. But when the producer looked up, a hint of a smile glimmered behind her dark eyes.

'I'm amenable to the idea,' she said. 'But Joshua may take some convincing. In fact I'm waiting for his call right now. He's been busy all day entertaining an executive visiting from our parent company in Los Angeles. Ah! That may be him now.'

The phone was ringing. Jardin picked it up. He listened and passed the instrument to Sorensen. 'It's Joshua, for you,' he murmured.

Sorensen spoke into the phone. 'Hello, Joshua, I've got Tanya Trevino here now,' she said. 'Or perhaps I should say I've got Katrina Cortez in my office! You'll notice a big change when you see her.'

Sheila Sorensen swivelled round in the chair and gazed unseeingly out of the floor-to-ceiling window. 'I talked with the two women at the club, Dupree and Angelo, and they confirmed everything that Tanya said. They have quite an operation there. I also called Pease. He denied everything, and gave a completely different version. According to Hiram, Tanya is the evil witch, plotting and scheming behind our backs.' She turned to wink at Tanya, who listened closely.

'But,' she said decisively, 'I tend to believe Tanya and the club owners. It tallies with other things I know about Pease.' She listened as he responded. 'Yes, Joshua,' she sighed, patiently. 'I *know* he's your fraternity buddy, and yes, I know you're borrowing his limo and his driver today to impress our visitor.' She laughed. 'You're right. It is embarrassing to fire the man one day and return his car the next, but that's what I'm going to do. I simply can't trust him to be straight with us on anything.'

The woman listened again for a few moments. 'All right. How about this? Come over here in half an hour with limo, driver and our guest. Then we'll go out to dinner. Tanya can talk to you herself. I'm ready to go ahead and get her to sign a contract now. There's no point in waiting . . . OK. Bye.'

Sheila Sorensen swung round as Jardin slipped some sheets of paper on to her desk. The older woman picked them up and handed them to Tanya. 'You'll want to look this over. When you're ready, sign and date both copies.'

Tanya glanced at the contract and looked up, startled. 'You had this prepared,' she said, excitedly. 'You'd already decided.'

Sheila laughed. 'Don't get too excited, Tanya. This contract represents a heavy workload. If you sign it, Katrina Cortez is going to rule your life for several months.' She leant over the desk and looked Tanya in the eyes. 'But yes, I had already decided to take a gamble on you. And,' she added, running her hand through her short curly brown hair, looking with twinkling amusement at the young woman before her, 'just between you and me, I've been looking for an excuse to dump Pease from our business relationship ever since he seduced me, several weeks ago.'

Tanya drew a second sharp intake of breath, but the older woman continued in an even voice that only hinted at anger. 'He fucked me once and then he wasn't interested anymore. I like to be the one who dumps people, not the other way round!'

'Oh, like Stephen Sinclair, you mean?' The words flew from Tanya's lips before she had time to stop them.

Sheila Sorensen looked up sharply. 'How did you know about that?'

Tanya winced at her careless tongue. 'Oh, I . . . I dated him for a little while,' she said vaguely. But inside she felt a sharp pang of jealousy and longing that appeared from nowhere.

Sheila shrugged, as if the matter was of no importance. 'Now,' she said, with an abrupt change of mood, 'if you'll excuse me, I have to call our dear Mr Pease and break the news to him.' She frowned. 'I wish we didn't have his damn limousine. That's a real embarrassment.'

She looked at Jardin. 'Michael, take Tanya down to the lounge. She can read and sign the contract there, and you can get her a drink. Oh,' she added with a grimace, 'get me a large scotch. I think I'm going to need it!'

Chapter Twenty
Tanya Goes Topless

Tanya was in the grip of twin cravings: for food and sex. Her experiences at the CowGirl Club seemed to have boosted her sex-drive into high gear, and she felt herself buzzing with a level of desire that even Hiram Pease's behaviour couldn't deflate.

The invitation to dinner had at least satisfied one of those cravings, for the time being. Settled with her companions in an upmarket restaurant in the Cedar Springs neighbourhood, Tanya sipped a glass of deliciously crisp white wine as the waiters cleared away their plates. Across the table from her sat Joshua McNally and the movie executive from Los Angeles. Tanya struggled to remember his name; in her elation at signing the contract, she had not paid sufficient attention when he was introduced. Eventually she gave up. She preferred to think of him as 'the stranger'. He fitted the part: tall, dark and debonair, with hard eyes that didn't soften when he smiled. She caught his glance and he studied her unabashedly. Locking her gaze with his, she challenged his stare. Eventually, 'the stranger' lowered his eyes and whispered something to Joshua.

'No,' replied Joshua so softly that Tanya strained to

hear his words. 'Not mine . . . changed a lot . . . hard and sexy . . .'

A small smile crept across the stranger's face and then was gone. Tanya gave no indication she'd heard their exchange and consciously focused her attention elsewhere.

Around the table were two other empty chairs. Sorensen and Michael Jardin had taken their cellular phone over to the bar, where Tanya could see them engaged in what appeared to be a heavy business discussion. Sheila was making expansive hand gestures and cradling the phone between ear and shoulder. Jardin was looking on, contributing the occasional comment to a question from his employer.

Tanya's eyes roved further, taking in the heavily panelled and wainscotted walls. She found the preponderance of dark wood oppressive. The hard surfaces echoed with the braying voices of the bourgeoisie in full cry, but at least they drowned out the endless strains of Frank Sinatra flowing through the ceiling speakers. At the far side was the glow of a wood-burning pizza oven, stoked by Mexican ex-stevedores as they ladled speciality pizzas with goat's cheese and sun-dried tomatoes. Beyond that was an exit door through which Tanya could glimpse the lighted parking lot. Somewhere out there was Pease's limousine and his driver Fernando Ramos, who had brought the party downtown from Las Colinas. Poor Fernando was probably sitting in the limo now, thought Tanya, eating a greasy cheeseburger from some neighbouring fast-food joint.

She had a sudden vision of the Mexican's strong body and sleek features. She had thought him attractive, the first time he'd driven her to lunch with Pease. He'd certainly checked out her body, that day. Maybe, she thought, he'd be fun for later in the evening. A wicked plan slowly formed in the back of her mind.

She transferred her attention to her more immediate

surroundings. On adjacent tables she typecast middle-aged businessmen rewarding their mistresses before going home to dutifully screw their wives; lawyers inflating their billable hours by falsifying meetings over dinner; and, close by, a table of overly earnest academics avidly discussing the importance of light rail transit in city design. Tanya felt bored and contemptuous of the patrons around her, with their petty personas and neatly packaged prejudices. She remembered the French poet and critic Baudelaire, who said the role of the artist was to shock the bourgeoisie. Tonight, they were going to be well and truly shocked.

A blast of heat from the pizza oven made her uncomfortably warm, and she shrugged her shoulders to rid herself of her tailored black lab coat. In a flash, the stranger jumped to his feet and helped her remove the jacket. His eyes hovered on the creamy surfaces of Tanya's torso now exposed by the skimpy camisole.

'You're quite a story-teller, young woman,' the Californian said quietly. 'Your tales of the GirlZone are very . . . interesting.'

'Is that a compliment?' she asked.

'Yes. Is your real life as daring?' The stranger sat down in the vacant chair next to her. His eyes now smouldered in contrast to their former coldness.

Emboldened by her fast-growing identification with her cartoon heroine, and stimulated by his hot eyes, Tanya toyed with the laces on her camisole. Her breasts were chafing under the newness of the material.

'Tonight it is,' she said. 'It's much more fun to be the real thing, rather than draw the story.'

The lust now transparent in the stranger's eyes made her feel sexy, in control. She stroked the tops of her breasts and unlaced two sets of eyelets, peeling the garment purposefully from her breasts.

The stranger's eyes dropped to watch her pink nipples emerge from their covering. 'Tell me more about yourself, my dear,' he instructed in a pleasantly authoritative way.

Tanya teased a nipple with her finger, making it stand proud to attention. 'My friend says my nipples are like strawberries to the cream of my tits,' she said teasingly, putting words into Carmen's mouth.

'Enchanting,' murmured her companion. 'Perhaps I shall be lucky like your friend, tonight.' Joshua was watching intently from across the table.

She unlaced more eyelets. 'Yes, perhaps,' Tanya suggested coquettishly. She leant back, holding her loose laces in her hands. She enjoyed the luxurious feeling of the two men's hungry stares raking her body.

Now Joshua moved to her side. 'Let me assist you with that,' he said. 'Are you still too warm?'

'Yes,' she replied. And quite moist, too, she thought, smiling to herself.

Joshua placed his strong warm hands on her shoulders and ran his fingers down her breasts, bending forward to unthread the remaining laces of her camisole. He carefully picked them apart, all the way to her waistline.

There was a quick intake of breath from her audience when her tits emerged to full view. Joshua and the stranger together eased the camisole's thin straps over Tanya's shoulders and down her arms. Tanya stretched her arms wide and her naked breasts jiggled, freed from the garment. The stranger laid the crumpled camisole conspicuously on the table.

'Oh, yes,' he murmured, his eyes locked on Tanya's nipples. 'Definitely strawberries and cream for dessert.' A stir was felt throughout the elegant, coolly formal, and very expensive restaurant. Then all was hushed. All faces were turned towards her. 'When may we taste?' enquired the stranger.

Tanya smiled enigmatically, basking in the attention of her companions and now of the entire clientèle. Sheila Sorensen and Michael Jardin were watching with rapt attention from the bar, their phone call forgotten. The *maître d'*, passing by Tanya's table stood stock-still, a look of utter panic on his face.

'Madam, your . . . your . . .' His voice faded away in confusion. He unfolded a damask serviette and started to spread it across her breasts. But he hesitated; her assertive demeanor stilled his protests.

Tanya laughed. 'Do you wish to cover me, sir? Shall I wear the cloth like a bib?' The pliant flesh of her naked bosom jiggled delicately.

'N . . . n . . . no, Madam,' the *maitre d'* stuttered, his mouth watering at the sight of her nipples.

'Good, I prefer them uncovered.' Tanya's eyes flashed, and she arched her back so that her breasts were emphasised.

The man balled up the serviette and blotted his brow.

Tanya stroked her breasts, making her nipples enlarge. 'Bring us another bottle of red, please,' she ordered gently. 'A Cabernet.'

He bowed. 'Which vintage does the lady wish to try?'

'Estancia Estates, 1995, please. It's a particularly velvety Cabernet Sauvignon,' she said. 'Lush and complex.'

'As you wish, Madam,' he complied with a bow, summoning the *sommelier*.

Throughout the restaurant, several tables ordered fresh rounds of drinks. The *maître d'* paused beside one group, where the head of the table waved a clutch of thick theatre tickets. 'Give these away!' cried the diner. 'We'd rather watch the floor show here!' With a nod towards Tanya's now notorious table, he continued breathlessly, 'That topless chick is a sensation!'

Tanya looked appraisingly around the room. The men circling her wore stupid grins; the women seemed both fascinated and jealous at the same time. She dipped her fingers in the wine and circled her nipples; the stranger bent to lick them with his tongue.

'Definitely an excellent vintage,' he declared.

A buzz ran through the audience. Tanya smiled and sipped the Cabernet appreciatively. She raised her glass to her companions. 'Here's to Katrina Cortez and her exploits.'

'To Katrina.' The two men at the table were rejoined by Sheila Sorensen and Michael Jardin. 'To our very own Katrina,' toasted Sheila, with a sexy smile. 'I can see this is going to be a very interesting relationship.'

Several patrons at adjacent tables raised their glasses in companion toasts. 'To Katrina,' shouted one young man, before being slapped down by his girlfriend.

Tanya drained her glass. It was time to go. She stood up, gesturing for her companions to follow. She adjusted her skirt and reached for her discarded camisole where it lay on the table top. As her hand closed upon the soft fabric, the stranger took her by the wrist.

Moving his hand up her arm, the man paused to tease the side of one full breast. 'Please don't dress,' he pleaded in mock supplication. 'Let me carry that for you.' He held out his open hand.

'Well . . . ' Tanya began.

When his finger grazed a nipple, she sighed voluptuously, feeling a quiver of lust shoot through her loins at the casual touch. She balled up the camisole and handed it to him. Her nipples were hard, her thong soaked with dew.

Tanya reached for her jacket. But Joshua McNally claimed that article of clothing. With a naughty grin, he said, 'You don't need this, either. It's warm out, tonight,' he coaxed. 'Don't cover your beautiful tits. They are so perfect.'

Tanya shrugged and turned away. Naked from her lovely neck to her swaying hips, she moved gracefully across the restaurant floor, her uncovered breasts swinging. All eyes were upon the slender statuesque woman who walked with sensual pageantry past the tables of staring diners. Not even the clatter of a fork shattered the silence of the restaurant.

Pausing near the open door, Tanya welcomed the feeling of fragrant warm night air as it blew across her nakedness. She turned to look behind her. Joshua and the others were delayed by the matter of the bill. Walking half-naked and alone into the night, Tanya's supple figure was illuminated by the soft glow of lights in the parking lot as she scoured the space, looking for the limo.

A wave of sound burst from the restaurant as the diners all started talking at once. 'Did you see those nipples?'

'I'd like to get my hands round a pair like that!'

'Would you strip like that for me?'

'Do you think I can get her number?'

'Put it away! Wait till we get home!'

'Well, I just think it's disgusting!'

Alerted by a familiar purring nearby, Tanya swung round to face the source of the sound and, in an instant, her nakedness was floodlit by the twin beams of the limo's headlights. Tanya stood still and signalled the driver. He rolled the car forward a few yards and came to a stop. In the full glare of the lights, Tanya calmly unzipped her skirt and stepped out of it. Wearing only her skimpiest of thongs, she stood beside the car. 'Twenty-eighteen, Rosedale Avenue, please, Fernando,' she ordered calmly. 'Let's lose the rest of these guys. I want to fuck you!'

Chapter Twenty-One
The Limo Driver

Fernando Ramos couldn't believe his eyes when Tanya turned and walked towards his vehicle, caught full in his headlights; she was half-naked! He watched spellbound as the young woman calmly stripped off her skirt and opened the car door to sit next to him. His eyes swivelled on stalks to follow every movement, capture every detail.

He drew on his leather driving gloves, his excitement growing. She really made his untamed dick rear up; he felt its pulsing hotness through the layers of his uniform. God, what breasts! She had an incredible body. Beneath her taut belly, a minuscule thong clung to high hipbones, revealing the full outlines of her pubic mound.

As she glanced through the windscreen, Tanya saw that the others hadn't yet left the club. Turning to the aroused and bemused driver, she asked, 'Can you lose McNally and the rest of them?' Her voice was steady, in control. She leant across the seat and touched Fernando's bulging dick.

Tanya knew what she wanted: to exercise the power of her body over her colleagues, to lead them on, to tease them – just like Katrina. But she also wanted some rampant sex, and Fernando was just the man for her.

'I want you to take me directly home,' she said, giving him a big smile. 'Then I want you to drop off the others and come back for me. Got it?'

He nodded.

'I'm going to play some games with my colleagues, but I want you for later. All to myself. *Comprendo*?' This was pure Katrina Cortez, she thought proudly. 'If I get too . . . preoccupied back there – ' she gestured at the expansive back seat ' – send me a signal when we get to my street.' Looking into the handsome Latino's eyes, Tanya murmured, 'I want to make it good for you.'

He opened his hand, and Tanya bent forward to lay her right breast in his leather-covered palm. 'How will you make it good?' he asked with a sexy purr. His hand caressed her breast.

'Just take me home and you'll see,' she coaxed softly.

His dark eyes caressed her body like a tactile touch. 'Listen for the music to change, *chica*. I'll switch from classical to rock-and-roll just before I stop,' he said.

'How will you dump the group?'

'Don't worry,' he replied with a wicked grin. 'I have an idea. Just don't be surprised if you see blue flashing lights. My *compadre* is a cop. When we stop, just open the door and run. I'll take care of everything else.'

He smiled knowingly and gently squeezed her breasts, his breath quick. Tanya's flesh was on fire beneath his touch. Their attention was diverted by sounds from the other end of the parking lot; she sat up, away from his hands.

Damn! thought Tanya. The others were back. She watched Joshua McNally bustle out of the restaurant with Sheila and the other two men in tow.

McNally charged towards the vehicle, braying, 'Tanya!'

Stepping out of the shiny car, Tanya casually waved to the group.

The quartet focused all their attention on Tanya's almost naked body, outlined in the light before them.

'Bewitching,' said the stranger, hoarsely. Sheila Sorensen surveyed Tanya's nakedness, eyes glittering in the halogen glare.

Tanya didn't miss the older woman's greedy inventory of her body. 'Get in the car, guys,' she ordered.

They obeyed meekly, entranced by Tanya's unselfconscious nudity. Pushing Sheila inside first, Tanya gestured to the three men to follow. She tumbled in after them and rapped on the glass partition. The driver acknowledged and flipped the radio to light classical music.

Tanya had her plans mapped out, and first was her game with the men and woman in the back seat. She sat between Sheila Sorensen and the stranger. McNally and Jardin were on folding seats facing backward across the plush interior. They stared at her nakedness. Tanya merely smiled and laid her hands casually on the thighs of the man and woman next to her. As she stroked Sheila's bare skin, she was pleased to feel a quiver of nervousness from the woman who had so brazenly taken Stephen Sinclair for her own, several nights ago. Tanya was surprised how much that episode rankled, and how each time she thought of Stephen, something inside her turned a little somersault. She looked around rather nervously, feeling her Katrina persona slip a little bit, and shivered as her nipples stood on end.

She raked Sheila's thigh with her nails, sliding beneath her skirt to feel the soft silk of the older woman's panties. Sheila moaned and pressed Tanya's hand over her mound. To her left, Tanya noted the bulge in the stranger's lap, and she dexterously opened his fly and took out his dick.

'Let me taste,' she ordered, licking her lips.

The man eagerly complied, dropping his trousers and proffering his long, hard penis to her waiting mouth.

Taking her hand from his cock, Tanya pulled off her panties, parted her legs, and urged the now panting Sheila to the floor between her knees. Tanya guided the woman's mouth to her pussy-lips, and held her face to her quim. With barely concealed delight, Tanya acknowledged that her intuition was correct. Sheila moaned softly, her tongue lapping Tanya's pussy eagerly, obviously well versed in pleasuring a woman.

Tanya's juices flowed, her clitoris swelling under the woman's expert attention, and she tasted the heady musk of the stranger on her tongue. Licking him lollipop-style, she gently stroked his shaft and cupped his balls with her left hand. She glanced towards the other two men; both had their dicks in their hands, masturbating eagerly. McNally's eyes were fixed on the spectacle before him. Jardin was clearly more interested in McNally's handsome erection. As Tanya watched, Jardin palmed a small sachet of oil and anointed his penis so it glistened in the flitting rhythm of the street lights. He pumped it slowly, never taking his eyes from McNally's massive member.

Tanya switched her attention to McNally. She gestured the publisher to the seat beside her, desiring to fondle his balls, creating symmetry with the stranger on her left. Between her thighs, her own climax was building under Sheila's rapt attention; she shuddered in delicious anticipation. The other woman frantically fingered herself inside her panties.

Tanya felt like Katrina enacting a moment of high seduction, a maestro conducting a four-part concerto of sex.

In the front seat, Fernando, increasingly horny, looked in his rear-view mirror. God, she was a wild woman! The men and the woman were all over her. Rubbing his erection through his pants, Fernando could hardly wait to fuck that horny girl. He grabbed his car phone and punched in the number of his buddy Gino's pager. Moments later, the call was returned.

'Hey, Gino, man.'

'Hey, man. What's up?'

'Hey man. I am *up!* I need a favour, big time. I've got a cute, wicked little girl in the back seat. She is eating up my passengers back there.'

'Yeah. So? Do I need to arrest them?'

'No, man. You see, I want to fuck her myself. But first I've gotta lose the other four. Could you just pull us over so she can jump out at her place, over on Rosedale, and then detain these good folks long enough for me to get back to her?' He spoke fast and eagerly.

Gino laughed knowingly. 'I get it, man. I know that car you drive. What's with this "cute, wicked little girl in the back seat"?' he asked. 'Big tits?'

'*Si, campanero*!' his friend replied. 'And she's buck-naked.'

'Jesus! How tall is she?'

Fernando knew Gino liked tall women. 'She's too small for you, big boy. Anyway, she's mine tonight.'

Gino sniggered. 'I'd like to see for myself.'

'OK. Sure, *amigo*, sure you can look,' Fernando agreed. 'But that's all.'

'OK. I'll stop the car for reckless driving or whatever. I'll get a good look at the girl, let her go, and take the others to the station on some pretended charge of lewd behaviour. I can probably hold them an hour,' he told Fernando. 'Will that do it for you?'

Fernando laughed. 'I'll owe you one!'

'Hey,' said Gino, suddenly more serious. 'There's something you can do for me in return, man. Can you talk to that cute chick in your apartment house? Tell her what a great guy I am? I'd love to go with her. You do that for me, and we're equal.'

Fernando chuckled again. 'It's a deal. I'll see what I can do. Rosalita and me, we go back a long way. Can you meet us at Hillcrest and Rosedale in about five minutes?'

'Got it.' The cop signed off with a laugh.

Fernando put down the phone, grinning broadly at his cleverness. Sure, his buddy could check out the pair of tits on the chick in the back seat. He looked again at the sex-mad covey in his mirror. It was getting pretty wild back there. He played impatiently with his cock, stiff in his pants.

In the back seat, Tanya was near to coming, but it was Sheila who demanded her own satisfaction first. Taking her mouth from Tanya's vulva long enough to instruct her assistant Jardin, she pulled down her panties and flipped up her skirt, exposing her trim arse to full view. Her fingers worked her clitoris in a frenzy.

'Do me, Jardin. Fuck me like you do your boyfriends,' she demanded.

With a wry smile, her handsome assistant lubed his dick one more time and eased a slick finger into Sheila's anus, teasing the tight muscle in preparation to receive his long dick. With practised ease, he mounted his employer, slowly penetrating her secret passage, easing his penis in and out in a sensual rhythm. The combined motions of his cock and her fingers sent the producer over the top. Sheila screamed, and nibbled fiercely on Tanya's love-bud, her face buried in the younger woman's juices as Tanya, her lips still around the stranger's cock, came herself.

Tanya's orgasm precipitated a chain reaction.

Michael Jardin withdrew his cock from Sheila and, with urgent strokes, ejaculated across his employer's naked bottom. Sheila thrashing, naked and eager, was begging for more. 'Fuck me,' she cried out, for someone, anyone.

The stranger still had not come. But as she sucked him, Tanya knew it was only a matter of moments; he was groaning with lust. Sheila, at her feet, lay moaning for a cock, any cock. Tanya rolled aside as the stranger eased his dick from her lips and moved towards the wailing, wanton Sheila. He eased his pulsing penis into Sheila's liquid channel, coming within seconds.

Tanya reached for McNally's balls and fondled them sensuously, inviting the finale. McNally obliged, pumped his member in urgent strokes and showered his semen across Sheila's hair and face, completing the carnival of carnality.

Tingling from sensual overload, Tanya watched fascinated as satiated bodies tumbled around her. At that moment, the limousine's piped music changed from classical to rock-and-roll. Tanya sat up, alert to Fernando's signal. Like magic, the flashing blue lights of the police car materialised behind them. With one deft turn of the wheel, Fernando manoeuvered the long car round a corner and pulled over. They came to a dead stop on Tanya's street.

'Where are we?' Joshua cursed, hastily dressing himself. Blue lights washed the scene of frantic reclothing. The limo sat idling as the cop got out of his car. He walked towards the driver's side.

Tanya slithered into position beside the back door. She gripped the handle. Across the seats, the three men and Sheila became miraculously sober and partially dressed when the policeman appeared at Fernando's window. Tanya caught the flicker of a signal from Fernando in the rear-view mirror.

Gino cast his torch into the back seat. The beam fell upon Tanya. She licked her lips and blew the cop a kiss. She grasped the handle and opened the door. Grabbing her clothes, she propelled herself against the door and leapt, stark naked, from the limo.

Tanya hit the pavement with a skidding flurry.

Despite her spiked heels, she ran the few hundred feet to her apartment building. Behind her she could hear Joshua's pleading voice cut short by the baritone laugh of the cop asking for his identification. She heard the words, 'Let her go, gentlemen . . . It's you I'm interested in, tonight.'

She raced down the street to her apartment, but through the still-open door Tanya heard the stranger's voice raised in a final comment. 'That Tanya Trevino is a wild woman.'

'I know,' she heard McNally reply. 'She's an artist.'

Within a few minutes, Tanya had clattered upstairs to the safety of her flat, still flushed and ready for more sex. With a gleeful if slightly hysterical chuckle, she spoke to her naked reflection in her full-length mirror. She smelt of sex. 'Now Katrina wants a fuck,' she exclaimed. 'Hurry back, Fernando.' Her labia tingled. How like Katrina she was feeling!

Ten minutes later, the sound of a car horn brought her to the bay window. She had washed herself and made her body sweet for her lover-to-be. Her clitoris was once more a hard bud between her legs, craving the full satisfaction of a man's touch. At the kerb she saw the limo. Fernando held open the car door like a model chauffeur. He tipped his hat to the naked woman caressing herself in the first-floor window.

Neither party noticed a small dark Honda that drove slowly by and parked a few doors down. The driver switched off the lights but did not get out. In the driver's seat, Stephen Sinclair turned his head. He had seen a striking naked woman with cropped dark hair standing at the window of what he thought was Tanya's apartment. Carmen had told him that Tanya's bay window was located at the top left, when seen from the street. But who was the naked black-haired beauty? And who was the man waiting for her at the kerb with the flashy limousine?

His heart in his mouth, he watched the front door open. The black-haired woman walked to the long car. To his amazement, on the pavement, she stripped off her light raincoat and stood stark naked under the street-light, handing her coat to the uniformed chauffeur, who bowed politely and laid the garment over his arm. Despite the strange, jagged black hair, Stephen now had no difficulty recognising his one-time lover, Tanya Trevino. She looked the very embodiment of Katrina Cortez, but there was no mistaking that lovely body and beautiful breasts. He cried out loud in his anguish, watching the woman he'd come to see, to apologise to, to beg forgiveness from, embrace the limousine driver and allow the man to fondle her naked breasts right there on the street, before guiding his hand between her legs. He watched in silent desperation as Tanya got in behind the wheel, still naked. With tears of frustration and misery in his eyes, he put the car in gear and drove slowly off in the opposite direction.

'Let me drive.'

Fernando smiled at the slender naked beauty behind the wheel of the long and ostentatious limousine. He chuckled as he adjusted the driver's seat for her smaller figure.

'What's so funny?' she asked.

'You,' he said. 'A naked chauffeur.'

Expertly, she drew the long car from the kerb. She parted her legs and rubbed herself delicately. She looked over at him, asking, 'Anything you want to show me?'

'Gladly,' he said, unzipping his trousers. Ever ready, he wore no underwear. 'I want to show you *mi polla*.' He pulled out his enlarged phallus, slid closer, and placed its throbbing reddened head against her thigh.

She gasped. It was a beauty.

He laughed. 'Didn't know it would be this big, did you, *chicita*?' Clasping the shaft in his hand, he bobbed its hardness rhythmically against her leg.

Pulling over, she stopped under the trees of a darkened stretch of road. Switching off the motor, she turned to him. 'Lick me,' she ordered, spreading her legs wide. Fernando's mouth covered her moist labia. He tasted her juice and smelt her musk. Her lust was clearly unabated by the evening's exertions.

'Let's get in the back,' he murmured, stripping off his clothing and helping Tanya out, still the perfect chauffeur.

On the site of the evening's earlier orgy, Tanya enjoyed another hour of very satisfying sex. In the capacious back seat, her new lover needed no instruction; his prominent penis pleasured her, probing the luscious folds of her vulva, her ready mouth and, finally, with gentle persuasion, the tightness of her anus. Tanya's sharp memory of Michael Jardin's cock sliding into Sheila Sorensen's arse peaked her curiosity about this new sensation. She groaned with surprise and pleasure as Fernando's dick stretched her passage, venturing where no other had penetrated. It was fun, but on the whole she decided she preferred the sheer joy of having her vagina filled to bursting with a throbbing male member. She lost count of the times she came, her body wracked with exquisite torment, her juices staining anew the fine leather of the seats.

Afterwards, she lay wet and panting across the seat. She stroked the driver's penis between her fingers. It stirred willingly. 'You have a beautiful big dick, Fernando,' she purred. 'If we go home, can you do it again?' The man smiled sweetly and jumped behind the wheel.

They ran naked across the lawn, then raced up Tanya's stairs, falling over each other to fuck on the floor of the living room like rampant animals in heat. They lubricated their lust by finishing Tanya's stock of tequila and

Tanqueray; a small pile of bottles accumulated beside them. At last satiated and sexually replete, Tanya gently eased the inexhaustible young man out into the night. It was three a.m. '*Hasta luego*, Fernando,' she said sleepily. '*Tu polla es magnifico!*'

Alone in bed at last, she dreamt about the young driver's constant erection. Pease, McNally and several other men laughed heartily from a darkened audience pit as she performed live sex acts with Fernando and Sheila Sorensen on stage. Then, on a large bed with a mirror above it, she alternated having sex with Stephen Sinclair and with Fernando, finally doing it with both of them at once. She looked upward in the mirror, and saw only the reflection of Katrina Cortez grinning wolfishly down at her.

'Welcome to my world,' said the decadent detective. 'You'll fit in very nicely here!'

Chapter Twenty-Two
Man to Man

Stephen hopped on the famous McKinney Street trolley, his briefcase over his shoulder. Carmen had thrust some papers from the fax machine directly into his hand with instructions to deliver them to Pease immediately. 'He'll be where he always is at this hour,' she told him, with a dismissive shrug of her shoulders. 'Propping up the bar at the Gentleman's Club in the Crescent, looking at the pretty girls' tits.'

Stephen had looked so miserable from his awful experience the night before that Carmen had taken pity on him. 'Don't torture yourself about Tanya,' she had urged. 'This may be a phase she's going through. She thinks she's a mature woman, but she's only a few years older than you, *chico*, and she's out of her depth with the success of *Katrina Cortez*. She wasn't prepared for it.'

Stephen remembered how much he'd wanted to believe those words of advice, but he couldn't get the image of a raven-haired Tanya throwing her naked body at the chauffeur, inviting him to finger-fuck her right there on the street. It had been like a scene directly from one of those damn comics.

The trolley clattered along the brick-paved street,

through the State-Thomas neighbourhood, past Starbucks on the corner of McKinney and Howell Street, past Beth-Ann's apartment building and the Bar of Soap. At five o'clock, the sidewalks were filling with office workers headed for the gym or for happy hour. A little knot of pedestrians clustered around the trolley-stop outside a looming grey building that resembled a French chateau on steroids. The Crescent was a swanky locale, a huge shopping and office complex north of downtown, built in the form of a ludicrously vast country house lifted from the Loire valley. Fifteen stories of fake stone, cascading mansard roofs and dangling wrought-iron balconies shaded the pavement, beckoning the passer-by out of the tortured late afternoon heat and humidity, and into a world of chic chrome and glass boutiques, selling jewellery and furs at unmarked prices.

Inside this monstrosity, in air-conditioned comfort, Hiram Pease sat at the bar of the Dallas Gentleman's Club. Like many local establishments, the club's ambience relied heavily on Texan motifs. Representations of the single-starred battle flag of the old republic lined the walls, including a neon version that competed for attention with advertisements for Budweiser and Corona beers, and outlines of cowboy boots, all in similar media. Fearsome horns of long-dead Texas cattle mingled with old photographic prints of even longer dead Indian chiefs.

These tragic chapters of American history were lost on Hiram Pease. He liked looking at the waitresses' tits, only half concealed by skimpy outfits. And he approved of the affluent ambience that buffered him from thinking too much about his own problems. This evening, he intended to get drunk and to get laid. He didn't care in which order, though he was closer to the first. He was in a foul mood. The stinging words of Sheila Sorensen still rang in his ears. 'There's no place in my organisation for a double-dealer like you. You're out of the picture!' That's what she'd had the audacity to tell him, in her preppy-fucking-Californian accent. She wasn't even that good a lay, he thought savagely.

Lush green Boston ferns and several sorts of succulents and cacti bedecked the polished mahogany bar with brass fittings where Pease rested his elbows. A stray frond tickled him in the face and he batted it away impatiently, glowering into his third glass of Californian Cabernet. He grimaced at the thought of that ungrateful little bitch Tanya Trevino. He had known Trevino would be trouble, ever since she'd got away from him at that first dinner meeting. So high and mighty, that one, fancied herself a real artist. More like a fucking prima-donna, and one who obviously preferred fucking women! Despite his foul mood, he couldn't resist a smile at the memory of Trevino and that little minx Carmen Sierra masturbating together, their legs spread wide and their fingers in their pussies. Trevino was so different from his favourite, Beth-Ann, who'd fuck him at the drop of a fifty-dollar bill, or three.

The thought of some casual sex to ease his woes stirred Pease's dick, and spurred him to lift his eyes from his glass and survey the possibilities. He liked the masculine aura, the muted sounds, the excellent wine list, and the attractive girls, who managed to suggest high class and sexual availability at the same time. The word among his cronies was that special unadvertised services were available to gentlemen of means in this up-market celebration of maleness.

He eyed his waitress appraisingly from several tables away; she was a little brunette with big tits. Just his type. He imagined how she would undress for him, cupping her breasts coyly in her hands, letting him play with them as she divested herself of her remaining clothes. Then she would go down on him, drawing every inch of his magnificent manhood into her mouth. He waited to catch her eye, to start the subtle ritual of sexual liaison, but she was serving other customers several tables away and failed to glance in his direction.

Glumly, he returned his attention to his drink, and his imagination to the revenge he would wreak upon Tanya Trevino. That lifted his spirits. He'd make that little tart unemployable in this city. He had only to spread the word among the tight-knit circle of designers here in the Dallas-Fort Worth Metroplex that she was a back-stabbing little thief, and she'd be history. A warm glow of hatred flooded his veins and welled up in his loins. He became fully hard, and he trawled the room for available females.

Alas, no one was paying him any attention. Several well-dressed sophisticated-looking women sat at the bar, chatting happily among themselves. Perhaps, Pease considered, they were some high-class escort agency girls. That could be his solution for the evening. Paying for sex had become a habit, a business expense. He liked to think of Beth-Ann's blow jobs as being tax-deductible.

His predatory survey of the bar did reveal a male acquaintance from SMU days at a nearby table. Pease smiled and waved nonchalantly. 'Waiting for a client!' he answered in reply to the other man's polite question. The two men nodded civilly to each other and returned to their private worlds, but Pease's thoughts switched to another old school buddy: Joshua McNally, that double-crossing bastard. How the hell could McNally dump Pease and side with that haughty west coast bitch Sorensen? Fraternity brothers were supposed to stick together, through thick and thin. You made your pledge for life.

And to boot, Pease had loaned McNally the use of his limousine and driver for a couple of days just so his old buddy could impress some visiting big-shot from LA! Pease scowled and squirmed in his seat with indignation at this further evidence of treachery. Fernando had delivered the car without a word this morning, but Pease knew something had been going on. There had been dark rings under his driver's eyes, a fatigue belied by the transparent swagger in his walk. Pease knocked back the Cabernet without tasting its rich oaky flavour and poured himself another from the fast-emptying bottle at his table. McNally was another person to get even with.

A discreet cough at his elbow jerked him from his bitter reverie. 'Good evening, Mr Pease. Carmen said I'd find you here.'

Pease looked up in surprise to find Stephen Sinclair standing at his table. 'Sinclair! What the hell are you doing here?' He certainly didn't want to talk to this young twerp just now.

But Stephen held out an envelope for Pease's attention. 'I'm sorry to bother you, sir, but this came by fax just before the studio closed. Carmen said it was important, and asked me to bring it by.'

Pease overlaid his irritation with a veneer of hospitality. The kid was only trying to do him a favour. 'Sit down, Stephen. Sit down. Take the weight off your feet. It's been a long hard day.' Pease became expansive. 'Here, have some wine.' Before Stephen could demur, his employer signalled the waitress for another glass and another bottle of the same vintage. The young woman presented the bottle for Pease's appraisal and uncorked it with a flourish and a satisfying pop.

Pease sniffed the cork ostentatiously. 'Try this, Stephen. The Cabernet from Mendocino County was very good in ninety-three; I think you'll enjoy it.' He raised his glass and Stephen, rather awkwardly, did the same.

'Er, cheers, Mr Pease. Thank you.'

'Bottoms up! And call me Hiram. We're out of the office now. No need to stand on formality. In a place like this, we're all men together.' Pease accompanied this last remark with a sly grin and a man-to-man wink. 'Look at these waitresses, Stephen,' he continued, warming to his theme. 'And those rare bits of arse propping up the bar. If you and me play our cards right, we could be sleeping with one of them, this evening. I bet those girls could show you a few things about Dallas you haven't experienced yet.'

Pease snorted his amusement into his glass. 'Yes, it'd do you good to go to bed with a real red-blooded Texas woman. They're not like your frigid southern belles from Atlanta.' Pease upended his glass and poured himself another in quick succession.

A new thought swam its way visibly across Pease's face as his alcohol-slowed brain grappled with something from his memory. He looked up at Stephen with another of his sly lascivious grins. 'But of course, my boy. I forgot. You don't need old Hiram to tell you about beautiful Texas blondes, do you?' He tapped his nose knowingly. 'I know what goes on in my studio, and some little birdie told me that you and Beth-Ann are more than friends. In fact, this little birdie told me that the pair of you fuck like rabbits.' Pease gurgled in delight at his humour. One or two heads turned their way from other tables.

Stephen's embarrassment was obvious in his hesitant reply. 'Well . . . Mr Pease . . .'

'Hiram. Call me Hiram.'

'Well, yes . . . Hiram. Beth-Ann and I have dated a few times,' Stephen mumbled.

'Pah! *Dated?* Don't give me dated. Beth-Ann doesn't "date"! She fucks your socks off.' Pease's voice grew in volume.

Stephen was stunned into silence. More heads looked their way, some annoyed and some amused. 'Mr Pease . . . Hiram, perhaps –'

But Pease interrupted his young employee. 'I bet you're wondering how I know about Beth-Ann, aren't you, Stephen?' Pease mistook Stephen's silence for agreement. 'Do you want to know where those Godiva chocolates came from?' Pease stabbed his chest with his stubby forefinger. 'From me. They came from me. And do you know why? Eh? Do you know why?'

Stephen gripped the arms of his chair, and made to rise.

Pease grabbed him by the arm and pushed him back in his seat. 'Don't leave yet. I'm just coming to the best part.'

Stephen subsided back into his armchair. At that moment, the waitress appeared at his elbow and refilled his empty glass. He smiled a weak thank you.

'I'll tell you exactly how Beth-Ann got those chocolates, Stephen.' Pease lowered his voice and leant forward confidentially. 'She lay buck naked on my desk and masturbated with a vibrator. That was after I fucked her rigid, but she's an insatiable bitch. But boy, does she give a great blow-job. One of the best in Dallas. And I should know. Every day, just like clockwork.' Pease grinned with pride at his sexual accomplishments.

Pease switched his sexual monologue to the brunette artist. 'Now, my little Tanya, she's different. You always know where you stand with Beth-Ann: fifty bucks a blow and it goes up from there. But Tanya, little Miss High-and-fucking-mighty Trevino, she's sneakier.' Pease paused, organising his thoughts amid the haze of alcohol. He took another swig of the excellent Cabernet, swirling it round his mouth and swallowing it with a large burp. Stephen winced at the waste of good wine.

'Stephen, take a piece of advice from someone who's been round a bit, you know what I'm saying?' Pease put his arm around Stephen in a burst of besotted benevolence. 'I can tell you, man to man, I've screwed my share of beautiful women.' He barked a short laugh, completed by a hiccup. 'I was going to get my way with pretty little Tanya, too. There we were, all at dinner . . .' He struggled to get Stephen in focus. 'You were there. Do you know what she did to me?' Pease's tone was now one of hurt misunderstanding. 'We had this agreement, see? I said I wouldn't stand in her way with those damn film people.' Pease paused momentarily to reflect on the perfidy of his former partners, 'I paved the way for her, but hey, one favour deserves another, and I said, "Let's get to know each other better." And do you know what she did? Do you know what that little bitch did?'

Stephen shook his head.

'She played all lovey-dovey at first, put her hands right here, on my dick.' Pease pointed at his groin, and patted himself, as if to ensure his penis was still in place. 'She pulled my pants down, played with my dick, got me all excited and then she just upped and left.'

Pease seemed baffled by the memory of this rejection, but then his face hardened. 'Worst of all, that little bitch lied about me to McNally and Sorensen, and they've backed out on the deal. *My* deal.'

Stephen stood up. 'I don't want to hear any more, Mr Pease,' he said, not caring who eavesdropped. 'You're drunk, and you should just go home and sleep it off. I've heard Tanya's side of that sordid little story, and I believe her. You were just trying to force her to sleep with you in return for giving her the credit she deserves for *Katrina Cortez*. That was a lousy thing to do. Now, if you'll excuse me, I must be going.'

Pease's voice stopped him in his tracks. 'She's a lesbian, you know.' There was a trace of drunken triumph in the older man's voice. 'Your fancy girlfriend's a lesbian.'

Stephen flung himself back into his seat and gripped Pease by the arm. 'What the hell do you mean? Who's a lesbian?'

A slow smile spread over Pease's face. 'Got you there, didn't I? You know who I mean. Precious little Tanya is a lezzie!' He cackled drunkenly.

'How do you know she's a lesbian?' He shook Pease roughly.

Pease smiled an aggravating little smile, and took his time answering. 'Just ask Carmen,' he said slyly. 'She knows.'

'You mean Tanya and Carmen . . .' Stephen couldn't finish the sentence.

Pease was gloating now. 'Yes, that's exactly what I mean. Only last Sunday I caught them both at it, in the CowGirl Club. They're all lesbians there,' he said disdainfully, warming to his tale. He could see he had Stephen's full attention. 'I walked right in on them. There they were, together, panties off, legs wide apart, masturbating for each other.' With gleeful exaggeration, Pease continued, 'Oh, boy, were they going at it, screaming at the top of their little lezzie voices!'

Before he knew what he was doing, Stephen swung back his right arm and planted his fist firmly in Pease's slack face. His employer slid from the chair and crumpled to the floor, with a look of stupefaction. 'You're despicable, Pease. You're a complete and utter bastard!' Stephen's furious exclamation fell into the deafening silence of the club's lounge. 'I quit! You can keep your fucking job! And you can keep Dallas, too.' He glared around the bar, daring anyone to stand in his way, and stalked from the room.

As soon as his feet hit the pavement outside, Stephen started to run, without direction, anywhere to get away from this terrible place and that disgusting man. But his brain kept repeating Pease's drunken singsong giggle from his seat on the floor, mindlessly nursing his bruised cheek. *Couple little lezzies. Couple little lezzies.*

When Stephen calmed down sufficiently to think straight, he took the trolley back to his car, and drove home like an automaton, paying little attention to his surroundings. Bitterly, he totted up his accomplishments from his few weeks in Dallas. He worked for a foul-mouthed creep – no, correction, he *had* worked for Pease;

that punch in the mouth had been a resignation in no uncertain terms. He had been sleeping with a girl who gave paid blow-jobs to the boss on a daily basis; and the woman he had fallen in love with was a lesbian. He knew of course she wasn't, but it must mean that she was bisexual. Like many males, Stephen had fantasies about girls going down on girls but, in the context of his feelings for Tanya, this only confirmed the woman's sexual wantonness, and her lack of interest in a stable relationship. She would obviously rather be Katrina Cortez than Tanya Sinclair.

Stephen wasted no time in further deliberations, and packed his clothing and the few personal belongings he'd brought with him into the storage boxes he'd used on his journey from Atlanta. He would load his car first thing in the morning, and drive over to see his sister in Atlanta. She'd put him up for a few days, while he sorted out what to do with his life.

He looked around his spartan little house. He wouldn't miss Dallas, and he certainly wouldn't miss Tanya Trevino.

Chapter Twenty-Three
Working Freelance

Tuesday passed for Tanya in a hangover daze: all she did was crawl into a cab and retrieve her car from Las Colinas. It was well into Wednesday before she finally rejoined the world. Even then, she felt detached from reality, both by her behaviour and by her complete absorption in the character of Katrina Cortez.

In some ways, Tanya rather liked transforming into 'the wild woman', and had enjoyed the enthusiastic responses of the restaurant revellers when she went topless. She laughed at the memory of the men falling over themselves to ogle her nude tits.

Her answering machine messages bore out this assessment of her admirers' lusts, although their compliments did not rise above the level of patronizing cliché.

'Tanya, baby, you were great!'

'Hey, *chica*, you and me, we make sweet music together, no? The next time you want to party, call your man Fernando.'

'Ms Trevino? You don't know me, but I saw you at the restaurant Monday night. You're the prettiest, sexiest woman I've ever seen!'

'I'd like to fuck. Call me!'

It's the thought that counts, mused Tanya wryly.

One message, however, snapped Tanya back to reality. Although friendly, Sheila Sorensen's recorded memorandum was underlaid with sternness. 'Tanya, we had a good time last night. I enjoyed it.' The executive made a seamless transition from sex to business. 'I hope you haven't forgotten the Tuesday deadline for preliminary storyboards. I look forward to seeing them on schedule.'

'Yeah, yeah, yeah,' muttered Tanya. 'I'll have your fucking drawings; you don't have to push me.' She remembered the delicious sensation of Sheila's tongue lapping at her clitoris: now this brusque business tone. The producer was one strange lady.

Tanya quickly showered, wolfed down a grapefruit and, clad only in a long T-shirt of black silk, settled down in the large bay of her living room where her drawing table was illuminated by morning sun slicing in the side windows. Wincing at the brightness, Tanya angled the wooden blinds to cut the glare.

Flipping through her sketchbooks, Tanya made notes and jottings on a larger pad. She worked steadily for several hours, until dissatisfied with a detail, she pushed her sketches aside. Standing, she lifted two illustrated volumes from her shelves, *Phoebe Zeit-Geist* and *Omaha the Cat Dancer*.

Amid the pages of the Cat Dancer's adventures, Tanya found a hedonistic scene depicting Omaha, the sexy female 'cat-human', climaxing under the tongue of her girlfriend Joanne, who in turn was being rampantly mounted by Omaha's human-tabby boyfriend Chuck. These explicit figures writhed against a jet-black background, occasionally punctuated with realistic definition of their surroundings.

Tanya made some jottings of her own and switched her attention to Phoebe Zeit-Geist, another comic-book heroine, whose adventures were often undertaken in complete nudity and bordered on the supernatural.

Suddenly a shock ran through her body and, with a start, she dropped her pencil.

Vividly, she recalled Stephen Sinclair standing beside her drawing board in Studio V, his arousal physically apparent. Tanya could hear his voice in her head commenting on her Katrina Cortez drawings: 'Sort of *Omaha the Cat Dancer* meets Dashiell Hammett and *Phoebe Zeit-Geist?*' Closing her eyes, Tanya could imagine his shy smile and guileless soft-blue eyes. With a clarity worthy of Proust and his Madeleine, Tanya recalled the love-making that had resulted from their spontaneous mutual lust. She recalled the gorgeous details of Stephen Sinclair's body, the slight uplift of his penis, the veins along his shaft, the lovely full purple tip, and the warmth and tenderness of his hands.

Quivering with lust, Tanya leant back in her chair and splayed open her legs, propping her feet on her drawing board. She lifted the hem of her T-shirt to finger her mons. From her second-floor vantage point she stared wide-eyed, not seeing the people and cars in the street below her window. She caressed her stiffening bud, allowing memories of Stephen to fill her mind from a reservoir of repressed recollections. The intensity of these thoughts unleashed a torrent of desire, and she came in only a few short moments, with tremors of such force they left her breathless.

Sitting slumped at her board, Tanya tried in vain to reorganise her thoughts, but her concentration was shot for the day. She could think of nothing but Stephen Sinclair, and how much she wanted to see him. She didn't care about his behaviour with Beth-Ann, nor about her own doubts that had pushed him away. She just wanted him. A glance at the clock told her that Stephen should be home from Studio V in about an hour. She showered again, freshening herself; her greatest desire at that instant was to feel Stephen's cock inside her.

Mindful of Katrina, she dressed in her new skimpy black clothes that matched her recently dyed hair. She wore no underwear, and her sensual curves announced themselves provocatively. She wore patterned black ankle socks under short black leather boots and, for a final touch, she pulled on thin black leather fingerless gloves. Slinging a small black purse over her shoulder, she casually spiked her short cropped hair with the fingers of one hand and stepped out into the heat of the late afternoon.

Tanya drove fast through the late-afternoon traffic, taking chances, weaving, zigzagging across town, expertly wheeling towards Stephen's neighbourhood. Without her panties, she ground herself into the seat fabric, enjoying the texture of the material against her sensitive flesh. She felt in control again; she could easily find his place from his description. 'It's a crummy little house, three down from the corner of McCommas and Greenville,' he'd said. *No problemo*, thought Tanya.

Turning on to McCommas, Tanya looked for Stephen's car, but didn't see it. She checked her watch; he should have been home by now. She cruised slowly down the block, looking for a place to park and watch for his arrival. But what caught her eye instead was a small sign that took her breath away, and left her cold despite the warmth of the afternoon sun. She stamped on the brakes in the middle of the street.

At the edge of the front yard of 'the crummy little house', a cheap 'For Rent' sign was stuck in the dirt. The house looked empty, its windows blank. There was no comforting hum of an air-conditioner. Tanya's eyes roved wildly up and down the street, as if she might see him turn the corner. She ran to the dwelling and hammered on the door. She peered in the windows to see empty rooms, no furniture, no belongings of any kind. Panic rose in her throat, followed closely by anger. How could he do this to her? Now that she wanted him so badly, the stupid kid was gone!

Tanya's anger was supplanted in turn by a deep and aching sense of loss, which she instantly tried to repress. Katrina Cortez wouldn't get sad, she'd get even! Tanya snapped the catch of the glove compartment and grabbed the portable car phone. Plugging it in the power socket, she dialled Carmen's home number. To her relief, her friend answered.

'Tanya! How are you? Where are you?' Eagerness and anxiety competed in Carmen's voice. Anxiety won.

Tanya ignored her friend's questions. 'Where's Stephen?' she demanded. 'I'm at his house, but it's empty. He's gone!'

The worry in Carmen's tone deepened. 'Tanya, Stephen has left Dallas. He had a row with Pease, on Tuesday night after work. He hit Pease! I don't know the details, but he dashed in first thing this morning and grabbed his things. He threw a letter on Pease's desk, and stormed out again. He said he'd had enough, was quitting, couldn't stay another day. He left me a post office box number in Atlanta to forward his mail. Then he was gone.'

'Did he . . . say anything about me? Or leave me a message?'

'No, *chicita*, no. He said a funny thing about *us* though; he said he hoped we'd be very happy. He looked sad and angry. Then he stamped out. Beth-Ann was *furiosa!* She went screaming into Pease's office. But being the boss man's whore really pays dividends. Pease has promoted Beth-Ann to be his personal assistant. I think it's to keep her quiet.' Carmen's voice held a strange bitterness in contrast to her usual good humour.

Tanya's blood alternately froze and boiled at this bevy of news. But one thing stood out above all else: Stephen Sinclair was gone; vamoosed; decamped; fled. Just plain quit! 'Carmen,' she said, 'what do you think Stephen meant by our "being happy"? Do you think that bastard Pease told him about us being together at the club?'

Carmen's voice was resigned. 'That's all I can think of. Pease was really mad with you for turning Sorensen and McNally against him. He fired Fernando, too. He heard about something you did in his precious limo.' Carmen hesitated before continuing in a small angry voice. 'The bastard also fired me. Today was my last day.'

Tanya was stunned. 'He can't do that! What reason did he give?'

'You, *cara mia*, you. He said anybody who was your friend was infected with evil. I couldn't reason with him.'

'Wait there, Carmen,' she said. 'I'll drive over right now. What will you do for money? Will you be OK?'

'For a while,' Carmen replied. 'I'm not too worried. I can do more hours at the CowGirl Club, and Vivienne said I could dance if I wanted to. I can get more tips that way. It might even be fun.'

'Hold on. I'll be there in twenty minutes,' Tanya said. 'I've got to stop at the liquor store first.' She snapped off the phone.

'You don't look like Natalie Wood any more,' said Carmen, by way of greeting.

Tanya frowned. 'Is that the first thing you can say?' she asked.

'Well, it's the first thing I thought,' Carmen responded, gesturing for her friend to enter. They hugged each other and walked arm-in-arm into Carmen's tidy kitchen. 'I am glad to see you, *chicita*, but you are hollow-eyed and pale,' Carmen commented, appraising her friend.

'I'm not pale. I'm just not Latina. Let's drink,' said Tanya.

Tanya hefted a large bottle of finest Cuervo Gold Tequila on to the kitchen counter. 'You don't look different,' she said. 'Maybe getting away from Pease is the best thing that could happen to you.' Tanya looked squarely at her friend. 'Do you want me to see Pease? I've already got him fired from the movie deal, but I could get the word out about him; make things difficult for him.'

'No, gracias, carina,' murmured Carmen. 'I want to put it all behind me. I don't want to think of him ever again.'

Tanya and Carmen blended margaritas with shaved ice and increasingly large quantities of tequila, called in pizza, and drank to their shared misfortune. Tanya felt responsible for her friend's problems. 'I even feel sorry for Fernando. He was a great lay,' she confided. But most of all she felt sorry for herself. Beneath her façade of lust and braggadocio was a good old-fashioned desire for one man: her man. The one who was gone.

Carmen rested on the sofa, listening to Tanya swear she'd forgo every man she'd had sex with in exchange for one more chance with Stephen Sinclair. 'Carmen, I'm cursing myself for being a fool to let him go, for allowing Beth-Ann to throw a spanner into my own little paradise.' Tanya gave a bitter little laugh. 'I must be getting drunk. I'm mixing up my metaphors.'

But Carmen, exhausted, was asleep. It was past midnight when Tanya gently tucked a light blanket over her friend. She locked the front door behind her and walked outside. The soft summer air did little to sober her, and she drove erratically back to her apartment. Luckily, none of Dallas's finest were patrolling her neighbourhood.

The alcohol had softened Tanya's hurt for the evening but, in the light of morning, her pain flared forth again. A myriad of gloomy thoughts roiled in her fevered brain all day, and the next day, and the days and nights after that. She slept little, dividing her time between drawing in the studio and working out in the gym. She ate whatever was at hand, whenever the mood took her. The bottle of tequila was her constant companion. A week without sun faded her normal tan, and her complexion became wan and pale.

Despite her frantic pace, Tanya produced little work to her satisfaction. Stephen Sinclair became a constant inhabitant of her most sensual fantasies, and she began drawing the chestnut-haired man into the comic strip, where she depicted him making love to Katrina at every opportunity. But none of these drawings were quite right, not quite up to her increasingly perfectionist standards, and though her Tuesday deadline with Ganymede drew near and then passed, Tanya trashed the sketches again and again.

In the middle of one drawing blitz, the phone rang. It was Sheila Sorensen. 'Tanya? I was expecting the drawings today. They were really due yesterday. Have you got them?'

Tanya fumbled for an excuse. 'No . . . not exactly. They're coming together but it's slow. I want it to be just right.'

Sorensen was exasperated. 'How long am I going to have to wait for it to be "just right"?'

'I don't know. I'm not a bloody machine!'

Sheila kept her voice calm with exaggerated patience. 'Don't snap at me, Tanya. I pay your fees, remember?' She waited for Tanya's acknowledgement.

'Yes, Sheila. Sorry.'

'Right. Now let's be realistic. You've missed this deadline. I'm going to give you another one. Seven days. One hundred and sixty-eight hours.' Sorensen's tone was firm; it brooked no compromise. 'We really like your work, but if you can't do this we'll have to give it to someone who can. You have seven days to get the boards to us, or your contract is terminated. Do you understand?'

Tanya put the phone down silently. Seven days!

She cast aside all her dreamy attempts to depict Stephen Sinclair fucking Katrina Cortez in the urban jungle, unplugged the phone, and got to work. She answered the door to no one, and went out only at night to scour the alleys and bars of the city's sleazier neighbourhoods. She avoided contact and conversations; her only companions were her sketchbooks, into which she poured a fevered array of characters and stories, filled with angst and pessimism.

'The Urban Castle,' wrote Tanya on a fresh page. In her drawing, Dallas was reborn as a post-modern Gotham City on steroids, a glitzy and decadent urban compound of corruption. In bitter contrast to this shiny yet tawdry world of wealth, avarice and sex, creatures barely human lurked in the shadows of the city's dark and dank undercroft of filth, corruption and squalor.

Katrina Cortez strode through this desperate degeneration, unrepentantly sacrificing human pawns to their fates in her mission to crush Pete Regan. This was no longer a police operation to Katrina. This was a personal vendetta. Two particular characters, rejected flotsam cast up by the savage tide of lawlessness and greed that swept this alternative metropolis, were none other than fictional counterparts of Beth-Ann Bodine and Hiram Pease. Lemming-like, the hapless pair, increasingly courted by ruination, found themselves at the mercy of Pete Regan, the heartless drug baron. Beth-Ann and Pease were drawn by Tanya's pen as the evil man's flunkies, used for the devil's errands and for amusement.

Originally cast in Tanya's brutal sketches as a vain and seedy businessman, operating on the edge of the law, Pease in cartoon form became ensnared in the cartel. Encouraged by the undercover agent's sly promptings and promises of 'quick and easy money', Pease made several bad deals and his fortunes plummeted. Plundering his own business accounts for cash, in desperation he turned to Katrina for help.

Katrina used her blatant sex-appeal with devilish

delight, dressing up as the Black Widow of Death. Masked, and all in black, save bare white breasts, rouged nipples and red-painted lips, she exploited Pease's weaknesses to double-cross both him and Regan, cleverly entwining them in her web of chicanery.

Having dropped her former boss from her affections early in his progress to penury, Beth-Ann spent most days in Regan's office, splayed upon his desk or kneeling naked in a familiar pose between his legs. She was rewarded not in fancy chocolates and crisp bills but in lines of cocaine, which Regan doled out stingily for her sexual services.

Pitilessly, Tanya portrayed the fantasy Beth-Ann as out of work and on the street, reduced to stripping in Regan's clubs to earn enough money for rent and food. Drugs and disease took their toll. The once-buxom blonde became thin, even emaciated, her formerly fulsome figure sagging in a catenary of despair. She lost the rapacious sexual sparkle that had trapped so many men in her carnal snare; she was relegated to warm-up acts on seedy stages. Her future looked indefinite. And short.

The imaginary Pease fared worse. Ruthlessly, Katrina exposed his duplicity to Regan. The doomed fool lived only long enough to flee the drug lord's thugs down a dead-end alley where he was beaten senseless and left to die in a garbage dumpster.

From the darkness of the alley came a piercing flash. A hand-held flashlight illuminated the nipple ring embellishing Katrina's right breast as she walked silent and semi-naked from the shadows to gaze at the body of the man she hated. The ring contained a minuscule electronic homing device inside the large false diamond that glittered so dramatically; when activated, the signal enabled the drug task-force commander to monitor his agent's whereabouts.

Katrina impatiently unfastened the silver circlet from

her breast, heedless of the stab of pain in her sensitive flesh. She switched on the device and tossed it contemptuously into the dumpster; before too long the police would notice the unusually stationary signal and investigate. She wrote Regan's name and secret address on a scrap of paper, slipped it into a small bag of cocaine and, bending over the body, placed the bag in Pease's pocket. Taking from her purse a fragment of cloth ripped from Regan's favourite suit just hours before, she placed it between Pease's clenched and nerveless fingers.

'Goodbye, Hiram, you miserable bastard,' she sneered, staring down at the forlorn and crumpled body. 'And goodbye soon to you too, Mr High-and-fucking-Mighty Regan.' She raised her eyes to the upper reaches of a dark forbidding office building that loomed over the alley. 'You deserve each other. Let the cops put two and two together and get five.' She bared her teeth in a predatory smile. It was nearly over.

Katrina stood at the window of a corner office in an anonymous suite on the thirtieth floor of the same dark tower flanking Central Expressway. The tinted glass imparted a morbid hue to the night-time landscape of metropolitan activity on the streets and alleys far below.

In the dim light Katrina perched on the edge of her companion's large desk, deliberately teasing him with a lingering glimpse of her breasts, bare beneath her dark pinstripe jacket. With its flared shoulders and cinched waist, the double-breasted lightweight wool garment matched her trimly tailored skirt. High-heeled suede slingbacks – black, of course – completed her outfit. Just one hour ago, the detective had cast aside her alley cat's garb in favour of this chic seductive ensemble, but she had the feeling she would be naked by the conclusion of her plan.

She knew that Regan kept this enclave secret from all but his most trusted associates. He listened as she said,

'Now we've got rid of Pease, we can move ahead with the next shipment.'

Sensing the man's unease, Katrina calmed his fears. 'You can trust me, Pete. It was necessary to rid ourselves of that slimeball. He had no business knowing what he did, and he'd have blabbed all over the city.' She spoke slowly for emphasis. 'If I'd wanted to hurt you, I could have taken that information to the cops, or to one of your rivals.' She smiled without humour. Regan had never realised it was she who tipped off the cops to arrest his Mexican counterpart at the airport. She continued, 'There are plenty of folks out there who would only be too glad to see the great Pete Regan brought to his knees, or worse.' And I'm one of them, you bastard! she gloated silently.

Katrina switched on the desk lamp, girding them both in a tight halo of amber, and the walls of the room receded to their crepuscular margins. The drama unfolded in the centre of the space as Katrina unbuttoned her jacket, letting it fall open to expose her breasts. Regan moved close, to caress the porcelain flesh, to bring her nipples to instant arousal.

'I can give you more pleasure than any of your other women, Pete,' she whispered. 'You don't need them now you've got me.' She stroked Regan's fast-rising dick. 'Let's fuck,' she breathed in his ear, shrugging her jacket to the floor and wriggling out of her skirt. She wore no panties and revelled in her nakedness. 'I want to come,' she hissed. 'I want to come and think of Pease's body rotting in that dumpster!' Vampire-like, Katrina's dark indigo-blue eye shadow emphasised her hollowed black eyes set deep in their sockets, implacable, merciless and predatory.

Katrina smiled at Regan as he threw his suit jacket on top of the growing pile of discarded clothing. He hadn't noticed the tear. Nor was he paying much attention to the screaming police sirens heading up Central Expressway. Katrina reckoned she had about five minutes. She consumed Regan's cock inside her with a mirthless growl of satisfaction.

'These are great, Tanya!' Sheila Sorensen was euphoric. 'This is just what we had in mind. Hell no, it's better!' She laughed, and paced around her office, gesticulating energetically, excitement flowing to her fingers like Frankenstein's sparks. 'Just wait till poor old Pease sees this in the movie. Of course, we'll change the character a little, and the name, to protect ourselves legally, but it serves that selfish prick right for trying to cheat us on the deal.' She stopped her perambulations and studied Tanya thoughtfully. 'I knew you didn't like him, or that silly tramp Beth-Ann. But I didn't know you hated them.'

Tanya stared back, unblinking and unrepentant. 'Haven't you ever hated anybody for what they did to you?'

Sorensen looked uncomfortable. 'Yes, but . . .'

'Then you know what it's like. I was taught to love my enemies, and forgive the people who did me wrong,' Tanya sneered. 'But that's strictly for losers. The only thing that matters is getting even, and that slimy bastard and his slut deserve every bad thing I could wish on them, and more!'

With her dark flashing eyes and heavy make-up, her chopped black hair and her minuscule black outfit, the artist looked every inch the figure of Katrina Cortez. 'We're not doing Quentin Tarantino, dear,' Sheila commented dryly.

But Tanya merely shrugged and crossed her legs so that her black denim micro-skirt rode higher, exposing a long portion of thigh. Tanya's wardrobe *de jour* was completed by calf-length black suede boots with three-inch stacked heels and a thin black halter top that displayed her jutting breasts.

'I'll call our finance department immediately, Tanya,'

Sheila said, 'and authorise payment of your full fee straight away. You won't have to wait the usual thirty days, and all that nonsense. You can pick up the cheque later today.'

Tanya merely nodded and yawned insolently.

'This work is superb and shocking. Yes, shocking. But superb! Right on target. I'll activate the bonus clause in the contract, too, my dear.'

Tanya's eyes flickered, her air of cool detachment faltering. 'Thank you, Sheila. This was the hardest thing I've ever done. But I want to do more. I've got all sorts of ideas for sequels!' Her voice rose in excitement.

Sorensen caught a glimpse of the fresh young artist she had met only a few short weeks ago, before the mask snapped back into place, freezing Tanya's beautiful features into their cynical caste. Her eyes once more were bleak and cold, as if she regretted the brief flash of humanity.

'We'll do more projects together, Tanya. We'll want you to work with the screenwriters to develop the screenplay. I want the finished film to look exactly like these drawings,' Sheila said, brandishing the sheets in the air. 'They're frightening, but beautiful. This is going to be brilliant.' Sorensen studied the calendar on her desk. 'Call me tomorrow for a meeting with Joshua to discuss this in detail.' She paused and added, 'Tanya, girl, you did good!'

This down-home pleasantry left no mark on Tanya's controlled features. She nodded coolly and headed for the door. 'Till tomorrow, Sheila. I'll collect my cheque this afternoon.' And she was gone.

Chapter Twenty-Four
Desperately Seeking Stephen

Carmen studied Tanya's copies of the new drawings. Putting them down, she sat back and regarded her friend, who sprawled provocatively across the down-stuffed velvet-covered cushions strewn on the old but sturdy sofa. Tanya was garbed as usual in a minimal black outfit, today's version comprising merely a black silk tank-top cut short to display her trim waist, and a denim mini-skirt that revealed her lean hard-muscled thighs. In deference to Carmen's furniture, Tanya's black leather boots lay discarded to one side. An empty bottle of white Caymus vineyards' *Conundrum* stood up-ended in a makeshift ice bucket.

When Carmen spoke, it was with a mixture of admiration and admonition. 'Tanya, these are beautiful and well drawn,' she said, 'and I can see why they went over so well with *Señora* Sorensen and *Señor* McNally. But *chicita*, they scare me! They are so, so . . . *aspero*, so harsh, unforgiving. That bastard Pease can burn in hell, but you are too cruel to Beth-Ann.'

Tanya was unrepentant. 'Ha! That bitch deserves everything she gets. She sabotaged my relationship with Stephen, and messed up my drawings. All the time she was fucking Pease for money on the side. Probably other men, too. No wonder she could afford that new car and fancy apartment.'

Tanya's eyes shone with a wild glare. 'But now I've got the money and the credit I deserve. *Katrina Cortez* is successful, and this movie will make me rich. I'll rub Pease's face in the dirt, with his lousy "fuck me" deals. That chubby little whore Beth-Ann and Pease will be the laughing stock of Dallas. Thanks to Katrina Cortez, everyone will know about them.'

'No. Not due to Katrina. Due to you.' Carmen's voice rose in vexation and passion. 'These drawings have consumed you; Tanya, you are not Katrina. She is just a cartoon; she is not real. You cannot live like this, without love, thinking only of sex and money. When you dump dirt on people like *Señor* Pease and Beth-Ann, you become no better than they are.'

Tanya was not dissuaded by her friend's outburst. 'You can't count on love in this life, Carmen. Everybody's out to screw everybody else. Sex and money make the world go round. Folks like you and me had better jump on for the ride while we can.' Tanya looked fiercely at her friend. 'Nobody loves us, so we might as well take what we can get: sex, money and recognition, in that order.'

'You're wrong, Tanya, dear silly, silly, Tanya. There is one person who loves you, and I know another does, too.'

Tanya's diatribe froze on her lips. She looked at Carmen as if seeing her for the first time. 'Who . . . loves me?' she asked, haltingly.

The pretty Hispanic woman looked down at her hands, smiling shyly. 'Tanya,' she said, 'I care about you deeply. Surely you know that.'

'You want to go to bed with me?' Tanya asked, a brazen smile slowly replacing her frown. 'I'd like that. I understand that. I like you too, you know.'

Carmen gave an impatient sigh. 'No, Tanya, that isn't what I mean. Just because I care for you doesn't mean I want to have sex with you. We've done some wild things together, and I like sex just as much as you do.' She smiled a slow conspiratorial smile. 'But I wouldn't want to get into a tug-of-war with the man you need in your life, especially right now.'

'Ha! Stephen, you mean.' Tanya gave a dismissive snort.

'Don't be so hasty,' replied her friend. 'It wasn't just Beth-Ann and Pease who drove Stephen away from Dallas. It was you, too.'

'Me? *I* drove him away? What do you mean?'

'He really cared for you, Tanya, but Katrina Cortez scared him off. He saw that side of your personality taking over. Rampant sex and a "fuck you" attitude do not sustain a relationship. Surely you know that?'

At Tanya's silence, Carmen continued, 'Come Tanya, *carina*. You talk so rough, so harsh, but underneath this aggression you are not Katrina. You made her hard and sexy and she became a success, but that doesn't mean you have to be so hard, so nasty. Yes, *Madre de Dios*, so nasty! Where's your softness gone?' Carmen looked deeply into Tanya's eyes with an unblinking stare.

The younger woman's voice broke with emotion. 'If I'm as nasty as you say, why do you love me?' She swung back to face Carmen.

'Tanya, my dear friend, *you* are not nasty! I want *you* back: not this lost soul in black.' Carmen reached to touch her companion's face, which was suddenly streaked with tears. Carmen embraced the younger woman affectionately. '*Calmate, chicita,*' she said. 'Calm down, my sweet. It is late, and you're in no condition to drive home. You must stay here tonight. There's only one bed, and we have to share it. But we lie together as friends, not as lovers. This is a lesson for you, I think. Come, let's get undressed.'

Carmen led a more docile Tanya by the hand into the bedroom, where she took off her own clothes quickly, and wrapped herself in a robe. She handed its twin to Tanya. 'You undress while I use the bathroom, and then it's all yours,' she said simply.

Through a mist of tears, Tanya nodded dumbly. As she undressed, she heard water running. Suddenly, Tanya's façade crumbled, and her body was rent by a series of racking sobs. She ran into the bathroom, and buried her face in her friend's shoulder. 'Oh, Carmen. I've been such a fool!' Her tears coursed down her cheeks and trickled over Carmen's breasts.

'Oh, Tanya, Tanya, *querida,*' murmured Carmen. Standing firm, she stroked her friend's cropped black hair. 'It's time for bed,' she said softly. 'Let's talk about it some more in the morning. *El sol*, he will make us all feel better, no?'

Carmen gently led Tanya to the bed, and they lay still, except for Carmen's soothing caresses and Tanya's muffled sobs. Before long, Tanya's breathing became quiet and regular. Carmen leant over and bestowed a soft kiss on the woman's cheek. 'Good night, Tanya,' she whispered. 'You silly, silly girl.'

Carmen woke only once during the night, to find Tanya curled against her like a child, lips against her breast. With a smile, Carmen closed her eyes. Tomorrow she would help Tanya start putting her life back together.

The sun was indeed shining brightly the following morning and Carmen suggested they had breakfast outdoors, on the apartment's semi-sheltered wooden deck. They set a simple table, and consumed toast and coffee in companionable silence. The tensions of the night before had eased, and Carmen was pleased to see that Tanya's spirits had lightened considerably. Across the table, her friend relaxed in the sun, face tilted up, eyes closed, the borrowed robe fallen open, exposing the tops of her shapely breasts to the tanning rays.

Carmen was wearing only an old T-shirt, and her own pert breasts were clearly visible beneath it. The deeply scooped neckline was loose and too big to stay on her round shoulders. Tanya's voice cut through her lazy thoughts. 'Carmen, your nipples are nearly poking through your shirt,' she said. 'Why don't you just take it off?'

Carmen inched the baggy neckline downwards, revealing most of one breast. 'I thought your eyes were closed!' she said accusingly.

Tanya smiled. 'I've been watching you watching me.'

Carmen stretched like a tawny pussycat. 'I love being in the sun,' she said. 'It cheers me up.' With a swift movement, she drew the baggy shirt over her head and tossed it on to a vacant chair. 'If you are sad, *amiga mia*, just let the sun get to your tits! The neighbours, they have left for work. No one will see.'

Carmen relaxed for a few moments longer, and then sat up, a business-like look in her eye. 'Alas, Tanya, we have to sort some things out.'

Tanya grimaced. She put down the cup. 'Now? It's such a lovely morning.'

But Carmen was not to be dissuaded from her self-appointed task. 'To my way of thinking, the most important thing to do is to locate *Señor* Steve,' she said, turning in the chair to retain the sun on her breasts. She donned her sunglasses, and said in a firm tone, 'Listen up; now listen carefully to *Tia* Carmen.'

This brought a glimmer of a smile to Tanya's face. 'You're some auntie, sitting there showing off your tits!'

'Like in the Green Room, eh? When *Señor* Pease walked in,' Carmen cupped her breasts theatrically and swivelled her torso back and forth, pouting her lips in an exaggerated kiss. 'You like my tits, no? Your Auntie Carmen can be very naughty!'

Tanya burst out in a giggle, which became a full-throated laugh, and she leant back in her chair, a large grin spreading like the sunshine across her face. Carmen's face lit up to match, and she reached to grasp Tanya's hands in hers, holding them tightly across the chequered tablecloth.

'Oh, *chicita*, it is a long time since I heard you laugh. It is good to see you smile. You are a beautiful woman, and it's wrong for that face of yours to be scrunched up in a scowl.' She patted Tanya's hands and released them, her expression more grave, but her eyes still twinkled sexily. 'Now, we must be serious for a little while, and you must listen. And not interrupt,' she added sternly.

Tanya nodded acquiescence.

'Young Stephen does care about you, I know he does.' Carmen raised her hand to forestall Tanya's question. 'Let's be realistic. Your situation is far from being the mess you describe. You must not think such foolish things, Tanya. Be honest with yourself about what is good and what is not so good; then we can start to sort your problems out.'

'But I –'

'No questions!' Carmen's playful slap turned into a lingering squeeze of Tanya's wrist. 'Now,' Carmen continued purposefully, 'let's make a list of the good things and the bad things.' Tanya nodded silently. 'First you are beautiful, even if you have messed up your lovely hair.' Carmen grimaced, and ran her fingers through Tanya's chopped and dyed hair. 'I want to help you get back to being the Tanya I love and *Señor* Stephen loves, but there will always be a little bit of Katrina in you.' Sitting upright, Carmen made a dismissive gesture with her hand. 'Come. Let me finish my list; things like your hair are minor worries.'

Tanya stood and stepped off the deck. She spread the robe on the grass and lay on it naked, soaking up the morning sun. 'I'm listening,' she said. 'Carry on.'

'OK. First, you are beautiful and sexy; that we know. Second, there is a lovely man who is very attracted to you. Third,' she persisted, before Tanya could say anything, 'you have just finished some very good work; fourth, your colleagues loved it and you got paid in full, with a bonus. And fifth –' Carmen held up her hand with fingers spread wide, tapping her thumb with the index finger of her other hand '– your colleagues want more work, giving you the prospect of continued employment. Am I right, so far?' Carmen thrust her chin forward and glared at Tanya, as if daring her to disagree.

Tanya grinned. 'Right so far,' she agreed.

'Good. Those are the good things. Now let's count the bad ones.'

Tanya's smile faltered. 'I can start that list,' she said. 'Stephen Sinclair. I don't know where he is, and I don't really know what he thinks about me.'

'True, we don't know where he is,' agreed Carmen. 'He left only a box number at the post office, in Atlanta. Studio V has no phone number or address for him.' She didn't seem too upset about it.

'And?' asked Tanya, sensing there was more to come.

A coy smile curled the edges of Carmen's mouth. 'You could, of course, just write to him, and hope he answers.' She sensed Tanya's impatience and continued. 'But no, *Tia* Carmen has a better idea.' She paused for effect. 'Stephen has a sister in Atlanta, who runs an art gallery, remember?'

'Of course!' exclaimed Tanya, and jumped up from the grass. 'He might even be staying with her.' Tanya ran naked into the apartment and grabbed the telephone directory from a side table. Carmen picked up their discarded clothing and followed her indoors.

Tanya turned quickly to the Yellow Pages under 'A' and ran a finger down the art gallery listings. 'Umm. Nothing under Sinclair. That would have been too easy.

But there are only about thirty art galleries listed here. It shouldn't be too difficult to track down Ms Sinclair.'

Tanya sat down at the table and avidly perused the list. 'Bamberg Gallery, Dalton Gallery, Georgia State Gallery, Ginger Root Gallery . . .' She paused. 'Now why would anyone call a gallery "Ginger Root", for heaven's sake! Oh, it's no good guessing which one it might be.' She tossed the heavy volume aside. 'I'll just have to call them all and ask ever-so-politely if a Ms Sinclair works there.' She looked at Carmen. 'Stephen never mentioned his sister's name, did he?'

Carmen frowned. 'Yes, come to think of it, he did. I remember thinking it was a nice name, something Biblical.'

Tanya tapped her finger impatiently against the side of her coffee mug. 'Mary? Ruth? Esther?'

Carmen shook her head. 'No, none of those. Give me a minute.'

But Tanya persisted. 'What other biblical women can we think of? Eve? Was it Eve?'

Carmen snapped her fingers. 'Got it,' she said proudly. 'It's not Eve, but that's close. It's Eden. Eden Sinclair.'

'Let's start calling right now!'

Carmen held up her hand in a gesture of caution. 'Not so fast,' she advised. 'Let's take some time and plan out what to ask. What would you say if you dialled one of these galleries and Stephen answered the phone?'

'You're right,' Tanya admitted with a rueful grin. 'If Stephen answered the telephone, I'd be like a tongue-tied teenager. I do need to get things straight in my head before I talk to him.' She poured herself another mug of Carmen's strong coffee. 'What if he won't speak to me?' Her expression was sober.

'Don't worry, be happy,' joked Carmen. 'You'd think of something. Back to our lists, remember? We got to number one on your bad side; there's plenty more to deal with. Now be still and pay attention.'

'Yes, Auntie Carmen,' said Tanya sheepishly, the grin back on her face.

'Tanya, admit it. While you've been acting wild for the past month or so, you've upset several people, and probably made some enemies, both professionally and personally. Pease has blackened your name all over town among his cronies. He's calling you a whore and a thief. Your reputation is bad news in some quarters.'

Tanya exploded. 'Talk about pots calling kettles black! He'll fuck anything that moves, but that's OK because he's a guy. I have some fun, and all of a sudden I'm a whore.' She scowled sulkily.

Again the voice of reason, Carmen scolded, 'Look, *novia*, sweetheart, there's no point in putting on your "poor little Tanya" act. You acted wild, and we want to make sure you don't mess up again.'

Watching her friend's reactions, Carmen continued, 'I want you back as my sexy Anglo friend Tanya, not as Katrina *la hechichera negro*. To act like a cartoon is bad for you. Katrina lives on the page, in the movies, but not in your heart.' She took both of Tanya's hands in her own. '*Cara mia*, look into my eyes. Promise me, your best friend, that you'll do as I say. Keep Katrina in your sketchbooks.'

The urgency in her voice obviously took Tanya by surprise, as tears sprang to her eyes. 'Oh, Carmen, why didn't I listen to you earlier?' Tanya cried. 'Yes, I promise. I promise with all my heart. I can't tell you how much I appreciate your love.'

The two women embraced, unheeding of their mutual nakedness. Carmen led Tanya to the bathroom and pulled back the shower curtain. 'Let's shower quickly and get dressed, *carina*,' she said, stepping into the small tub. 'You've got some fast talking to do.'

'Excuse me. I'm sorry to trouble you, but I'm trying to reach Eden Sinclair. Can you tell me if she works in your gallery? No? Do you know her gallery? OK. Thanks anyway. Bye . . . bitch!' Tanya mouthed the last word, put down the phone and crossed Bamberg Gallery off her list with a scowl. 'I hope they don't treat their customers like that,' she said. 'They were really rude.'

Carmen smiled from where she stood at the kitchen sink, washing their few breakfast dishes.

Tanya contemplated her friend, and felt a nagging stab of guilt. 'I've been so wrapped up in my own personal problems, Carmen. I haven't asked how you're faring since your departure from Studio V.'

'I still enjoy working at the CowGirl Club. It's OK.'

'Perhaps there'd be a better job with Sheila Sorensen or McNally for you. Would you be interested?'

'First find Stephen Sinclair,' replied Carmen. 'Then, we'll see.'

Giving Stephen top priority, Tanya dialled again. 'Hello. I'm trying to reach Eden Sinclair . . . Oh, she's with Ginger Root Gallery? Yes, I have their number. Thank you very much.'

Tanya swallowed hard. Carmen watched from the doorway, drying her hands. 'Good luck,' she said and blew a kiss.

Tanya's finger trembled as she punched the buttons. She misdialled, cursed and tried again. The phone in Atlanta rang for a moment before a pleasantly southern-accented voice answered, 'Good morning, Ginger Root Gallery. How may I help you?'

'Hello. My name's Trevino, and I'm trying to reach Eden Sinclair. Is she available, please?'

'Yes, she's here. May I tell her what it's about?'

'Umm . . . it's personal. Just say it's about her brother.'

There was a pause filled with Mozart and a new voice came on the line, precise and professional, but tinged with concern. 'Ms Trevino? I'm Eden Sinclair. How may I help you? You said it's about Stephen. Is he OK?'

'I don't know,' Tanya said. 'I was hoping you could tell me.'

'I'm sorry, I don't understand. Where are you calling from?' Was there a sharper tone to Eden Sinclair's voice?

'From Dallas.' Tanya thought she heard a soft sigh. Could it have been of relief?

'What do you want with Stephen?' Now Tanya was sure. There was a definite edge of hostility in the other woman's voice.

'Ms Sinclair, please bear with me a moment.' Tanya gulped and took the plunge. 'I'm a friend of Stephen's, or at least I was. We were lovers, but, well, I'm afraid I'm one of the reasons he left Dallas.'

Silence swallowed the distance. Tanya closed her eyes. Eden Sinclair could have been in the room with her. All Tanya could hear was the beating of her heart in her throat. 'Hello, Ms Sinclair?'

'Yes, Tanya. I'm here. Stephen told me . . . about you.'

Tanya clenched the phone at the unexpected use of her Christian name. Eden Sinclair's tone was softer, but what had Stephen told his sister?

In answer to the unspoken question, Eden Sinclair proceeded, 'I'm sure he didn't tell me everything, even though I am his big sister. But he told me two important things: you hurt him badly, and you still mean a lot to him.'

Tanya concentrated on finding the right words. 'Ms Sinclair, he's right. I mistreated him. He has every right to be mad at me.' An invisible dam broke inside her, and words tumbled breathlessly. 'I was a fool. I put my work above everything else to impress some people. I didn't see past my own selfish ambition. I just wanted credit for my art; my boss tried to seduce me and everything went berserk.'

Tanya continued, 'I liked Stephen. I broke up with my boyfriend, who threatened me, and Stephen was really brave; he protected me and gave Eric a bloody nose.' She paused, sweating, and heard a soft chuckle from the other end.

'Stephen didn't tell me that part! Go on.'

'I wanted Stephen and took him to bed. But when he tried to get close, I wanted to be the one in charge; I was wild and sexy and unrestrained, like . . .' She paused and looked helplessly towards Carmen.

'Yes?' Eden's voice floated over the wire.

'Like a cartoon version of a private investigator chick I draw . . . I sort of became this person, like a fantasy in my own mind.'

'Like Katrina Cortez, you mean?'

Tanya gasped out loud. Eden Sinclair laughed with a soft open sound. 'Oh, yes, Tanya,' she explained. 'I know your work. Stephen showed me some photocopies of your drawings. They're very good; very sexy, too.'

Tanya struggled to put her chaotic thoughts into coherent speech. 'Thank you,' she exclaimed. 'I appreciate your opinion. Are you an artist, too?'

'Oh yes, whenever I can get away from running the gallery. My husband and I share a studio together.'

Tanya thought it sounded wonderful to make art with the man you loved. 'What kind of work do you do?' she blurted.

'I used to do a lot of figurative painting, but recently I've gone back to abstraction. I still like to do figure studies, but I keep those sketches private.' The gallery owner laughed again. 'But now I've seen your work, perhaps I'll reconsider.'

Carmen was telegraphing frantically across the room. 'Get . . . the . . . address!' she mouthed.

Nodding, Tanya refocused her attention and addressed the phone. 'Ms Sinclair? Thank you for taking the time to speak with me. It's easier to talk to you than I expected. I'm anxious to reach Stephen, to tell him how sorry I am, to find out if he will speak to me. Do you have an address or a number where I could contact him? To reassure him that I'm Tanya again, and not Katrina.'

There was a pause at the other end. Tanya grew nervous again. Finally, Eden Sinclair said, 'All right. You seem very nice, and genuinely sorry. I've enjoyed talking with you, and I do really like your work.'

'Thanks, Ms Sinclair.'

'I must warn you, Tanya, he's still pretty bitter. I don't think he knows whether to love you or hate you. But he continues to think about you a lot.'

Tanya was thrilled and humbled at the same time. 'I've got a pencil right here,' she prompted.

'He's in Little Rock, Arkansas, working as a graphic artist for the firm of architects designing the Clinton Presidential Library, down by the Arkansas River.'

Tanya heard the rustle of pages turning. Eden's voice came back on the line. 'I can give you his work phone.' Eden dictated the information and Tanya eagerly scribbled it down. 'Thank you, Ms Sinclair,' she said. 'You don't know how much I appreciate this.'

Eden Sinclair laughed. 'Oh, I can guess! Good luck. Stephen is a good kid.' Her voice grew serious again, even stern. 'I'm trusting you to treat him right, this time.'

Tanya felt her cheeks burn with embarrassment, and was glad that Eden Sinclair couldn't see her. 'Yes, Ms Sinclair, I understand.' A moment passed before she added, 'I hope Stephen will forgive my stupidity. Thank you for your help and encouragement.'

'Give him my love when you speak to him. Oh, and call me Eden next time. All this "Ms Sinclair" stuff makes me feel old!' The phone went dead with a click, and Tanya was left sitting on Carmen's sofa, a foolish grin on her face.

Chapter Twenty-Five
Epiphany

'Well, what did she say? What was she like, this sister of *Señor* Steve?' Carmen questioned, 'Why is he in Little Rock, of all places? Arkansas? Pouf! There is nothing there.'

Tanya laughed. 'Spoken like a true Texan, Carmen.' But she saw her friend's expression transform into one of worry. 'What's wrong?'

'Just that I'm *not* a Texan! My immigration status is a worry, Tanya,' she said. 'Now I work only at the CowGirl Club, I do not have a sponsor for my Green Card. My visa expires soon, and I want to live here permanently. Hiram Pease was going to be my sponsor, but when he fired me, all that went down the tubes. I don't think the Immigration people will approve of me working in a place like the CowGirl Club. I may have to become illegal. I certainly don't want to be sent back home.'

Tanya slapped her head in annoyance. 'See, I'm doing it again. I'm so wrapped up in my own business that I completely forget about your problems. But I have an idea. My stock is pretty high with McNally and Sorensen, right now; everybody's so crazy about Katrina Cortez. I can ask them if they have an opening for you, and even if they'll sponsor you with the Immigration and Naturalization Service.'

'Oh, *chicita*, that would be wonderful! Let me get my resumé.' Carmen jumped up and ran to the adjacent room, returning a moment later. 'This will tell them what I can do,' she said, thrusting a slim document into Tanya's hand. 'It's got all my business experience on it.'

Tanya picked up the phone again. 'I'll call them now, before I try Stephen. Actually,' Tanya admitted, 'now I can get hold of him, I'm nervous. I'm glad of the excuse to put phoning him off for a little while,' she said, and opened her handbag. Reading the publisher's number from her diary, she punched the buttons.

'Joshua? It's Tanya . . . Doing just great. And yourself? . . . Good. No, there's no trouble. I just need to ask you a favour. I might be doing you a favour, too.' Succinctly, Tanya explained Carmen's predicament and qualifications. 'Any chance you or Ganymede could use someone in your accounting or financial departments?'

There was a silence in the room punctuated only by audible squawks from the handset. Tanya nodded and murmured agreement a few times. 'Yes, she could do that.' Carmen looked on apprehensively. Finally, Tanya smiled. 'Thank you, Joshua. I'd take that as a personal favour. I'll wait to hear from you.' She put down the phone.

'Well?' Carmen was eager.

'Well,' replied Tanya, 'McNally says he could take on a new bookkeeper, rather like the work you did for Pease, but he thinks Sheila Sorensen might be needing another personal assistant. He'll call her and one of them will get back to me. He sounded optimistic.'

With a yelp of joy, Carmen flung her arms around Tanya and bubbled over with gratitude and giggles. She was a far cry from the wiser older woman who steered Tanya through her crisis. She kissed Tanya and hugged her, her fingers running up and down Tanya's spine, leaving a delicious trail of tingling sensation.

'Tanya, Tanya, Tanya,' chortled Carmen. 'I love you all over again! Thank you, *cara* Tanya! Now you do me this favour and we are equal, yes?'

Tanya nodded, smiling at her friend's happiness. 'This has been worrying you a lot, hasn't it?' she asked.

Carmen nodded. 'Yes, *chicita*, a great deal. But, come, let us celebrate. It's past lunchtime. We can have a beer.' She fetched a frosty pair of Negro Mondelos from the refrigerator, popped the tops, and handed one to Tanya. 'Here's to new beginnings.'

'Here's to Green Cards, love, and sex,' retorted Tanya, with a big grin. 'First we get you a proper job, then we get you a boyfriend.'

Carmen settled back in the sofa and took a swig of her beer straight from the bottle. 'It's been a long time since I had a steady relationship with a guy. I met one or two guys working at the club, but we had only casual sex, just for fun. And I've had a couple of girlfriends, too. There was never any commitment. But now,' Carmen said with a smile, 'I think there's a new one.' Her eyes twinkled.

Tanya was all ears. 'Who?'

'Well, Skip Braddock asked me out,' Carmen replied.

'Ooh, sexy,' exclaimed Tanya. 'The cute actor guy? He's coming over?'

'Yes, in a few moments,' said Carmen.

'Oh!' Tanya exclaimed, and rose quickly. 'Time for me to go.' She paused in the doorway and smiled at her friend. 'I'm going home to call Stephen. I love you, Carmen. Good luck with Skip.'

It was early afternoon before Tanya settled back in her apartment with the portable telephone by her side. Sitting close to the window air-conditioner that tried vainly to keep pace with the scorching heat of the Dallas summer, she thought about Skip and Carmen furiously fornicating back in Carmen's bed. She felt an aching emptiness in her own loins. With a chilled glass of mineral water in her hand, she stared at the phone for several minutes, unable to will herself to pick up the instrument.

Outside, the summer heat had driven all pedestrians inside, into their air-conditioned buildings or their cars. Several dogs lay panting in the shade of the oak trees and crepe myrtles that were all the landscape offered in terms of natural habitat.

Tanya checked the setting of her air-conditioner, hoping there would be an extra notch for cooling, but it was set to the max. She mopped her brow and swallowed a large gulp of iced water, rose, refilled her glass, returned to the chair and sat down, only to rise again immediately and traipse to the fridge for some more ice. She tried Mary Chapin Carpenter and LeAnn Rimes on the CD player, but neither singer's lyrics matched her mood, and she silenced them with the remote control.

The phone sat like a miniature black obelisk on the small cherry-wood table. Tanya was consumed by doubt. Was this agony of indecision better than the agony of rejection if Stephen turned her away? She laughed out loud at her weakness, a hard bitter little sound, devoid of humour. 'Jesus, this is stupid,' she cursed herself. With an angry gesture, she snatched the phone and stabbed out the area code for Arkansas, followed by the number.

'Good afternoon, Proctor Walters Architects. How may I direct your call?'

'Er . . . Stephen Sinclair please.'

'Thank you. Hold, please.' A Scarlatti harpsichord sonata tinkled meaninglessly in her ear.

'I'm sorry, he's not answering. Do you want to leave a message?'

Tanya felt an absurd sense of relief. 'No, no message. Thank you.'

She sat in her window looking at the street below without seeing it. She berated herself as a coward, disgusted by her lack of courage. She set down her water glass, went to the refrigerator and took out the nearly empty bottle of Tanqueray. She sloshed the remaining measure in a glass, added ice and a minuscule portion of tonic, didn't bother with the lime, and drank deeply. 'OK,' she said with new resolve. 'This time.'

'Hello, Proctor Walters.' A different voice.

'Stephen Sinclair, please.'

'He isn't in, right now. Would you like his voice-mail?'

Tanya muttered assent.

'Hello, you have reached the desk of Stephen Sinclair. I'm not available to take your call right now, but please leave a message with your name and number and I'll get right back to you.'

Tanya was mesmerised by the sound of Stephen's recorded voice, delaying her response. Precious seconds ticked by before she spoke. 'Stephen? This is Tanya. Tanya Trevino. I'm in Dallas at 214–555–1212. I'd like to talk to you. Please call –.' The machine clicked off before she could finish. She hung up with a sense of frustration. It was impossible to explain her feelings, or what she wanted to say, in a disembodied message. She crossed her fingers and prayed that he'd call back.

Tanya stayed glued to the phone for the rest of the day and that evening, watching it, willing it to ring. By eight p.m. her spirits were flagging, her stomach growling and her hopes fading. There was no food in the house, but she didn't want to go shopping in case he called, and she didn't want to use the phone in case he called. Eventually hunger won out, and she ordered a pizza. Ten o'clock came and went, and then midnight brought the end of the day. With a sigh, Tanya turned off the light and lay down on her bed. The message was clear. She sobbed herself to sleep in her pillow.

The morning brought some return of spirits. She called the architectural firm again.

'Sorry, he's in a meeting. Would you like to leave a message?'

'I left a message yesterday, Has he checked his voice-mail?'

'Oh, yes, I heard him checking it when he got back yesterday afternoon. Do you want to leave another one?'

'No, thank you.'

Tanya threw the phone on to the lumpy stuffing of her sofa, where it bounced to the floor and beeped in an offended tone. She picked it up and snapped it off. 'Shut up, you stupid machine. I'm getting out of here!' She grabbed her gym bag from the closet, picked up her car keys and stalked out, slamming the front door behind her.

She was too late for the morning classes at Gold's Gym, and too early for the lunchtime sessions, so Tanya rode the exercise bike, ran the treadmill, and sculled the rowing machines for over an hour. Despite her angry mood, she took time to stretch, and it was when she was lying on the floor, bending up and over to stretch her obliques that it came to her. She was too shy or scared to speak to Stephen, and she couldn't communicate her feelings through voice-mail. She could, however, express herself in drawings. She could create a whole new set, just like those for *Katrina Cortez*, but this time they would be about Tanya and Stephen.

She grabbed her towel and ran downstairs to the changing room. She showered in record time and, not bothering to fix her hair or make-up first, drove home like a woman possessed, stopping only for tonic water and another bottle of Tanqueray.

At home she flung her bag at the washing machine and left it where it fell. She raced to her desk and searched frantically for the sheets of precut vellum left over from her last *Katrina Cortez* series. In prearranged storyboard format, their vacant squares waited for their drama to materialise.

Tanya believed she had become identified in Stephen's mind with the dark and decadent side of Katrina's personality. To change his perception of her, to reveal the full truth of her actions and feelings, she had to be absolutely honest about her emotions and activities.

Sketching rapidly, Tanya draughted a storyline that depicted the sequence of events since that first fateful day when she had talked to Stephen at her drawing board. She left nothing out, making sure that the full context of the events was clearly portrayed.

She depicted her false bargain with Pease, and was brutally honest in portraying herself in a quandary about whether or not she should have sex with the boss for professional advancement. She drew Beth-Ann and Stephen together, interspersed by the buxom blonde servicing Hiram Pease and her imaginings of Stephen's canalside tryst with Sheila Sorensen. She drew her stormy relationship with Eric Janovich, her lust for Stephen, and her selfish rejection of his love. She portrayed, with harsh realism and no excuses, her own sexual adventures in the CowGirl Club, including the lesbian sex with Carmen. She illustrated her descent into fantasy, her exhibitionism at the restaurant, her licentiousness in the limousine, and her rampant coupling with Fernando.

In her pictures, Tanya portrayed her desolation at Stephen's departure, her troubles as a freelance, and her relief at eventually producing good storyboards for the movie script. She illustrated the conversation with Eden Sinclair when she learnt Stephen's whereabouts, as well as her embarrassed inability to communicate with him at work. Finally, she drew herself at home, alone, with Stephen featured exclusively in her daydreams and night-time fantasies. Her line was crisp, her blacks deep and saturated, her highlights piercing. Above all, her drawings told Stephen how much she loved him and how much she wanted him back.

In a great burst of cathartic energy, Tanya drew and wrote frantically all weekend, taking breaks only to eat and sleep. She called Carmen to bring in food; sometimes her friend stayed for a while, but usually she left immediately with a kiss and a wave. Tanya was in no mood for conversation. On Monday morning she reviewed the sketches, made minor amendments, photocopied them at the local copy shop, and mailed them to the address of Stephen's employer in Little Rock, express delivery. She felt as if a great weight had lifted from around her neck.

She phoned Carmen. 'Carmen, let's get drunk!'

'But, *chicita*, it's not even lunchtime.'

'So what? I've just sent the best drawings of my life to Little Rock. In fact, I've sent my life, all poured out for Stephen to see. I'm empty. Come and fill me up.'

Chapter Twenty-Six
Drawn Together

Tanya put down her drawing tools and studied the couple she was illustrating. They relaxed from their provocative embrace on her living room couch. Tanya sighed. They looked so much in love. And in lust.

Tanya was working on her current commercial commission, a series of soft-focus yet realistic illustrations for *La Femme et L'Homme,* a line of 'exclusive sensual products for loving couples'. Carmen and Skip Braddock had gladly accepted Tanya's invitation to pose for a series of sexy couplings. Despite Pease's lies and badmouthing, Tanya had been able to pick up a few commercial clients, fitted around her work on the movie. Most had come by recommendation from Joshua McNally, who now took it as a personal mission to compensate for his fraternity brother's malice towards Tanya.

'I think it's time for us to change the background,' she announced to the cuddling couple. 'Let's try another venue and move to the bedroom. I need a break myself. You two must be getting stiff.'

Carmen Sierra's distinctive giggle accompanied the sound of Skip Braddock's sultry laugh. 'You could say that *he* is stiff,' said Carmen. Tanya saw the Hispanic woman's hand drift under the stylised toga that Skip wore above his sculpted loins. The outline of Skip's penis was very clear, as was Carmen's loving manipulation of his shaft. Tanya found Carmen and Skip very alluring as a couple, especially in the nude. Tanya sighed again. How she wanted to be a couple, too. With Stephen.

She left them to each other for a few minutes and stepped to the bathroom. As she washed and freshened up, she wondered, with increasing desperation, whether Stephen would ever reply to her drawings. For nearly a fortnight, Tanya had received no reply to the elaborate visual message she had mailed to Stephen and, in a fever of anticipation, had nearly called his office on several occasions. But always she retreated, preferring ultimately to let her drawings tell the story. She could add nothing that wasn't already in the cartoon; her true feelings, her blunders, and her heart's greatest desire were depicted there.

During many of the long, lonely days, Tanya worked hard with Sheila and Joshua. The demands of the movie script, along with the distractions of the freelance commercial illustrations she was doing at home, served to keep Tanya's longing for Stephen temporarily at bay. But at times like today, with a pair of passionate and lusty lovers lying half-naked in her living room under a subdued light, she got really horny for Stephen.

Each night, she slept alone, and dreamt of her absent lover. Usually she masturbated, filling her mind with images of his body. One such lonely night, on a whim, Tanya recovered the teddy bear wedged in the bottom drawer of her dresser and hugged him tightly to her chest. She brushed his soft fur and whispered, 'Oh, Edward Bear. You won't ever leave me, will you?' She felt she was talking to an old friend. The bear's small paws seemed to cling to her warm skin, affirming his devotion. Tanya removed the image of Katrina Cortez that was still tacked to her mirror, and turned off the light.

Tanya shook herself from her reverie and examined her face in the bathroom mirror. Her hair, still very dark, was beginning to grow out to its natural sheen and colour. She combed it into a semblance of its former style. It would take a long time indeed to return to its original state. She grimaced at the legacy from Katrina and walked slowly back to her board.

'Time to go into the other room,' she said.

Carmen and Skip broke their embrace and looked towards the artist. When the man stood, his erection jutted in front of him. Carmen reached out to pat the rampant member.

'You said fully nude, right?' asked Skip.

'Yes,' Tanya said with a nod. 'I've changed the sheets on my bed. You can use that for the poses . . . and afterwards, if you like.' It was obvious that her friends wouldn't be able to hold themselves in check very much longer.

As the duet posed in each other's arms on her bed, Tanya drew them coupling in various positions of simulated sex. The action was getting hot. Skip and Carmen were both excellent life models and enjoyed posing in the nude, so much so that their physical attraction to each other was becoming more urgent by the minute. The sight of their naked bodies increased her arousal, and again Tanya put down her drawing tools. She saw Skip slide his penis into the spread pink lips of Carmen's pussy.

'I think I'm taking another break,' she said, 'and leaving you two to it.' It was obvious they were going to fuck, whether she was in the room or not. She thought it best to leave them alone for a while. She blew a kiss at the copulating pair, closed the door and went back to the kitchen.

Tanya felt very lonely. She could stay in the house and

listen to their lovemaking through the walls, if she so desired. They probably wouldn't mind; in fact, they probably wouldn't mind a threesome. Tanya was tempted for a moment to take off her clothes and join her friends on the bed, but she put the thought out of her mind. She didn't want to start that scene again. Not now.

Tanya drank a glass of lemonade and walked downstairs for a breath of 'fresh' midsummer Dallas air. The heat was considerable, but she hardly noticed it in her distraction. She'd give the lovebirds a good twenty minutes, this time. Then she could return to complete the sensual illustrations without the distraction of full-blown sex while working. As usual, a deadline loomed in her immediate future.

She watched the mailman drive away from her block after completing his deliveries. Tanya's rational mind told her there was no reason for this morning to be any different from all her previous disappointments, yet she quickened her pace to the mailbox at the kerb. The large black metal container nailed to its timber post was stuffed with sundry mail for her and the other apartment-dwellers, but her heart jumped to her throat when she unearthed a large manila padded envelope at the bottom of the pile. Her name, rendered in stylish lettering, caused her to disregard everything else in a frantic scrabble to uncover the contents. There was no doubt it was from Stephen!

Rushing indoors with the large flat parcel, Tanya tore it open to find a slender hand-bound volume containing several beautifully drawn comic strips on fine paper. In response to her drawings, Stephen had illustrated a folio! Entitled *Katrina Cortez and Her Lover*, the suite featured the main character, her own Katrina Cortez, rendered as a softer, warmer woman. Tanya turned the pages. The investigator took a new lover, a man who resembled Stephen.

This Katrina Cortez allowed the man to become close to her, to enter fully her life and her heart. Rendered in Stephen's delicate line, in a flowing, more curvilinear style than Tanya's aggressively angular characterisation, the cartoon imagery was transformed from its *noir* origins into the forms and colours of Maxfield Parrish opulence.

This new lover was a helpmate who responded avidly to Katrina's new softness. Stephen drew him having rampant sex with Katrina, most beautifully illustrated. This alternative Katrina Cortez, Tanya realised, represented the woman who Stephen loved.

The fully illustrated episode of *Katrina Cortez and Her Lover* was an emotionally moving series of pictures, and Tanya sat down with a lump in her throat and tears starting in her eyes. All was quiet from Carmen and Skip in the bedroom; Tanya had forgotten their existence. She studied the drawings more carefully, her heart beating loudly in her chest. When did Stephen send them? She turned over the padded envelope, looking for a postmark. To her shock, the envelope bore no postage stamps; it had been delivered by hand.

The meaning of this discovery froze Tanya in her seat for a moment before she jumped excitedly to her feet. No stamp! She rushed to the window.

Stephen was outside, leaning against the mailbox.

Tanya hurled herself down the stairs and raced into the street. Stephen stood halfway along the garden path, blushing, with a shy smile on his face. Tanya's momentum carried her to him like a cannonball. There was no time for words.

Stephen braced himself and cushioned Tanya's charge as she crushed herself to his chest. Tanya flung her arms around his neck and sobbed tears of joy on to his shoulder, making large damp patches on his crisp blue shirt. He just stood there, holding Tanya, absorbing her emotion.

After what seemed an age, Tanya released her vice-like grip and stepped back. She held on to Stephen's hands, frightened he'd vanish again if she let go.

'You delivered it in person,' she said, stating the obvious with the delight of one who has made a startling discovery.

'I needed to see you,' he said simply. 'I came to see if my Tanya was back. Once I had worked out what I really felt for you, and that took me quite a while, I couldn't bear to wait any longer. I drew those drawings in two days, and then drove right down. I left at 3 a.m. and came straight down I-30. I haven't had much sleep,' he added apologetically, as a yawn stretched his facial muscles. He looked appreciatively at her face and her firm athletic body. 'Underneath all those tears, you're looking good, Tanya,' he said. 'It's so good to see you, and touch you!' He pulled her close again and kissed her with a passion that threatened to melt Tanya's heart.

'I was afraid I'd never see you again, Stephen!' she said when they came up gasping for air. 'I was afraid. Me. Tanya, that is. Not Katrina,' she said softly. She wanted to touch his skin and caress him all over. She nuzzled up close, oblivious to the amused stares of passing drivers.

'I became Katrina to overcome my shyness, but I lost myself in my own fantasy,' Tanya continued, eager to make sure Stephen understood. 'Carmen helped me a lot. Eventually I realised I was more content as myself –' she paused '– except that you weren't around.' Tanya gazed intently up at the handsome man next to her. 'Please don't go away again. I don't think I could bear it. Please stay with me!'

Stephen grinned broadly. 'Katrina would have to get a whole team of wild horses this time,' he said, 'and even then they wouldn't manage it.' He squeezed his companion in his arms. 'No, this time I'm here to stay.' Gently, he elaborated his feelings. 'I didn't fall in love with a comic-book heroine. I fell in love with you!' he murmured softly. 'I wanted you so badly, but you were so convincing as Katrina. I couldn't compete with that. But now I want you. Now! Let's go inside.'

Tanya panicked and grew stiff beneath his touch. How would she explain the naked couple, probably having sex, in her apartment? If they went into her apartment now and found Carmen and Skip in her bed, she feared that Stephen would think that she was engaged in the same old wanton behaviour that characterised Katrina. She was silent, tongue-tied.

'Oh, please, Tanya, let's make love,' Stephen said. 'Now.'

She tried to lead him away. 'Let's go for a drink . . . to, er, celebrate.'

Stephen stood, puzzled by the sudden change of mood, but then walked alongside as the pretty dark-haired woman headed for her car. Then Tanya stopped herself. 'Wait a minute,' she said to Stephen, turning and touching his arm to stop him, too. 'Excuse me, Stephen. I'm doing it again.'

'Doing what?'

Tanya opted for honesty and explained her quandary. 'I'm playing a silly game again,' she admitted. 'After being honest in my drawings about how I feel, I'm trying to hide something from you. It's very stupid of me.'

'What's going on?' he asked.

They stood still on the pavement. She told him in a rush, holding him tight, her eyes squeezed shut. 'Let's go inside, Stephen. If there's a naked couple in my bedroom, making love, please don't be alarmed. It's only Carmen and her new boyfriend, Skip. He's an actor, and they're posing together for my illustrations for a new line of sensual body products. They've been naked all morning and are horny as hell! But I'm only drawing them. Honest.' She opened her eyes to see a smile spreading over Stephen's face.

'I always fancied seeing Carmen naked,' he said with a grin. Then he laughed out loud at the confusion on Tanya's face. 'Oh, darling Tanya! Don't worry. I believe you. Thank you for telling me what's going on and trusting me. That proves that Katrina's long gone.'

Tanya was all eagerness. 'Come on,' she said, and led him indoors by the hand.

Inside the apartment, she put her finger to her lips. 'Wait here a sec.' Tanya peeked into the kitchen and was not surprised to meet Carmen, naked, preparing a post-coital snack to take back to bed. She was carrying a tray holding an ice-bucket and two glasses. The couple had finished making love, obviously, but it looked like they might be considering more. Carmen looked up. 'Oh, *chicita*, is our break over?'

'Stephen's here,' said Tanya abruptly.

Carmen's eyes widened as the tall chestnut-haired artist stepped into view behind her friend. 'So I see,' she chirped excitedly. The little dark-haired woman looked over Tanya's shoulder at the young man, who stood, staring at her naked body, his eyes popping from nipples to pubic hair. 'Oh, Stephen,' Carmen cried, 'I'm so delighted to see you!' She put down the tray and ran to greet him with a big hug.

Stephen didn't know where to put his hands.

Tanya said, 'Um, Carmen, why don't you and Skip take another break . . .'

Carmen picked up the tray and scurried out the door. Skip was calling her.

Laughing, Stephen and Tanya followed Carmen into the hall. She entered the bedroom where she placed the tray on a table beside the rumpled bed.

Oblivious to the new member of the audience, Skip, eyes closed, lay prone among the pillows, one arm behind his head. His other hand caressed his cock, which stood proud above his belly. He opened one eye and sat up, temporarily withdrawing his hand. He reached for

Carmen before noticing the clothed couple standing in the doorway to the room. If he was startled, he disguised it well. His experiences being nude before the camera had long ago stripped him of embarrassment about his naked body. 'Oh, hi, Tanya. And, er . . .'

'Skip, this is Stephen,' explained Tanya above the sound of Carmen's giggles.

As if shaking hands with a naked man in your lover's bedroom were the most normal thing in the world to do, Stephen stepped forward and grasped Skip's large paw. 'Nice to meet you,' he said with a straight face.

Perfectly at ease with their nakedness, Skip and Carmen sat side by side on the bed. Skip openly admired Stephen's body, but Carmen slapped him down playfully. 'Aren't I enough for you, big boy?' she asked. 'Anyway,' she added, 'Tanya and Stephen have a lot of making up to do. I expect they'd like their bed back.' She held out her hand to help her lover to his feet.

'No, please. The two of you stay right where you are,' said Tanya. 'I'll take Stephen next door. I'm sure he won't mind the spare futon, this one time.' She looked up at her lover's eyes and down at his groin, where a lovely solid bulge was forming as the penis she remembered so well struggled against its confines.

'Looks as if your boyfriend's ready and willing, Tanya,' said Skip mischievously.

'And I want some more of that delicious cock of yours,' Carmen purred, and pushed Skip back to the futon, her bare bottom sticking up as she bent forward to take his penis deep into her mouth.

Stephen and Tanya laughed as Skip surrendered to the inevitable, bringing Carmen's bottom over his face and propping himself on the pillows to lap at her pussy.

Hand in hand, Tanya and Stephen entered the spare room next door to Tanya's bedroom. They stripped naked in seconds flat and fell into bed. They had quick, hard sex. Tanya came almost as soon as Stephen penetrated her, all her weeks of longing and frustrated desires washing out of her body in one long shuddering orgasm. Stephen held himself in check until he was sure of Tanya's satisfaction, and then he came himself, with quick long thrusts of his cock. He felt his lover spasm around him in aftershock as he finished pleasuring her.

They lay exhausted for a few moments. Stephen turned to stroke his lover's breast, taking her nipple gently between his teeth. 'Did you want to join them next door?' he murmured.

Tanya opted for full frankness. 'Part of me did. They're both attractive. As you know,' she said, blushing slightly, 'Carmen and I have played around together a bit, and I've seen Skip having whipped cream licked off his cock, so I know them pretty intimately.'

Stephen stroked her other breast, and ran his hand softly between her legs, parting Tanya's renewed growth of pubic hair to caress the hard bud of her clitoris. She held his hand there. 'That feels so good. Don't stop!' she whispered huskily. She thought carefully before continuing.

'Part of me loves sex so much that any opportunity for physical satisfaction is exciting, but in the past few weeks, all I got out of my wild variety of sexual experiences was a heartache.' She grinned at Stephen and challenged him. 'But don't tell me you haven't fancied three- or four-way sex. That one evening, with Carmen and me, you were practically drooling at the thought of having both of us.'

Now it was Stephen's turn to blush. 'That's true,' he admitted. Even now his dick was stiffening at the thought of a four-way romp. 'Why aren't we in there with them?' he asked.

'Because I want you here, all to myself,' Tanya said. 'I've done those things I thought I wanted to do, and I've come back wiser and sometimes chastened by the experiences. I've done things sexually I didn't know I was capable of. But now I want to channel all my sexual energy into one relationship. For keeps. With you.'

The handsome man smiled contentedly. 'I guess we're just "drawn together", like two characters in a comic book,' he said, caressing his lover's beautiful body. 'But now I'll be able to draw you for real.' He hugged her close. 'You know, the drawings you sent me are brilliant,' he said softly. 'But when I first received them I was shocked. They were so frank, so honest! It hurt to read them. You stripped yourself naked in more ways than one. It took me a long time to digest everything you poured on to the page. I think you're a great artist. You should exhibit that work somewhere; perhaps at my sister's gallery.'

But Tanya shook her head. 'You're very kind. I love your drawings, too. You're no slouch with a pencil! But those drawings of mine are just for you. They show you my soul, my heart; the real me, as best as I can tell my story.' She fluffed her short brown-black hair with one hand. 'The silly, confused and greedy little girl under this dumb disguise is gone forever, but I'm not ready to expose my stupidity to the rest of the world. Not just yet. Maybe some time later, after we've been married for a while.'

Propped up on her elbow, Tanya enjoyed the looks of amazement, disbelief, confusion and joy that raced across her lover's face in quick succession. She leant over to kiss him gently on the lips.

'Yes, Stephen, I'm ready at last to make the commitment you wanted weeks ago, when I so stupidly turned you down.'

Stephen demurred. 'That was partly my fault, too,' he said. Tanya silenced him with another kiss.

'Will you have me?' she asked. 'We could be partners, just like your version of *Katrina Cortez*. But you must know I'll be very demanding. I'll want sex all the time, at least twice every day.' She giggled at the luscious thought.

'I thought you'd never ask,' said Stephen, lying back and fondling his cock to full hardness. 'Here it is,' he said, holding his seven inches of rigid flesh vertically in his hand. 'It's all ready for you, and there's plenty more where this comes from.'

Tanya sighed with joy and went down on her man. She might even be able to teach the formidable Katrina Cortez a thing or two about love.

Epilogue
Midnight Swim

Katrina Cortez tossed her clothing on to the bar top. Wearing only a black bikini bottom, she reclined in *Cabana Noir* Bar next to the glistening waters of the rooftop hotel pool. Now deserted, this wonderfully kitsch concoction, complete with trees and coloured lights, a waterfall and rock grotto, simulated a pirate's lair for what was now an intimate audience of two.

Katrina's breasts were exposed to the evening breezes of autumn as the torrid summer heat at last surrendered its grip on the city. She surveyed the empty poolside, the darkness surrounding the solitary figure of her new lover, the only other person remaining from the crowd of cretins who celebrated the capture of Pete Regan and the smashing of his notorious drug cartel.

The cops had gone home, or back to the precinct house; the politicians to their mistresses; and the media to scavenge at new sites of scandal. Katrina breathed a long low sigh of relief at their departure. Sometimes it was hard to tell the good guys from the bad guys. Beside her casual heap of clothing rested her official Certificate of Appreciation, presented to her by the Dallas Police Department. Wryly, she recalled how the paunchy

Police Commissioner had spent the entire ceremony looking down her cleavage, lifting his face only briefly from her patently bra-less breasts to leer into her eyes when he exchanged the parchment for a kiss on the cheek.

Katrina found no thrill in being thrust into the spotlight; she preferred to inhabit the darkened margins of the case, unseen and unknown by friend and foe alike. But public relations and Dallas politics dictated otherwise. To be seen with 'the tough, heroic female PI' was a photo opportunity few politicians and their spin doctors could resist. 'Dallas's own *La Femme Nikita*!' ran one headline from a local tabloid.

Katrina discarded the newspaper, and regarded instead her brown-haired lover, who lay stretched out by her side. Relaxed and trusting, he lay flat on his back. She stroked his naked torso, running her fingers down his chest to fondle the developing bulge in his swimming trunks. She pulled the elasticated waist down to expose first the tip of his long, handsome dick, and then its full length. His plump balls clustered amid chestnut curls at the base of his shaft. Katrina thought it was the most beautiful dick she'd seen for a long, long time. It was special, like this man. At her touch, he raised his hips to facilitate his unclothing.

She stroked his shaft with her fingers, knelt over him, and took the succulent member deep into her mouth. Katrina flicked her tongue around his glans, bringing low moans of pleasure from his recumbent form. After a few minutes, he eased her face from his cock and spoke softly, looking into her eyes with condensed urgency.

'I want you. I want you all to myself, you little witch,' he said, with a smile that made his phrase a compliment. 'I want to fuck you all day, every day; in every possible position known to woman and to man.' He paused, then took the plunge. 'But I want you to promise me one thing.'

Katrina looked into his eyes and felt herself melting.

She knew what was coming; although she'd fought this promise, another part of her accepted, even desired, this portent of commitment, and had done so ever since the first day she let this handsome man share her body. But still a part of her resisted. She valued independence; it defined her. 'Ask me what you want,' she whispered huskily, softly stroking the still-plump penis nestling in her hand. 'I'll promise what I can.'

'Promise you won't go with other men; or other women. Can you do that for me?' He paused, his eyes dark with lust and tender with devotion. 'In exchange, I swear to be faithful. Always. Forever.'

Katrina surrendered as she knew she would. The stirrings deep within her were new, unknown. They might be love, and she was warmed by the thought. 'I promise, baby,' she said. 'I want you, too. But . . . there has to be one condition.'

The man studied the raven-haired beauty lying on his thigh, this woman whose body he'd explored in its minutiae, mapping the geography of every crevice, tunnel and peak, but whose mind remained a mystery. He raised a single eyebrow. 'Name it.'

Katrina dropped her eyes but lifted them again. It was important to see her lover's reaction. She spoke slowly, choosing her words with care. 'I promise never to have sex with anybody else but you,' she reiterated, 'except, sometimes, just sometimes, on very rare occasions, if my job demands otherwise. And I swear to tell you if I ever have to make that decision.' She wondered if that would be enough.

He stood and raised her from her knees. Slowly he stooped to undress her, matching his nakedness, exposing her black triangle of trimmed curls to his heavy-lidded gaze. With his tongue, he traced the sinuous line of the tattooed serpent on her thigh, following the inky curves of black to the very opening of her vagina.

She was already wet, and he tasted her musk, savouring the sweet nectar on his tongue. He nuzzled and sucked, nibbling her bud and sliding his fingers inside her flowing channel.

Katrina threw back her head. The glimmering stars hung in her hair, its darkness lost in the vault of midnight indigo that spanned the halogen city. The fingers within her, the tongue that lapped her, brought pleasure beyond her dreams. She howled into the night, her banshee cry of lust blown through the silent streets below.

In the creeping chill of the darkness, they slid sensuously, sleek as otters, into the warmth of the water, its steam wrapping their naked bodies. They swam beneath the waterfall to the darkened grotto, where the black-eyed beauty tasted his lips. 'I love you,' she said. 'I'm scared of what that means. Please fuck me so I know you're real.'

Katrina Cortez spread her legs and felt the tip of his penis probe her pussy. She closed her eyes, clinging tightly to her lover's arms. 'Fuck me baby. Make me come!' That was real.

LOOK OUT FOR THE ALL-NEW BLACK LACE BOOKS – AVAILABLE NOW!

All books priced £6.99 in the UK. Please note publication dates apply to the UK only. For other territories, please contact your retailer.

LIBERTY HALL
Kate Stewart
ISBN 0 352 33776 1

Vicar's daughter and wannabe journalist Tess Morgan is willing to do anything to pay off her student overdraft. Luckily for Tess, her flatmate Imogen is the daughter of infamous madam, Liberty Hall, who owns a pleasure palace of the same name that operates under a guise of respectability as a hotel. When Tess lands herself a summer job catering for 'special clients' at Liberty Hall, she sees an opportunity to clear that overdraft with a bit of undercover journalism. But when she tries to tell all to a Sunday newspaper, Tess is in for a shocking surprise. **Fruity antics aplenty in this tale of naughty behaviour and double crossing.**

THE WICKED STEPDAUGHTER
Wendy Harris
ISBN 0 352 33777 X

Selina is in lust with Matt, who unfortunately is the boyfriend of the really irritating Miranda, who was Selina's stepmother for several years until her poor old dad keeled over years before his time. When Miranda has to go to the US for three weeks, Selina hatches a plan to seduce the floppy-haired Matt – and get her revenge on the money-grabbing Miranda, whom Selina blames for her dad's early demise. With several suitors in tow, the highly sexed Selina causes mayhem, both at work – at the strippergram service she co-runs – and in her personal life. **Another hilarious black comedy of sexual manners from Ms Harris.**

Coming in March

EVIL'S NIECE

Melissa MacNeal

ISBN 0 352 33781 8

The setting is 1890s New Orleans. When Eve spies her husband with a sultry blonde, she is determined to win back his affection. When her brother-in-law sends a maid to train her in the ways of seduction, things spin rapidly out of control. Their first lesson reveals a surprise that Miss Eve isn't prepared for, and when her husband discovers these liaisons, it seems she will lose her prestigious place in society. However, his own covert life is about to unravel and reveal the biggest secret of all. **More historical high jinks from Ms MacNeal, the undisputed queen of kinky erotica set in the world of corsets and chaperones.**

LEARNING THE HARD WAY

Jasmine Archer

ISBN 0 352 33782 6

Tamsin has won a photographic assignment to collaborate on a book of nudes with the sex-obsessed Leandra. Thing is, the job is in Los Angeles and she doesn't want her new friend to know how sexually inexperienced she is. Tamsin sets out to learn all she can before flying out to meet her photographic mentor, but nothing can prepare her for Leandra's outrageous lifestyle. Along with husband Nigel, and an assortment of kinky friends, Leandra is about to initiate Tamsin into some very different ways to have fun. **Fun and upbeat story of a young woman's transition from sexual ingénue to fully fledged dominatrix.**

ACE OF HEARTS
Lisette Allen
ISBN 0 352 33059 7

England, 1816. The wealthy elite is enjoying an unprecedented era of hedonistic adventure. Their lives are filled with parties, sexual dalliances and scandal. Marisa Brooke is a young lady who lives by her wits, fencing and cheating the wealthy at cards. She also likes seducing young men and indulging her fancy for fleshly pleasures. However, love and fortune are lost as easily as they are won, and she has to use all her skill and cunning if she wants to hold on to her winnings and her lovers. **Highly enjoyable historical erotica set in the period of Regency excess.**

Coming in April

VALENTINA'S RULES
Monica Belle
ISBN 0 352 33788 5

Valentina is the girl with a plan: find a wealthy man, marry him, mould him and take her place in the sun. She's got the looks, she's got the ambition and, after one night with her, most men are following her around like puppies. When she decides that Michael Callington is too good for her friend Chrissy and just right for her, she finds she has bitten off a bit more than she expected. Then there's Michael's father, the notorious spanking Major, who is determined to have his fun, too. **Monica Belle specialises in erotic stories about modern girls about town and up to no good.**

WICKED WORDS 8

Edited by Kerri Sharp

ISBN 0 352 33787 7

Hugely popular and immensely entertaining, the *Wicked Words* collections are the freshest and most cutting-edge volumes of women's erotic stories to be found anywhere in the world. The diversity of themes and styles reflects the multi-faceted nature of the female sexual imagination. Combining humour, warmth and attitude with fun, imaginative writing, these stories sizzle with horny action. Only the most arousing fiction makes it into a *Wicked Words* volume. This is the best in fun, sassy erotica from the UK and USA. **Another sizzling collection of wild fantasies from wicked women!**

Black Lace Booklist

Information is correct at time of printing. To avoid disappointment check availability before ordering. Go to www.blacklace-books.co.uk. All books are priced £6.99 unless another price is given.

BLACK LACE BOOKS WITH A CONTEMPORARY SETTING

❑ THE TOP OF HER GAME Emma Holly	ISBN 0 352 33337 5	£5.99
❑ IN THE FLESH Emma Holly	ISBN 0 352 33498 3	£5.99
❑ A PRIVATE VIEW Crystalle Valentino	ISBN 0 352 33308 1	£5.99
❑ SHAMELESS Stella Black	ISBN 0 352 33485 1	£5.99
❑ INTENSE BLUE Lyn Wood	ISBN 0 352 33496 7	£5.99
❑ THE NAKED TRUTH Natasha Rostova	ISBN 0 352 33497 5	£5.99
❑ ANIMAL PASSIONS Martine Marquand	ISBN 0 352 33499 1	£5.99
❑ A SPORTING CHANCE Susie Raymond	ISBN 0 352 33501 7	£5.99
❑ TAKING LIBERTIES Susie Raymond	ISBN 0 352 33357 X	£5.99
❑ A SCANDALOUS AFFAIR Holly Graham	ISBN 0 352 33523 8	£5.99
❑ THE NAKED FLAME Crystalle Valentino	ISBN 0 352 33528 9	£5.99
❑ ON THE EDGE Laura Hamilton	ISBN 0 352 33534 3	£5.99
❑ LURED BY LUST Tania Picarda	ISBN 0 352 33533 5	£5.99
❑ THE HOTTEST PLACE Tabitha Flyte	ISBN 0 352 33536 X	£5.99
❑ THE NINETY DAYS OF GENEVIEVE Lucinda Carrington	ISBN 0 352 33070 8	£5.99
❑ EARTHY DELIGHTS Tesni Morgan	ISBN 0 352 33548 3	£5.99
❑ MAN HUNT Cathleen Ross	ISBN 0 352 33583 1	
❑ MÉNAGE Emma Holly	ISBN 0 352 33231 X	
❑ DREAMING SPIRES Juliet Hastings	ISBN 0 352 33584 X	
❑ THE TRANSFORMATION Natasha Rostova	ISBN 0 352 33311 1	
❑ STELLA DOES HOLLYWOOD Stella Black	ISBN 0 352 33588 2	
❑ SIN.NET Helena Ravenscroft	ISBN 0 352 33598 X	
❑ HOTBED Portia Da Costa	ISBN 0 352 33614 5	
❑ TWO WEEKS IN TANGIER Annabel Lee	ISBN 0 352 33599 8	
❑ HIGHLAND FLING Jane Justine	ISBN 0 352 33616 1	
❑ PLAYING HARD Tina Troy	ISBN 0 352 33617 X	
❑ SYMPHONY X Jasmine Stone	ISBN 0 352 33629 3	

- ❑ STRICTLY CONFIDENTIAL Alison Tyler ISBN 0 352 33624 2
- ❑ SUMMER FEVER Anna Ricci ISBN 0 352 33625 0
- ❑ CONTINUUM Portia Da Costa ISBN 0 352 33120 8
- ❑ OPENING ACTS Suki Cunningham ISBN 0 352 33630 7
- ❑ FULL STEAM AHEAD Tabitha Flyte ISBN 0 352 33637 4
- ❑ A SECRET PLACE Ella Broussard ISBN 0 352 33307 3
- ❑ GAME FOR ANYTHING Lyn Wood ISBN 0 352 33639 0
- ❑ FORBIDDEN FRUIT Susie Raymond ISBN 0 352 33306 5
- ❑ CHEAP TRICK Astrid Fox ISBN 0 352 33640 4
- ❑ THE ORDER Dee Kelly ISBN 0 352 33652 8
- ❑ ALL THE TRIMMINGS Tesni Morgan ISBN 0 352 33641 3
- ❑ PLAYING WITH STARS Jan Hunter ISBN 0 352 33653 6
- ❑ THE GIFT OF SHAME Sara Hope-Walker ISBN 0 352 32935 1
- ❑ COMING UP ROSES Crystalle Valentino ISBN 0 352 33658 7
- ❑ GOING TOO FAR Laura Hamilton ISBN 0 352 33657 9
- ❑ THE STALLION Georgina Brown ISBN 0 352 33005 8
- ❑ DOWN UNDER Juliet Hastings ISBN 0 352 33663 3
- ❑ THE BITCH AND THE BASTARD Wendy Harris ISBN 0 352 33664 1
- ❑ ODALISQUE Fleur Reynolds ISBN 0 352 32887 8
- ❑ GONE WILD Maria Eppie ISBN 0 352 33670 6
- ❑ SWEET THING Alison Tyler ISBN 0 352 33682 X
- ❑ TIGER LILY Kimberley Dean ISBN 0 352 33685 4
- ❑ COOKING UP A STORM Emma Holly ISBN 0 352 33686 2
- ❑ RELEASE ME Suki Cunningham ISBN 0 352 33671 4
- ❑ KING'S PAWN Ruth Fox ISBN 0 352 33684 6
- ❑ FULL EXPOSURE Robyn Russell ISBN 0 352 33688 9
- ❑ SLAVE TO SUCCESS Kimberley Raines ISBN 0 352 33687 0
- ❑ STRIPPED TO THE BONE Jasmine Stone ISBN 0 352 33463 0
- ❑ HARD CORPS Claire Thompson ISBN 0 352 33491 6
- ❑ MANHATTAN PASSION Antoinette Powell ISBN 0 352 33691 9
- ❑ CABIN FEVER Emma Donaldson ISBN 0 352 33692 7
- ❑ WOLF AT THE DOOR Savannah Smythe ISBN 0 352 33693 5
- ❑ SHADOWPLAY Portia Da Costa ISBN 0 352 33313 8
- ❑ I KNOW YOU, JOANNA Ruth Fox ISBN 0 352 33727 3
- ❑ SNOW BLONDE Astrid Fox ISBN 0 352 33732 X
- ❑ QUEEN OF THE ROAD Lois Pheonix ISBN 0 352 33131 1

- ❑ THE HOUSE IN NEW ORLEANS Fleur Reynolds ISBN 0 352 32951 3
- ❑ NOBLE VICES Monica Belle ISBN 0 352 33738 9
- ❑ HEAT OF THE MOMENT Tesni Morgan ISBN 0 352 33742 7
- ❑ STORMY HAVEN Savannah Smythe ISBN 0 352 33757 5
- ❑ STICKY FINGERS Alison Tyler ISBN 0 352 33756 7
- ❑ THE WICKED STEPDAUGHTER Wendy Harris ISBN 0 352 33777 X
- ❑ DRAWN TOGETHER Robyn Russell ISBN 0 352 33269 7

BLACK LACE BOOKS WITH AN HISTORICAL SETTING

- ❑ PRIMAL SKIN Leona Benkt Rhys ISBN 0 352 33500 9 £5.99
- ❑ DEVIL'S FIRE Melissa MacNeal ISBN 0 352 33527 0 £5.99
- ❑ WILD KINGDOM Deanna Ashford ISBN 0 352 33549 1 £5.99
- ❑ DARKER THAN LOVE Kristina Lloyd ISBN 0 352 33279 4
- ❑ STAND AND DELIVER Helena Ravenscroft ISBN 0 352 33340 5 £5.99
- ❑ THE CAPTIVATION Natasha Rostova ISBN 0 352 33234 4
- ❑ CIRCO EROTICA Mercedes Kelley ISBN 0 352 33257 3
- ❑ MINX Megan Blythe ISBN 0 352 33638 2
- ❑ PLEASURE'S DAUGHTER Sedalia Johnson ISBN 0 352 33237 9
- ❑ JULIET RISING Cleo Cordell ISBN 0 352 32938 6
- ❑ DEMON'S DARE Melissa MacNeal ISBN 0 352 33683 8
- ❑ ELENA'S CONQUEST Lisette Allen ISBN 0 352 32950 5
- ❑ DIVINE TORMENT Janine Ashbless ISBN 0 352 33719 2
- ❑ THE CAPTIVE FLESH Cleo Cordell ISBN 0 352 32872 X
- ❑ SATAN'S ANGEL Melissa MacNeal ISBN 0 352 33726 5
- ❑ THE INTIMATE EYE Georgia Angelis ISBN 0 352 33004 X
- ❑ HANDMAIDEN OF PALMYRA Fleur Reynolds ISBN 0 352 32951 3
- ❑ OPAL DARKNESS Cleo Cordell ISBN 0 352 33033 3
- ❑ SILKEN CHAINS Jodi Nicol ISBN 0 352 33143 7

BLACK LACE ANTHOLOGIES

- ❑ CRUEL ENCHANTMENT Erotic Fairy Stories Janine Ashbless ISBN 0 352 33483 5 £5.99
- ❑ MORE WICKED WORDS Various ISBN 0 352 33487 8 £5.99
- ❑ WICKED WORDS 4 Various ISBN 0 352 33603 X
- ❑ WICKED WORDS 5 Various ISBN 0 352 33642 0
- ❑ WICKED WORDS 6 Various ISBN 0 352 33590 0

❑ WICKED WORDS 7 Various ISBN 0 352 33743 5

❑ THE BEST OF BLACK LACE 2 Various ISBN 0 352 33718 4

❑ A MULTITUDE OF SINS Kit Mason ISBN 0 352 33737 0

BLACK LACE NON-FICTION

❑ THE BLACK LACE BOOK OF WOMEN'S SEXUAL FANTASIES Ed. Kerri Sharp ISBN 0 352 33346 4 £5.99

To find out the latest information about Black Lace titles, check out the website: www.blacklace-books.co.uk or send for a booklist with complete synopses by writing to:

Black Lace Booklist, Virgin Books Ltd
Thames Wharf Studios
Rainville Road
London W6 9HA

Please include an SAE of decent size. Please note only British stamps are valid.

Our privacy policy
We will not disclose information you supply us to any other parties. We will not disclose any information which identifies you personally to any person without your express consent.

From time to time we may send out information about Black Lace books and special offers. Please tick here if you do not wish to receive Black Lace information. ❑

Please send me the books I have ticked above.

Name ....

Address ....

....

....

....

Post Code ....

Send to: Cash Sales, Black Lace Books, Thames Wharf Studios, Rainville Road, London W6 9HA.

US customers: for prices and details of how to order books for delivery by mail, call 1-800-343-4499.

Please enclose a cheque or postal order, made payable to Virgin Books Ltd, to the value of the books you have ordered plus postage and packing costs as follows:

UK and BFPO – £1.00 for the first book, 50p for each subsequent book.

Overseas (including Republic of Ireland) – £2.00 for the first book, £1.00 for each subsequent book.

If you would prefer to pay by VISA, ACCESS/MASTERCARD, DINERS CLUB, AMEX or SWITCH, please write your card number and expiry date here:

....

Signature ....

Please allow up to 28 days for delivery.